Monster Problems

Books 1-3

Monster Problems: Vampire Misfire

Monster Problems 2: Down for the Count

Monster Problems 3: Prince of Dorkness

By

R.L. Ullman

But That's Another Story... Press

Cover designs by Yusup Mediyan
All character images created with heromachine.com.

Published by But That's Another Story… Press
Ridgefield, CT

Printed in the United States of America.

First Printing, 2020.

ISBN: 978-1-7340612-7-7
Library of Congress Control Number: 2020910990

PRAISE FOR MONSTER PROBLEMS
Readers' Favorite BOOK AWARD WINNER

"I absolutely loved Monster Problems. The story is action-packed and fast-paced. The characters were unique and lovable, as well as great role models. I was hooked by the first page and never wanted to put it down." **Rating: 5.0 stars by Kristen Van Kampen (Teen Reviewer).**

"Ullman spins a monstrosity of a tale in the first book of his new series. It reminds me of Harry Potter with a twist. Hilarious and so unexpected. This book is one to believe in." **Rating: 5.0 stars by Gail Kamer.**

"From the first sentence it draws you in and doesn't let go until you've come to the very end. Ullman hits all the bases with this one. I can't recommend this supernatural adventure highly enough!" **Rating: 5.0 stars by Sarah Westmoreland.**

"All the characters are portrayed so well they'll remain fresh in the minds of readers. Like me, readers will be keen to grab book 2 to see what happens next." **Rating: 5.0 stars by Mamta Madhaven.**

"Monster Problems is a grand romp that will thrill kids and forever-young adults alike. I'm thrilled it's just the first book in Ullman's new series. Most highly recommended." **Rating: 5.0 stars by Jack Magnus.**

To Esther and Lillian,
thanks for looking out for me

TABLE OF CONTENTS

Monster Problems: Vampire Misfire

CHAPTER ONE

MY LIFE BITES

Clearly, I won't be getting any sleep.

Not after the thundering crash of my door against the wall. Or the snap of my window shade, which is now rapping annoyingly against the glass pane. Or the bright light shining in my eyes as daylight streams over my face.

Note to self: stop sleeping in rooms that don't lock from the inside.

"Well, well," comes a nasally voice. "This must be the special one himself."

Okay, here we go. I roll over reluctantly, squinting at the two goons hovering over me. Needless to say, their expressions are less than warm-and-fuzzy.

The first guy reminds me of a shark, with his pale, unblinking eyes and long, thin nose. He's short and wearing the most disturbing Christmas sweater I've ever seen, featuring a snowman swallowing a reindeer. For some reason, he's studying me like I'm some kind of a zoo animal while frantically scribbling notes on his clipboard.

The second guy could pass for Mr. Clean's stunt double, minus the earing and the charm. He's bald, dressed in all white like an orderly at a psychiatric hospital, and his biceps are twice the size of his head.

After our awkward three-way staredown, shark-face finally puts down his pen and says, "Mr. Abraham Matthews, I presume?"

"My friends call me Bram," I say. "So, you can call me Abraham."

Shark-face doesn't crack a smile. Instead, he looks down at his clipboard and presses on, "I see, Mr. Matthews, that you arrived in the wee hours of the morning. The night guard informed us you were hand-delivered by the police."

"Yep," I say. "They were in the neighborhood. Nice of the boys to give me a lift."

"I also understand," he says, "that you ran away from your group home three weeks ago—in Arizona."

"Ah, Arizona," I say. "Quite an interesting place. Did you know they'll arrest you for cutting down a cactus? Or that crazy roadrunner bird from the cartoon is actually real? Dynamite-carrying coyotes, however, not so much."

"You do realize, Mr. Matthews, that you are now in Massachusetts? That's over two-thousand five-hundred miles away."

"Really?" I say, faking a shiver. "No wonder I'm so darn cold."

"You're a funny guy," shark-face says. "But we can

be funny too. Isn't that right, Mr. Snide?"

"Hilarious," the bald guy says, cracking his knuckles.

"Do you know where you are?" shark-face asks.

"Well, I'm no detective," I say, taking a look around, "but I think you just told me I'm in Massachusetts." Other than these bozos and the giant daddy-long-legs hanging from the ceiling, the place has an all-too-familiar sparseness. There's a bed, a desk, and a closet, but that's about it.

"I'll be a little more specific," shark-face says. "You are at the New England Home for Troubled Boys. I am Mr. Glume, the Director, and my esteemed colleague here is Mr. Snide, the House Manager."

"Honored to make your acquaintance," I say. Truth be told, I've bounced around group homes like this my entire life. There was the one in Arizona. And before that California. And before that Oregon, and so on. I've been in so many of these joints I've lost count.

And they're all the same. They claim they'll find you a loving family. They claim you're just one step away from enjoying family movie nights and roasting marshmallows over a fire. But trust me, it never happens.

Not for kids like me.

Don't worry, there's no need to break out the violins. I'm a realist, so I know the odds are against me. After all, I'm twelve now, which means no first-time parents would touch me with a ten-foot pole. Think about it. Why would any wide-eyed, bushy-tailed couple looking to adopt take on a troubled teen when they could drive off the lot with a brand-new baby instead? Trust me, they wouldn't. As soon as you're out of diapers, you're considered damaged goods.

Plus, I've got my, well, other quirks…

As Glume flips through the mountain of paperwork on his clipboard, his whisper-thin eyebrows rise higher and higher. Clearly, he's got my whole case file.

"You've been in the foster system since you were an infant," Glume says.

"Yep," I say. "Guess that makes me the poster child."

"It says your parents died in a house fire," he continues. "What a shame."

"I've come to grips with it," I say quickly.

"I'm sure you have," Glume says. "But it also says you have quite a long history of causing trouble. Lots of trouble. In fact, the director of your former group home doesn't want you back. She says you have… unusual habits?"

"Like she should talk," I scoff. "She didn't get the nickname 'Beast of Bourbon' for nothing."

"She says you stay up all night. You refuse to go to bed during mandatory lights out."

"I'm a night owl," I say. "I catch my 'z's' during the daytime. Otherwise, I get cranky. Like now, for instance."

"She says you avoid sunlight."

"I burn easily," I say. "I'm delicate."

"And you only eat food that is red in color?"

"Okay, now even I have to admit that's a weird one. She's got me there."

Glume flips through more pages. "It seems several reports are accusing you of property damage—like flooding the basement."

"Not true," I say. "I walked in just as some kid threw the fire extinguisher into the washing machine. No one expected it to go off like that. The bubbles were insane."

"And the broken windows on the second floor?"

"Purely an accident," I counter. "They told us to do a craft project. Who knew taping worms to glass would attract so many birds?"

"And the bed bug infestation?"

"A complete misunderstanding," I say. "I was the one warning those kids to leave their pillows in the garbage dumpster."

"Mr. Matthews, you are not taking responsibility for your involvement in any of these incidents."

"That's right," I say. "Because I wasn't responsible."

"Clearly," Glume says. "In fact, you don't seem to be responsible for anything."

"Whew!" I say, wiping my brow. "I was worried we wouldn't understand each other."

"Well, you're in luck," Glume says. "I do understand you. I understand you perfectly. And fortunately for you, you've come to the right place."

"It sounds like it," I say relieved. Just then, my

stomach rumbles. I can't remember the last time I ate. "Hey, this has been a great kumbaya session, but how about we wrap it up and head to the kitchen for a hearty breakfast?"

"Excellent idea, Mr. Matthews," Glume says. "We shall adjourn to the kitchen where we will begin your education."

"Great, I could eat a—wait, did you say education?"

"Oh, don't panic, Mr. Matthews," Glume says with a sinister smile. "Here at the New England School for Troubled Boys, you'll get a steady diet of exactly what you need."

"And what's that?" I ask suspiciously.

"Responsibility," he says.

"Is this the hilarious part?" I ask.

"I guess that depends on which side of the clipboard you're standing on," Glume answers. "Now you can choose to get up on your own or, if you would like, Mr. Snide would be more than happy to assist you."

The bald guy steps forward and I realize this could get real ugly real fast. But I'm not looking for any trouble.

"Okay, hold your horses, cue ball," I say, throwing my legs over the side. "There's no need to get personal. Let's get this education thing over with so I can eat."

***

I don't think I've ever seen so many dishes in one

kitchen sink before. They're piled sky-high like Glume had been waiting for my arrival for weeks. And it isn't just plates. There are stacks of dirty cups, and hundreds of used forks and spoons scattered all over the place. At least they know enough to use plastic knives.

"Your first lesson begins now," Glume says gleefully. "Every one of these items needs to be hand-washed, hand-dried, and returned to its proper place."

"Hand washed?" I exclaim. "You mean, there's no dishwasher?"

"We just got a new one," Snide says, throwing a dish towel over my face. "Have fun."

"But… this will take hours," I say. "What about food?"

"Oh, you'll find plenty of leftovers," Glume says, "if you *lick* the plates clean. You'd best get started, Mr. Matthews. And please, no spots on the silverware."

As they exit, I hear them snickering down the hall. Well, this is a major bummer. I had hoped this would be a longer stop—get in a few square meals, sleep in a warm bed—but now I need to rethink my plans. After all, I didn't volunteer to be the resident Cinderella.

As I turn on the faucet, I catch my reflection in the stainless tea kettle. Not surprisingly, I look as tired as I feel. My skin is thin and pale, my dark hair is a tangled mess, and my eyes look like brown half-circles.

I take in the ceramic carnage around me and exhale.

I'm in no mood to do this chore the conventional

way, so I open the cabinets to see where everything is supposed to go, and peer over my shoulder to ensure the coast is clear.

Then, I get busy.

Remember those quirks I mentioned earlier? Well, sometimes they come in handy. Like right now.

You see, I have some strange abilities.

Super speed happens to be one of them.

Now I'm not claiming to be the Flash or anything, but I can really motor when I need to. I've never told anyone about it. I mean, people think I'm weird enough already. But when a situation calls for it and no one's around, I like to indulge a little.

The only problem is that using my super speed wipes me out. Especially if I haven't eaten in a while. But this task is simply too inhumane not to go for it.

So, despite some ear-jarring dish clinking, I manage to wash, dry, and put away every item in less than two minutes with no spots on the silverware. I stand back and admire my handiwork.

Even though I'm feeling drained, it was worth it. And the best part is that no one will be the wiser.

At least, that's what I think.

Until I turn around.

That's when I find a blond, curly-haired kid standing behind me with his jaw hanging open. He looks a few years younger than me, and he's holding a dirty plate.

I curse under my breath for being so careless.

Time to play it cool.

"Thanks," I say, taking the plate out of his hands as if nothing happened. "I must have missed that one."

I turn back to the sink and begin washing it—at normal speed. Okay, don't panic. Maybe he didn't see anything.

"D-Do you have superpowers?" he stammers.

Or maybe not.

"What are you talking about?" I say, grabbing the dish towel to start drying.

"Y-You just cleaned that mess up ridiculously fast," he says. "I-I saw you do it."

"Really?" I say, putting the plate away. I hate lying to the kid, but what choice do I have? "So, let me ask you something. If I could move like that, do you think I'd be hanging around this joy factory? Believe me, I'd take off so fast all you'd see is a cloud of dust."

"Well," the boy says, thinking it over, "I-I guess that's true."

"Believe me, I wish I had superpowers like that. Yet, here we are. Hey, are you feeling okay? You look kind of green. Maybe you need to sit down?"

The boy looks confused. "I… but… I… Maybe I'm not feeling so well."

"Here," I say, pulling over a chair from the table in the corner. "Take a load off."

As he slumps down, I fill a glass with water and get him some ice. "Drink this. Maybe you're dehydrated.

Kids today don't drink enough water."

"Thanks," he says, downing half the glass in one gulp. "Sorry, I… must be losing my mind."

"No problem," I say, taking a seat beside him and reaching out my hand. "My name is Abraham. But you can call me Bram."

"I'm Johnny," he says, shaking my hand. "You're that kid who came in late last night. With the police."

"The one and only," I say. "Sorry if I woke you."

"No big deal," he says. "I sleep with one eye open anyway. Have for a while."

"Yeah," I say. "I get it."

"So, how'd you end up here?" he asks, taking another sip.

"Incredible luck?" I say, causing Johnny to spit take.

"Seriously," I continue. "I don't know. I've been in foster care as long as I can remember. I've probably lived with twenty foster families. Eventually, no one wanted me anymore, so now I just kind of go from group home to group home."

"Twenty families?" he says, either shocked or impressed. "That's a lot of foster families."

"I guess," I say with a shrug. "I never really thought about it. I mean, it's all kind of a blur now. I just remember it was hard to keep track of all the different rules. What was okay in one house would be against the law in the next. I guess I never felt settled, you know? How about you? How'd you get here?"

"I got labeled a 'bad kid' a few years back,'" he says, sitting back. "I had just gotten to a new family. Nice couple who already had a biological son. At first, I thought I had a chance. Well, I guess the kid wasn't so happy I was there and claimed I stole his mom's necklace. It was ridiculous. I've never stolen anything in my life! Anyway, he wasn't going anywhere so I got the boot. Been here ever since."

"That's rough," I say. "I can't even tell you how many times I've been blamed for stuff I didn't do. I actually had one parent tell me if her daughter and I were hanging off a cliff and she could only save one of us, she'd save her kid every single time. Like, isn't that obvious? But I always wondered why she had to say it. It's just cruel, you know?"

"I guess kids like us don't get to have real families," Johnny says, his face falling.

For some reason, his words hit me hard.

"Yeah," I say. "I guess so."

We sit in silence for a minute when I notice a newspaper on the table. The headline reads:

GRAVE ROBBERS EXHUME BODY OF MILITARY HERO

"Well, that's creepy," I say.

"Yeah," Johnny says. "It was all over the news. It was the grave of some old military sharpshooter who helped win a bunch of wars. Someone dug him up and took all his bones. I think it's the second grave robbery in the last two weeks. People are weird."

"Totally weird," I agree, wondering why anyone would even think about doing something like that.

"Well, it's not so bad here," Johnny says, trying to change the subject. "As long as you follow the rules."

"Guess I'm in trouble then," I say. "Because I'm not much of a rule-follower."

"I wasn't either," he says. "Until I got here."

Just then, the door bursts open, and Snide barges in. "How're the chores go—What?"

The ogre stops short, taking in the scene.

"Oh, I'm all finished," I say quickly. "Guess I'm more of a Type A personality than I thought. I was just using my free time here to meet some of my fellow inmates."

"But that's impossible!" Snide says furiously. "You couldn't have done it all alone." Then, he wheels on Johnny. "You helped him!"

"No," I interject. "He didn't lift a finger."

"I think I'll be going now," Johnny says, standing up quickly. He shoots me a look, mouths 'good luck,' and makes a brisk exit.

"I don't believe you," the brute says.

"It's all in the magic of the suds," I claim, holding out my arms. "And look, no dish-pan hands."

"That's it, wise guy!" he says. "You're coming with

me!"

"To where?" I ask, as Snide opens the kitchen door and waves me into the hallway.

"You'll see," Snide says, as we walk down the hall and past an office where Glume is on the phone.

"Oh, yes, Officer Smith," Glume says into the receiver. Then he catches sight of us and breaks into a weird smile. "Mr. Matthews is having a great time. He's learning the ropes quickly."

Snide chuckles and leads me down a flight of stairs.

"Hope you're not afraid of the dark," he says.

Well, he's right about one thing, wherever he's taking me is dark—pitch dark even. But not for me. For some reason, I've always been able to see perfectly in darkness. It's like my eyes never need time to adjust. Of course, I have no idea why. I guess it's just another one of my strange quirks.

But when we reach the bottom, Snide flicks on a dim light, and my stomach drops. The basement is totally creepy, with cement-block walls and a way-too-low ceiling. It smells musty down here, like mold has been brewing for centuries.

Then, I notice a row of steel doors lining the walls.

What are those for?

Snide reaches into his back pocket and pulls out a set of keys. As he jingles them around the ring, they echo through the narrow chamber. Finally, he finds the one he's looking for.

"Um, is this some kind of a kid dungeon?" I ask. "Because I don't think state-sponsored group homes are supposed to have kid dungeons."

"You think you've got it all figured out, don't you Matthews?" he says, unlocking the steel door to our left. "Well, keep thinking that way and you're gonna have problems around here. Serious problems."

"C'mon," I plead, "you're not really gonna—"

But before I can finish my sentence, he nudges me inside the tiny cell. And then he slams the door shut behind me.

Suddenly, a small slat opens at the top of the door, and Snide presses his ugly mug into the opening.

"Do you know what we do with problems here at the New England Home for Troubled Boys?"

I'm about to provide an eloquent response when I realize the question is rhetorical.

"We keep 'em down here in solitary," he says. "Until one way or another, they aren't problems anymore."

Then, he slams the slat closed.

And I'm locked inside.

Foster Care Profile

Case No: 66649666

Name: MATTHEWS, ABRAHAM
Nickname(s): BRAM
Yrs in Care: 12 years
Difficulty: HIGH

VITALS:
Height: 4'10"
Weight: 95lbs
Hair: Black
Eyes: Brown

FOSTER CARE R
ARIZONA, PHO
CALIFORNIA,
OREGON, SALE
IDAHO, BOISE
NEVADA, RENO
CALIFORNIA,
UTAH, LOGAN
WYOMING, CA
NEW MEXICO, ALBEQUERQUE
PENNSYLVANIA, ERIE (ran away after 3 mo.)
(Please see pages 2-4 for additional foster locations)

Matthews, Abraham (Bram) pg 1/56

CHAPTER TWO

BREAKING AND EXITING

You'd be surprised how time doesn't fly when you're locked inside a basement prison cell.

Let's just say there's way too much time to think. In fact, I've spent so much time thinking, the mere thought of thinking absolutely exhausts me. Especially after holding a spirited debate with myself about whether I'm hungrier or thirstier. Now I fear I'm drifting into a dangerous state of delusion.

Case in point, there seems to be a hunk of crusty bread lying by the foot of the door. I haven't got the foggiest idea how it got there. I mean, I certainly would have noticed if someone had opened the door or dropped it through the slat.

Or would I?

I stare at the bread for a good long while, questioning if it's even real until I muster enough energy to poke it with my foot. The bread tumbles across the floor, hits the wall, and comes to a dead stop.

Okay, at least I'm not seeing things.

Unfortunately, the sight of the bread utterly repulses me. Look, I don't know why I can only eat red-colored food. Again, I had hours to contemplate that one too. My conclusion—I'm a freak. So, I'm clearly going to starve to death unless I can get out of here.

Looking up, I notice a small spider weaving an intricate web in the corner of the ceiling. For some reason, wherever I go spiders seem to follow.

Maybe they're my spirit insect.

I wonder why this one is so darn industrious. After all, there aren't any flies buzzing around. And every time I check in on the little guy, its web is not only getting larger, but closer. So, either we'll die in here together, or it's plotting to take early retirement from its largest catch ever—me!

So yeah, I'm a little delusional. But what happens next pushes me over the edge.

First, I hear little pitter-patter noises. Like something is scampering across the cement floor. I sit up and look around, but I don't see anything.

Then, they come into view.

Two hairy rats are inspecting the bread. One is tall and thin, the other small and fat. They sniff it with their pink noses, sinking their claws into the hard crust. They squeak back and forth, chattering away when suddenly their squeaks turn into… words?

"See here food me told you me smelt," the fat one says.

"Right you be," the thin one says, looking at me. "Pink one eat not."

I clean out my ears with my fingers. Are they actually speaking English or am I actually nuts?

"Lose out does he," the fat one says, taking a big bite. "Stupid maybe he be."

"Blind maybe he be," the thin one says, taking a bite of his own.

"Stupid and blind maybe he be," the fat one says, and they both cackle at my expense.

Okay, that's enough. After the day I've had I'm not about to sit here and get insulted by vermin.

So, I lean over and interject, "Pink one bread no like maybe?"

They freeze.

A piece of bread drops from the thin one's mouth.

Then, they look at each other, and then back at me.

"P-Pink one talk us like?" the thin one stammers.

The fat one swallows hard and slowly backs up. "P-Pink one … me understands?"

"Look, you can have the bread," I say. "Seriously, I'm not going to eat it."

"Impossible this be!" the thin one says.

"Unless … unless …" the fat one says, staring at me. Then, he takes off like his ears are on fire, disappearing through a narrow crevice between the cement blocks.

"Hey, wait!" I call out. "Unless what?" I look at the thin one. "What's he talking about?"

The rat looks at me, then at the bread, then back at me. Then he grabs a chunk of crust and hightails it after his friend.

At this point, I realize my mind is playing tricks on me and I can't distinguish between fantasy and reality. I mean, I'm so far gone I'm speaking Rat!

Suddenly, the room starts spinning. I'm guessing starvation has finally caught up with me. My body starts trembling and I can't seem to keep my eyes open.

I'm losing consciousness.

Fading out.

I look up to say goodbye to my spider friend, but to my surprise, its web is still there, but the spider is gone.

Then, everything goes black.

***

It takes all I have just to open my eyes, but the bright light overhead forces them closed again. My head is throbbing, and I feel like I've been run over by a steamroller. It's not until I try sitting up that I realize I'm not lying on a cement floor anymore, but on a bed. I'm tucked under the covers and my head is resting on a soft pillow. I try propping up again, but I don't get far.

"Take it easy," comes a familiar voice.

I pry my eyes open to find Johnny sitting beside me. He's holding out a plate with something red on it.

Swedish Fish candies!

"H-How did you know?" I ask.

"You kept moaning for something red to eat," Johnny says. "I didn't have much time, so I snuck down to the kitchen and grabbed these. Although technically I'm not sure Swedish Fish actually qualify as food."

"It's perfect," I say, inhaling the delicious treats. After being so hungry for so long, I can feel the sugar entering my bloodstream, re-energizing my body. "Where am I? What are you doing here?"

"After you passed out, they pulled you out of the dungeon and brought you back to your room. I felt bad seeing what they did to you. So, after everyone went to bed, I snuck in to check on you. But I can't stay long. Snide's on night duty."

Out of the corner of my eye, I catch a digital clock sitting on a desk. It reads: 12:49 am. It's the middle of the night. "How long was I down there?"

"Sixteen hours," Johnny says. "I think that's a record. By the way, why do you only eat red stuff?"

"Because I'm weird," I say, swallowing the last Swedish Fish. "Thanks for getting this for me. I was starving."

"Clearly," Johnny says. "They put all the new kids in the dungeon. Although they usually spring them after four hours. So, you must have made one heck of a first impression."

"Well, my first impression will be my last," I say. "Because I'm getting out of here. ASAP."

"What?" Johnny says. "Are you nuts? Where are you going to go?"

"Doesn't matter," I say, peeling back the covers and getting to my feet. I stand up, although I feel pretty shaky. "But wherever I'll be, it won't be here."

"But how will you survive?" Johnny asks. "If you're here, at least you've got food and shelter."

"Let's get something straight," I say, looking him straight in the eyes. "Some things are more important than food and shelter. Just because they put every kid in a dungeon doesn't make it okay. We're human beings, not monsters."

Johnny's lips quiver as he tries to respond, but he can't. I didn't mean to upset him, but what's happening here isn't right. It's like the old story of the frog and the pot of boiling water. If you put the frog straight into a pot of boiling water, it'll feel the heat and jump right out. But if the frog is put into warm water and you turn up the heat slowly, the frog won't notice the temperature rising and will end up being boiled alive.

Johnny's been here so long everything seems normal to him, but I'm not going to wait around until I get cooked. I look out the window. We're on the third floor, which is way too high to jump. If I'm going to make my exit, I'll have to do it through the front door.

Which means I'll need to dodge Snide.

"Thanks for your help," I say, grabbing my gray hoodie from the back of the door. "Do you want to come with me?"

At first, Johnny looks stunned by my question. Then, he sits quietly for a moment, deep in thought.

"No, but thanks," he says finally. "I kind of watch over some of the smaller guys here. I guess this is my home now."

His answer doesn't surprise me. Kids like us tend to accept our situations, no matter how bad they may be. But over time I've learned to follow my instincts on what I think is right, not comfortable. Still, I can't just leave him and the other kids in this horrible mess.

Then, I get an idea.

"Don't worry," I say. "I'll help you out before I go."

"Thanks," he says. "So, is this the part where I see a cloud of dust?"

I smile. Clearly, I never had him fooled.

"Something like that," I say. "Take care of yourself."

He nods, and I enter the hall.

It's pitch black, but again, darkness isn't a problem for me. Johnny was right though. I could turn on my super speed and make a clean getaway, but I plan on saving it for later. After all, that's how I ended up here in the first place. I got too tired to outrun the police.

Since everyone is asleep, I tiptoe down the stairs, passing Glume's room on the second floor. The door is cracked and old shark-face is peacefully snoring away. Sleep while you can because your whole world is about to change.

When I reach the bottom step, I have a clear pathway to the front door. My instincts tell me to go for it, but I can't. I promised Johnny I'd help him out.

So, I turn the corner and head for the office. The door is open, and the lights are on, but no one is inside. Snide must be doing his rounds.

I enter the room and duck behind the desk. Then, I pop up to dial the phone and pull the receiver back down with me. The phone rings once before someone picks up.

"This is 9-1-1, how can we assist you?" the female operator says.

"Yes, hi, I'm calling from the New England Home for Troubled Boys. I'd like to report on the improper treatment of children here."

"Are you a child?" the operator asks, her voice sounding surprised.

"Yes," I say. "I'm a resident here."

"Oh," she says. "What kind of improper treatment?"

I don't have much time, so I cut to the chase. "Just get the police here. Tell them to go straight to the basement. There's a kid dungeon down there no one knows about. You'll see. Just hurry."

"I've already sent a notification to the police," the operator says. "They should be there shortly. Are you okay? Can I have your name?"

I think about giving my name, but instead, I say, "Look, I represent all the kids here. Good kids that just need a helping hand."

Then, I hang up. I need to split before Snide shows up. But when I leap back into the hallway, I discover a large figure blocking my path to the front door.

Snide!

"What were you doing in my office, Matthews?"

"I'm a night owl, remember?"

The oaf smiles. "Are you looking for your file, Matthews? Are you trying to find out why no one loves you?"

"Shut up, Snide," I say.

"That's Mr. Snide," he says.

"Shut up, Mr. Snide," I say.

"Well, I'll tell you something you probably didn't know," Snide says. "Because I did a little research on you myself."

"Congratulations," I say. "Because I didn't think Neanderthals could read."

"Ha," Snide says. "Then I guess you're not interested in what I found out. It's about your daddy."

He stands there with a big, stupid grin on his face. He's baiting me. Sucking me in. But what could he have found out about my dad? I mean, he's long dead.

"Okay," I say, my curiosity getting the best of me. "I'll bite, what is it?"

"Get this," Snide says, folding his immense arms. "You weren't put into foster care by just anyone. Your very own father dropped you into the system."

What?

I'm stunned. That's not what I'd been told. I was told my parents died in a fire that I somehow survived, and then I was put into foster care. So, what he's saying can't be true.

"You're lying," I say.

"Am I, Matthews?" he says. "Well, I did some digging. Your case is so darn thick and convoluted it took a while. But I went all the way back and found your very first record and guess what? Your daddy's signature was right on it. Mr. Gabriel Matthews. He gave you away like a smelly carpet."

No way. That's impossible.

"Must be tough," Snide continues, "but I guess you can say you've been unwanted your whole life."

"Liar!" I yell, red hot. All I want to do is get out of here, but Snide is blocking the hallway.

"Now go back to your room, Matthews," he orders.

"No," I answer.

"I was hoping you'd say that," he says.

Then, he cracks his knuckles, and charges at me!

Without thinking, I react.

Just before Snide reaches me, I turn on my super speed and somersault between his legs in a flash. Snide thunders over me and crashes into a table which breaks beneath his considerable weight.

"I don't know how you did that," he says, standing up, his muscles rippling. "But you're going to pay."

If he catches me, he'll tear me limb from limb.

Suddenly, the hall light clicks on.

"Snide?"

That's Glume's voice!

"Snide, what's all the ruckus?"

As Snide looks up, I realize this may be my only chance. The Swedish Fish aren't going to last in my system for long, so my speed powers will be nearing the end of their shelf life. If I'm getting out it has to be now!

I bolt down the hall and plow into the front door, knocking it clear off its hinges. Oh well, I guess Glume can add that to my list of property damage. My shoulder is throbbing but I don't stop. I book down the street as fast as I can, my speed waning with every step. When I think I'm a good enough distance away, I duck behind a parked pickup truck.

Just then, I hear SIRENS—police sirens!

Four patrol cars pull up in front of the group home. I peer around the truck as a bunch of police officers sprint up the front steps, disappearing through the open door frame I left behind. I watch anxiously from my hiding spot, hoping the boys in blue got my instructions.

After what seems like an eternity, there's movement.

First, I see Glume, and then Snide. They're being led out of the building—in handcuffs!

It worked!

Suddenly, boys spill out of the house onto the front steps. They all look shell-shocked as they watch Glume and Snide get pushed into the back of a police car. But there's one boy in the middle of the pack who is wearing a different expression.

He has blond, curly hair. And he's smiling.

***

As I roam the city in the dead of night, I'm feeling pretty lost. After all of this, there's no way I can ever go to another group home again. Plus, I'm pretty sure if the police catch me, I'll be charged with reverse breaking and entering.

So, for the first time, I'm truly on my own.

And what's worse, I can't stop thinking about what Snide said. Was everything I thought I knew about my life a lie? Did my father really put me into foster care? Did my parents really not want me?

Suddenly, a HOWL in the distance snaps me back to reality. It sounds like a wounded dog. Looking around, I realize I wandered into a graveyard of all places.

Lucky me.

I keep walking, reading the tombstones around me. Some are really old, like as far back as the 1800s. Then, I remember that eerie story about the graverobbers and a chill runs down my spine.

I can keep going, but I'm pretty hungry. If I don't eat something soon, I'll pass out. But the graveyard just seems to go on and on, and my chances of finding a pizza joint in a place like this are slim to none.

I turn to head back when another HOWL pierces the night air, making the hairs on the back of my neck stand on end. That one seemed a lot closer than the last one.

Looking up, I realize there's a full moon.

Wonderful.

I pull my hood over my head and start walking double time. To my relief, I finally find the exit and step through the gates, only to hear RUSTLING behind me.

I spin around and gasp.

Because standing in front of me is a hunched figure.

At first, I think it's a man, but there's something wrong with his head. Then, he steps onto the pavement and I realize it isn't a man at all. His head is shaped like a wolf, and every inch of his muscular body is covered in matted, brown fur.

My jaw hits the floor.

Holy cow!

I can't believe what I'm seeing.

It's a… a… werewolf?!?

The beast stares at me with his bright red eyes as a long string of drool drips from the corner of his mouth, splattering onto the pavement.

I want to move, but I'm glued to the spot.

Then, he lets out an ear-piercing HOWL.

And to my horror, several creatures HOWL back.

MONSTEROLOGY 101
FIELD GUIDE

WEREWOLF

CLASSIFICATION:

Type: Shapeshifter
Sub-Type: Lycanthrope
Height: Variable
Weight: Variable
Eye Color: Red
Hair Color: Variable

KNOWN ABILITIES:

- **Transformations typically occur during a full moon**
- **Superhuman Strength, Speed, Reflexes, Agility, and Healing**
- **Heightened Sight, Smell and Hearing**

KNOWN WEAKNESSES:

- **Vulnerable to silver objects (e.g. bullets or blades)**
- **Susceptible to injury in human form**
- **Wolfsbane is rumored to reverse lycanthropy**

DANGER LEVEL:

HIGH

TIPS TO AVOID AN UNWANTED ENCOUNTER:

- **Remain inside during a full moon**
- **Mask your scent**
- **Travel in large crowds**
- **Stay far away from wooded areas**

CHAPTER THREE

HERE A WEREWOLF, THERE A WEREWOLF

Despite my limited knowledge of low budget B-movies, I'm pretty sure the creature staring me down meets all the criteria for a bonafide werewolf.

Angry wolf face. Check.

Smelly, furry body. Double check.

Clear intention to kill me. Triple check.

That's when my fight or flight mode kicks in. There's no question I'm choosing flight, but I'd already used up my super speed escaping from Snide. I've got nothing left in the tank!

Based on the look in the beast's eyes, I have no doubt he'll tear me to shreds as soon as I move a muscle. Then again, if I just stand here doing nothing, I'm pretty sure he'll tear me to shreds anyway. So, I guess this is a lose-lose situation.

Maybe Johnny was right. Maybe I should've just stayed at the New England Home for Troubled Boys. After all, what's a little torture compared with losing your life forever?

Then, I realize something.

The werewolf hasn't attacked me.

Why hasn't he attacked me?

I mean, he's got me cornered. He easily could have gobbled me up by now and had cheesecake for dessert. Yet, he hasn't moved. Why not?

At this point, I've got nothing to lose, so I figure I'll test the waters.

"Um, if you don't mind," I say, "I've got to go. You see I've got this huge book report on some dead guy due tomorrow, and I haven't even started the darn book yet. You look like you've been in that situation a few times yourself. So, anyway, I hope you have a great night."

I take a step backward and the werewolf lets out a deep-throated growl. Then, he steps towards me.

Okay, he didn't like that. But then again, he still hasn't pounced on me either.

That's when I get a crazy thought.

I take a step to my left.

The werewolf steps right, staying in front of me.

Weird.

I step right. He steps left.

Still in front of me.

Great. I'm square dancing with a werewolf.

For some reason, wherever I go he wants to keep me dead in his sights. But there's one direction I haven't tried yet. Of course, this could mean certain death.

Here goes nothing.

I say a prayer and take a step forward.

The werewolf's eyes grow big, and he leaps ten feet backward, snarling. Well, I wasn't expecting that! It almost seems like he's afraid of me.

How's that even possible?

But I'll have to figure that out later because this might be my only chance to escape. I wheel around to bolt when, to my surprise, two other creatures leap out of the woods, scaring the bejesus out of me.

More werewolves!

These two are just as big as the first one, except one is black and the other is light brown. And now, with his buddies present, werewolf number one seems to have regained his confidence, because he lets out a series of sharp hoots, like he's barking orders.

Suddenly, the three spread out around me.

I'm surrounded!

If I don't come up with a plan, I'll be mincemeat. Maybe I can get the first one to back up again so I can make a break for it? I step towards him, but this time he doesn't budge. Instead, he roars back with such foul-smelling ferocity it makes me wish I was wearing a gas mask.

Well, that didn't work.

In fact, I think I made him angrier.

Suddenly, panic sets in. How could I be so stupid to think a kid-eating werewolf was scared of me? He was probably just keeping an eye on me until his friends showed up. After all, who likes dining alone?

Then, they move in.

I start hyperventilating.

Everywhere I look, all I see are teeth, fur, and claws. Is this how it's going to end? I can see the headlines now: *Loner Kid Mauled by Angry Gang of Werewolves.*

I close my eyes and brace myself for the first slash of claws. But instead, I feel something… different.

Something light lands over my head and body.

I open my eyes to find I'm covered in a thin, white netting. It's sticky and sort of tickles where it touches my skin. What's going on?

The next thing I know, the net tightens, cinching my arms against my sides. I try extending my elbows, but I can't. It's too strong.

Suddenly, I'm lifted clear into the air and over the surprised faces of my wolfish friends. I'm flying high above the trees, far away from danger.

Yes! I'm saved!

But then I realize I'm not getting any higher. I hang in the air for a moment and my stomach lurches.

And then gravity does its thing.

No! I'm going to go splat!

My stomach drops, and I start plummeting towards the ground at ridiculous speed, my arms still pinned to my sides. So, I do what any reasonable person would do in a situation like this—I scream my lungs out!

The ground is approaching fast, and depending on which end I land on, I'll either break my head or my legs. I close my eyes, seconds away from impact. But instead of bouncing off the ground, someone catches me in the nick of time.

In fact, it seems like a whole group of people catch me all at once because I feel multiple arms cushioning different parts of my body. I'm so relieved I decide right then and there to dedicate the rest of my life to every person who saved me.

But it's not until I open my eyes that I realize I'll have more free time on my hands than I thought, because I'm not lying in the arms of multiple people, but rather one person with multiple arms!

I do a double take.

Okay, I'm clearly being held by a man. I mean, he looks like a normal man, with dark hair, a bushy beard, and a warm smile. But then I realize he's holding me in all of his arms, two of which are completely normal, but the other four looks like the appendages of… a spider?

I nearly pass out.

"Don't worry," he says. "I've got you."

"A-Are you Spiderman's brother?" I stammer.

"Something like that," he says with a wink.

He swipes down with one of his spider legs and cuts the strange wrapping from my body. Finally, my arms are free! I touch the material. It's a spider web! The thickest spider web I've ever seen.

It's only when he sets me on my feet that I realize how massive he is. He's tall and super muscular. But of course, his size isn't his most notable feature. That distinction belongs to his limbs. There are eight in total: two normal arms, two normal legs, and four spider legs—two on each side of his torso.

I close my eyes. Maybe this is all just a weird dream. But when I open them again, he's still standing there—spider legs and all.

"You okay?" he asks.

"Me? Oh, I'm great," I say. "Just another day talking casually with an enormous man-spider."

"Did the werewolves bite you?" he asks.

"No," I say. "They didn't touch me."

"You're lucky. If a werewolf bites you, you'll likely turn into one yourself."

"Well, isn't that a kick in the pants," I say.

"Listen, we've got to get out of here," he says.

I agree with that. But to where? And I don't even know this guy's name. If I can just get some food in me, I can use my speed and make my getaway.

"Yeah," I say. "About that. Look, I really appreciate you saving me and all, but I think I'm just gonna go solo from here on out. You wouldn't happen to have a tomato or a red pepper on you?"

The giant looks down at me and shakes his head.

"Kid, do you really think you're going to just walk out of here like nothing happened? Do you even know why those hounds are after you?"

Well, now I feel totally stupid.

"Of course I know," I say, faking it. "It's because, um … one time I … okay, I've got nothing."

"Let me simplify it," he says. "They're after one thing and they won't stop until they get it. And that's you."

"Me? Why would those shag carpets be after me? What did I do to them?"

"You were born," he says. "And now you've been discovered."

"Um, could you possibly be any more cryptic?"

"Okay, listen up because I'm gonna have to make this quick," he says, his eyes darting all around. "You see, we've been watching you. We knew this would happen one day. We just didn't think it would be today."

"Wait," I say. "What do you mean you've been watching me?"

He puffs up his chest and says, "Let's just say I have an extensive net-work." Then, he wiggles his spider legs.

"Net-work? What are you—"

Then, it hits me.

I suddenly realize what he's talking about. He's part spider. There was a spider in my room when I got to the New England Home for Troubled Boys. There was a spider in the dungeon. Then my mind flashes back to all of the spiders I've seen throughout my life and I realize they've always been there. Every foster family. Every group home. Everywhere.

Holy tarantulas!

Those spiders weren't random. They were a network of spies! My entire life has been bugged!

I back away, my heart racing. "Who are you? What do you want from me?"

"I go by Crawler," he says. "For obvious reasons. I know I look strange and what I'm telling you may sound crazy, but I'm what's called a 'Supernatural.' And so are you."

"A 'Super-what?'" I ask, totally lost. "What are you talking about?"

"You're a Supernatural, Bram," Crawler repeats.

"How do you know my na—?" I start, but then I remember. "Right, your spider spy network thingy."

"Here's how it breaks down," he says. "In this world, you're either a 'Natural,' which is a person without special abilities, or a 'Supernatural,' otherwise known as a person with special abilities. Guess which you are?"

"Normal?" I say.

"Really?" Crawler says. "My mistake. I thought you were the kid with super speed and a bad habit of getting burned in sunlight."

Well, I guess he knows me alright.

"Okay," I say. "So, let's just say I'm one of those things you mentioned. I still don't get why this is all happening now."

Crawler smiles. "Let's just say that 'now' we're not the only ones who know about you. You're a special kind of Supernatural."

"Special?" I say with a laugh. Now I'm convinced this is a case of mistaken identity. "And by the way, who is this 'we' you keep talking about?"

But before he can answer, there's a SNAP!

The werewolves have found us!

"We've wasted too much time," Crawler says, stepping in front of me. "Stay back."

I see the two brown werewolves, but where's the—

"Duck!" Crawler yells.

I hit the deck just as Crawler swings two of his spider legs over my head, firing off a series of webs. When I look up the black werewolf is pinned to a tree, only a few feet behind me. The creature struggles to get free, but the webbing is too strong.

Then, Crawler spins and lets loose an onslaught of spiderwebs. But the other two are too fast, disappearing into the brush.

"We've got to get out of here," Crawler says. "They'll be back soon. They're probably marshaling reinforcements."

"Wait, you mean there's more of them?"

"A lot more," he says. "It's time to go. Come on."

Then, he reaches out his hand.

But for some reason, I hesitate.

"Aren't you coming?" he asks.

I don't know why I paused. Maybe it's because I'm nuts. Or maybe it's because I don't know who he's working for. But deep down, I sense that if I go with him, everything in my life will change—and it may not be for the better.

Suddenly, HOWLS fill the air.

"Let's get out of here," I say, grabbing his hand.

Crawler scoops me onto his back and sprints. With his long stride and extra limbs, the guy can really move. I hold on for dear life, dodging branches as we weave through the trees. A few minutes later, we come upon a clearing where a motorcycle is parked. It's a chopper, with a long front-end and extended handlebar. For a second, I wonder if I'll be riding piggyback, but as we get closer I see a sidecar.

Crawler climbs on and lowers me into the seat. Then, he buckles my seatbelt with his spider legs and pops a helmet onto my head.

There are a series of HOWLS behind us. I turn to see a swarm of dots in the distance: four, then ten, then twenty.

The werewolves are heading straight for us!

"Gun it!" I yell.

"Hang on," Crawler says coolly. Then he puts on a pair of sunglasses, kickstarts the engine, and we're off.

CLASSIFIED

Person(s) of Interest

CODE NAME: CRAWLER

REAL NAME: UNKNOWN

BASE OF OPERATIONS: VAN HELSING ACADEMY

FACTS: Crawler operates as a field agent for Headmaster Lothar Van Helsing. Crawler's skills are primarily utilized for a variety of sensitive assignments including rescue and stealth missions. Crawler is armed and dangerous and should be approached with caution.

Category:	Abnormal
Sub-Type:	Not Applicable
Height:	6'5"
Weight:	240 lbs

FIELD OBSERVATIONS:

- Possesses four spider appendages with super-human strength
- Can shoot webs and climb walls
- Communicates with all types of spiders

STATUS: ACTIVE TARGET

DEPARTMENT OF SUPERNATURAL INVESTIGATIONS

CHAPTER FOUR

WELCOME TO WEIRDVILLE

I wake with a start.

Unfortunately, I'm not lying in bed at the New England Home for Troubled Boys just having a bad dream. Instead, I'm riding shotgun with a man-spider on a motorcycle. My head is throbbing, and my tongue feels like I've been chewing on a sock. I must have passed out, which isn't surprising given all of the energy I expended during the whole werewolf incident.

Speaking of werewolves.

I take in our surroundings and realize we're driving down some deserted road without a werewolf in sight. I don't know how long I've been out, but it must have been a while because the sun is now peeking over the horizon. I have to give major props to Crawler for getting us to safety relatively unscathed, my long-term therapy bills notwithstanding.

I slump back into the sidecar. So much has happened it's hard to process it all. According to Crawler, I'm some kind of a 'Supernatural,' whatever that means. And because of that, I'm now kidnapping target numero uno for a band of rabid werewolves.

That alone is crazy, but toss in Snide's comments about my dad being the one who dropped me into foster care and I'm still reeling. I mean, was Snide telling me the truth, or was he just pushing my buttons?

I need answers, and I'm about to ask Crawler some very pointed questions when he suddenly announces—

"We're here."

I look up just in time to see a black sign on the side of the road. At first, it's blank, but then bold, white letters appear out of nowhere. That's weird. My eyes must be playing tricks on me. Anyway, the sign reads:

VAN HELSING ACADEMY

Van Helsing what?!?

"Wait a minute," I yell over the engine. "Are you taking me to a school?"

"Something like that," Crawler yells back.

My back tenses up. School is not—and never will be—my thing. I'm not a good student, which is probably because I never spent any meaningful time at one school. Moving from family to family meant moving from school to school. And when you spend your life being fumbled around like a football, you tend not to make friends or get attention from teachers who think you're just passing through.

So, if this is where he's taking me, I won't be sticking around for long.

Suddenly, Crawler goes off-roading through the woods, bouncing me along some bumpy path I didn't see before. And the next thing I know, we're riding beside a huge brick wall. It's thirty feet tall and several miles long, with barbed wire wrapped around the top. Okay, I don't know any schools that need this kind of security. I mean, if I didn't catch the sign on the way in, I'd think we were visiting a prison.

Crawler rolls up to the main entrance. The massive front gate is closed shut, and the security booth is unmanned. Then, I notice a giant, yellow sign plastered front-and-center on the gate door. It reads:

RESTRICTED AREA.
DO NOT ENTER.
AUTHORIZED PERSONNEL ONLY.

Well, that's unwelcoming.

Needless to say, this doesn't look good.

"We're not seriously going in there, are we?" I ask.

"Yep," Crawler says. "We seriously are."

The next thing I know, a small device extends from the side of the security booth. At first, I think it's a microphone, but then it emits a thin, red light—like a laser. Crawler puts his face in front of it and it scans his pupils. Seconds later, the gate slides open with a slow and eerie screech.

Before I can object, Crawler powers us forward and I watch the gate close quickly behind us. Great. I guess there's no turning back now. But when I face forward, my jaw drops, because what's on the inside looks nothing like what's on the outside.

In fact, it looks like we're riding onto the movie set of an amazing prep school campus, with rolling green hills, expertly trimmed hedges, and stately brick buildings. Now I'm totally confused. Why would a place as nice as this need so much security?

We motor down the smooth driveway towards three massive buildings surrounding a perfectly manicured lawn. In my mind's eye, I can picture kids hanging out here, chucking Frisbees, and relaxing on the grass. Except, at this early hour there's no one around. Which reminds me I don't want to get a sunburn.

Crawler pulls around the circular driveway and parks in front of the center building. As I remove my helmet and step out of the sidecar, I can only marvel at the gigantic structure before me. The building is five stories high and half a mile long. The exterior is red brick, with crisp white windows, and a cupola adorning the roof. The giant, double-doored entrance is flanked by marble white columns. I've got to admit, this place is downright swanky.

"What do you think?" Crawler asks.

"I suppose it's nice," I say, "for a school."

"Glad you like it," Crawler says. "But it's not just any school. Come check it out."

Crawler pushes the doors open with his spider legs, and my eyebrows go up. The entrance hall is simply enormous, maybe bigger than a basketball court, with a giant, iron chandelier hanging over pristine marble floors. Two intricately carved wooden staircases flank the sides, leading several stories high. Perched along the walls are massive, stone statues of creatures with wings that look like gargoyles. I count six in total.

On the back wall hangs a large black banner with a white shield. The inside of the shield is very detailed, almost like a coat of arms, with old-looking symbols and mosaic patterns in the shape of strange creature's heads. Dead center is the school's name—Van Helsing Academy—in bold, gothic type. Beneath the shield is a saying, which reads:

YOU MUST BELIEVE IN THINGS YOU CANNOT IMAGINE.

Huh? What's that supposed to mean?

"This is the main building," Crawler says. "Our students take all of their classes here. This building also houses the cafeteria, the library, the auditorium, and the gymnasium. Oh, and a pool."

"You have a pool?" I say, almost too excitedly. "I mean, that's very interesting," I say, more matter-of-factly. Honestly, I'm impressed. I've never seen a school as decked out as this one.

Crawler looks amused. "Our faculty wing is also on the ground floor," he says. "Let's head that way. There's someone I'd like you to meet."

As we walk, our footsteps echo through a series of grand, dimly lit hallways. In one, I see a grandfather clock ticking away and check the time. It's four in the morning.

"Are you sure people are up at this hour?" I ask. "It's awfully early."

"Oh, don't worry," Crawler says. "He's up."

He? Who's 'he?'

Several minutes later we enter another wing. A plaque on the wall reads:

FACULTY OFFICES

We pass several closed offices with nameplates posted on the front doors. They read:

PROFESSOR LAWRENCE SEWARD
PROFESSOR QUINCY MORRIS IV
PROFESSOR LUCY HOLMWOOD
PROFESSOR ALASTAIR HEXUM

Strangely, there's one door with several locks and chains on the outside. The nameplate reads:

PROFESSOR CLAUDE FAUSTIUS

But that's not all, hanging from Faustius' doorknob is another sign that reads:

ENTRY FORBIDDEN

Strange.

We keep walking until we reach a final office at the end of the hallway. It's different than the others, with large, black doors and a rounded archway. The nameplate on the door reads:

HEADMASTER LOTHAR VAN HELSING,
MD, JD, Ph.D., D. Th., Etc., Etc.

Van Helsing? Hang on. Isn't that the name of the school? Suddenly, my stomach drops. I feel like I'm about to see the principal, except this time I didn't do anything wrong. I mean, I don't even go here.

So why am I so freaked out?

My gut tells me to split, but before I can move, one of Crawler's spindly legs RAPS on the door.

We wait for a response, but there's nothing.

"Shucks," I say. "I guess we should come back another time."

"No, go ahead," Crawler says. "He's in there."

"But nobody answered," I say.

"The door is warm," Crawler says. "He's in there. Good luck."

"Wait," I say, "aren't you coming with me?"

"Uh-uh," Crawler says. "He wants to see you alone."

Of course he does.

"Oh, and get ready," Crawler continues, "it's toasty in there."

Toasty? I grab the doorknob and it's super-warm to the touch. I guess he's not kidding. Well, here goes nothing. I pull open the door and step inside. But instead of entering a room, I find myself standing in a dark corridor.

What's up? Doesn't he pay the electric bill?

Fortunately, my eyes don't need to adjust, but as I turn back to question Crawler's assertion that someone is actually in here, the door slams shut in my face.

Great.

I guess there's only one way to go.

Well, Crawler was right about one thing, it's like a sauna in here! Sweat starts dripping from my body so I pull off my hoodie. I feel a bit cooler in my t-shirt, but I'm still sweating like a pig. Unfortunately, it looks like humidity isn't the only obstacle I'll have to deal with.

That's because this place is a hoarder's dream.

Everywhere I look are books—on shelves, on surfaces, even on the floor. In fact, I've never seen so many books stuffed in one place before. There are thick ones, thin ones, old ones, and really old ones. Well, I can say this about Van Helsing, he's certainly well-read. There's a narrow pathway cutting through the center, just wide enough to squeeze through.

Lucky me.

I make my way forward until the corridor ends in a small room that looks like a mad scientist's lair. Test tubes of various colors line the walls. Microscopes, Bunsen burners, and other scientific equipment cover every square inch of table space. There are all sorts of unfinished inventions scattered about, including a broom attached to some kind of a rocket.

That room then connects to another narrow hallway littered with medieval weaponry. There are swords, and axes, and spears, and all sorts of ancient armor you'd find in a museum or something. I move cautiously, trying not to get diced like an onion.

Finally, I enter a chamber that's considerably more open than the rest. Strangely, it's also way more organized. I see books neatly arranged on shelves, mugs hanging handle-side up, color-coordinated arrows resting in quivers, a raging fire, and…

My heart skips a beat.

A man with piercing blue eyes is staring at me.

His gaze is so intense all I can do is freeze and stare right back. He's bald on top, with long, gray hair falling along the sides and back. While his face is wrinkled and weathered, his body is stocky and strong, with a barrel chest and thick arms. Despite the oppressive warmth, he's sitting by the raging fireplace, bundled up in a sweater, gloves, and a scarf. Yet, he's not sweating at all.

"Welcome, Bram," he says. "Welcome to the Van Helsing Academy."

I'm stunned.

"How do you know my name?" I ask.

"All will be explained in due time," he says. "But first, it would only be polite to introduce myself. I am Headmaster Lothar Van Helsing."

I was right. This is his school. But I can't place his accent. It's not French. Maybe German? Or Dutch?

"Please, join me," he says, beckoning me inside. "We have much to discuss. Including your recent werewolf encounter."

"What do you know about that?" I ask anxiously. "Do you know why they were after me?"

"Indeed, I do," he says. "And I am afraid this is just the beginning. You see, the werewolves are merely pawns of a far greater danger."

A chill runs down my spine. I mean, what could be more dangerous than werewolves?

"But I do not wish to alarm you so soon," he says, offering me a chair across from him. "Please, have a seat. Let us get acquainted."

Okay, everything about this guy has me fairly creeped out, but I need to get answers and he seems like my best bet. So, I sit down across from him.

"Would you care for a beverage?" he asks.

"Yes," I say. "That would be great." My throat is really dry. I could use some water.

He leans towards the fire and scoops a ladle into a cauldron, pouring a steaming red liquid into a teacup. Then, he passes it to me.

"What's this?"

"Frog tea," he says. "It is steeped in the skin of the northern red-legged frog who makes his habitat from British Columbia to Northern California. I made it especially for you."

Did he just say red-legged frog skin? Gross!

"Thanks," I say, putting the cup on the floor. "I think I'll let it cool down first."

"As you wish," he says, taking a sip from his cup. "Ah, delicious. I am sure you have many questions. But first, perhaps you will allow me to begin with a brief history lesson, and then we will discuss how it relates to you."

"Um, sure," I say. Truthfully, history was never my best subject, but I'm willing to see where this goes.

"Excellent," he says. "My tale begins way back in the fifteenth century, where a boy named Vlad Dracul was born to a powerful lord in the ancient land of Sighisoara. Unfortunately, the boy's life was cursed from the start, as his father gave him away as a hostage to appease the Sultan of the Turks who ruled all of the lands."

"Wow, that sounds rough," I say.

"It was," Van Helsing says. "Poor Vlad grew up as a

prisoner, and I will spare you the details, but let us say the Sultan did not treat him well. Around the time Vlad became a young man, the Sultan turned on Vlad's father, destroying his kingdom and leaving Vlad an orphan. From that day forward, Vlad swore he would avenge his family, but it was only a fantasy, as Vlad remained a prisoner for another decade. That is, until one night…"

For some reason, Van Helsing trails off.

"Until one night, what?" I ask, surprising myself by how much I'm into the story.

"Until one night," Van Helsing continues, "a band of his father's loyalists snuck into the Sultan's palace and set Vlad free. They escaped to a land called Wallachia, where Vlad became their ruler. There they built a fortress that became known throughout the land as Castle Dracula."

Castle… Dracula?

"Sorry," I interrupt. "But you just said 'Dracula.' Are you talking about 'the' Dracula? Like, you're saying there was a real Dracula or something?"

"Yes, I am speaking of 'the' Count Dracula," Van Helsing says. "And he was as real as the werewolves you encountered today."

I'm speechless. Is he serious? But then again, if I hadn't seen those werewolves with my own eyes, I'd think he was a crackpot.

"Unfortunately," Van Helsing continues, "Vlad Dracul never got his revenge, because he was killed on the battlefield fighting against the Turks. Rumors of his death, however, seemed greatly exaggerated, because when his grave was exhumed months later, his coffin was found empty."

Empty? Suddenly, my mind races back to that newspaper headline about the grave robbery.

"Stories began to circulate," Van Helsing continues, "that Vlad's followers had used an enchanted artifact known as the Blood Grail to bring Vlad's body back to life, returning him once again to the land of the living, but not as a living being. Instead, Vlad Dracul returned as something else entirely—a vampire—and he took a new name, Count Dracula, the King of Darkness, Lord of the Undead."

Well, this has certainly turned gloomy.

"What do you mean by 'undead?" I ask.

"The undead are beings who were once deceased," he says, "but are brought back to life."

"Seriously?" I say. "You're saying this is all real?"

"As real as you and me," Van Helsing says.

Van Helsing pauses, not for dramatic effect, but because I probably look like a deer in headlights. I'm also feeling lightheaded.

"Are you okay?" Van Helsing asks. "Perhaps you need some nourishment?"

"Yeah, good idea," I say, picking up the teacup with a shaky hand. I don't want to drink it, but it's my only option. Plus, it's red. That's weird. Does Van Helsing know about my red-food thing, or is it just a coincidence?

I take a sip. Surprisingly, it's good.

"Wow, this doesn't stink."

"Thank you," Van Helsing says with a wink. He raises his cup. "Cheers. Shall I continue?"

"Yes, please," I say, drinking the rest.

"Very well," he continues. "Soon, strange things began happening across the land. People started disappearing in the night, only to return as vampires themselves—servants of Dracula's ever-expanding army of the undead. He was unstoppable, rumored to possess remarkable powers: shapeshifting, mind control, super strength, super speed, the power to control vermin, and an unrelenting thirst for blood. But even with all of this, his most dangerous asset remained his mind."

Van Helsing stops momentarily and takes another sip. I'm on the edge of my seat waiting for him to continue.

"You see," Van Helsing says finally, "Count Dracula was as ambitious in death as he was in life. He was a conqueror by nature, and his desire for power was unrelenting. But he also learned his new form had weaknesses. For example, he could not operate in daylight or pass over bodies of water. But most of all, he was afraid of dying again."

Can't blame him there. I'm not a fan of dying myself.

"Not willing to risk himself," Van Helsing continues, "he operated only in the night. But with rapid changes in science and technology, he needed allies to help him conquer the world and keep his operation moving during the day. So, he amassed a cult of human followers to assist him. He promised them riches, land, and power. They called themselves the Dark Ones."

For some reason, I shudder. Why would humans help Dracula? At first, I can't think of any logical reasons, but then I remember all of the power-hungry people I've met in my life, like Glume and Snide, and I realize maybe it's not so far-fetched after all.

"But there were always forces to oppose them," Van Helsing says. "My ancestors were at the forefront of those battles, fighting for the lives of the living over the undead. And as recently as a hundred years ago, they believed they had finally defeated Count Dracula and his minions once and for all. But they were wrong."

Van Helsing looks into the fire.

"The Dark Ones are on the rise again," he says. "But no longer just in Europe. Now they are emerging here, in the United States. And they are building strength rapidly."

Hold on. The Dark Ones are here in America? That doesn't sound good, but there's something I still don't understand, so I just blurt it out.

"Look, this is an incredibly disturbing story, but I still don't understand what it has to do with me?"

"Is it not obvious, Bram?" Van Helsing says, leaning towards me, the fire crackling in his eyes.

"You are the last vampire."

CHAPTER FIVE

THIS MUST BE A JOKE

"Um, do you mind going over that last part again?" I ask. "Because I think you just mistakenly called me a vampire."

Now I've been called plenty of things in my life, but 'vampire' has never been one of them. At this point, I'm totally doubting Van Helsing's sanity, but he just leans back in his chair and smiles. There's a twinkle in his eye, like he was expecting me to react like this.

What's his problem?

"I understand why you are surprised," he says. "After all, vampires are horrible creatures. But trust me when I tell you there is no mistake. You *are* a vampire. Would you like me to prove it to you?"

Prove it? I don't know what kind of 'proof' he's got, so this should be entertaining. I nod my approval.

"Very well," he says. "Let us begin with your physical characteristics. They are not as pronounced as other vampires I have seen before you, but all of the key markers are there, though more subtly. For example, you possess the trademark dark hair and dark eyes of a vampire, but one could argue those features are commonplace among the general population. However, if I go a level deeper, the upper helix of your ear has a pronounced point, but not so much as to seem unusual to the untrained eye. Similarly, the canine teeth of your upper jaw are ever-so-slightly elongated, but again this would not appear as meaningful to the unsuspecting."

I pinch the point on my right ear and suddenly feel self-conscious. Yeah, I noticed that stuff about me too, but I didn't think it qualified me as a vampire.

"Then, there is the matter of your skin tone," he continues, "which is as pale as bone. This complexion is quite rare amongst the general population, but a telling feature amongst vampires. Of course, this paleness has an unfortunate side effect. You burn easily when directly exposed to sunlight."

Now I realize I'm rubbing my left arm. Okay, he nailed that one. This Van Helsing guy is crazy observant.

"Let us move on to your behavioral characteristics," he says, "which I believe will be far more revealing. For the sake of expediency, I will summarize them. You have more energy at night than during the day, at times you can move at remarkable speed, you can see perfectly in the dark, and you only crave food that is red in color. That last one is novel even for me, but it still fits the overall pattern."

"Which is?" I ask.

"Vampires feed on blood," Van Helsing says. "And as you know, blood is red."

Whoa! Is that why I only eat red things? Because I'm … a vampire?

I feel the sudden urge to throw up.

"In addition," he continues, "we have recently learned you can communicate with rats, yet another telltale characteristic of a vampire. By the way, those rats you conversed with in the group home dungeon are the very reason you were identified by Dracula's minions in the first place."

"Wait, you mean those rats were real?"

"Quite real," he says. "You should note that rats are generally a disloyal lot. Those two sold their information directly to the Dark Ones and were handsomely rewarded. Have I succeeded in convincing you yet?"

Unfortunately, I can't argue with anything he's told me. Then, a strange thought crosses my mind.

"But if I'm a vampire, how come I'm not sucking people's blood?"

"An excellent question," Van Helsing says. "Perhaps now is the appropriate time to discuss your lineage. But before we do, it is important to remember that numerous tales have been told about Count Dracula, but I can assure you they are all just fiction. What I am about to share with you is the cold-hearted truth."

What does that mean? But I'll have to wait as Van Helsing takes another sip of his frog brew. Meanwhile, my mind flashes through all of the pop culture references I know about Dracula. The movies, the comic books, the novels. I know they're only stories, but they all have one thing in common—Count Dracula is always pure evil.

Van Helsing finishes his drink and begins again. "In the world of the Supernatural, you may be surprised to learn that you come from royalty. You see, your great-grandparents, Jonathan and Mina Harker, played a central role in the downfall of Count Dracula himself, but not before suffering greatly at the hands of the fiend."

Great-grandparents? I've never heard of any great-grandparents.

"The time," Van Helsing continues, "was the late nineteenth century, and Count Dracula was looking to exert an even greater influence over the world. To accomplish this, he moved his base of operations from the remote wilderness of Wallachia to London, a densely populated city where he could easily add unfortunate victims to his undead army. Before long, his forces swelled and the city was in complete disarray. Dracula's victory over humanity would have been assured had he not met your great-grandmother."

His statement shocks me. What did my great-grandmother have to do with this?

"Mina was bright and attractive," Van Helsing says, "and Dracula took a special interest in her, so much so that he did not turn her into a vampire with just one bite. Unbeknownst to Mina, the villain visited her repeatedly during the night, preying upon her, taking his time in transforming her into one of his loyal, undead subjects. That is, until his actions were discovered by your great-grandfather."

"What did he do?" I ask, fascinated.

"Jonathan Harker was a brave man," Van Helsing continues, "and when Mina's behavior grew odder and odder, he realized something was wrong. Soon, he uncovered Count Dracula's nefarious plot but could do nothing to stop the monster. Jonathan, however, would not give up until he found a way to save his beloved wife. He searched frantically, sending letters around the globe until he found a Dutch man with intimate knowledge of how to destroy Dracula. That man was my grandfather, Abraham Van Helsing, an expert in all things Supernatural."

"Hold the phone," I say. "Are you saying my ancestors knew your ancestors?"

"Indeed," Van Helsing says. "And if it weren't for the combined daring of those two men, your great-grandmother would have succumbed to Dracula's power, and the world would have plunged into darkness. But under the tutelage of my grandfather, Jonathan Harker did the impossible. He destroyed Count Dracula. And once Dracula was vanquished, his army of the undead turned to dust. Fortunately, Mina had not been transformed into a vampire, and upon Dracula's demise, she reverted to her natural state. She was saved."

"So, she lived a normal life?" I ask.

"For a while," Van Helsing says. "But then things took a turn for the worse. As you can imagine, news of Count Dracula's 'death' swept far and wide. Your great-grandparents wanted to live a quiet life, but instead, they became unwilling celebrities across all of Europe. And while some still believed Dracula was only a character in a bedtime story, the Dark Ones knew the truth, and they sought revenge against Jonathan and Mina."

"What kind of revenge?" I ask, cringing.

"The worst kind of revenge," Van Helsing says. "But fortunately, they failed, and Jonathan and Mina realized they were no longer safe in Europe. With the help of my grandfather, they changed their names to Joseph and Miriam Murray and booked passage to America to start life anew. But even in the new world, they could not escape the curse of Count Dracula."

"Why not?" I ask.

"Because it was always with them," Van Helsing responds. "You see, while Mina, now called Miriam, had never transformed into a full vampire, she had come so dangerously close that unbeknownst to them, her blood had been forever contaminated. She was now the only surviving carrier of the vampire pathogen—a virus she passed down to your grandfather, and then to your father, and now to you. By blood, your ancestors were half-vampire, and so are you."

Half-vampire?

I'm half-vampire?

"Y-You're kidding?" I stammer.

It's strange to even think about, but deep down I know it's true. And then it hits me. Maybe what Snide said about my father is also true. Suddenly, I feel angry.

"It figures my father was part vampire," I say. "He never loved me. He abandoned me."

"That is partially true," Van Helsing says. "Your father abandoned you, but he did it because he loved you."

"That's a lie!" I yell, surprising myself by my reaction. "How could anyone abandon someone they love?"

"To save your life," Van Helsing says. "Your father was stubborn, but he was a good man who valued your life more than his own."

"What are you saying?" I ask. "You're talking like you

knew him."

"That is because I did know him," Van Helsing says. "Your father, Gabriel Murray, was once a student here."

What? Now my mind is blown. My father was a student here? At the Van Helsing Academy? I thought there couldn't be any more shocking news about my life, but it just keeps on coming. Then, I realize he said my father's last name was Murray. But my last name is Matthews?

"Hold on," I say. "Gabriel Murray. Jonathan and Mina Murray. Are you saying my real last name isn't Matthews? It's … Murray?"

"Yes," Van Helsing says. "Your given name is Abraham Murray. Your father was one of my very first students. His parents had passed away, and he was on his own then. Just a teenager—a lost soul. He had no idea how special he was."

Van Helsing looks longingly into the fire.

"What do you mean?" I ask.

"In the beginning," he says, "this school was intended for Natural students. We did not teach the things we do now. We did not have to. But when I discovered Gabriel, I realized the Supernatural world of my grandfather was still very much alive, and I knew it was my duty to help your father. Your father was our first Supernatural student and he had the spirit of a wild horse. Gabriel knew he was different from the others, but I never told him why. The Dark Ones were non-existent in America, and since there was no imminent danger, I decided he was better off not knowing his true heritage."

"Wait, you never told him he was half-vampire?"

"No," Van Helsing says. "And as he grew into a young adult, he began feeling confined behind our gates. He became increasingly rebellious, challenging the way we did things. He called this place a prison and demanded to leave. I tried to convince him to stay, for his own safety. But he did not understand and one night he ran away. I never saw him again."

I see the sadness in his eyes.

"We… I… lost track of him," Van Helsing says. "At the time I did not have the resources to find him. It was only through a chance encounter with an old colleague that I learned what had happened to Gabriel. He had gone far away, met a Natural girl, and fell in love. He got a job, they married, bought a house. Life was normal for a while."

"That's good, right?" I ask.

"Yes, of course," Van Helsing says. "I wanted him to be happy with his choices. But, unfortunately, it did not last. At that time the Dark Ones were returning to prominence in Europe. Employing new methods, they retraced Count Dracula's final steps, leading to the mysterious disappearance of your great-grandparents. They discovered Jonathan and Mina's new identities, followed their path to America, and tracked down their descendants. By the time we figured out what was happening, the Dark Ones had discovered your parents and… we were too late. They perished in a terrible fire."

I had always been told that's how they died. I just never knew the story behind it.

Van Helsing looks down and I can see he feels horrible. Like it was his fault.

"From that point forward," Van Helsing says, "I changed everything. I dedicated my life to protecting those who could not protect themselves—Supernatural children. They were innocent outcasts in society, abandoned by their very own families. They were labeled as monsters and left to survive on their own, hunted by human predators who wanted to destroy them."

I'm shocked. I had no idea all of that was happening. I mean, I've survived pretty much on my own, but I never had people hunting me down.

"My academy became a haven for these special children," Van Helsing says. "A place where they could master their gifts while defending themselves against the prejudices of the Natural world. And one day, they will be called upon to save those who shunned them."

Wow. If that's what this school is about it's kind of inspiring.

"But despite our success," Van Helsing continues, "we still did not have the means to defeat a nebulous organization like the Dark Ones. And then, one day, our network provided intelligence that a child with strikingly similar characteristics to Gabriel was discovered in foster care. And that child was you."

For some reason, I feel tingly all over.

"I realized that, in some way, my training had paid off," Van Helsing continues. "Your father must have sensed danger and placed you into foster care, giving you a new last name to conceal your identity. It was likely his final act before facing the Dark Ones."

I'm stunned. So, my father didn't abandon me? He put me in foster care to save me? Then, I have a strange thought. What about my mom? Did she know who my father was? Did she know he put me in foster care?

"Did you know my mom?" I ask.

"No, I never had the pleasure," Van Helsing says. "But now we knew of you."

I'm confused. "So, if you knew I was out there, why didn't you bring me here? Like all of those other kids you were talking about."

"Because you were different. It was clear from the beginning that you shared the same restless spirit as your father. Vampires are notoriously independent, and I swore I would not make the same mistake twice. It was a difficult decision, but I feared if I brought you here too young, you would grow to resent it, just like your father. So, instead, we kept a careful watch on you."

Whoa! What? Suddenly, I'm red hot.

"You mean you decided to let me suffer out there?" I say, my voice rising. "You just sat here and watched me burn through all of those foster families? All of that bullying? And you didn't even have the decency to tell me who or what I really was?"

"Yes," Van Helsing says. "I decided it was best for you to live free for as long as you could. To experience the world your father longed for. I do not regret this decision."

"I do!" I say. "I can't believe this."

"I understand your outrage," Van Helsing says. "But the timing was not right. Now things are different. The Dark Ones will not stop until they bring Dracula back."

"Bring him back?" I say. "How's that possible? I thought you said he was destroyed."

"Only his mortal body was destroyed," Van Helsing says. "But his soul is immortal. The Dark Ones are working to bring him back to life, and they might succeed if they find the Blood Grail."

"What's a Blood Grail?" I ask, remembering Van Helsing mentioning it before.

"It is the cursed artifact that brought Count Dracula into existence in the first place. If the Dark Ones find it, they may be able to resurrect him once again. It is up to us to stop them."

"Us?" I say. "Hang on a second, I didn't sign up for this. I didn't say I'd help you."

"I know I have shared a lot," Van Helsing says. "Most of which is a surprise to you. But remember, if the Dark Ones succeed, Count Dracula will ravage America and everything we know will be in peril. You must join us, Bram."

"I don't have to do anything," I say. "On second thought, I think I will do something. I'm getting the heck out of here."

I stand up and head for the exit.

"Bram, wait," Van Helsing says. "You are making a mistake. It is dangerous out there. The werewolves work for the Dark Ones and they will pursue you relentlessly. We can train you here. We can teach you how to use your abilities. There are other students here who—"

But I never hear Van Helsing's last words because I'm gone, squeezing my way out of his cluttered office. Once outside, I take a deep breath. My head is throbbing and my clothes are dripping with sweat. Man, it feels good to get out of there.

This whole thing is nuts. I mean, what's wrong with that guy? He knew everything about my life but chose not to tell me about it. Who does that?

Anyway, I was expecting Crawler to be waiting for me, but he's not around. I don't know how long I was in Van Helsing's office, but now the sun is up. I'm tired and hungry, but I've got to keep moving. I need to get as far away from this place as possible.

I retrace my steps as best as I can remember, sprinting past the faculty doors—all still closed—and turning down a long hallway. I run through a bunch of corridors hoping to find the front entrance, but instead, I wander into a large space that looks like a gym.

Standing in the center is a girl. She's walking in the opposite direction, but maybe she knows the way out.

"Excuse me," I call out.

The girl turns around, and I hate to admit it, but she kind of takes my breath away. She's really pretty, with bright blue eyes and long brown hair. She's wearing a black sweater with some kind of a silver badge on it.

"Yeah?" she says. "Do I know you?"

"W-Well, no," I stammer. "But I—"

Just then I notice a huge block hanging by a thin rope from the ceiling, about fifty feet high in the air. How did I miss that? It looks like it weighs a ton and it's hovering right over her head. Does she even know it's there? I mean, if that thing drops, she'll be crushed!

"Do you need something?" she asks, putting a hand on her hip. "Because I'm kind of busy right now."

I'm about to answer, when…

The rope snaps.

CLASSIFIED

Person(s) of Interest

CODE NAME: HEADMASTER

REAL NAME: LOTHAR VAN HELSING

BASE OF OPERATIONS: VAN HELSING ACADEMY

D.S.I.

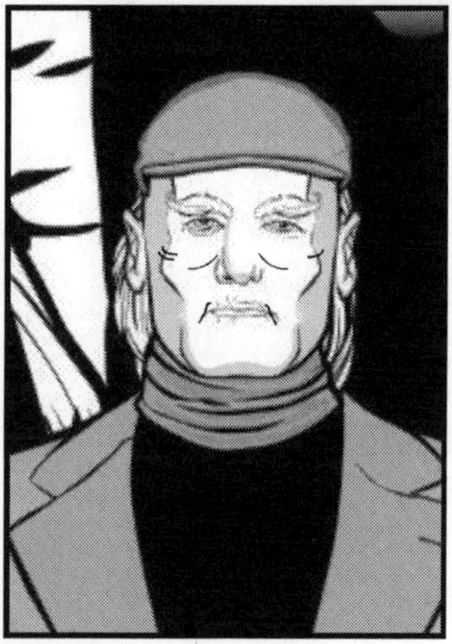

FACTS: Van Helsing is the third generation in a family of infamous monster hunters. Van Helsing founded the Van Helsing Academy to harbor and train Supernatural children. The purpose of this training is unknown. He is under constant surveillance.

Category: Natural

Sub-Type: Not Applicable

Height: 5’11”

Weight: 215 lbs

FIELD OBSERVATIONS:

- Carries a silver crossbow
- Dresses in winter clothing, regardless of the season
- Exceptionally intelligent and evasive

STATUS: ACTIVE TARGET

DEPARTMENT OF SUPERNATURAL INVESTIGATIONS

CHAPTER SIX

TALK ABOUT EMBARRASSING

"Look out!" I yell, pointing up.

The blue-eyed girl stares at me quizzically, but when she looks up her expression changes to horror as she sees the massive block falling over her head. She's about to be squished like a grape!

Without thinking, I launch into action.

I race towards her, kicking into super speed mode, everything around me moving in slow motion. I'm not sure where I'm getting this extra energy from because I thought I didn't have anything left.

But I can't figure it out now, because if I mistime this rescue by even a fraction of a second, we'll both be pancakes.

As I peek up, the block is halfway there and the girl is reeling back in shock, her brown hair bouncing dramatically like she's in a shampoo commercial.

This is gonna be close.

Then, everything around me darkens.

I'm right under it!

I might get crushed, but I can't break my stride.

I pump my arms and legs harder.

She's inches away.

I feel the block pressing down on my hair.

It's on top of me!

I reach out to wrap her up, hoping my momentum carries us both out of harm's way.

But I come up empty!

I narrowly clear the block's path before it CRASHES to the gym floor, vaulting me sky high. I land hard on my stomach and get the wind knocked out of me, tumbling head over heels until I smash into a blue-padded wall.

I'm bruised, but that doesn't matter.

What happened to the girl?

She was right in front of me. All I had to do was grab her. There's no way I could have missed.

So, does that mean she's…?

I sit up nervously, fully expecting to find a big, disgusting mess. But there's… nothing? I mean, that big old block is there, sticking halfway out of the gym floor. But there's no girl. Or girl parts.

Holy cow. She must be under the block.

Suddenly, I hear a muffled noise. Strangely, it almost sounds like… giggling? And then, to my astonishment, a figure steps out of the center of the block itself.

My jaw drops.

I-It's the girl!

But instead of walking, she floats in the air straight towards me, hovering a few feet away. Then, she lands gently, her hands on her hips.

It's her! But then I realize she doesn't seem like she's here. I mean, I can actually see right through her, like she's transparent!

"A-Are you an angel?" I ask.

"Nope," she says, "Just your friendly neighborhood ghost."

Wait, did she just say… ghost?

"And by the way," she continues, "I didn't need to be saved. I can take care of myself."

Then, I notice the silver badge on her black sweater. It has a big letter 'M' that looks like it was engraved by the claws of a lion. And there's a word beneath it. It reads:

AURA

"Who's that guy?" comes a boy's voice.

"He ruined everything!" another boy says.

Suddenly, there's a whole group of kids gathered around me. But then I realize they're not kids at all.

They're… monsters?

And all of them are wearing black sweaters, just like the ghost girl, with their own silver badges.

I take in the scene.

To the girl's left is a big kid whose entire body is covered in brown fur. His shaggy face sort of looks like an ape, with a thick brow, small nose, and large jaw. He's not wearing any shoes, and his feet are absolutely enormous. For some reason, he reminds me of Bigfoot, only smaller. His badge says:

HAIRBALL

Behind him is a skinny kid who makes me do a double take. He sort of looks like that fish guy in the Creature from the Black Lagoon movie. He has green scaly skin, black eyes, and large pointy ears. His entire head is encased in a clear, round helmet filled with water, and gill-like flaps are opening and closing on the sides of his neck. His badge reads:

STANPHIBIAN

To the girl's right is a kid wrapped in white bandages from head to toe, except for a giant pair of sunglasses covering his eyes. What's up with this guy? Is he trying to be a mummy or something? Anyway, his badge reads:

INVISIBILL

Finally, a smaller boy with rosy cheeks, messy blond hair, and a worried expression peers cautiously around the bandaged kid. He's wearing blue-rimmed glasses with a cord connected to each earpiece. Compared to the rest of them he looks downright normal. But for some reason his badge says:

RAGE

Rage? Why is that little guy called Rage? And Aura? Hairball? Stanphibian? InvisiBill? Are these their real names?

Strangely, they're all staring at me, like I'm the weird one. Unfortunately, I can't even stand up because I'm totally wiped out. And I still don't know how I managed that last burst of speed considering I'm running on fumes. All I know is that I'm breathing hard and feeling incredibly woozy.

"He ruined everything!" Hairball says.

"Yeah," InvisiBill says. "It took Stanphibian over an hour to get that block up there."

"Two hours," the fish-kid says, with a sad fish face.

"Okay, dude," Aura says. "You ruined our training exercise. Now spill it, who the heck are you?"

"Do you even go here?" Rage asks.

"Of course he doesn't go here, bonehead," Aura says. "He's not wearing a house badge."

"Sorry," I say. "I wasn't trying to ruin anything. I just thought she… she…"

Suddenly, I'm not feeling so good. My skin feels hot like it's on fire. Then, my stomach starts quivering like I'm going to… to…

"Oh god, he's hurling!" Hairball says.

"So nasty!" InvisiBill says, blocking his sunglasses.

"Shut it, you morons," Aura says. "He needs help. Someone get a bucket."

"On it," Rage says, running off.

I don't know what's wrong with me. I'm in a full sweat and my body is shaking like a leaf. Oh no. Not again! Here it—

"Seriously?" Hairball says. "You know, I can't unsee this."

This is so embarrassing, but I can't stop myself.

Finally, Rage shows up with a bucket, pushing it in front of me with his foot.

"Here you go," he says.

"Th-Thanks," I say, wiping my chin. Everything starts spinning and I pull the bucket close.

"You okay?" Aura asks.

"N-N-No," I stammer. Everything is definitely not okay. I close my eyes, but the spinning sensation doesn't stop. In fact, it's only getting worse, like I'm on a roller coaster and can't get off.

When I open my eyes, the kids are still there, but they look like they're upside down. Aura's mouth is moving, but I can't hear what she's saying.

Then, everything goes dark.

***

"He sure doesn't look like a vampire," comes a boy's voice. "He doesn't even have fangs. Aren't vampires supposed to have fangs?"

"His ears are pointy," a girl says. "But I think they're too big for his head."

Now hang on a minute! I don't know who's talking, but I'm not going to just stand here and be insulted. I try opening my eyes, but my head is pounding. Then, I realize I'm not standing at all. I'm lying down on something soft.

Where am I?

Then, I remember. The gymnasium. Those strange kids. Ugh, I must have passed out. As if that whole scene wasn't humiliating enough.

"Still," the boy says. "He doesn't look like a vampire."

"You of all people should know you don't have to look like a monster to be a monster?" the girl says.

"True," the boy says. "But fangs would be cool."

Okay, that's enough. I force my eyes open and, to my surprise, the first thing I see is a red tube sticking out of my arm. What's that? Is someone drugging me?

Instinctively, I reach up to pull it out.

"He's awake!" the girl yells. "Doctor!"

Suddenly, I feel someone pulling my arm back. It's that Rage kid. And Aura is floating behind him.

"Stop it!" Rage yells. "They're feeding you through that tube!"

Feeding me?

"So, you're not drugging me?" I ask.

"No," Rage says. "That tube is pumping tomato puree into your system."

"Oh," I say. "Really? My bad." Wait a minute, how did they know to give me red food?

"Chill, Bram," Aura says. "You're safe here. They know what you need."

"How do you know my name?" I ask.

"Headmaster Van Helsing told us," she says.

Van Helsing? I guess my face betrays me, because then she says, "He's a good man. We know what you're going through and trust us, you're safe here. Okay?"

I don't know why, but when I look into her blue eyes, I feel calmer. Rage lets go of my arm.

"Where am I?" I ask.

"The infirmary," Aura says. "You were in really bad shape, but now you've got a little color in your cheeks, which isn't bad for a vampire."

I must admit I'm feeling a lot better. I guess I pushed myself too hard. I've never felt like that before.

"How's the patient?" comes a woman's voice.

I turn, and my eyes bulge out of their sockets.

A woman with jet black hair, green skin, and a giant wart on her nose is checking my vital signs. She looks like a… a….

"I'm Dr. Hagella," she says. "And yes, I'm a witch. But I'm also a doctor, which technically makes me a witch doctor." She cackles loudly. "I know, it never gets old. How are you feeling, young man?"

"Better," I say, smiling reluctantly.

"Great," Dr. Hagella says, adjusting the feeding tube. "Your blood count was low. Probably because you hadn't eaten for days. You can't go that long without food."

"I wasn't trying to," I say. "It just happened."

"The vampire-side of your physiology requires you to constantly produce red blood cells. When you don't eat, it slows the production of blood cells leading to aplastic anemia, which can cause dizziness, vomiting, and possibly death. So, you'd better make sure you don't skip meals."

Well, I didn't know that. But I guess that explains my delusional state when I was trapped in that dungeon at the New England Home for Troubled Boys.

"Dr. Hagella is the best," Rage says. "She knows everything."

"Thanks, dear," Dr. Hagella says, patting Rage's head. Then, she turns to me and says, "I'm feeding you with enriched tomato puree. It contains additional proteins that should help your bone marrow start producing red blood cells at a faster rate. Now you need your rest. Hint, hint, little monsters, it's time to leave the patient alone. Don't worry, I'll check on him later."

Dr. Hagella scoops up a few papers and leaves.

"Okay, we'll let you rest," Rage says. "We just wanted to make sure you were okay. Aura and I need to head back to Monster House anyway."

"Um, what's Monster House?" I ask.

"It's the name of the Residence Hall," Rage says. "It's where we live."

"Wait," I say. "You guys live here?"

"Yep," Aura says. "The Van Helsing Academy is our school and our home. It's the only place in the world for kids like us."

"And what kinds of kids are those?" I ask.

"Supernatural kids," she says. "Just like you."

"Yeah," Rage says. "Maybe you'll stick around."

"Um, maybe," I say.

"Great," Rage says. "Well, good luck."

"Hope you recover," Aura says. "We'll probably be up all-night practicing that rescue mission you screwed up for us. We have a test on it tomorrow."

"Sorry about that," I say.

"Not as sorry as we are," Aura says. Then, she disappears through the wall.

Rage shrugs his shoulders and walks out the door.

I'm alone. And totally confused.

Maybe I'm dreaming, but even this is too bizarre. I mean, monster kids? And Aura said this place is not just their school, but also their home. I mean, I've lived in houses before, but never one that felt like home.

But I know I can't stay here.

This place just isn't for me.

"Have you forgiven me yet?" comes a man's voice.

Startled, I look up to find Van Helsing standing in the doorway, still wearing his winter gear. The last thing I want to do is talk to him.

"The doctor said I needed rest," I say.

"She is right," Van Helsing says, entering the room anyway. He takes the seat Rage vacated and adds, "She is an expert on monster biology."

Monster biology? Wait a minute!

"Are you calling me a monster?"

"I am," he says. "And you should get used to it. It is what the world outside will come to know you as. You are different, and you will always be different."

"I'm no monster," I say.

"Not in the traditional sense," Van Helsing says. "After all, I do not know many monsters who would try to save the life of an innocent girl. That shows me you are far from a monster at heart. You are a hero."

"A hero?" I scoff. "I'm no hero."

"Helping those that cannot help themselves is the definition of a hero," Van Helsing says. "You acted because you believed Aura needed help, and I am here because I also need your help. And I believe you need mine."

"I don't need anything from you," I say.

"You may not think so," Van Helsing says. "At least not now. But when the Dark Ones come for you, and come for you they will, you may feel differently."

Images of werewolves flash in my brain, and I know

he's right. I mean, what chance do I have out there on my own? I already know the answer.

None.

"Bram," he continues. "I built this place to be a sanctuary for Supernaturals like you. Danger lies outside these walls. There are monsters, but there are also men who behave like monsters. Men who will stop at nothing to destroy you, or to use you to get what they want. Here you will be safe. Here you will learn to master your skills and properly prepare for the war that is coming."

"I don't want to fight in any war," I say.

"Neither do I," Van Helsing says. "But it is an unavoidable war. It is our responsibility to do something about it, not because we can, but because we must. There are far too many innocent lives at stake. But we cannot win this war without you."

"Why not?" I ask. "You're training all these other kids. Why do you need me?"

"Because you are special," Van Helsing says.

"And why is that?" I ask.

"You are the last of the vampires," Van Helsing says. "You bring special skills no one else can duplicate. You are essential to defeating Count Dracula."

"B-But how?" I ask, my heart suddenly racing.

Just then, the monitor over my head starts BEEPING.

"What's happening?" Dr. Hagella asks, rushing in. "Headmaster, are you over-exciting our patient?"

"I am educating our patient," Van Helsing says, standing up. "Bram, I will explain more when you are stronger. But neither of us should forget the Dark Ones are gathering strength as we speak. We cannot sit back and let them take over the world. It is up to us to stop them. We need you on our side. Will you join us?"

Van Helsing looks me in the eyes and extends his hand, and a million things jump into my head at once.

The parents I never knew.

All of my failed foster families.

Johnny and those innocent kids at the group home.

Aura, Rage, and the other strange kids here.

It's a weird feeling. I mean, I've never been wanted before. I've never been part of a team.

But what if I fail?

Well, I guess if I fail, I'll be toast one way or the other. So, what do I have to lose?

I reach out and shake Van Helsing's hand.

"Okay," I say. "Let's give it a shot."

VAN HELSING ACADEMY

STUDENT ASSESSMENT

VITALS:
NAME: Aurelia Spector
EYES: Blue
HAIR: Brown
HEIGHT: 4'8"
WEIGHT: N/A

CODENAME: Aura

NOTES: Phases through objects and floats on air. Shows potential for telekinesis. Can't touch physical objects. Purpose as ghost is unknown.

CLASSIFICATION TYPE:
Spirit – Ghost

SUPERNATURAL ASSESSMENT:

STRENGTH	●○○○○
AGILITY	●●●●○
FIGHTING	●●●○○
INTELLECT	●●●●●
CONTROL	●●●●○

TEACHABLE?	Yes	No
VAN HELSING	●	○
CRAWLER	●	○
HOLMWOOD	●	○
SEWARD	●	○
MORRIS	●	○
HEXUM	●	○
FAUSTIUS	●	○

RISK LEVEL: LOW

CHAPTER SEVEN

THE MONSTROSITIES AND ME

The next morning I'm officially discharged from the infirmary. Dr. Hagella said I looked appropriately pale for a vampire and sent me straight to the admissions office located in the building next door.

As I step onto the quad, the scene is totally different from when I first arrived at the Van Helsing Academy. This time the sun is shining, and dozens of students are walking across the green wearing backpacks and carrying books. If I didn't know better, I'd think I was strolling through the campus of your average, upscale school.

Except, there's one little thing shattering the illusion.

All of the kids are monsters.

Now, for some of the kids, it's not so easy to tell. You really have to look closely to find an unusual feature or two, like claws, horns, or a tail. But for other kids, you know right away they're different.

Very different.

Like the girl running across the green covered head-to-toe in some kind of bluish armor. Or the kid lying on his back who looks like a cross between a boy and a monitor lizard. There's even a guy flying overhead with giant wings.

It dawns on me that if I were anywhere else, I'd have bolted by now. So, I guess I'm getting used to it.

Sort of.

Then, I notice they're all wearing badges like Aura and Rage, but in different colors. Some badges are bronze and others are blue or green. I wonder what the colors mean?

Because the sun is shining, I don't want to linger too long or I'll get a major sunburn. So, per Dr. Hagella's instructions, I follow the driveway to the large building on the right. According to her, this is the Residence Hall where the students live year-round.

The place Rage called 'Monster House.'

As I climb the stone steps, I feel a sense of awe. The group homes I've been crashing in are dumps compared to this place. I mean, the outside has the same pristine, ivy-league feeling as the other buildings, with red brick, white window frames, and perfectly trimmed hedges.

But as I approach the large double doors I stop.

I mean, do I really belong here?

I guess I'll find out. Besides, it's not like I've got anywhere else to go. So, I pull open the large double doors, step inside, and gasp.

The entrance hall is so enormous I think I could fit two group homes inside of it. My eyes wander from the dark wood walls to the white marble floors to the large windows letting in lots of natural light. There's an extra-wide staircase leading upstairs, and the room is outfitted with comfy sofas and chairs. There's also a big bulletin board filled with flyers. I squint to read one. It says:

MOVIE NIGHT DOUBLE FEATURE
TEEN WOLF & TEEN WOLF 2
THIS THURSDAY

Movie night? Okay, I can get used to this! Well, I can say one thing, these students certainly aren't slumming it.

Then, I notice a familiar-looking banner hanging on the back wall. It's the Van Helsing Academy crest with that strange motto:

YOU MUST BELIEVE IN THINGS YOU CANNOT IMAGINE.

I suppose it makes a little more sense now. To my left is a door with a sign for the Administration Office. Bingo. Well, I guess it's time to make it official. I walk over, step inside, and nearly faint.

Standing behind the counter is the largest "person" I've ever seen. She's bald, with humungous shoulders, and one giant red eye sitting smack in the middle of her forehead. She's wearing a long, blue tunic and bright red lipstick.

I open my mouth to say hello, but no words come out. She must be, like, twenty feet tall. But then I realize she isn't even standing, she's sitting!

The nameplate on the counter reads:

MS. VIOLET CLOPS

MONSTER HOUSE MANAGER

"Alright, stop yer gawkin'," she says, in a surprisingly deep voice. "I can see yer, y'know?"

"I-I'm sorry," I stammer. "I didn't mean… It's just that…"

"Keep your flap shut before yer says somethin' yer gonna regret," she says. "My name's Ms. Clops. But after a week, if I haven't eaten yer, yer can call me 'Vi.' Yer must be Murray, the new kid."

I'm about to tell her my last name is Matthews when I remember it's not. This is going to take some getting used to. Then, she hands me a big yellow envelope that looks like a Tic Tac in her massive mitts.

"Inside is yer room key, class schedule, and student handbook. Now if yer like most kids, yer stick the handbook in yer desk drawer and forget it existed, so let's get two things straight. One, the basement is off limits. Don't forget. I'd hate for yer to be the second kid in Van Helsing Academy history that gets lost forever on some stupid dare. Is that clear?"

"Um, yes," I say, swallowing hard.

"Two," she continues, "Lights out means lights out. There's no scampering around campus after hours like those kids in them wizarding books. If I catch yer, I'll eat yer on the spot. Is that clear?"

"Y-Yes," I say, overwhelmed by all the new info.

My eyes drift back down to her nameplate.

Violet Clops. Vi Clops. Then, it clicks.

Vi-Clops is like Cy-clops. She's a female Cyclops! And an angry one at that.

"Good," she says, pointing at her eye and then back at me, "because I got my eye on yer. And here's yer backpack. It's got all yer need inside, including yer books, pens, and notebooks."

She tosses it like it's weightless, but when I catch it it's so heavy I nearly fall over.

"Now yer may wanna hit the showers before class. A zombie could smell you coming a mile away. Room number thirteen. Up the stairs, third level on the left. Good luck, Murray."

"Er, thanks," I say.

Well, she's frightening.

I head back to the entrance hall and tackle the staircase. A group of students coming down shoot me odd looks, including a girl with a trunk for a nose who whispers, "Pee-ew," to her friend.

Now I'm feeling self-conscious and I realize it's been days since I've showered. Finally, I reach the third-floor landing and hang a left. There's a handwritten sign on the wall that reads:

HOME OF THE MONSTROSITIES.
KEEP OUT!!!
YES, THAT MEANS YOU!

Okay. That doesn't look promising.

For a second, I consider going back downstairs to ask Vi Clops for another room assignment, but that just might give her an excuse to eat me. So, I press on, passing several doors until I hit room number thirteen. I pull out my key when it dawns on me that I've never held one before. I rub my finger along the metal edges.

Funny, I've probably stayed in hundreds of rooms, but no one has actually ever given me a key. I guess this is a major step up.

I unlock the door and push it open, slamming it into the face of some blond-haired kid who was about to exit.

He falls to the ground backward.

Hang on. I know that kid.

It's Rage!

I'm about to tell him how sorry I am when he lowers his arm from his face and I realize something is seriously wrong. He's bent over, breathing heavily like I've clobbered him with a baseball bat. Then, I notice his entire face is… purple?

"Butterflies and puppies," he pants. "Just think about… butterflies and puppies."

"A-Are you okay?" I ask. "I'm so sorry." I have no idea what's going on. But by the color of his face, it looks like he's going to self-combust or something.

"Butterflies…," he says, breathing in and out slowly. "Just think… happy thoughts."

"Um, maybe I should come back later," I say, backing into the hallway.

"N-No," Rage says, waving his arm. "Come in. I-I'm good. I'm good."

I step inside as Rage gets to his feet. He leans over a chair, catching a second wind. He's sweating profusely, but his face looks like it's back to its natural coloring.

"I'm so sorry," I say. "I was told this was my room."

Then, I notice it's a double. There are two beds, two dressers, and two desks.

"I guess we're going to be roommates," I say.

"Really?" he says. "That's great news! When I first got here, they told me I couldn't have a roommate. I guess I've gotten better."

Oookaaaayyy. What's that supposed to mean?

"That's your half," he says, pointing to my left. "I tried to keep it neat, just in case they changed their minds. My side looks like a train wreck. Sorry."

"No problem," I say, sitting on my bed. Well, he's right about the train wreck part. While my side is empty, his side is an absolute disaster zone. His bed is unmade, his clothing is strewn all over the floor, and his books are scattered everywhere. I wonder if Van Helsing gave him decorating tips.

"Can I see your class schedule?" Rage asks.

"What schedule?" Then I realize it's probably in the envelope Vi Clops 'the boy-eating monster' gave me. I open it up and pull out a bunch of papers. One of them looks like a class schedule, so I hand it to him.

"Interesting," he says, studying it intently. "We're in the same section. That's pretty surprising since they usually group kids by skill level and you haven't even been assessed yet. Oh well. Here you go." Then, he hands it back to me.

I look at it, fully expecting to see the usual subjects like Math and Social Studies, but this class schedule isn't like any schedule I've seen before. It reads:

MONSTEROLOGY 101	09:00
SUPERNATURAL HISTORY 101	10:30
PARANORMAL SCIENCE 101	13:00

SURVIVAL SKILLS I 16:30

"What's with the weird timings," I ask.

"It's a Van Helsing thing," Rage says. "He likes to use military timing."

"Well, these classes certainly look interesting," I say.

"They are," Rage says, "but the teachers are really tough. Especially Hexum. He teaches Survival Skills. I thought I'd die in his class like, five times."

I wait for him to laugh, but I realize he's serious.

Then, I notice the clock. It reads: 8:23 AM.

If I'm going to de-stink before our first class at nine, I'll need to shower now.

"Hey, where's the bathroom?" I ask. "I'd love to shower and feel like a normal person again. Well, sort of normal, I guess."

"Down the hall and to the right," he says. "But you'd better hurry. Oh, hang on." Then, he races to his closet. "Here's one of my towels. I just did laundry so it's clean. And here's a fresh bar of soap and some shampoo."

"Gee, thanks," I say, taking the toiletries. Then I realize I don't have any clothes to change into. "Ugh, I guess I'll have to put these back on afterwards."

"No, wait," he says excitedly, digging into his dresser. "I wondered why all this stuff showed up last night. Now it makes sense. It was way too big for me, so they must have left it for you."

He hands me a pile of clothes. There's a shirt, pants, socks, and clean underwear. I've never been so happy to see clean underwear in my entire life.

"Thanks," I say.

"You better be fast," Rage says. "You've only got about fifteen minutes. Oh, and look out for InvisiBill, he likes to play practical jokes."

I don't know what that means, but I grab all of the stuff and head for the shower.

***

Let me tell you, there's nothing better than a warm shower after spending days caked in your own sweat. I can't remember the last time I felt so clean. I probably stayed in there longer than I should have, but the water felt great against my skin, and I really needed it.

What I don't need, however, is to be late for my very first class. I dry off quickly, and for the first time in a long time, I'm feeling surprisingly optimistic. Despite all of the craziness, maybe this will work out after all.

Then, I rip open the shower curtain and realize something is wrong.

My clothes are missing.

What happened to my clothes?

I know I set them down on the bench right outside the shower. They couldn't have walked off on their own.

Then, I remember Rage's warning.

InvisiBill.

Wait a minute.

Invisi – Bill?

As in, 'Invisible?'

Seriously? That kid with the sunglasses must be invisible under all those bandages! He must have snuck in here and stolen all of my clothes. There's no way I'll make it to class on time now. So much for feeling optimistic.

"Hey!" I call out. "InvisiBill! Bring my stuff back!"

But there's no answer.

I bet that jerk is having the time of his life right now, laughing at my expense.

I don't know what to do. If I use my super speed, I can probably make it back to my room before anyone notices. But then I'll have to put my old, stinky clothes back on.

I call out again, but InvisiBill still doesn't show up.

There's no choice, I'll have to go for it. I tighten the towel around my waist and throw open the bathroom door. Only to find—

"Surprise!" comes a chorus of voices.

Rage is standing there, along with Stanphibian, Hairball, and… Aura! They're all grinning ear to ear.

This is so embarrassing.

Then, to their right, I see my clothes!

They're floating in mid-air.

"Is this a bad time?" Hairball asks.

I'm so humiliated I don't know what to say.

"When you attend the Van Helsing Academy," Aura says, "you're taught to believe in things you can't imagine. That means you can't let your guard down. Not even in the shower. It could mean the difference between life and death."

"I tried to warn you," Rage says.

He warned me, but he could've been more specific.

"Don't be angry at Rage," Aura says. "Let's just say you've been taught your first lesson. You'd better learn it fast if you want to join the Monstrosities."

"What are 'the Monstrosities?'" I ask.

"Not 'what,'" Aura says, "but 'who.' We're the Monstrosities. It's the name of our section. We consider ourselves to be the best of the best. But just because you're in our section doesn't mean you're one of us. You've got to prove yourself first. So, I guess we'll see what you're made of. InvisiBill, give him his clothes back."

Suddenly, my clothes come flying at me. I catch them all, nearly dropping my towel in the process.

"And you get one of these," Rage says, putting a black sweater on top of my pile. It's just like the sweaters they're wearing, but without a badge.

"Silver badges are for Monstrosities only," Aura says. "If you want one, you've got to earn one. Got it?"

"Yep," I say. Although I have a distinct feeling that's not going to be so easy.

"By the way," Rage says. "The closet in our room is filled with new clothes for you."

"Of course it is," I say.

"See you in class," Aura says. "And don't be late. Detention is with Headmaster Van Helsing himself."

VAN HELSING ACADEMY

STUDENT ASSESSMENT

VITALS:
NAME: Billy Griffin
EYES: Unknown
HAIR: Unknown
HEIGHT: 4'10"*
WEIGHT: 90 lbs*
* Estimates

NOTES: Lives in a constant state of invisibility. Casts no shadows. Can be tracked by scent. Is unable to revert back to visible state.

CODENAME: InvisiBill

CLASSIFICATION TYPE:
Abnormal – Invisible

SUPERNATURAL ASSESSMENT:

STRENGTH	●○○○○
AGILITY	●●●●○
FIGHTING	●●○○○
INTELLECT	●●○○○
CONTROL	●○○○○

TEACHABLE?	Yes	No
VAN HELSING	●	○
CRAWLER	○	●
HOLMWOOD	●	○
SEWARD	●	○
MORRIS	●	○
HEXUM	○	●
FAUSTIUS	○	●

RISK LEVEL: MEDIUM

CHAPTER EIGHT

A CRASH COURSE IN VAMPIRE

Thanks to my super speed, I make it to class with seconds to spare. That was fast, but I realize even faster that my education at the Van Helsing Academy is going to be unlike anything I've ever experienced before.

Case in point, my first class is Monsterology, the study of monsters, taught by Professor Lucy Holmwood, a middle-aged woman with green eyes, red hair, and an unusually cheery disposition given the macabre nature of her subject matter. It takes me a few minutes to get used to her English accent—I mean, is 'gobsmacked' really a word? But as soon as she launches into the four categories of monsters, I'm hooked.

The first group she describes are shapeshifters, which are creatures who can take on other forms. There are two types of shapeshifters: lycanthropes and doppelgangers.

Lycanthropes turn into monsters when naturally occurring events happen, like full moons. Werewolves are the most popular type of lycanthropes, but other 'were' creatures are known to exist, like wererats for instance.

Yep, you heard me. I said wererats.

The other type of shapeshifter is a doppelganger. This creature replicates the exact physical and vocal characteristics of someone else. Professor Holmwood explains that doppelgangers are rare and there are several sub-types although none have been seen in the last century. But then again, how would anyone know for sure?

The next category is spirits. Spirits were once living people whose souls never moved on to their next destination. Now they just hang around, haunting the living. In fact, some spirits don't even know they're dead—talk about awkward conversations! Spirits come in two types: ghosts and skin-riders.

Ghosts are exactly what you think they are, bodiless souls that can drift through walls, windows, and your local McDonalds. Typically, they're stuck here for a reason, but whatever that reason is, it's usually a mystery to them.

A skin-rider, on the other hand, is a nastier kind of spirit. They're stuck between worlds like ghosts, but they can possess the body of a living person, using them to carry out devious deeds, like monopolizing your video game console.

The third category of monsters is the undead. These are the ones Van Helsing talked about earlier. These fun-suckers were once dead, but now they're back alive again.

This group includes all of your Halloween favorites, like vampires, mummies, and zombies. No need to go into the gory details, we know these guys all too well.

The fourth and final group are the abnormals. Abnormals are a catch-all category for anything that can't be classified into one of the previous buckets. In here you'll find your one-of-a-kind beasts, science experiments gone wrong, and bizarre freaks of nature. Think Frankenstein, Godzilla, or the Blob.

It's not until the bell rings that I'm able to put down my pen. I've never taken so many notes in my life! It seems like the ninety minutes flew by in a snap, and I can't believe everything I just learned. Apparently, there's a whole secret monster world out there I never knew existed—and a rather frightening one at that.

But before I can process it all we're off to Supernatural History. With the word 'history' in it, I thought it would be a real snoozer, but boy was I wrong. The class is taught by Professor Lawrence Seward, a heavy-set man with a thick, handlebar mustache. With his red bowtie and tan duster jacket, it looks like he fell out of a 1920s photograph.

Professor Seward starts lecturing before we even take our seats, sending everyone scrambling for their notebooks. And what he's teaching is simply incredible. I had no idea how far back monster history went. Van Helsing told me the whole vampire thing started in the fifteenth century, and I thought that was old. But according to Professor Seward, monsters have been running around for ages.

I learn about the Zombie Crusades of the 1100s, the Werewolf Inquisition of the 1200s, and even the Ghost Rebellion during the Revolutionary War. They never taught us this stuff in public school!

Then, Professor Seward sidetracks into a discussion about Supernatural items. Apparently, certain household items have powerful effects on certain monsters. For example, silver destroys werewolves, salt repels spirits, and garlic can hold a vampire at bay. I guess the trick is remembering not to spray garlic on a werewolf or throw salt at a vampire.

Then, Professor Seward offers bonus points for anyone who can answer questions about ancient Supernatural artifacts, like:

"What is the Spear of Darkness?"

"When would you use Holy Water?"

"What is the Crossbow of Purity?"

Of course, I'm clueless, but Aura's hand shoots up after every question. I have to admit I'm impressed. This girl definitely has game. Then, Professor Seward asks a question that really gets my attention.

"What is the legend of the Blood Grail?"

The Blood Grail? I remember Van Helsing talking about the Blood Grail. The Dark Ones are searching for it. Of course, Aura is all over it.

"According to legend," she begins, "during the War

of the Turks, King Vlad Dracul of Wallachia knew his armies were far out-numbered by his Turkish enemies and were likely to be destroyed. Trapped in a narrow mountain chasm, the King bled a quart of his blood into an empty wine chalice and had his sorcerers perform an ancient spell over it."

Whoa! Van Helsing didn't give me that kind of detail.

No wonder it's called the Blood Grail.

"Then," she continues, "Vlad Dracul ordered a contingent of his best men to take the chalice and sneak through enemy lines, returning it safely to his kingdom in Wallachia without spilling a single drop. In the darkness of night, the men did just as the King instructed. And the very next day, just as Dracul predicted, his forces were overrun, and he was killed on the battlefield."

Well, most of that matches up to what I was told.

"But before the Turks could claim his body," Aura continues, "his loyal subjects retrieved his remains and returned them to Wallachia. There, they collected the chalice—now called the Blood Grail—and poured King Dracul's blood over his lifeless body, miraculously returning him to life from the dead. From that moment forward, he became known as Count Dracula, King of Darkness, and Lord of the Undead."

So that's the legend of the Blood Grail, huh? And to think, the Dark Ones are out there looking for it right now. I hope it's smashed into so many pieces Gorilla Glue couldn't put it back together.

After class, we break for lunch. As I enter the cafeteria, I'm shocked to discover dozens of tiny winged creatures with pointy ears and horns on their heads fluttering all over the place. One of them lands on a table and picks up a dirty fork with both hands.

"Imps," Rage says. "They work in the cafeteria. But look out, they like to play pranks. Last week they put strawberry jelly on my hamburger instead of ketchup. I nearly barfed."

"Great," I say.

I move through the buffet looking at all of the options. There's more food here than I've seen in my entire life, including chicken, steak, salads, and sandwiches, but nothing for me. Then, at the end of the line, I see something bright red. It's pizza but without the cheese! I grab a few slices when one of the imps comes flittering around the corner with a large silver shaker that says: Red Pepper Flakes.

Before I can react, it hovers over my pizza and turns the shaker over. But before the flakes hit my food, Rage sticks his hand over my plate.

"Yuck!" Rage says, smelling the specks on his palm. "These aren't red pepper flakes. They're chopped liver flakes. Now shoo."

The imp sticks out its tongue and flies away.

"Thanks," I say.

"Told ya," Rage says. "Now I've got to wash my hands."

When he comes back, we sit together in the crowded cafeteria. Hairball and Rage have steaks larger than their heads, Stanphibian slurps some algae concoction through a straw, and we're all forced to watch InvisiBill chew his chicken fingers into mush before swallowing them down his invisible gullet.

But Aura isn't eating anything at all. She's just sitting there, watching us with her sad, blue eyes.

"Aren't you hungry?" I ask.

"Nope," she says, pushing back her hair. "Ghosts don't get hungry."

Suddenly, it hits me. All of those monster classifications I just learned about apply to us as well! Which means—

"S-So, you're, like, dead?"

"I suppose," she says casually. "I don't remember much about it. Headmaster Van Helsing has been trying to help me figure out what happened. Just like Professor Holmwood said, I'm probably still here for a reason. I just don't know what it is."

"Wow," I say. "I'm sorry."

"Don't be," she says. "It happens to everyone eventually. My turn just came a little early."

I manage to smile, but I feel terrible for her. I mean, she looks like she had everything going for her: smarts, good looks, confidence. Yet, here she is—or isn't.

After lunch, we have Paranormal Science with Professor Quincy Morris IV. He's an athletic-looking man with white, slicked-back hair and a nasty scar running from his forehead down to his chin. He speaks with a thick southern accent, and uses phrases like: "over yonder," "fixin' to," and "y'all."

Today's lesson is all about conducting Supernatural crime scene investigations, and we spend most of our time learning how to properly secure a crime scene. According to Professor Morris, the biggest problem isn't the crime itself, but keeping first responders off the scene. You see, in normal crime situations, firemen, paramedics, and police officers are essential to solving the case, but in a Supernatural crime scene, they typically end up ruining all the evidence.

That's when Professor Morris introduces a lollipop-looking device called a Hypno-Wipe. Under its power, you can hypnotize a whole bunch of people at once, which is great for lots of purposes, like helping them forget everything they just saw. Professor Morris lets us practice using it, which leads to some good laughs, like when Rage hypnotizes Hairball into thinking he's a grizzly bear.

After that, Professor Morris lets us play with a Spirit Sensor. The Spirit Sensor looks just like a watch, but it's really a GPS for tracking ghosts. Professor Morris explains that in most Supernatural crime scenes ghosts are often your best witnesses. The Spirit Sensor detects the presence of ghosts in the area by measuring molecular disturbances. All ghosts have a unique molecular signature. The Spirit Sensor reads that signature and matches it to the appropriate ghost.

Thanks to Aura, we get to try it out firsthand. Professor Morris gives her a five-minute head start and then turns it on, leading to an hour-long ghost chase through the entire building. Every time we think we have her cornered, she just laughs and phases through another wall. That girl is way too competitive.

Unfortunately, the fun and games eventually come to an end, because the bell RINGS and class is over.

Next up is Survival Skills.

"Get ready," Rage warns.

"For what?" I ask.

"For anything," he answers. "Hexum is a mentalist."

"What's that?" I ask.

"You'll see," he says.

To my surprise, Survival Skills isn't taught in a classroom, but in the gymnasium, which looks dramatically different from when I saw it a few days ago. Instead of a large, enclosed room with wood floors and blue-padded walls, the space has been transformed into an open-air dirt field.

How's that possible?

Standing in the center is a tall figure wearing all black and a red flowing cape. He has a narrow face, angular cheekbones, and a pointy chin. His hair and beard are white, and his lips are curled into a strange smile. He's leaning on a black walking stick, his long fingers tapping impatiently on the silver cap. As we approach, I can't help but notice that his green eyes are focused only on me.

I have a bad feeling about this.

We fan out side-by-side, and no one says a word. Clearly, there aren't going to be any friendly introductions. Finally, Hexum breaks the silence.

"There is a rumor that we have a real vampire in our midst," he says, his raspy voice barely above a whisper. "Is that true?"

I peer at Rage who mouths, 'don't take the bait.'

"No answer?" Hexum continues, pacing back and forth. That's when I notice he walks with a pronounced limp, so I guess that walking stick isn't just for show.

"How disappointing," he continues. "I always thought vampires were kings of the monsters. Perhaps ours is more of a court jester."

Hang on. Did he just insult me? Then, I remember what Rage said, so I do my best to stay calm.

"I assume all of you know how rare it is to even glimpse a vampire in this day and age," Hexum says. "After all, vampires were thought to have been extinct, only existing in our nightmares. Yet, we supposedly have one right here in our presence. What an honor."

What is this guy's problem?

"The abilities of vampires are legendary," Hexum says, stopping suddenly in front of me and looking me dead in the eyes. "Are yours?"

Okay, this guy is getting under my skin.

"Here in Survival Skills," Hexum continues, "we will put your abilities to the test. We will see if you can live up to the standards of your ancestors. Shall we begin, Mr. Murray?"

I shoot a sideways glance at Rage and the others who are all staring at their feet. Clearly, no one is going to help me out here.

"I guess so," I say finally, my voice surprisingly soft.

"Ah, he speaks," Hexum says. "I was afraid you might be mute. Very well then, Mr. Murray, your first test is a simple one. Control the wolves."

Wolves? What wolves?

Suddenly, Hexum snaps his fingers and two gigantic, gray wolves appear out of nowhere across the way. Where'd they come from? The wild animals crouch low and start growling, looking at me like I'm their next meal.

"Ready, Mr. Murray?" Hexum says. "Go."

Um, what?

Just then, the wolves leap up and start chasing me.

So, I do what comes naturally. I take off.

"Stop it!" I hear Rage cry.

"Quiet!" Hexum barks. "I must see what he can do."

What I can do? All I can do is run for my life. I turn on the speed jets, putting as much distance between us as possible. But when I look over my shoulder, the wolves are still right on my tail. How is that possible?

"Cease!" Hexum commands.

Suddenly, the wolves vanish into thin air.

What's happening? And why am I still standing in the same spot? I mean, I must have run for miles.

"Strike one, Mr. Murray," Hexum says. "You failed to control the wolves. Now let us move to your next test. Free yourself from the glass container."

Did he say container?

Suddenly, a giant, glass tube drops from the sky, trapping me inside. I push against it, but it won't budge. I notice there's a small hole at the top, big enough for a mouse to squeeze through, but I can't reach it. And even if I could, I couldn't fit through it anyway.

Suddenly, my feet feel wet. I look down to find the tube filling with water! Where did that come from? The water is rising quickly, reaching the tops of my shoes, then my knees, then my waist.

Holy cow! If I don't get out of here, I'll drown!

I jump up to reach the hole, but it's too high!

"He's struggling!" Rage yells.

"Silence!" Hexum responds.

The water is up to my armpits! I'm going to drown in here! In front of everybody!

I close my eyes and scream.

"Stop!" Hexum commands.

Just like that, the water and the glass tube are gone.

And what's even weirder, my clothes are completely dry. It's like nothing happened.

"Strike two, Mr. Murray," Hexum says. "You have failed to escape from the glass container. Now for your third and final test. Fly."

Wait, what?

Suddenly, I'm standing on the edge of a high, rocky cliff. Where am I? I back away from the precipice and peer into the misty abyss. Great, it looks bottomless.

By now I know something bad is about to happen, I just don't know what.

Then, I hear an ear-piercing SHRILL behind me.

I duck just as a giant bat buzzes my head.

Gross!

The bat flaps off into the sky. Whew, that was close!

Suddenly, I hear more SHRILLS.

I turn slowly, only to find more bats heading my way.

Hundreds of them.

My heart starts pounding and I look for somewhere to hide, but there's no escape. The bats are coming so fast all I can do is shuffle back to the edge of the cliff.

My heel kicks a rock that tumbles over the edge.

I never hear it land.

I look back to find a nearly black sky. The bats are everywhere! My only option is to jump, but I can't!

There's no bottom!

Seconds later, they're on me. I kneel, blocking my face with my arms, but the creatures pummel me, pushing me backward. I try holding my ground, but I can't, and then…

I'm falling! I can't stop!

I'm going to die!

"Enough!" Hexum yells.

Just like that, the sensation of falling to my doom disappears, and I find myself lying on my back, my arms and legs spread out wide.

I'm alive! Thank goodness, I'm alive!

Then, I sense someone approaching.

"Strike three," Hexum says, with disappointment written all over his face.

"W-Why are you doing this?" I ask.

"Because my job is to sharpen your skills as a vampire," Hexum says. "The first test was to see if you could control wild animals. The second test was to see if you could turn your body into a mist and escape through a small opening. The third test was to see if you could transform into a bat and fly. These are the most basic abilities of a vampire. You, Mr. Murray, have none of them."

I look at the other kids who are just staring at me.

I feel so embarrassed.

"You may be a vampire by blood," he says, "but you are a rather limited vampire. If you wish to succeed in our line of work, you will need to push yourself harder than you have ever pushed yourself before. And if you don't, then you will die. And I don't think either of us wants that on our resumés, do we?"

But before I can answer he turns his back on me and claps sharply at the others. "This pathetic experiment is over. Students, take your places!"

CHAPTER NINE

STROLLING THROUGH THE GRAVEYARD

I don't think I could feel more useless if I tried.

The other kids attempt to cheer me up at dinner, but I'm not in the mood. In fact, I'm feeling so depressed I can't eat a thing. I try to smile and pretend everything is okay, but it's not.

According to Hexum, I'm a limited vampire. And what's worse is that I know he's right! I mean, how in the world am I supposed to battle the Dark Ones if I'm so pathetic? The short answer—I can't.

And the Monstrosities know it too.

I mean, they were forced to watch me make a total fool of myself. I'm pretty sure they won't be inviting me to join their team any time soon.

Some vampire I turned out to be.

As we head back to our rooms, I decide I'm going to run away once everyone has gone to sleep. I mean, why should I bother hanging around this joint? Plus, at this point, I'm pretty sure no one would miss me anyway.

Rage unlocks our door and flops onto his bed. As I head over to my side, I survey my things. I've never had so many clothes before. I could probably carry some of it, but the rest would only slow me down. I scoop a few pairs of clean underwear in my arms.

"You're taking this way too personally," Rage says.

"Taking what too personally?" I say, pretending not to know what he's talking about.

"Hexum's assessment," Rage says.

"How else am I supposed to take it?" I snap. "I failed every one of his tests. Every single one. Am I supposed to be happy about it?"

"It's your first day," Rage says. "Don't be so hard on yourself."

"Hexum called me 'limited,'" I say. "How'd you feel if he said that to you?"

"He has," Rage says. "Look, I failed all of my first tests too. And so did Stanphibian, and Hairball, and Aura. I warned you, you can't win with that guy."

"Hang on," I say. "Aura failed a test?"

"Yep," Rage says. "We all did. I told you, Hexum is a different kind of teacher. He pushes you hard. But he does it to make you better."

"He crossed the line," I say.

"Think so?" Rage says. "On my first day, I cried in front of the whole class. But look at me now. I'm still here, aren't I? I didn't quit. Will you?"

Darn it, he's on to me.

I never thought of myself as a quitter, but maybe I am. I mean, every time things get hard I take off. Hexum was tough on me, but is it really the end of the world?

I turn to find Rage looking at me earnestly, like a puppy wearing blue glasses. I drop the underwear.

"Okay, okay," I say. "I won't quit. I just don't get how he did all of those crazy tests. I mean, where did those wolves come from? And the creepy bats?"

"From your brain," Rage says, pointing to his head.

"What?"

"I told you," Rage says. "Hexum is a mentalist. He can tap into your brain and make you think that all of that stuff is really happening. We didn't see a wolf or a bat. Everything that happened was happening inside your own mind."

In my own mind? I'm so shocked I sit down. Is that why those wolves were right behind me even though I was running at top speed. And I guess that explains why my clothes were bone dry after the water test. Or why I didn't go splat after the bats knocked me off the cliff.

"I must have looked like a complete dweeb," I say.

"A total dweeb," Rage says. "But Hexum makes all of us look like dweebs now and then. He knows what buttons to push. He's a master at it. But if you stick with him, you'll get stronger."

"Yeah," I say. "I guess."

I'll need to get a whole lot stronger if I'm going to survive this nuthouse. I lay down on the bed and stare at the ceiling. I have that same itchy-feet-feeling I'd always get when living with a foster family got rough. But this time that feeling is being squashed by another one.

A feeling that I should stay.

I mean, I've never felt like I belonged anywhere before until I got here. I've never met kids like these.

Kids like me.

"By the way," Rage adds, "if you think Hexum is bad, you should have been here when that Faustius guy was around. Supposedly, he was a lunatic."

Faustius? Who's that? But then I remember seeing his name on that door with all the locks on it.

"How so?" I ask.

"Because he used to teach a subject called Black Magic," Rage says. "You know, evil incantations, curses, demon summoning. Stuff like that."

"Wow," I say. "That sounds hard core. What happened to him?"

"No one knows for sure," Rage says. "He was gone before I got here. But I heard he was more brutal than Hexum. Van Helsing has been looking for a replacement ever since."

I couldn't imagine anyone more brutal than Hexum.

Rage puts his arms behind his head and settles into his bed. He seems like a good kid, but I don't know much about him.

"So, what brought you here?" I ask.

Rage chuckles.

"What's so funny?" I ask.

"Nothing," he says. "It's just the way you phrased the question. I guess I literally *was* brought here. You see, I don't remember anything before the Van Helsing Academy."

"Seriously?" I ask.

"Yep," Rage says. "One day I opened my eyes, and I was lying in the infirmary with tubes sticking out all over the place. Van Helsing was there, with Crawler, and Dr. Hagella. They were telling me to stay calm, that everything was going to be okay. Of course, I was scared out of my mind. I remember the machines blaring and Crawler holding me down while they amped up the medicine. Eventually, I calmed down and they asked me a lot of questions, but I couldn't remember anything. I didn't even know my own name, let alone the names of my parents, or even my home address."

"Wow, is that still true?" I ask.

"Yep," he says. "Everything before here is gone. So, they enrolled me. They said this was the perfect place for a kid like me. Because of my powers, I got the code name Rage. And now here I am."

"I was going to ask about that," I say. "Does everybody get a code name?"

"Oh yeah," he says. "You'll get one eventually. But it has to relate to your abilities."

"So, why are you called Rage anyway?"

"Well…" Rage starts.

But just then, Aura phases through the door.

"Get up, people!" she orders. "Time to get moving! Monsters are on the prowl!"

"Aura, I told you to knock!" Rage complains. "I could have been naked!"

"Whatever," she says, rolling her eyes. "Get up, we've got a cemetery to visit. Hairball, InvisiBill, and Stanphibian are already downstairs."

"Um, sorry, but what's going on here?" I ask.

"There's another grave robbery in progress," she says. "This is the third one in the last two weeks. This time we can catch the thieves red-handed."

"And how do you know that?" I ask.

"I'm a ghost, remember? I'm wired into the spirit network."

"Gotcha," I say.

"Okay, okay," Rage says, hopping off his bed and pulling on his sweatshirt. "How far away is it?"

"We're in luck," she says. "This one is only a few towns over. Hurry up. Hairball's driving."

"Hang on," I say. "I thought we weren't supposed to be running around at night, especially off campus. What about Vi Clops? You know, that scary gigantic mountain-of-a-woman with the enormous eyeball. Remember her?"

I certainly did. She pretty much told me she'd swallow me whole if she caught me wandering around after curfew.

"Seriously?" Aura says, arms crossed.

"Um, yeah," I say.

"Okay, then you stay here," she says. She turns to leave, then stops and throws me an icy stare. "Maybe Hexum was right about you."

Then, she phases through the door.

Seconds later, Rage is right behind her. He opens the door, shrugs his shoulders, and leaves.

I'm all alone.

Great.

I'm sure Aura thinks I'm a total loser. First, I looked like a complete dork in Hexum's class, and now I'm just lying here while the rest of the Monstrosities try to stop a grave robbery.

My chances of making the team just keep shrinking. I stare at Rage's empty bed. Then, I remember what Aura said: *Maybe Hexum was right about you.*

Darn it!

I grab my hoodie and bolt out the door.

***

Thankfully, the kids are still in the lobby. I catch Aura half-smiling when I show up, but she quickly wipes it from her face.

"Sorry," I whisper. "I'm a bonehead, okay?"

"Apology accepted," she whispers back. "And yes, you are."

"Why didn't you leave yet?" I ask.

"We were about to," she says. "But we can't find InvisiBill. Feel free to help us look around."

While the team searches for InvisiBill, I'm sweating bullets. In my mind's eye, I see Vi Clops rounding the corner, her angry red eye heading straight for me. I guess Aura senses my nervousness because she just shakes her head and points towards the Administration Office.

Just then, I hear a SAWING noise coming from the partially open door. I tiptoe over and peek inside. To my surprise, Vi Clops is lying face down on the counter, snoring like a busted vacuum cleaner. Next to her are a dozen empty pizza boxes.

"She'll sleep for hours," Aura says, scaring me out of my skin. "A cyclops always falls asleep after a big meal. It pays to know your Monsterology."

"Right," I whisper. "Good tip."

A few minutes later, Rage accidentally sits on InvisiBill, who was napping on one of the couches. Mystery solved, but boy did Aura rip into him.

After that, we leave the lobby and dash through a series of corridors. It feels like we're running through an endless maze, but the Monstrosities seem to know exactly where they're going, so I'm thinking they've done this before. Like, lots of times before.

Finally, we reach a solid stone wall and I think we've hit a dead end. But then Hairball pulls down a sconce, and the whole wall slides open, revealing a narrow hallway. Well, I wasn't expecting that.

We squeeze through one by one, and the next thing I know, we pop out the back of Monster House and onto the school grounds. We dart across the grass beneath a full moon and head towards a big building I've never seen before.

"Where are we going?" I yell out to Rage as my heart pumps a million miles a second.

"The garage," Rage whispers back.

The garage? That's the biggest garage I've ever seen in my life. We run through the open hangar door to find dozens of parked vehicles, like buses, jeeps, and Crawler's motorcycle. I run my hand along Crawler's sidecar. Seeing it again reminds me of just how freaked out I was when I first got here.

If only Crawler could see me now.

Aura tells us to keep watch as Hairball hotwires a nearby jeep. Rage and I take the hangar door.

"You sure this is a good idea?" I whisper.

"Probably not," Rage whispers back.

"Does Hairball have a driver's license?" I ask.

"Dude, don't let the facial hair fool you. The kid's only twelve-years-old."

"Oh," I whisper. "Wonderful."

Suddenly, the engine ROARS and we pile inside. I'm squished in the backseat between Stanphibian, who smells like an aquarium, and InvisiBill, who just plain smells.

The next thing I know, we're swerving down the driveway towards the front gate. I remember Crawler getting eye-scanned to open the campus gate, so I'm pretty sure this will be a short joyride. We pull up to the security booth, and right on cue, the eye-scanning device extends towards the car.

Well, I can finally breathe.

This should put an end to this little adventure.

But to my surprise, Aura crosses over to the driver's side and sticks her hand right through the scanner! Electric blue currents shoot across the face of the device and then there's a loud POPPING noise.

Suddenly, the front gate slides open.

She short-circuited the machine!

"Gun it!" Aura orders.

Hairball pounds the gas and we're off like a rocket!

As we drive away, I look back to see the campus getting smaller behind us, and I'm pretty sure Van Helsing wouldn't approve of what we're doing.

***

After a perilous drive going way over the speed limit, we finally arrive at the cemetery. Somehow, and I still don't know how, I manage not to toss my cookies.

Hairball rolls up to the iron-wrought front gate.

No surprise, it's locked.

A dense fog hugs the ground, adding an extra creepy dimension no one needs right now. Behind the gate, I can make out tombstones organized in neat little rows, but there's no sign of any grave robbers.

"What now?" Hairball asks.

"Now we go inside, fur brain," Aura says. "We won't stop any grave robbers sitting out here."

"Got it," Hairball says, slamming on the gas.

Before I can object, the jeep SMASHES through the gates, and I see InvisiBill's window go down. The next thing I know, I hear InvisiBill retching.

Great, invisi-barf.

Hairball flies through the cemetery with Aura shouting directions. The fog is so thick you can't see more than a foot in front of the jeep, and the two of them are arguing like crazy over which way to go.

Between Hairball's horrible driving and the stench coming from InvisiBill, I'm starting to feel nauseous myself. I'm about to tell Hairball to slow down when our headlights suddenly flash over a group of figures standing waste deep in a grave.

"Stop!" Aura yells. "Right there! Those people are the grave robbers!"

"Um," Hairball says, "Those aren't people."

"I-Is that …?" Rage stammers.

"Zombies?" Hairball says. "Yeah."

I look out the windshield and my stomach drops to my toes. Four hideous creatures stare back with red, unblinking eyes. They're disheveled looking, with wild hair, ripped clothes, and huge chunks of skin missing from their faces.

"I'm gonna puke," InvisiBill says. "Again."

No one moves. It's like each group is shocked to see the other. That's when I notice three of the zombies are males and one is a female. For a minute, they almost look like store mannequins at a Halloween costume shop. Then, out of the blue, the males start coming out of the grave, walking towards us in a slow, herky-jerky manner!

"Get us out of here!" Rage yells.

Hairball throws the jeep into reverse, and then lurches forward, SLAMMING into a tree!

My head smashes into Stanphibian's fishbowl and everything becomes a jumbled blur. For a second, all I see are stars. Then, I realize the jeep isn't moving.

Hairball turns the key and the jeep SPUTTERS.

"It won't start!" Hairball yells.

There's smoke coming from the hood.

"Monstrosities, move out!" Aura commands.

No one needs a second invitation. We jump out of the vehicle and scatter. Given my lack of fighting skills, I stick close to Hairball because he's the largest.

"Don't let them bite you!" I hear Rage yell.

The zombies spread out. One of them, wearing a suit and tie, approaches Hairball and me, arms outstretched. He smells putrid, like rotten meat. I'm about to bolt when I realize Hairball is standing his ground.

"Um, Hairball?" I say. "Shouldn't you—"

But before I can finish my sentence, Hairball rears back his giant fist and punches the zombie into the next zip code!

"Holy cow!" I say.

The other Monstrosities are equally as impressive. Aura and Stanphibian team up against a zombie to my left. I watch Aura bait it, but when the creature lunges it passes right through her. Then, Stanphibian takes over, spearing it with a giant branch. He spins around at incredible speed and then lets the branch go, launching the zombie high into a tree.

On the other side, I see the last zombie dude turning aimlessly in circles. Knowing InvisiBill, he's probably tapping it on the shoulder and running to the other side. But his fun and games are about to end as Hairball heads over to help.

Then, I realize I haven't seen Rage.

Where is he?

Suddenly, I remember there's one zombie left—the female! She was still in the grave, but when I look over, I can't see anything through the fog.

Then, a terrible thought crosses my mind.

What if she's got Rage?

Without thinking, I take off for the grave. When I arrive the zombie isn't there, but neither is Rage. I look into the grave itself and notice the coffin is busted open.

It's empty inside!

That zombie stole all of the bones!

I glance up at the tombstone, which reads:

DR. EUGENE ALBERT
INVENTOR, PHILOSOPHER, PHILANTHROPIST

Something moves behind a cluster of trees.

Is that the zombie? And does she have Rage?

I can't let her escape, but the other kids are too far away to help. I've got no choice.

I turn on my super speed and break for the woods, but the fog is so thick I can barely see where I'm going. I reach the area where I thought I saw the movement, but there's no sign of the zombie or Rage. I don't know what to do. I'm not trained to fight a zombie by myself, and I can't see the other kids. I could head back, but I'd risk losing the trail—and quite possibly Rage—for good.

There's only one choice.

I figure I can cover the woods quicker with my speed, but as soon as I power up, I feel myself powering down. What's going on? Then, I remember I was so upset about Hexum that I didn't eat dinner.

Genius move.

I could yell for help, but that'll just tell the zombie where to come eat me. Out of the corner of my eye, I spot a branch lying on the ground. It's long and sharp and looks like it can do some serious damage, so I pick it up and keep moving.

It's quiet. Eerily quiet.

The only sounds I hear are my feet crunching

through the leaves and the beating of my own heart. After a few minutes of aimless walking, I realize I've lost the trail.

There's no point in being subtle now.

"Rage!" I call out. "Rage, where are you?"

But there's no answer.

I take a few more steps.

Suddenly, I hear a CRACK behind me.

"Rage?"

I turn, hoping to see my friend, but instead, I see something far worse.

It's… a werewolf!

Seriously? Now?

The beast lets out an ear-piercing HOWL.

And five more pop up behind him.

MONSTEROLOGY 101
FIELD GUIDE

ZOMBIE

CLASSIFICATION:

Type: Undead

Sub-Type: Not applicable

Height: Variable

Weight: Variable

Eye Color: Red

Hair Color: Variable

KNOWN ABILITIES:

- Superhuman Strength
- Travels in packs
- Pursues victims relentlessly
- May bite victims, turning them into fellow Zombies

KNOWN WEAKNESSES:

- Low intelligence
- Vulnerable to fire
- Extremely slow with poor reflexes
- Brittle body can be easily destroyed

DANGER LEVEL:

MEDIUM

TIPS TO AVOID AN UNWANTED ENCOUNTER:

- Avoid cramped spaces
- Don't stand in front of windows
- Stay alert for large, slow-moving crowds
- Travel only during the daytime

CHAPTER TEN

SERIOUSLY NOT AGAIN

I've decided I really, really hate werewolves.

Not only do they eat people, but they also have a terrible habit of showing up at the worst possible times.

Like now, for instance.

With six of the hairy monsters surrounding me, I need to hit the pause button on my search for Rage and put all of my attention on the task at hand—staying alive!

I spin around, jabbing with my spear to keep the beasts at bay when I notice for the first time that werewolves come in all shapes and sizes. Some are tall and skinny, while others are short and stout. Three have brown fur, while two are red, and one is black. Then, it dawns on me that now probably isn't the best time to be making useless observations like this. I guess the mind works in funny ways when one is facing impending death.

As the creatures form a circle of teeth and claws around me, my heart is pounding out of my chest. I mean, all I have to defend myself is a stick! I hold it up high, ready to thrust at a moment's notice, but there's no way I can hold off one werewolf, let alone six!

The last time this happened I was miraculously saved by Crawler. But this time I'm not expecting miracles to strike twice. Then, I remember Hexum's class.

If I can turn myself into a bat, or a cloud of mist, then I could sail out of here scot-free!

But how the heck do I do that?

I mean, Hexum only told me it's possible for vampires other than me. But he didn't tell me how I can do it for myself.

Just then, the black werewolf grunts and they all take a step closer, tightening the ring around me. Now I barely have room to operate! They're standing just outside of my reach, but close enough that I can smell their stench—and boy do they need breath mints!

I sweep my spear, but they barely react, which tells me they're less than intimidated. If I don't do something—anything—fast, I'm dead meat.

Am I overthinking this vampire thing?

Maybe I just need to go for it.

"Be a bat, be a bat, be a bat," I chant quickly, but nothing happens! No wings. No tiny feet. No air time.

I'm still a kid.

Let's try the mist thing.

"Be a mist, be a mist, be a mist."

But no luck either.

Then, I remember Hexum's first test, controlling wolves! I pick out the black-furred one and send Jedi mind tricks its way.

Go home. Please, go home.

But it just narrows its eyes and lets out a ferocious growl. Okay, Hexum is right, I really suck at this whole vampire thing. Time for plan B—total panic!

"Help!" I yell. "Aura! Hairball! Stanphibian! Even InvisiBill! If you're out there, help!"

Unfortunately, no cavalry comes to the rescue, and I'm not surprised. I've probably drifted miles away from the cemetery and way out of earshot. The Monstrosities are either searching for me, or they figured I'm already zombie food by now and split.

A string of drool falls from the black-furred one's mouth, and then it bares its sharp teeth and SNARLS.

This is it!

I close my eyes, waiting for the end.

ROOOOAAARRRRRR!

Um, what's that?

That didn't sound like any werewolf.

Suddenly, there's a series of high-pitched YELPS, and when I open my eyes, I see werewolves scattering all over the place.

What's happening?

THUD!

The ground buckles, knocking me on my rear.

Was that… an earthquake?

THUD!

I bounce like a kernel in a popcorn popper.

Then, there's a loud SNAP, and I realize that's no earthquake. Something is heading our way.

Something big.

My instincts tell me to run, but I stay put. For some crazy reason, I feel like I need to see what's about to happen next. And apparently, the werewolves feel the same way, because instead of fleeing, they're huddling up, preparing themselves for whatever is coming.

Then, the footsteps stop.

The werewolves sniff the air and shoot each other nervous looks.

It's super quiet. Why's it so darn—

BOOM!

I crabwalk backward as two gigantic trees come toppling to the ground like twigs, nearly crushing the werewolves. I get back on my feet, and when I look over at the brush, out steps the biggest, baddest, most horrific monster I've seen yet!

I pick up my jaw and try to take it all in. It must be ten feet tall, with curly, blond hair, purple skin, and an unfriendly scowl. Its body is inexplicably humungous, with boulder-sized muscles bulging from its arms and legs. And strangely, its clothes are shredded across its broad chest and thick thighs.

With a thundering step, the giant strides into the center and glares at me. My legs turn to jelly and I seriously consider asking the werewolves to adopt me.

But then I notice the glasses.

There's a pair of blue glasses wrapped tightly around its neck by a cord. And if I didn't know better, I'd say they looked like… Rage's glasses?

Suddenly, two werewolves jump on the monster's back and begin clawing at his skin. The behemoth lets out a tremendous ROAR and reaches back, grabbing the werewolves by the scruffs of their necks and tossing them into the trees so hard the trunks splinter.

The werewolves crumble to the ground.

Neither gets back up.

Seconds later, the four remaining werewolves approach at once, two from the front and two from the back. The monolith holds its ground, watching them closely. It's like they're playing a game of chicken, waiting to see who will make the first move.

Then, the red werewolf charges from the front. With shocking speed, the purple giant steps aside and grabs him from behind. The others jump in, but the brute uses the red werewolf like a baseball bat, clobbering the others into the air and out of sight. When he's done, he chucks the red werewolf into the night sky.

Well, so much for the werewolves.

Now it's just us!

I put my hands in the air.

"Rage?" I say. "Is that you? It's me, Bram."

It steps towards me with a curious expression, and as I look into its blue eyes, I realize that this monster is, in fact, my friend Rage.

"Rage?" I ask. "Are you hurt?"

But he doesn't answer. He just stares at me.

"Rage? Remember me? I'm your roommate."

His brow furrows, and he ROARS, blowing my hair straight back.

"Um, you do remember me, don't you?"

The creature raises his massive fists.

He's gonna pound me!

Suddenly, I hear a THWIP and feel something buzz by my ear. The next thing I know, Rage CRIES out so loud the trees shake. And when I look up, I see a large dart sticking out of his arm.

Rage looks at me with an odd expression.

"Get out of the way!" comes a familiar voice.

Something grabs me from behind right before the giant comes crashing down, smashing face-first into the ground.

I breathe a sigh of relief. There's no doubt that if I were still standing there, I'd be a kid pancake.

"Just in time," Crawler says.

The man-spider is holding a huge smoking gun the size of a bazooka. I look back at the monster, but he's gone! And in his place is a small, blond-haired boy.

Rage!

But he's not moving.

"D-Did you…?" I stammer.

"No," Crawler says. "I used a tranquilizer strong enough to knock out a herd of elephants. He'll be okay, but he'll be out for a while."

"I-I can't believe that was him," I say. "Now I know why he's called Rage. I thought he was going to kill me."

"He might have," Crawler says. "He has no control of his emotions when he's in that state. He's dangerous. But that's just one reason you kids shouldn't be sneaking around alone at night. Those werewolves are another."

"Yeah," I say. "I seem to have a thing with werewolves. Maybe I need to change my brand of deodorant."

"Werewolves have an incredible sense of smell," Crawler says. "They know your scent by now."

Then, I have a weird thought. "So, if they know my smell, how come they haven't tracked me down at school yet?"

"The Van Helsing Academy is protected by Supernatural artifacts that shield it from evil," Crawler says, slinging the gun over his shoulder. "When you're on campus, you're safe. But once you exit those gates, all bets are off. Remember that, because Van Helsing may not send me to rescue you next time."

"I will," I say. "Wait, Van Helsing sent you?"

"Yep," Crawler says, scooping up Rage. "Up until about an hour ago, I was enjoying a pretty relaxing night. So, I think you owe me one. Now tell me, what exactly were you kids doing out here?"

"Um, well, we—"

"—were just looking for a late-night snack," comes

Aura's voice.

I turn to find the Monstrosities walking towards us.

I can't even tell you how happy I am to see them!

"You know how it is, Crawler," Aura says. "We were studying late for one of Professor Seward's pop quizzes and got a little hungry. We just took a wrong turn on our way to a fast food joint. Isn't that right, Bram?"

Aura shoots me a serious look. That's a cold, hard lie. But if I don't back her up, she'll never trust me again.

"Um, yeah," I say, swallowing hard. "That's it in a nutshell."

"Is that so?" Crawler says, eyeing me warily. "Seems like a shaky story coming from a ghost who doesn't eat. So, which one of you jokers is responsible for damaging the jeep?"

"Jeep?" Hairball says, his voice cracking. "What jeep?"

"That one," Crawler says.

Just then, the jeep comes rolling towards us. The hood is popped open, the windshield is smashed, and the bumper is hanging halfway off the front. It looks so badly damaged I don't know how it's running at all, until I realize it's not being driven, it's being carried—by a gazillion spiders!

"Uh oh," Hairball says.

"I hope you've got car insurance, Hairball," Crawler says. "Because I can't wait for Van Helsing to see this one."

***

The other kids get to see Van Helsing as a group, but I'm not so lucky. Instead, Crawler instructs me to wait outside until Van Helsing is finished with them. I don't know what's worse, getting the punishment, or being forced to think about getting the punishment.

An hour later, the door finally opens, and my friends file out with their heads down. Strangely, no one says a word so it must have been pretty bad. Aura doesn't even look my way.

The only one spared is Rage, who is recovering in the infirmary. Dr. Hagella thinks he'll be okay, but only time will tell. He still hasn't woken up yet.

I watch as the Monstrosities walk away, except for InvisiBill, who I can't see at all. Then, they round the corner and disappear from view.

It's my turn.

I know I need to go inside and face the music, but for some reason, my eyes are fixated on Professor Faustius' door across the way. I study the 'Entry Forbidden' sign hanging from his doorknob and wonder what happened to that guy. Rage told me he used to teach Black Magic, so maybe he summoned a demon who gobbled him up or something?

Well, whatever it is, I'm sure it's not good.

Okay, I figure I've stalled long enough.

I take a deep breath and enter Van Helsing's office.

It's just as warm as I remembered, with piles of junk precariously balanced upon other piles of junk. How he finds anything in this place is a mystery to me. I carefully pick my way through the clutter, nearly making it through unscathed until I step on something that SQUEAKS and scampers away, nearly giving me a heart attack!

Once I regain my composure, I pause before turning the final corner because I know what's waiting for me on the other side. Then, I step out to meet my fate.

Van Helsing is sitting in his chair, feeding logs into the fire. He's as heavily dressed as before, complete with a sweater, scarf, and gloves. The flames from the fire cast dancing shadows on his furrowed brow. His blue eyes meet mine, but he doesn't say anything, so I take a seat across from him and await my sentencing.

It's so unbearably warm that sweat starts dripping from my forehead. I wait for Van Helsing to start talking but he simply stares at me. In the meantime, a hundred horrible scenarios unfold in my head, each more terrible than the one before.

Is he going to tell me he's disappointed in me? Is he going to throw me in a dungeon? Is he going to expel me from the academy?

Suddenly, he breaks the silence.

"What should your punishment be?" he asks.

My eyebrows go sky high. Um, what? Did he just ask me what my own punishment should be? Was he serious?

I mean, no one has ever asked me to pick my own punishment before. I must have misheard him.

"I-I'm sorry," I stammer. "Did you say you wanted me to decide my own punishment?"

"Yes," he says. "At the Van Helsing Academy, students are accountable for their behavior and misbehavior. Therefore, it falls on you to pick your punishment. I only ask that you weigh the transgression and pick the most reasonable punishment."

Wow, that's amazing!

My mind fills with possibilities.

Maybe a day of television? Or no homework for a week? Or maybe all of the Swedish Fish I can eat?

But when I look at Van Helsing, I know those aren't punishments at all. He's expecting me to be responsible—to find a punishment that fits the crime.

So, let's see. We snuck off campus, wrecked his jeep, and put all of our lives in danger, including Crawler's life.

What punishment is worthy of all of that?

Suddenly, the worst thing possible pops into my head.

"An extra session with Professor Hexum?" I blurt out unexpectedly. "Just him and me."

I regret it as soon as I say it.

This time Van Helsing raises his eyebrows. "That is a fair punishment. Your session will be scheduled for tomorrow afternoon. Thank you for being accountable for your actions. You are now dismissed."

Really? That's it? I'm so shocked I sit there dumbfounded for a minute before standing up.

Then, a curious thought springs to mind.

"Headmaster, can I ask you something?"

"Yes, Bram."

"What happened to Professor Faustius?"

Van Helsing's left eyebrow raises for a second, and he says—

"Professor Faustius is no longer employed here."

But before I can follow up, he turns away and looks into the fire.

It's clear he doesn't want to talk about it.

So, I take the hint and leave.

VAN HELSING ACADEMY

STUDENT ASSESSMENT

VITALS:
NAME: Unknown
EYES: Blue
HAIR: Blond
HEIGHT: 4’4”/10’3”
WEIGHT: 72/615 lbs

NOTES: Kind and docile in human form. Transforms into angry, uncontrollable beast with extraordinary strength. Has no memory of transformation.

CODENAME: RAGE

CLASSIFICATION TYPE:
Abnormal – Jekyll/Hyde

SUPERNATURAL ASSESSMENT:

STRENGTH	●●●●●
AGILITY	●●○○○
FIGHTING	●●●○○
INTELLECT	●○○○○
CONTROL	●○○○○

TEACHABLE?	Yes	No
VAN HELSING	●	○
CRAWLER	●	○
HOLMWOOD	○	●
SEWARD	○	●
MORRIS	●	○
HEXUM	○	●
~~FAUSTIUS~~	~~○~~	~~○~~

RISK LEVEL: HIGH

CHAPTER ELEVEN

BAT-TERED AND BRUISED

It's the wee hours of the morning and we're all in the infirmary checking up on Rage. Dr. Hagella said he's stabilized, which is great news, but he's been sound asleep for at least four hours. He has way more color in his cheeks than the last time I saw him—which thankfully isn't purple.

No one is feeling particularly chatty. After our discussions with Van Helsing, we're all lost in our thoughts. Not surprisingly, I can't seem to get my upcoming punishment with Hexum out of my mind. I'm kicking myself for not coming up with something—and I mean anything—else.

After a while, Stanphibian, Hairball, and InvisiBill head back to Monster House for some shuteye. Aura isn't ready to go back yet, so I decide to keep her company.

The two of us sit in silence as Rage snores like a baby hog. I want to say something to break the noticeable tension in the air, but she doesn't seem so interested in talking to me.

Finally, I can't take it anymore.

"Are you mad at me or something?" I ask.

"Mad?" she says. "Why would I be mad at you?"

"I don't know," I say. "You've been awfully quiet since you left Van Helsing's office."

"Don't be ridiculous," she says. "I'm not mad at you. I'm mad at myself. This whole mess was my fault. I'm the one who found out about the grave robbers. I'm the one who forced everyone to go. I'm the one responsible for Rage getting hurt."

"Don't be so hard on yourself," I say. "You didn't know that would happen."

"But it was my responsibility," she says. "I knew going to the cemetery would be risky, and I should have made sure we were better prepared. But I didn't, and Rage nearly got killed. Anyway, I let Van Helsing know that I'm the one to blame, so I should face all of the consequences."

"What did he say about that?" I ask.

"He thanked me for my honesty," she says. "But he still made everyone come up with their own punishments. He said none of them had to follow me. He said they were responsible for making their own decisions."

She pauses, clearly upset.

"I'm sorry I asked you to lie to Crawler," she adds. "That wasn't right either."

"That's okay," I say. "But to Van Helsing's point, I guess I could've decided not to do it. But I still don't understand why you wanted me to lie to Crawler in the first place?"

"I don't know," she says. "I guess I thought we could handle it. I mean, if we could solve the mystery, we could show Van Helsing how capable we are."

"I think everyone knows how capable you are," I say. "You're the smartest person in our class. Like, it's not even close."

"Thanks," she says, brushing a strand of hair from her forehead. "But I don't feel very capable. I mean, look at me, I'm a freaking ghost. I'm here, but I'm not. I used to love to dance and act. Now I'll never be able to do those things again. I go crazy thinking about all the things I'll miss out on. Like driving a car, or going to prom, or my first kiss—"

She stops and shoots me an embarrassed look.

If I weren't so pale, I'm sure I'd be beet red.

"It… it must be tough," I manage to say.

"Yeah, it stinks," she says.

She looks depressed, so I figure I should try changing the subject. "So, about that mystery. Why do you think those zombies wanted those bones anyway?"

"I've been trying to figure that out," she says, her eyes widening with excitement. "Like, is there a pattern? The first grave they hit was of a man named Jonah Covington. I did some research on him. He was an Olympic gold medalist in the late nineteenth century who is still considered to be the greatest athlete of all time. He was supposed to be really tall and strong. He set all kinds of records."

"Really?" I say. "I didn't know about that one."

"Yeah," she says. "And the second grave belonged to a military corporal named Lloyd McAdams. He was a sharpshooter during World War I and was known as the best shot of the twentieth century."

"Totally weird," I say. I remember seeing the newspaper headline for that one back at the New England Home for Troubled Boys.

"Very weird," she says. "But it gets weirder. Tonight, they stole the bones of Dr. Eugene Albert. He was a brilliant scientist who won the Nobel Prize for his work in physics and quantum mechanics."

"What would a bunch of zombies want with the bones of an athlete, a sharpshooter, and a brainiac?" I ask. "I thought they only cared about eating flesh."

"Exactly," she says. "I've been wondering the same thing. But then I realized the zombies probably didn't want the bones for themselves. They must be working for someone else."

"Like who?"

"Like the Dark Ones," she says matter-of-factly.

A chill runs down my spine. The Dark Ones? Could they be behind this? And what about those werewolves? Van Helsing told me they worked for the Dark Ones too. Clearly, they're still after me.

Suddenly, Dr. Hagella pops in. "You both should go

to bed. Rage needs his rest, and so do you. Goodnight."

"Okay, Doc," Aura says. "You know I can't sleep, but I get it. Goodnight."

As we head out, the sun is climbing over the horizon. I can probably get in a shower before breakfast, but there's no way I'll be getting any rest. Today is going to be a busy day.

Especially with Hexum.

"Just out of curiosity," I say, "what did you pick for your punishment?"

"I told Van Helsing I'd alphabetize his private library for him," she says, rolling her eyes. "You've seen the state of his office, right? Trust me, his library is much, much worse."

"I can't even imagine," I say. "But how can you do that? I mean, you're a ghost. Sorry."

"No, it's okay," she says. "Hexum has been teaching me how to use my own 'aura' to control the molecules around me and move objects around. He calls it 'telekinesis.' I'm still learning how to do it. It takes a lot of concentration, but that's how I keep my Monstrosities badge on."

"Really?" I say, noticing for the first time that her silver badge isn't pinned to her sweater, but floating in front of her body. "Wow. That's cool."

"Thanks," she says. "I'm no pro yet, but I figure I can handle moving some books around. It'll be good practice anyway. And since I don't need sleep, I figure I can tackle it over a few nights. How about you? What punishment did you pick?"

"A one-on-one with Hexum," I say sheepishly.

"Seriously?" she says. "Boy, you must really feel guilty about what we did."

"Either that," I say, "or I'm a big dope."

"No comment," she says.

"Gee, thanks," I say.

Our eyes meet, and we laugh.

***

I'm pretty much a train wreck all day. All I can think about is my dreaded appointment with Hexum, which pretty much makes me a space cadet in all of my other classes.

In Monsterology, Professor Holmwood makes me write 'I will pay attention in class' one hundred times on the chalkboard after I fail to respond to her questions. In Supernatural History, I struggle through Professor Seward's pop quiz on monsters in the medieval era. And in Paranormal Science, I manage to temporarily blind myself with a flash bomb.

It's hard to imagine things getting worse.

But then comes Survival Skills.

No sooner had we lined up, when—

"Attention!" Hexum commands. "Today's class is canceled. I expect all of you to practice your exercises on your own."

What? Really?

This is incredible news!

"Except for you, Mr. Murray," Hexum says. "Today, you and I will be having a private, double session."

Wait, what?

A double session? That's totally unfair! I told Van Helsing I'd have one extra session for my punishment, not two. This is injustice! This is criminal!

"The rest of you are dismissed," Hexum says.

As I jealously watch the others walk away, I catch Hairball snickering. Oh, when I get my hands on that giant, flea-bitten rug…

But then I see Aura.

She mouths 'good luck,' and then floats away.

Luck? I suspect I'll need more than luck if I'm going to survive this. The door SLAMS shut behind the last kid, echoing through the chamber.

Great, my worst nightmare has come true.

I'm alone with Hexum.

For two flippin' hours.

My back tightens up.

Hexum paces back and forth like some kind of a predator, which I guess makes me his prey. But I'm not opening my mouth. The more time he wastes doing this, the less time I'll have to interact with him.

Then, he wheels on me.

Uh-oh.

"Mr. Murray," he says, "I suspect you do not like me. Would I be correct in this assumption?"

I'm stunned. Of course he's correct, but am I supposed to tell him that? This feels like a trap. If I tell him the truth, I'll lose. But if I lie, somehow I'll lose again. But maybe bigger.

"Mr. Murray, I asked you a direct question. It would be polite to provide an answer."

What should I do? I have no choice but to go for it.

"You're correct," I say firmly. "I don't like you."

"Thank you," he says, raising an eyebrow. "I respect your brutal honesty, and I certainly understand if you left our last meeting feeling frustrated. No doubt it was a difficult day for you. But I am afraid your difficulty is just beginning. You see, Mr. Murray, my job is not to like you or dislike you. My job is to teach you how to get the most out of your abilities so you do not die. Do you understand, Mr. Murray?"

Strangely, I do.

I nod.

"Excellent," he says. "So, our first encounter was difficult out of necessity. After all, we needed to understand where the bar was set. Do you agree?"

I nod again.

"Excellent," he says. "I am glad you agree. Unfortunately, what we learned is that the bar is set so low, I am doubtful we will be able to raise it."

Speaking of low, that's pretty much how I'm feeling.

"But it is my job to try, Mr. Murray. So that is precisely what I will do. Now, perhaps we should start with something a bit more elementary this time. Do you know our motto here at the Van Helsing Academy?"

His question catches me off guard. Motto? What's that? But then I remember the black banner and the saying beneath the Van Helsing crest.

"You must believe in things you cannot imagine."

"Very good, Mr. Murray. Yes, that is correct. You must believe in things you cannot imagine. Do you know what that means?"

He's got me there. I've never really thought about it.

"I suppose it means there's more to this world than meets the eye," I say.

"In part," Hexum says, his lips curling into a thin smile. "It means there are things in this world that cannot be explained by science. You see, Mr. Murray, there are two types of creatures in this world, and they live by entirely different sets of rules. There are the Naturals, ordinary creatures, living their pedestrian lives according to the laws of nature. You know them well. They go to school, they go to work, they have offspring, they die."

Well, that makes being human sound lovely.

"But there is another type of creature," he continues. "The Supernatural creature, who lives by a force far more chaotic and unpredictable than nature. A force so powerful it can give life back to the dead. Tell me, Mr. Murray, which set of rules do you live by?"

"The Supernatural one?" I say.

"Very good," Hexum says. "You are a Supernatural, after all. But you do not think like a Supernatural. No, no. You think like a Natural. And when you think like a Natural, it is hard to 'believe in things you cannot imagine.' Do you understand, Mr. Murray?"

"I-I think so."

"If you are truly going to be a Supernatural, you must learn to think like a Supernatural. This will be the focus of our lesson today."

Suddenly, a lightbulb flashes in my head. Maybe that's why this vampire thing isn't working. Maybe it's because I'm not thinking like a vampire. I'm thinking like a normal kid—a Natural—but I'm not.

"Enough talk," Hexum continues, "now we begin."

Hexum taps his walking stick on the floor, and I realize my pain is about to begin.

***

At dinner, I can barely lift my fork to my face.

And it's not just because my arm is sore, which it is, but also because I don't have an ounce of brainpower left. After an afternoon with Hexum, I'm mentally fried.

"You okay?" Hairball asks. "You look like a zombie."

"I'm not sure," I murmur. "I just experienced the worst two hours of my entire life."

"What did he make you do?" Aura asks. As usual, she's not eating anything.

"Turn into a bat," I say.

"How'd that go?" InvisiBill asks. I can't see him, but a slice of pizza magically lifts off of his tray.

"Not well," I say. "Over and over and over again."

"I'm so sorry, Bram," Aura says.

"I think Hexum is convinced I'm a complete waste of vampire DNA."

"Ouch," Stanphibian says.

Well, if I didn't know how bad it was, I know it now because Stanphibian rarely says anything. But is it my fault I can't turn into a bat? Maybe not all vampires are meant to be bats. Maybe I'm just not your typical vampire. I mean, look at me now. It's not like I'm sitting here sucking blood for dinner.

"Hey, gang!" comes a familiar voice.

"Rage!" we all exclaim.

"It's great to be back," he says, sliding his tray onto the table and squeezing in between Stanphibian and Hairball.

"How do you feel?" I ask.

"Great!" he says, stabbing into his steak with his fork. "Better than great actually. I needed that rest."

We watch him stuff his face like he hasn't eaten in days. He seems completely normal. Nothing like the purple beast that nearly squished me to death.

"Just out of curiosity, do you remember anything

that happened?" I ask.

"Nope," he says, looking at me with a screwy expression on his face. "The last thing I remember is that female zombie taking a swing at me. After that, nothing."

Wow. Okay then.

"Well, we're glad you're back," Aura says. "You scared us for a while."

"A long while," Hairball says.

"Dr. Hagella wants me to sit out of Survival Skills for a few weeks," Rage says. "She put this thing on me to monitor my blood pressure."

He raises his right arm to show us a device wrapped around his wrist with big, flashing numbers on it.

"Well, your blood pressure looks normal," Aura says.

"Thank goodness," I say, "for everyone's sake."

We all laugh, including Rage.

"So, I also have some exciting news," Aura says. "While Bram was being tortured by Hexum, I used my free time to start cataloging Van Helsing's private library. You'll never guess what I found."

"Van Helsing's sense of humor?" Hairball says.

"No," she says. "A copy of The Alchemy of Reanimation, Volume I."

"Reani-what?" Rage asks, his mouth full.

"Reanimation," Aura says. "It's the science of bringing the dead back to life."

Suddenly, I remember my conversation with Hexum. It sounds like some Natural was using science to bend the laws of nature, which probably isn't a good thing.

"It's a pretty fascinating read," she says. "It has all of this theory on how to do it, with charts and calculations and stuff. But to do it, you need the skeleton of a dead person."

"So?" InvisiBill says as we're forced to watch his chewed pizza rolling down his throat.

"So?" Aura says. "What's been going on around here lately?"

"Bones are being stolen," I say.

"Exactly," she says. "I think someone is trying to reanimate these dead people."

"Yuck," Hairball says.

"But that's not all," she says. "You'll never guess who wrote the book?"

Everyone looks at one another.

"Donald Duck?" Hairball guesses.

"No," Aura says. "Professor Claude Faustius."

My fork slips from my hand and clangs on my plate.

"Seriously?" I say. "The Black Magic guy?"

"Yep," she says. "He published it a few years ago."

"Maybe that's why he doesn't teach here anymore?" Rage says. "I bet Van Helsing didn't approve of that."

"That's probably why his office is locked up," I say. "So nobody can get inside to see what he did."

"But here's the thing," Aura says. "There are two volumes to the Alchemy of Reanimation. I could only find the first one in Van Helsing's library. The second volume is the one that actually tells you how to bring the dead back to life. I bet it's inside Faustius' office. I bet there's a clue in there about those grave robbers too."

"But we can't get in there," Rage says. "It says 'Entry Forbidden,' remember? Plus, it's locked up like crazy."

"Maybe for you," Aura says smiling, "but not for a ghost."

VAN HELSING ACADEMY

STUDENT ASSESSMENT

VITALS:
NAME: Harry Woolsey
EYES: Brown
HAIR: Brown
HEIGHT: 6'1"
WEIGHT: 205 lbs

NOTES: Yeti-DNA provides incredible strength and heightened sense of smell. Not very mobile and could become a large target. Requires a lot of food.

CODENAME: Hairball

CLASSIFICATION TYPE:
Abnormal – Yeti

SUPERNATURAL ASSESSMENT:

STRENGTH	●●●●○
AGILITY	●○○○○
FIGHTING	●●●●○
INTELLECT	●●●○○
CONTROL	●●●○○

TEACHABLE?	Yes	No
VAN HELSING	●	○
CRAWLER	●	○
HOLMWOOD	●	○
SEWARD	●	○
MORRIS	●	○
HEXUM	○	●
FAUSTIUS	●	○

RISK LEVEL: LOW

CHAPTER TWELVE

CREEPIN' IT REAL

I can't believe we're doing this.

I mean, we were just punished by Van Helsing last night! Yet, here we are, hiding in a row of thorny hedges, risking our necks on another one of Aura's crazy hunches. If we're caught it probably means the end of our little gang, but we've got to find out the truth. After all, there are just too many strange things going on.

First, zombies are digging up graves and stealing the bones of dead people. Then, Aura discovers that creepy book in Van Helsing's private library about bringing the dead back to life.

Are they related?

Maybe. Maybe not.

But here's the kicker.

The book was written by Professor Claude Faustius. The very same Professor Claude Faustius who used to teach Black Magic right here at the Van Helsing Academy. The very same Professor Claude Faustius whose office is in lockdown mode.

More than a coincidence?

Yeah, I'd buy that.

So, that's why we're camped out here in the bushes. Well, at least Rage, Stanphibian, Hairball, and I are camped out in the bushes. We're waiting for all of the teachers to go home so we can break into Faustius' office and solve the mystery once and for all.

Aura is on lookout duty, floating high above the main building. InvisiBill is stationed inside, scouting out the professors. The rest of us are stuffed inside this thicket, way too close for anyone's comfort.

Yet, surprisingly, everything is going smoothly.

At least, so far.

Getting by Vi Clops was pretty simple. All we had to do was deliver another dozen pizzas and she was down for the count. I never knew outwitting a cyclops would be so easy, but according to Aura I still have lots to learn.

We just need the professors to go home for the night. Since they keep different hours we brainstormed ideas on how to get them all out of the building at once. InvisiBill wanted to pull the fire alarm but we told him not to do it as it would just raise suspicions. I hope he listens.

In the end, we agreed our best option was to just wait them out. Which probably means we're stuck here for a while.

Suddenly, a horrific, fishy smell assaults my nostrils.

"Ugh! What's that?" Hairball whispers.

"Sorry," Stanphibian says.

"Seriously?" Rage whispers. "Are you trying to put me back in the infirmary?"

Before going on this crazy adventure, we debated if Rage should even come along. After all, he's supposed to be resting. But after arguing with each other for a whole thirty-minutes, Rage told us he was coming no matter what so that was a complete waste of time.

I look up at the cupola to see if Aura is giving us any signals, but she's facing the other way, keeping an eye out for unexpected stragglers. She sort of looks other-worldly in the moonlight, kind of like a guardian angel.

Just then, something comes crashing through the brush, knocking me and Hairball on our backsides.

"Hey!" Hairball yells.

"Shut it, fluffy cakes," InvisiBill whispers. "They're coming."

I glance up at Aura. She gives a thumbs up and phases through the wall.

Someone is exiting the building.

"No noises," I whisper, "from any body parts."

Just then, Holmwood and Morris step through the doors.

I'm the closest to the stairs, so I have the best vantage point. The two professors are having an intense conversation, but instead of heading over to the Faculty Residence Hall, they stop on the front porch.

What's going on? Why aren't they leaving?

They're speaking in low tones. I tilt my head, trying to make out what they're saying.

"—long did he say he'd be gone?" Professor Holmwood asks.

"He didn't," Professor Morris answers. "I offered to ride along, but he looked like he had a burr in his saddle and said he needed to go alone. All I could do was insist he take some special equipment with him. There wasn't much else I could do."

"He's so stubborn," Professor Holmwood says. "I certainly hope he's careful. This is a dangerous appointment with a most unsavory character."

"Like a snake in the grass," Professor Morris says.

"Please, Quincy," Professor Holmwood says, "if you hear anything, anything at all, let me know."

"Of course, Lucy," Professor Morris says. "Fortunately, he's a very competent fellow."

"Yes," she says. "That's precisely why I'm worried."

"Well, I'm going to take my evening stroll," Professor Morris says. "Would you like to join me?"

"No thank you," she says. "I need to do some lesson planning for tomorrow. It's skin-rider day."

"Exhilarating," he says, tipping his hat. "Well, goodnight."

"Goodnight," Professor Holmwood says.

Then, they go their separate ways.

"What was that all about?" Rage whispers.

"I have no idea," I answer.

"Shhh!" InvisiBill interjects. "Shut up."

Just then, Professor Seward exits the building carrying a tall stack of test booklets. I bet my 'monsters in the medieval era' pop quiz is in that pile. He's probably grading them tonight. Boy, did I screw that one up.

Suddenly, a strong wind kicks up out of nowhere, blowing several booklets from the top of his pile onto the front porch.

"Unbelievable," Professor Seward mutters.

As he bends over to pick them up, I spot something out of the corner of my eye and my heart stops beating. One of the booklets blew off the porch and landed right next to my foot! If Seward reaches into the bushes to get it, we'll be caught!

"HOOT! HOOT!"

Huh? What's that? It sounded like an owl caught in a blender somewhere high above.

"HOOT!" it repeats.

All of us look up, including Professor Seward.

And then, "SCOOT!"

Scoot? What bird says—?

Suddenly, I feel like a world-class dufus.

It's Aura! She's making a distraction.

I snatch the booklet and toss it back on the porch. Right on cue, Professor Seward scoops it up with all the others and goes merrily on his way.

Whew! That was close.

Now there's just one left.

The one I'm most worried about.

I hear Hexum before I see him, the TAPPING of his walking stick announcing his arrival. I hold my breath as he makes his way across the front porch.

C'mon. Keep going. Keep going.

Hexum walks down the front steps.

Yes!

He steps onto the driveway.

Yes! Yes! Yes!

And then he stops.

No! No! No!

Hexum stands there, his cape billowing in the wind.

What's he doing? Why isn't he leaving?

Then, he turns and my heart skips a beat!

He's staring into the bushes!

I freeze.

Does he see us? Is he looking at me?

I don't know what to do.

"HOOT!"

That's Aura! She's creating another diversion.

"HOOT!"

Hexum looks up and smiles. "A hoot indeed," he says loudly. Then, he extends his walking stick and continues on his way.

No one moves until he's clearly out of sight.

"Thank heavens," Rage whispers, collapsing onto my back. "I thought we were going to die."

"Stop yapping and get up," Hairball whispers.

"Before we do die."

After that, all of our best-laid plans for a 'slow and stealthy' break-in are chucked out the window. We race inside the building and book over to the faculty wing. Thankfully, no one is around. Nevertheless, I keep my eyes peeled for any of Crawler's critters who might report us via the world wide web.

Eventually, we reach Faustius' office and skid to a stop. After crashing into InvisiBill, I take a quick count. We're all here, except for one. Where's Aura?

Just then, a pair of legs materializes through the ceiling over our heads.

"Ahhh!" Rage screams.

Aura lands smack in the middle of us.

Suddenly, there's a loud BEEPING noise. We go into panic mode, trying to find the source.

"It's Rage's blood pressure watch," InvisiBill says.

"Turn it off!" Hairball orders.

"I can't!" Rage says. "There's no off button!"

"Give me that," Hairball says, ripping it off of Rage's wrist and crushing it in his hand. "There's your off button."

"Ow!" Rage says, rubbing his arm. "Did you have to take half my skin with it? And Aura, seriously? Was that necessary?"

"Sorry," Aura says. "I took a shortcut after making sure Hexum was gone."

"Hexum may be gone," Hairball says. "But what

about Van Helsing?"

We look down the hallway. Van Helsing's door is closed, but that doesn't mean he's not inside.

"I think he's gone," Rage says. "Didn't you hear what Holmwood and Morris were talking about? They said he went out for some kind of dangerous appointment."

"But they never said his name," InvisiBill adds. "Maybe it was Crawler and not Van Helsing?"

"Only one way to find out," I say, making my way down the hall.

I put my ear against the door. There aren't any noises coming from inside, not even a crackling fire. Then, I realize the door is cool to the touch.

"He's not there," I say.

"Are you sure?" Hairball asks. "Maybe Aura should phase in there."

"No need," I say. "I think we're good to go."

"Then let's get this over with," Rage says. "Before someone shows up."

We hustle back to Faustius' door. With seven locks and one 'Entry Forbidden' sign, Van Helsing couldn't have been any clearer.

"Are you sure you want to do this?" I ask Aura.

"Really, Bram?" she says, rolling her eyes.

Then, she steps straight through the door.

"Okay, this is really happening," Rage says, his head in his hands.

"I'll keep a lookout," InvisiBill says, his footsteps echoing down the hallway. "But make it snappy."

Making it snappy sounds great, but there's nothing the rest of us can do but wait. I mean, Aura's been inside only a few seconds, but it already feels like an eternity. That's when I realize we haven't heard from her.

I lean against the door. "Aura, can you hear me?"

But there's no response.

I knock hard. "Aura?"

"Cut it out!" comes her muffled voice. "I hear you. I'm just getting my bearings. It's dark in here."

Whew! She's safe.

"Can you see at all?" I ask, this time much quieter.

"A little," she says. "Some light is filtering through a boarded-up window, but that's about it. This place is big-time creepy and there's all sorts of scientific equipment in here. Microscopes and test tubes and beakers. Is that an operating table? Oh, yuck!"

"What? What is it?"

"Sorry," she says. "I-I think there's a whole shelf of brains. So gross."

"Do you see a book?" I ask. "Remember, that's what we're looking for."

"I know what we're looking for," she says. "I'm not a moron. Wait, here's a desk with all sorts of— Hang on! There's a book on it! Let me read the spine. Yes! This is it! The Alchemy of Reanimation Volume II! Let me see if I can open it somehow and—"

Suddenly, there's silence.

"Aura?"

No answer.

We all look at one another.

"Okay," Hairball says. "Where'd she go?"

"Aura?" I yell, knocking on the door. "Aura, are you okay? Aura?"

There's no reply.

"Something happened!" I say. "Hairball, bust it down!"

"But we'll get caught!" InvisiBill says. He must have come back down the hall.

"Dude, who cares?" I say. "Aura's in trouble. Take it down, Hairball!"

The furry giant rears back his fist and pounds the door. The next thing I know, Hairball is flying backward through the air, crashing into the opposite wall.

"That's Black Magic!" Rage says. "The door must be cursed!"

"Pull off the locks!" I say.

Stanphibian grabs a lock and tugs with all of his might, but it won't break off.

"Forget it," InvisiBill says. "We can't get inside. We've got to get the professors. Stanphibian, let's go!"

The two of them take off, but I have a feeling we can't waste time waiting for help to arrive. Aura is in trouble now! I pound on the door again.

"Aura! Are you okay? Are you still there? Aura?"

Still nothing.

I've got to help her. But how?

Then, I spin around and my eyes land on Hexum's door. Suddenly, I hear his voice inside my head:

'If you are truly going to be a Supernatural, you must learn to think like a Supernatural.'

He's right. That's the only way I'll ever believe in things I can't imagine.

While Rage is helping Hairball back to his feet, I close my eyes, tuning them out. I focus on one thought.

How can I best help Aura?

Suddenly, I envision a vapor cloud flowing beneath the crack of a door.

That's it! If we can't go through Faustius' door, maybe I can go around it?

I fixate on that vapor cloud.

I hold that image in my mind.

I focus everything I can on that image.

A cloud of mist.

Then, I start to believe.

Suddenly, I'm tingly all over.

I feel light—lighter than air.

My entire body feels like it's spreading out. Like my molecules are pulling apart!

"Um, Bram?" comes Rage's voice. It sounds distant.

I feel like I'm floating, like I'm high in the air, brushing against the ceiling. But my body feels scattered. Like I've dissipated into a gazillion, tiny particles.

I see Rage and Hairball looking up at me, their mouths hanging wide open.

I… did it?

"Bram, is that you?" Rage asks.

But I can't answer him.

First, I have no mouth.

Second, my thoughts are on Aura.

I've got to help her.

I focus my mind, clustering my atoms together.

Then, I flow through the cracks of Faustius' door.

VAN HELSING ACADEMY

STUDENT ASSESSMENT

VITALS:
NAME: Stanley Seawald
EYES: Black
HAIR: Green
HEIGHT: 4'7"
WEIGHT: 101 lbs

CODENAME: Stanphibian

NOTES: Can breathe underwater, limited breathing on land. Quick reflexes, excellent swimmer, super strong skin. Rarely speaks.

CLASSIFICATION TYPE:
Abnormal – Gill-man

SUPERNATURAL ASSESSMENT:

STRENGTH	●●●○○
AGILITY	●●●●●
FIGHTING	●●●○○
INTELLECT	●●●○○
CONTROL	●●●●○

TEACHABLE?	Yes	No
VAN HELSING	●	○
CRAWLER	●	○
HOLMWOOD	●	○
SEWARD	●	○
MORRIS	●	○
HEXUM	○	●
FAUSTIUS	○	●

RISK LEVEL: LOW

CHAPTER THIRTEEN

WELL, THAT SUCKS

As I drift into Faustius' office, I know I need to be ready for anything.

I also learn that maintaining my mist-form is tricky business. Half of me is hugging the ceiling while the other half is skimming the floor. I need to stay focused to keep my particles together, and after a few seconds of excruciating mental effort, I manage to pull myself into a fairly respectable vapor cloud.

It's dark in here, just as Aura said, but fortunately, I can still see even in mist form. And to my surprise, one major benefit of being a mist is that I can see in multiple directions at once.

The only problem is that I don't see Aura anywhere.

Where is she?

At first, I feel a flutter of panic, but then I realize I've got this. After all, I've paid attention in Professor Morris' class about Supernatural crime scene investigations. Now I just have to apply what I've learned. So, here goes.

Step one, secure the crime scene. Well, it appears I'm

the only one here so a big check mark for that one. Step two, sweep the crime scene, assess the environment, and look for clues. Okay, if I want to cover the most space in the fastest time possible I'll need to fan out.

That's kind of frustrating after working so hard to pull myself together, but what other choice do I have? So, I relax my concentration and feel myself spreading apart. The good news is that it only takes a few seconds to permeate the room. The bad news is that Faustius' office is as creepy as Aura said it was. Maybe even creepier.

I run down the list of what Aura reported seeing. Brains on a shelf. Check. Bizarre operating table. Check. Feeling totally freaked out. Double check.

But there's still no sign of Aura.

I wish I knew what step three of a Supernatural investigation was, but we haven't gotten that far yet.

Maybe Aura is just playing a practical joke, like when we tried tracking her with the Spirit Sensor. She's probably back at Monster House laughing her head off. Boy, that would be great. But I know it's not true.

Something happened to her.

Something bad.

Part of me feels like I should head back into the hallway, but I know it's fear talking. Aura needs my help and hovering like a cloud isn't going to get me any closer to solving this mystery. I need to get my sneakers on the ground. I just hope I can change back to normal, otherwise, I'll be stuck like this forever and get a code name like "Gas Boy" or something.

I concentrate hard, picturing myself as a regular kid. I put all of my focus on that mental image. Then, I start to feel tingly again, like my atoms are coming back together. I feel myself becoming heavier, more solid.

The next thing I know, I'm falling from the ceiling!

I SLAM hard on my backside and roll over.

Note to self: the next time I transition from mist to human form, make sure I'm near the floor.

Suddenly, I hear KNOCKING.

"Bram, are you okay!" comes Rage's voice.

"I'm good!" I yell. "Just fell from the ceiling. Only hurt my pride. I don't see Aura though!"

"Maybe you should get out of there," Rage says. "The guys are trying to find Van Helsing or Crawler. Let's let them handle it."

"There's no time!" I yell back. I have a bad feeling that if I can't figure out what happened to Aura, she'll be lost forever. I spin around the room. What was she doing when we last heard from her? Then, I remember.

The book!

It was on Faustius' desk.

Where the heck is that desk?

I'm about to make a mad scramble when I suddenly feel drained. Changing into a cloud and back again sapped my energy. But I can't stop now. I need to find that book.

Suddenly, I notice a piece of furniture sticking out from behind the shelf of brains. For some reason, I missed this area. So, I head over to explore.

Bingo! It's a desk alright.

It's positioned beneath a boarded window. The surface is large, and every square inch is covered with beakers, microscopes, and… a book!

Just then, I notice something shimmery on the floor.

It's Aura's badge!

Okay, that's not a good sign.

I pick it up and shove it into my pocket. Then, I get back to the book. It's thick, with a tattered black cover and yellowed pages. It's still closed, so I guess Aura never got it open. I check out the text on the spine. It reads:

THE ALCHEMY OF REANIMATION
VOLUME II
BY PROFESSOR CLAUDE FAUSTIUS

This is it!

I reach for it but then stop myself.

Aura was opening it when something happened to her—and she's a ghost! Maybe I shouldn't open it. I mean, if doors and locks can be cursed then who knows what kind of Black Magic is inside of this thing? Yet, this book is definitely linked to Aura's disappearance.

I just don't know how.

What should I do?

The way I see it, I have two options. Option one, leave the book here and mist my way out of Faustius' office for help. Since Van Helsing put the locks on Faustius' door, he'd know how to open them up so we could get back inside. The risk is that he's probably not around. I mean, according to Holmwood and Morris, he left the Academy for his appointment a long time ago. Plus, we'd lose precious time finding Aura.

Option two, stay in kid form, grab the book, and break out of Faustius' office. That way, even if Van Helsing isn't here, we can track him down and hand deliver the book as quickly as possible. The risk is that I'll have to ensure no one opens the book. Especially InvisiBill because he'd be the one to do something stupid like that. The problem is that I'm not sure I can unlock Faustius' door from the inside. After all, it's cursed.

Decisions, decisions.

Okay, option two it is!

I grab the book, and immediately I know it's a mistake! There's a strong force pulling me forward like I'm being sucked inside a vacuum cleaner!

What's going on?

I try releasing the book, but it won't let me go!

I'm slip—

***

I wake up in a fog.

I try opening my eyes, but my head is pounding so hard even my eyelids hurt. Nevertheless, as soon as I pry them open, I wish I hadn't, because it only takes a second to realize I'm in trouble. Serious trouble.

I'm in some kind of a circular chamber with stone walls along the perimeter and a domed, leaded-glass ceiling. Looking up, I see it's still nighttime, but not a star is hanging in the sky. All around me are various stations holding strange sciency stuff, like giant microscopes, bubbling beakers, and electric amps. To my left are two metal tables complete with wrist and ankle shackles. A small table between them holds an array of surgical tools, like scalpels, knives, and scissors.

By the looks of it, I'd say I'm in some mad scientist's laboratory, and that's probably not a good thing.

How did I end up here? Then, it hits me.

The book!

The last thing I remember is grabbing Faustius' book. Suddenly, it dawns on me that I'm not holding it anymore. Where did it go? I need to get that book to Van Helsing before it's too late to save Aura!

It's not until I get to my feet that I realize I won't be saving anyone anytime soon. That's because I'm standing inside a glass tube exactly like the one Hexum created in my mind, except this one is real and completely sealed at the top and bottom, making escaping in mist form impossible.

Not that I could turn into a mist anyway. I'm so wiped out I feel like I could sleep for days. Plus, I'm absolutely starving, which I've learned is never a good thing for a vampire like me.

I look around as best I can, but I don't see Faustius' book anywhere. I feel like such a dope. Clearly, you didn't have to open the book to be zapped by its curse. And the Black Magic must be powerful enough to work on ghosts too. So, Aura must be around here somewhere.

"Aura?" I yell, my voice echoing in the tube.

No answer.

Well, I can't stay trapped in here forever. Maybe I can knock this tube over and break it open? I lean up against one side of the glass and then launch myself against the other, pushing with all of my might, but the tube doesn't budge. I do, however, manage to bruise my shoulder.

Monster fail.

I've got to get out of here.

Just then, I hear a CREAK behind me.

"Aura?"

But instead of Aura, I'm suddenly facing two werewolves—one is red and the other is black! Where'd they come from? Fortunately, we're separated by glass, but they're looking at me like I'm some kind of a zoo animal. Shouldn't the roles be reversed?

"Hi guys," I say casually. "Great to see you. Hey, any chance you can spring me and let me walk out of here alive? Promise I'll get you all the dog chow you can eat."

The red one bares his teeth and ROARS.

"Okay," I say quickly. "Forget the dog food. Think

steaks. Thick, juicy steaks every night for the rest of your lives? Not bad, huh? I'll even throw in a bottomless salad bowl."

"Don't waste your breath," comes a voice. "You know you can't control them. You don't have the power."

I turn to find a hunched, bald man standing between the operating tables. His dark, beady eyes stare at me through gold-rimmed glasses, and he's wearing a white lab coat and cradling something in his arms.

"Who are you?" I ask.

"Who do you think I am?" the bent man answers.

I know I've never seen him before. But he has a distinct accent. It sounds different than Van Helsing's accent. Maybe… German? Then, I notice what he's holding.

It's a bundle of bones!

There's a skull, a femur, a collar bone…

Then, it hits me!

"Y-You're Professor Faustius!"

But Faustius doesn't respond. Instead, he carefully lays the bones down on one of the metal tables. Then, he reaches beneath and pulls out a bin filled with even more bones. After laying those out, he grabs another bin and then repeats this several more times. Minutes later, he's organized a complete skeleton.

This is weird. Where'd he get all those...

Suddenly, it all comes together.

Those must be the stolen bones!

"You robbed those graves!" I exclaim.

"Guess you caught me red-handed," Faustius says, waving a hand bone. "Allow me to introduce our guest. The legs, arms, and torso belonged to a man named Jonah Covington, a four-time Olympic gold medalist in the decathlon who set world records in the 100-meter sprint, long jump, high jump, javelin throw, and pole vault. The bones of the hands, wrists, and fingers belonged to a man named Lloyd McAdams, the most decorated sharpshooter in military history. And the skull belonged to a gentleman named Dr. Eugene Albert, Nobel prize winner in physics."

"Okay," I say, totally freaked out. "You have some really stiff friends."

"Perhaps," he says. "But they won't stay that way for long."

Okay, this guy is nuts. What he's planning to do with that skeleton is beyond me, but I don't want to stick around to find out. I've got to get out of here. I need a plan. Maybe I can bluff my way out.

"You might as well let me go," I say. "Van Helsing is on his way right now."

"Really?" Faustius says. "How could Van Helsing find us here, in the middle of nowhere?" He lifts a femur. "Are you pulling my leg?"

"No," I say. "He followed me here."

Then, I realize I made a big mistake. After all, I didn't exactly come here voluntarily. Faustius' cursed book sent me here.

"Your survival skills are very poor," Faustius says. "Hexum has not trained you well but I'm not surprised. That pompous bore took far more credit than he deserved. But I'm afraid your ruse is ineffective. For one, I have cast a spell banishing any of Crawler's eight-legged sentries from my lair. But even more importantly, I know for a fact that Van Helsing will not be coming to save you. We had an appointment to meet somewhere else."

An appointment? So Faustius was the person Van Helsing left the academy to meet? Now I know why Professor Holmwood was so nervous. This guy is a total wackadoo.

"Unfortunately, my invitation was only a decoy," Faustius continues. "Soon, we will no longer need to worry about your Headmaster."

"What?" I say. "What does that mean?"

"It means that several of my associates are waiting to greet him," Faustius says with a smirk. "I would have so enjoyed seeing the terror in his eyes as he's ripped limb from limb. But alas, I have other priorities."

"You're going to kill him?" I say, my voice rising.

"Are you fond of Van Helsing?" he asks. "I'm not surprised. I know firsthand how manipulative he can be. I'm sure he told you many false stories about the Dark Ones, portraying them as evil."

"They killed my parents!" I say.

"Did they?" Faustius says calmly. "Do you know that

for a fact? Or are you merely taking his word for it?"

His words catch me off guard.

"I know the Dark Ones are evil!" I snap back. "Van Helsing told me they're searching for the Blood Grail to bring Count Dracula back to life. I'd call that pretty evil."

"Perhaps you should understand both sides of the story before passing judgment on what is evil and what is not," Faustius says, walking towards me. "Yes, the Dark Ones are searching for the Blood Grail, but they are doing so for noble reasons. And I am leading them."

"Wait a second," I say. "You're a Dark One?"

"Not just any Dark One," he says, brushing the werewolves aside. "I am the High Lord of the Dark Ones."

"Th-The High Lord?" I stutter. "You mean, like, the person in charge? No wonder Van Helsing threw you out of the academy. You're a monster!"

Faustius puts a hand on the glass and smiles.

"And by coincidence, so are you," Faustius says. "Are you aware of how monsters were treated before the reign of Count Dracula?"

Suddenly, I remember Professor Seward's lectures about the great monster hunts, like the Zombie Crusades and the Werewolf Inquisition.

"They were persecuted," Faustius continues, "hunted down and destroyed by angry mobs of Naturals led by some Van Helsing ancestor or another. Their thirst for Supernatural blood was insatiable. It did not matter if you were a man or a woman, an adult or a child. Sometimes, it didn't matter if you were a monster at all. So, tell me, who are the real monsters now?"

I think about Aura, Rage, and even InvisiBill.

I couldn't imagine them being chased down.

Hunted.

"And now, here we are again," Faustius says, "with yet another Van Helsing leading the charge. But instead of angry mobs, this one is using Supernatural children to destroy other Supernaturals. It's a novel approach, but should we simply stand by and let history repeat itself? I don't think so. Instead, let's create a world where Supernaturals live in peace."

I'm confused. For some reason, he's making sense.

"It's all within our reach, Bram," Faustius says. "You see, because your great-grandfather was not a vampire, he only succeeded in destroying Count Dracula's mortal body. But Count Dracula's spirit wasn't destroyed. It lives on. That is why he can be resurrected. That is why he can be returned to life. And with my steady hand guiding him, we can show humanity that Supernaturals are once again the superior race."

Superior race? Hold on a second!

"You're nuts," I say. "That's wrong!"

"Is it?" Faustius says. "Is it any more wrong than what Van Helsing has planned for you?"

"What are you talking about?" I say.

"You mean, you don't know?" Faustius says, his

right eyebrow rising. "Are you saying your trustworthy Headmaster didn't tell you?"

"Tell me?" I say. "Tell me what?"

"Please, Bram," he says, looking into my eyes. "Heed my words, because unlike Van Helsing, you can trust me to always tell you the truth. Van Helsing may have told you that you are the last of the vampires, but I fear he neglected to tell you what that means."

"What are you talking about?" I ask, my heart racing.

"I am sorry, Bram," he says. "But only a vampire can truly kill another vampire."

Wait, what?

Van Helsing never told me that.

"W-What are you saying?" I ask, fearing the answer.

"Don't you see?" Faustius says. "Van Helsing is using you. Because you are half-vampire, Van Helsing is planning to sacrifice your life to destroy Count Dracula."

CHAPTER FOURTEEN

THE FACE OF EVIL

I'm utterly speechless.

I mean, this Faustius guy just dropped a bomb on me. First, he tells me only a vampire can truly kill another vampire. That's some pretty important information that Van Helsing forgot to mention. Then, Faustius claims Van Helsing is just using me to destroy Count Dracula—and he's willing to sacrifice my life in the process!

Why didn't Van Helsing tell me that? Was he afraid I'd run away? Or is Faustius just blowing smoke?

For a second, I don't know who to believe.

But then I remember Faustius saying he's the High Lord of the Dark Ones, the evil group that killed my parents. Plus, he confirmed the Dark Ones are still searching for the Blood Grail so they can bring Count Dracula back to life. And to top it off, he's got me trapped in his crazy laboratory.

I'd say that's three strikes.

Winner—Van Helsing.

I need to keep Faustius talking until I find a way out.

"Why are you so angry with Van Helsing anyway?" I ask. "What did he do to you?"

"He betrayed me," Faustius says, his lips quivering.

Wow, I can tell whatever happened between those two is still really bugging him. I need to keep him distracted. "What do you mean?" I say.

"If you must know, it all began decades ago," Faustius says, his eyes drifting into space. "At that time, I was just a boy, orphaned and alone, working as a clerk in the town library. For a hard day's work, I was paid in bread and allowed to sleep on the cold basement floor. Everyone assumed I was stupid, but I knew I had special talents. I had a gift for languages, and I was fascinated by books. They were my escape. My sanctuary."

Faustius heads towards the metal tables.

"At night, after everyone would leave, I would read by candlelight, consuming book after book, always wishing for a more adventurous life like my heroes in the great stories. And then, one day, almost by accident, I stumbled across a dusty book lodged beneath a bookcase. I had never seen it before. Its cloth cover was tattered, and the pages inside had strange letters and intricate drawings. It captivated me, and I wondered what this odd book was about."

For some reason, a chill runs down my spine.

"It took me months to decode it," he continues, "translating each page letter by letter, word by word. I quickly realized it wasn't a story at all, but rather an ancient book of Black Magic. I studied it carefully, committing every incantation to memory, but I was too timid to try any of them myself."

Okay, maybe getting him talking wasn't such a good idea because this is getting weirder by the minute.

"Until one day," Faustius says, his eyes narrowing. "I was sweeping the alleyway when I was accosted by a group of privileged and bored teenagers. I tried to ignore them, but they persisted. Things quickly turned physical, and they left me in a broken heap. As I stumbled back into the library, I swore things would be different from that day forward. I pulled out the book of Black Magic, turned to an entry entitled 'Spell of Summoning,' and carefully followed the instructions. Then, to my astonishment, a small creature appeared before me."

"Wait, what?" I blurt out.

"He was as big as a puppy," Faustius says, "with red skin, little horns and big, black eyes. Without uttering a sound, he left the library, and when he returned, I knew exactly what he had done. He had avenged me, and in return, I took him in. I hid him in the basement, never revealing his existence to anyone."

Okay, this guy is legitimately cuckoo. I rub my hands along the glass, looking for any crack I can mist out of, but it's perfectly smooth.

"Over time we grew close," Faustius continues. "I was the master and he was my pet. But things got out of hand. He would disappear often, and bad things began happening around town with greater frequency. I quickly realized he took joy in causing others misery. And as he grew bigger, his appetite for destruction grew larger. I didn't know what to do. So, I prayed for a miracle. And one evening, it came. There was a knock at my door."

Faustius picks up a scalpel. What's that for?

"Van Helsing was a younger man back then," he says, "he was carrying a knapsack and asked if he could come inside. He said he could help me with my problem. Of course, I had no other solution, so I let him in. We waited up all night until my creature returned home. Upon seeing it, Van Helsing wasted no time before destroying it with a silver arrow. To my surprise, he had concealed a crossbow in his knapsack, and in the blink of an eye, my problem was solved. And my only friend in the world was gone."

Wow, I can tell he's still heartbroken over this.

"You know, I was in a similar situation once," I say. "One of my foster families had a hamster, but it got free and we never saw it again. Guess who got blamed for that one?"

"Do not belittle me, child," Faustius says, gripping the scalpel tightly. "I was furious. Van Helsing called my pet a 'demon' and demanded to know how it was conjured. That is when I showed him my book. Van Helsing was both surprised and impressed by my talent. He asked if I would be interested in becoming his apprentice at a special school he was starting. I was shocked. Me? A poor boy joining a prestigious academy? I couldn't believe it. Of course, I agreed at once, but I never forgave him for what he did."

I can see the anger seething in Faustius' eyes.

"Van Helsing took me under his wing," Faustius continues. "I helped him establish his academy and recruit his other professors. But as I grew older, I knew I had more to offer. I begged him to make me a professor, but he refused. He would not admit it, but I knew he was afraid of what I might teach the children. It wasn't until I threatened to leave that he finally relented. I should have been happy. After all, I had finally achieved my goal. But instead, I felt hollow. It was then I realized Van Helsing never respected me. Since the day we met, he kept me close not because he liked me, but because he wanted to keep an eye on me."

I don't blame him.

"And then one night," Faustius says, "I had a dream. I realized I no longer needed to stand in Van Helsing's shadow. If he could build a school, I could build an empire. If he could teach monsters to live in society, I could teach them to dominate society. My power was stifled under Van Helsing's thumb. But to pull off my ambition, I needed operatives. So, I rekindled the Dark Ones right under Van Helsing's nose."

"You're a maniac!" I say.

"Perhaps I am," he says, approaching me, scalpel in hand. "Or perhaps I'm a visionary. When Van Helsing got wind of my plans, he forced me out of the academy. Fortunately, I escaped before he uncovered my true purpose—to capture Count Dracula's spirit and bring him back to life."

Spirit?

OMG! I almost forgot.

"Where's Aura?" I demand. "What did you do with her."

"Ah, your little ghost friend," Faustius says with a wicked smile. "I'm afraid she has left us."

"Left us?" I say. "What do you mean?"

"I mean she's gone," Faustius says. "She was a ghost, remember? Like all ghosts trapped on earth, she had a mission to complete. And now that her mission is done, her soul was released to the great beyond."

"What are you talking about?" I ask, totally confused. "What mission?"

"You *are* a naïve one, aren't you?" Faustius says, now standing on the other side of the glass. "Her mission was simple—to bring you to me."

"Liar!" I yell.

"I wish I were lying," Faustius says. "But again, I will only tell you the truth. Your friend was merely a pawn in this game of monsters. You see, one day, while I was traveling in the city, I witnessed her unfortunate demise. It was a terrible accident; one she never saw coming. Nevertheless, I was able to capture her soul with a simple spell before it left."

I shudder. Poor Aura.

"Through this spell, I could control her actions," Faustius continues. "Of course, she was none the wiser. I knew her powers may come in handy one day, perhaps as a spy, so I enrolled her in the academy. At the time I did not realize she would become such a valuable asset."

Faustius twirls the scalpel in his fingers.

"But after several failed efforts to capture you directly," he says, shooting annoyed looks at the werewolves. "I had to take a subtler approach. So, I used your ghost friend to lure you here."

My mind races into overdrive. I mean, Aura was the one who led us to that cemetery with the grave robbers and werewolves in the first place. She also discovered Faustius' book in Van Helsing's library. And it was her idea to break into Faustius' office. Could he be right? Was Faustius manipulating her the whole time?

And was this the reason she was still stuck here? I feel like I've been punched in the gut. I mean, she was my friend. Maybe my best friend. And now… she's gone.

"I hate you!" I scream.

"That's sad," Faustius says. "I was hoping we could work together."

"Never!" I yell.

"Very well," he says. "Have it your way."

Then, his mouth starts moving, but he's speaking so low I can't hear what he's saying. His lips are forming the same patterns repeatedly, like he's chanting. Then, I realize, he's putting a spell on me!

Suddenly, my whole body tightens up.

I can't move a muscle!

What's happening?

"Struggling is futile," he says, "I have employed a Curse of Immobility. You will be unable to move or use any vampire tricks. However, I have allowed you the ability to breathe and to speak if you wish. In case you change your mind before it's too late."

"No way!" I yell.

This is ridiculous, my arms and legs are locked in place. I can't move at all.

"There is no chance for escape now," Faustius says. Then, he snaps his fingers and my glass prison is gone! The werewolves grab my arms and lift me into the air.

"Wait, what are you doing?" I protest.

"Don't worry," Faustius says, "this part will be quick and relatively painless."

I want to fight back, but I can only watch as the werewolves carry me towards the metal tables.

Strangely, Faustius is busy fitting a robe around the skeleton. "There, now you are dressed. That will save any embarrassment."

"What are you doing?" I ask.

"Preparing the bones," Faustius says. "It's the respectable thing to do after I reanimate them with Count Dracula's spirit."

Reanimate?

Wait a minute! He's actually going to try this? But instead of using Count Dracula's bones, he's going to use the bones of these dead heroes. If he pulls this off, Count Dracula will be smarter and stronger than ever!

The werewolves lay me down on the empty table, shackling my wrists and ankles. Okay, I've seen enough horror movies to know where this is heading.

My heart is racing.

"Let me go!" I demand.

"Sorry, but no," he says. "I've worked too hard to acquire you. You see, you play a pivotal role in my plans. Plans that begin right now."

Faustius closes his eyes and begins chanting in a language I've never heard before. It's another spell but based on his reddening complexion this one is taking a big toll on him.

I can't understand what he's saying, except for one word I keep hearing over and over again.

DRACUL.

Suddenly, there's a loud CRASH overhead, and when I look up, I see shards of glass falling from above. There's a giant hole in the domed ceiling, and cold air is flooding into the room.

But Faustius just keeps on chanting, his voice rising louder and louder.

Just then, a black mist swirls over my body, setting the hairs on the back of my neck on end.

"W-What's that?" I ask.

But deep down, I know the answer.

The black cloud circulates throughout the room, leaving a trail of darkness in its wake. And as it passes over me again, I'm overcome by a wave of negativity.

"Yes!" Faustius screams, his eyes wide with delight. "He is here! The King of Darkness is finally here!"

The King of Darkness?

Dracula's spirit is here!

But then I remember there's no Blood Grail. When Aura told Dracula's tale back in Professor Seward's class, the Dark Ones needed the Blood Grail to restore him to life. But Faustius told me he's still searching for it. So, I don't know how he thinks he's gonna pull this off.

"These are great parlor tricks," I say, "but let's face it, you still haven't found the Blood Grail. So why don't we stop this whole thing before somebody loses an eye."

Suddenly, Faustius stands over me, scalpel in hand.

"I'm afraid you couldn't be more wrong," he says. "My quest for the Blood Grail has finally ended."

Then, I notice he's holding a golden chalice!

Oh no. It can't be.

"I-Is that the Blood Grail?" I stammer.

"No," he says, laughing. "This is merely a cup."

"So, you don't have it!" I say relieved.

"You still don't understand, do you?" Faustius says. "You are the last of the vampires. Dracula's Supernatural blood is flowing through your veins. Bram, the Blood Grail is you."

CLASSIFIED

Person(s) of Interest

CODE NAME: None

REAL NAME: CLAUDE FAUSTIUS

BASE OF OPERATIONS: CURRENTLY UNKNOWN

FACTS: Faustius is a former professor at the Van Helsing Academy responsible for teaching Black Magic. At one time, Faustius was a trusted confidante of Lothar Van Helsing, but Faustius was dismissed from his post over a year ago. His current whereabouts are unknown.

Category:	Natural
Sub-Type:	Not Applicable
Height:	5'9"
Weight:	175 lbs

FIELD OBSERVATIONS:

- Fluent in multiple languages
- Seen conducting meetings with known operatives of the Dark Ones organization
- Very intelligent
- Anxious and paranoid

STATUS: ACTIVE TARGET

DEPARTMENT OF SUPERNATURAL INVESTIGATIONS

CHAPTER FIFTEEN

COUNT DOWN

My mind is blown.

Faustius just told me I'm the Blood Grail!

What?

At first, I think he's nuts. But the more I think about it, the more it makes perfect sense. After all, I'm supposedly the only living ancestor of Count Dracula. So, if Faustius needs Count Dracula's Supernatural blood to bring him back to life, there's only one place to get it from.

Me!

Suddenly, everything that's happened becomes crystal clear. Now I understand why those werewolves wanted me. Faustius sent them to capture me alive so he could get my blood. When that failed—twice—he manipulated Aura to find his cursed book and teleport me into his lab. I've got to hand it to him, he's persistent.

But that's not all he's been up to.

Faustius was also the one who sent the zombies to rob those graves. And if his master plan comes to fruition, he'll stick Dracula's spirit into their bones and take over the world!

Now, if I wasn't watching Dracula's spirit ping-ponging around the room, I'd say the whole thing was impossible. But this looks like it's about to go down!

Faustius lifts my arm and positions the chalice beneath it. Then, he raises his scalpel.

Holy cow!

He's really going to do it!

He's going to cut me!

I feel like I'm about to pass out, but I can't. I've got to stop him before it's too late!

"Faustius," I plead, "think this through. Is this really a good idea? Let's say your theory is correct and I'm the Blood Grail. If you bring Count Dracula back to life do you really think you can control him? I mean, he's Count. Freaking. Dracula. You know, the King of Darkness. Do you think he's going to listen to you?"

"A valiant attempt," Faustius says. "But I am not worried. I can control Dracula."

"Ha!" I blurt out. "Just like you controlled that demon you needed Van Helsing's help to destroy?"

"Enough!" he says enraged. "You don't know what you're talking about! Without me, Dracula would remain an amorphous spirit. I will control him, and he will do my bidding!"

SLASH!

Ahhh!

My right arm is on fire!

I look down and see a thin cut on the top of my forearm. There's red liquid on Faustius' scalpel.

H-He cut me!

"Finally!" Faustius says, holding up my arm. "The sweet elixir I've been seeking."

I'm horrified. All I can do is watch as my blood drips into the chalice. Then, when he's satisfied he's collected enough, he drops my arm onto the table and walks over to the skeleton.

"Do not worry, Bram," he says. "When I am finished your pain will be over quickly. I will ensure Count Dracula sees to that. After all, only a vampire can truly kill another vampire."

My arm is throbbing, but I'm still strapped in, so I can't stop the bleeding. I'm woozy, but I need to stay conscious. I've got to get out of here before it's too late.

"Prepare, Dracula!" Faustius commands, pouring my blood over the bones of the skeleton. "Prepare to rejoin the land of the living!"

Dracula's spirit is swirling over the skeleton.

"Watch the boy," Faustius orders the werewolves. "I must focus on the task at hand."

Whatever hold Faustius had on me relaxes because I can suddenly move again. But I can't pull out of the arm or leg restraints. I'm losing blood quickly, getting dizzier by the second. There's no way I can use my vampire abilities even if I wanted to.

Faustius begins chanting, his voice growing louder.

Thunder CRACKS outside and the wind picks up, blowing into the room.

Faustius raises his arms. He's concentrating, eyes closed, repeating the same words over and over again.

The next thing I know, the black mist forms a shape. I-Is that a bat? But then it disperses rapidly, flowing over the bones, covering them completely. Then, the skeleton starts smoldering and black smoke billows into the air.

I-It's working!

I have to stop it!

I try sitting up to bust the arm shackles, but the werewolves GROWL and push me back down. My energy is sapped, and my eyelids are getting heavy. I try keeping them open, but I can't.

Everything is blurry.

I'm blacking out.

HOOT!

W-What's that? An owl?

HOOT!

That sounded louder. Strangely familiar.

I force my eyes open, and I can't believe what I'm seeing. It's a girl. Floating down from the ceiling.

I-Is that an angel?

"SCOOT!" she says.

Scoot?

OMG!

Aura!

She's alive! Well, I mean, she's not dead! Well… it's just great to see her!

I feel overwhelmed with emotion.

"Bram!" she yells. "Stop gawking and get moving!"

Aura furrows her brow and my restraints pop open!

But how? Then, I realize Aura used her telekinesis to free me!

"I'll distract these guys," Aura says, lowering herself to the ground. "You stop Faustius. Now catch me if you can you hairy morons!"

Aura takes off with the werewolves in hot pursuit.

She's right. I've got to stop Faustius. But blood is running out of the cut on my arm. First things first. I grab a bandage off the small table and wrap it around my forearm to stop the bleeding. Then, I glance over at Faustius.

He's so focused on what he's doing, he's got no idea what's going on over here. But something weird is happening to the skeleton. It's like it's being wrapped in layers of black energy. It almost looks like the energy is forming into… muscles?

Count Dracula!

Instinctively, I close my eyes and think.

How can I stop Faustius?

An image of a flying bat pops into my mind.

That's it! If I can turn into a bat, I can attack Faustius and stop all of this before it's too late. But can I turn into a bat? I mean, it's never worked before. But then I stop myself. There's no time to dwell on the past. I shake the negative thoughts from my mind and concentrate.

I focus like I've never focused before.

I picture a bat.

I can become a bat. I must become a bat.

I lock in on that image.

Then, I start to believe.

Suddenly, I feel my body… transforming? My limbs begin to recess. My fingers extend, curling into sharp claws. Something sprouts from the underside of my arms. Are those wings?

Then, the world around me changes.

I pick up sounds I've never heard before, like the wind swishing around the skeleton's body. Strange odors assault my nostrils, like the sweat from Faustius' skin. New colors from hidden spectrums strike my eyes with blinding intensity. It's like a sensory overload. What happened?

Then, I realize I'm a bat.

I-I did it!

But there's no time to celebrate.

I start flapping my arms and lift into the air. I beat my wings furiously, totally unsure of how to do this flying thing when my head SMASHES into the ceiling.

Ouch! Too much flapping.

I adjust my flutter rate, and then divebomb Faustius, digging my toes into his back.

"Ahhh!" Faustius screams, breaking his chant.

I flap my wings in his face, pummeling him as best I can, but he's inherently stronger and pushes me away.

"Is that you, Bram?" he says. "I don't know how you got free, but I'm impressed. Unfortunately, you are too late. The deed is done."

I want to respond, but I'm a bat. I manage a "SHRIEK!" and dive in for round two.

I get in a few more shots before Faustius grabs one of my wings and SLAMS me to the ground.

Ugh. My whole left side hurts.

I try righting myself, but I'm seeing stars. That really knocked me for a loop. Then, the area around me darkens. It's Faustius. And this time he's holding a large knife!

I try to fly away, but I'm in too much pain.

"I think it's time you were grounded," Faustius says. "For good."

He reaches up to deliver the final blow when a silver arrow suddenly penetrates his arm.

"Augh!" Faustius screams, the knife clanging to the floor.

What the—? What's going on?

"Step away from the boy," comes a familiar voice.

I turn to see Van Helsing standing in the doorway, a silver crossbow in his arms. Then, he fires two more arrows at lightning speed, and I hear werewolves YELPING in the distance.

Despite his gruesome injury, Faustius shouts out a

strange incantation, and the next thing I know, Van Helsing's crossbow leaps out of his hands and flies across the room, smashing into a wall.

I know I'm a sitting bat just lying here, so I focus my energy on turning back to kid-form. It's a struggle, but I concentrate hard. Just then, I feel my limbs expanding, my wings retracting, my body growing bigger.

And then, I'm back.

But I'm so weak.

"Bram, are you okay?" Aura asks, appearing next to me from out of nowhere.

"Not sure yet," I say, breathing heavily.

"How?" Faustius cries, backing up to the wall, his wounded arm hanging limply at his side. "How did you find me? I-I set a trap for you."

"Yes, you did," Van Helsing says. "But details were never a strength of yours. Let's just say your organization now has several dozen openings to fill. As to how I found this place, I used this." Van Helsing turns his wrist.

It's a Spirit Sensor!

"Professor Morris lent it to me before our so-called appointment," Van Helsing says. "Coincidentally, it was already set to track a certain ghost you have on the premises."

Aura looks at me and smiles.

But my joy quickly turns to horror as I look at the metal table. The skeleton… it's gone!

Just then, something huge drops from the ceiling.

"Headmaster!" Aura cries.

A robed figure lands in a crouch, cutting us off from Van Helsing. It's a man—an absolute giant of a man—with broad shoulders, wispy black hair, and a chalky white complexion. He's wheezing, and I can see his ribs expanding and contracting through his paper-thin skin—like he hasn't breathed for thousands of years. Then, he lifts his head, revealing wild, red eyes.

I-It's… Count Dracula!

"Heaven help us," Van Helsing mutters. "Faustius, what have you done?"

"Isn't it obvious?" Faustius says, grinning from ear to ear. "I have done the impossible. I have brought Count Dracula back from the spirit world. Now bow before me, King of Darkness. Bow and show everyone your gratitude towards me, your High Lord, the man who brought you back to the land of the living."

Count Dracula rises unsteadily, and I realize how shockingly tall he is. He hesitates for a moment, regaining his balance, and then steps towards Faustius.

"Yes!" Faustius screams. "Bow before your creator!"

To my amazement, Dracula approaches Faustius and kneels before him. Faustius' expression is one of pure glee. I-I can't believe it. He's doing it. He's actually controlling Count Dracula!

"M-My Lord," Count Dracula stammers. His voice barely a whisper.

"Yes," Faustius' responds. "Speak, my loyal subject."

Out of the corner of my eye, I catch Van Helsing quietly inching towards his fallen crossbow.

"My Lord," Count Dracula says, "I am forever in your debt for restoring my spirit and providing this magnificent vessel in which I can once again walk this earth. Were it not for you, I would be forced to live out my days as an ethereal being for all of eternity. Now I am free to repay you in any capacity you require. But at the moment, I am quite vulnerable and cannot help but notice there is a descendent of my ancient rival Abraham Van Helsing present. Therefore, I must make one small request before pledging my undying servitude."

"Yes," Faustius says. "Of course. What is it?"

"Sustenance," Count Dracula says. Then, he reaches up and runs a finger down Faustius' wounded arm. When he pulls it away, it's covered in blood.

Faustius recoils, his eyes wide.

"And that sustenance," Count Dracula says, licking Faustius' blood off of his finger, "will be you."

"Faustius!" Van Helsing yells. "Run!"

But Count Dracula grabs Faustius with remarkable speed.

"No!" Faustius screams, and then his eyes roll back in his head. He passed out!

Count Dracula catches Faustius' limp body and throws it over his shoulder. Then, he wheels on me.

Our eyes meet.

I can't look away.

I feel incredibly hot.

Feverish.

"Thank you," he says, revealing long, sharp fangs. "Like Faustius, you have fulfilled your role in the first phase of my plan."

Plan? What's he talking about?

"We shall meet again."

Then, with prey in hand, he jumps and breaks through the glass ceiling in one incredible leap.

Van Helsing grabs his crossbow and fires, but his arrow misses the mark.

They're gone.

And Count Dracula is free to terrorize the world.

"What now?" Aura asks.

"Now?" Van Helsing says solemnly. "Now we prepare for war."

It's all my fault. I feel like a failure.

"I-I'm sorry," I say.

"No, Bram," Aura says. "It's okay. It's not…"

But I never hear the rest of her sentence.

Because I'm out.

EPILOGUE

THE END OF THE BEGINNING

I'm running through the woods at incredible speed.

A full moon hangs in the night sky. There's a chill in the air, but it feels refreshing against my skin.

Everything is a blur as I weave through trees, duck beneath branches, and leap over fallen logs. I'm fast, but I've never run this fast before. The only sounds I hear are my feet crunching on fallen leaves.

As I run, my fists swing in front of me, but they don't look like my fists. They're much bigger than I remember, and they're chalky white.

I want to slow down, but I can't. It's like I'm not in control, like I'm a passenger in someone else's body.

What's going on?

Then, up ahead in the distance, is a building situated in the middle of a swamp. As I slosh through murky, ankle-deep water, it becomes clearer the building is an old manor covered by black vines.

What's it doing here in the middle of nowhere?

Just then, my facial muscles contort into a smile, and

my tongue slides over my teeth, slithering over two very sharp points.

They almost feel like… fangs?

OMG!

***

I spring up in a cold sweat.

What's happening?

Was that a dream?

Or…?

"At last," comes a gentle voice. "You are awake."

I turn to find Van Helsing staring at me. He's sitting in a chair, bundled up as usual, his neck wrapped snugly in a wool scarf. He's leaning forward with his fingers pressed in a steeple position. I notice his silver crossbow propped against the wall.

For a second, I'm totally lost. And then I realize I'm hooked up to several machines, which can only mean one thing. I'm in the infirmary. How did I get here?

Then, it all comes flooding back.

Faustius. The werewolves. Count Dracula…

"Aura!"

"Do not distress," Van Helsing says calmly. "She is fine. Perfectly fine."

I lie back down. Well, at least that's good news. But honestly, Van Helsing is the last person I want to see right now.

"Much has happened," he says. "I am sure you have many questions for me."

He's right about that. I have a million questions, but I don't think I can face him without losing my cool. After all, he lied to me. I wish he'd leave me alone.

"What would you like to know?" he asks. "You can ask me anything."

Too little too late is all I can think. But I figure I'll throw him a bone and maybe he'll leave.

"Is that the Crossbow of Purity?" I ask.

"Yes," he says, raising an eyebrow. "I didn't realize you knew about it."

"Seward covered it," I say. "He asked about it on one of his quizzes."

"Of course," he says. "Is there anything else?"

"Nope," I say. "I'm good. Thanks for stopping by."

"Bram," he starts, "I am—"

"If the next word you're going to say is 'sorry,' then don't bother." I'm fuming mad. I look down at my right forearm which is covered in bandages. That's where Faustius cut me and used my blood to resurrect the evilest villain in the history of the world.

"I am truly sorry," he says with deep sincerity. "I understand why you are angry with me. I am disappointed in myself."

I'm ready to fire back with all the fury I can muster, but I can't. His apology took the wind out of my sails. But I still can't forgive him.

"Well," I say, "I'm still upset."

"I understand," Van Helsing says, his head down.

"I mean, why didn't you tell me I was the Blood Grail? Don't you think that's something I should've known?"

"You are right," Van Helsing says. "I should have told you. It was unfair of me not to. The truth is that I thought it would be too much too soon. I never expected you to be so bold as to break into Faustius' office. Just as I never expected Faustius would lay a trap for you there."

"Right, then there's that creep," I say, feeling agitated all over again. "Faustius told me you're using me. He said only a vampire can kill another vampire. He said you'll sacrifice me to kill Count Dracula."

"I would never do that," Van Helsing says, shaking his head. "I hope you realize Faustius is an opportunist. He would say anything to sway you to his side. But he was not completely wrong."

"What?" I say, sitting up again. "What does that mean?"

"He was correct in saying that only a vampire can truly kill another vampire," Van Helsing says. "Make no mistake, as the last vampire you have a tremendous responsibility. Only you can destroy Count Dracula. But I would never use you. I only intended to train you, so you can come out of this alive."

"Great job you're doing," I mutter.

"I admit, things could be going better," he says, "but

I saw you transform into a bat. That tells me we have accomplished quite a lot. It also tells me your powers are within your control, a very positive development."

"A whole lot of good it did me," I say. "I just helped Count Dracula come back to life."

"You are not to blame," Van Helsing says. "We cannot rewrite the past, we can only shape the future. But yes, it is true, your blood is now running through Count Dracula's body. But you are not at fault. You fell victim to an evil plot far darker than even I could have imagined, yet one I should have seen coming. Do not give up, Bram. Never give up. Count Dracula is out there, growing stronger night by night."

At the sound of his name, I remember my strange dream. It actually felt like I was him. Like I was the one running through the woods in his body. And clearly, he was a lot stronger than when I saw him last. I want to tell Van Helsing about it, but something holds me back.

"What happened to Faustius?" I ask.

"I fear the worst," Van Helsing says. "He always teetered on the fringes of darkness—all the way to the bitter end."

"That's sad," I say.

"Indeed," Van Helsing continues. "But darkness is an unyielding adversary. It entices the weak—just as it enticed Faustius. Left to its own devices, it would doom us all. But together we can fight against it. Together, we can break its evil lure. I cannot force you to help us. I only hope that you will."

Despite my desire to run away, I know I can't.

After all, I'm the one responsible for bringing Count Dracula back to life. Everything that happens from here on out is my fault. I could never walk away knowing that.

So, no matter how dangerous it's going to be, I know I have to fix the problem I created. It's all up to me.

"Don't worry," I say. "I'll stick it out. But you're going to have to tell me everything from now on. And you can't leave anything out. Deal?"

"Deal," Van Helsing says, offering his hand.

We shake just as my friends pile through the door.

I see Rage, Hairball, and Stanphibian. And I'm sure InvisiBill is around here somewhere.

"Glad you're okay," Rage says, greeting me with a high five. "We were worried when we lost track of you in Faustius' office."

"Trust me," I say. "I'm glad to be back."

But someone is missing.

"Where's Aura?" I ask.

"Right here," she says, phasing through the wall.

"Please, not again," Rage says, holding his chest.

Everyone laughs.

Seeing her is a huge relief.

"I'm… happy you're okay," I say.

"I'm glad you're okay too," she says. "And thanks for trying to save me again. You're alright in my book."

"Please," InvisiBill says, "don't say 'book!'"

Everyone laughs.

"Oh, I've got your badge," I say, reaching for my pocket when I realize I'm in a hospital gown. "Well, I'm sure it's around here somewhere."

"Thanks," she says. "But we've got something for you."

For me?

"What is it?" I ask.

"Hairball," Aura says, "hand it over."

"Here ya go," Hairball says. "Catch."

Then, he flips a shiny object into the air. I catch it and turn it over. It's a silver badge!

Engraved in the center is the word:

BRAMPIRE

Brampire?

What's that? Then it hits me.

"No way!" I say. "Really?"

"Really," Rage says. "That's your new code name. Get it, Bram plus vampire equals Brampire. So Brampire, let me be the first to officially welcome you to the Monstrosities."

All the kids clap.

The Monstrosities? I made the team? I don't know what to say. I've never belonged to anything before. I feel tears welling up in my eyes.

"Congratulations, Brampire," Aura says with a wink.

"Thanks," I manage.

"Hey, don't get all sappy," Rage says, patting me on the shoulder. "You don't want Hexum seeing you like this."

He's right about that.

Then, I feel a hand squeeze my shoulder.

"Congratulations," Van Helsing says, leaning in. "Brampire. It has a nice ring to it."

As my friends start busting on each other, I lie back, holding my badge to my chest, happy to be part of the team.

And for the moment, I even forget about my looming destiny—my showdown with Count Dracula.

Monster Problems 2: Down for the Count

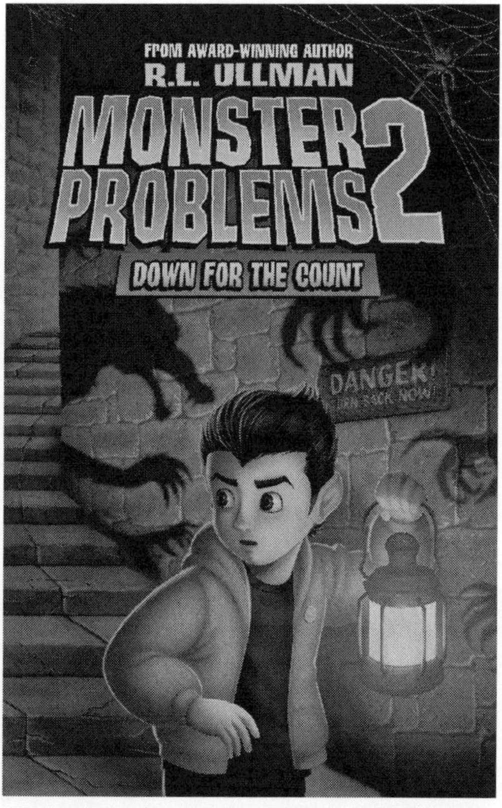

CHAPTER ONE

BLIND AS A BAT

"Come on, Brampire!" comes a voice from behind me.

Based on the nasally tone, it sounded like Rage.

"You've got this!" comes another voice.

That's definitely Aura.

"If you lose, you're a moron!"

And there's good old InvisiBill.

Well, I guess people have different ideas of what they consider motivating. But it doesn't really matter what they say because I've got all the self-motivation I need. After all, my entire team is counting on me not to blow it.

I look across the gym at my opponent, a bubbling mass of kid-flesh codenamed Blobby. His real name is Bobby Rotunda, and he's essentially a blob—a boneless, amorphous pile of goop categorized as an 'abnormal,' also known as a one-of-a-kind monster.

He easily weighs over a thousand pounds and is best known for gobbling up everything and anything in sight, which could include me if I'm not careful. At the moment, he's cheating ever-so-slightly, rolling inch-after-inch of his skin over the starting line.

I guess I could complain but I'm not too worried about it. I mean, I'm pretty confident I could dust him in anything other than a hot dog eating contest. But maybe I'm feeling too confident. After all, this isn't exactly a normal kind of competition.

Nope. It's a monster competition.

More specifically, it's the 42nd annual Monster Cup.

Apparently, the Monster Cup is a pretty big deal around here at the Van Helsing Academy. It's a two-week competition pitting different sections of the academy against one another in a variety of events like races, quizzes, and other spooky shenanigans. Whatever team tallies the most points at the end wins the Monster Cup—a big silver trophy with a tiny skull on top that you can display proudly on your dorm room floor.

Aura has been talking about it nonstop for weeks. Honestly, I don't think I've ever met anyone as competitive as she is. According to her, losing is not an option. So, she's woken us up early every morning before class to grill us on monster trivia and put us through grueling exercise drills. And if you thought getting up at dawn was painful, try standing next to Hairball before he's showered.

G.R.O.S.S.

Anyway, I had hoped the hard work would pay off, but we're currently trailing the Howlers 3-2 in our very first event! But I suppose I shouldn't be too surprised because the Howlers are older than us and have way more experience using their Supernatural powers. There's Blobby, my current opponent, but they also have Harpoon, a green-skinned harpy with wings, Putrid Pete, a decaying mummy, MinoTodd, who is half-minotaur, half-kid, Lucky, a goth guy with a cursed amulet, and Gnatalie, a teeny-tiny girl with big, buggy eyes.

I hate to admit it, but after watching the Howlers in action I have to say they're pretty impressive. But it's not like I can go over and shake their hands, or whatever appendage they offer me. First of all, my fellow Monstrosities would kill me. And second, bragging rights are on the line.

The smack talk between sections has been intense, and if we end up losing this round, the Howlers will tease us like crazy. Fortunately, Aura and Hairball won their heats to keep us in the game. But now it's up to me.

No pressure, right?

I have to win for us to save face and walk out here with at least a tie. And right now, my face, as well as the rest of my body, is in the form of a bat.

I flap my wings, hovering unsteadily behind the starting line. Let's just say that being a bat is something I'm still getting used to. Even though I've practiced a lot, I'm no expert—not by a long shot. And I've noticed I'm developing some really 'bat' habits in my human form, like the urge to hang upside down and just chill.

"Mr. Murray!" Professor Hexum barks. "Focus!"

I snap back to reality.

Looking down, I see Hexum's green eyes glaring back up at me. His eyebrows are furrowed and he's leaning forward on his walking stick, gripping it so tightly his knuckles are white. He's clearly not happy with me.

Surprise, surprise.

Ever since I came to the Van Helsing Academy, Hexum has been a major thorn in my side. He claims he's doing it to make me stronger, but I'm finding that increasingly hard to believe. In fact, torturing me seems to be his favorite pastime. Like now, for instance. For some reason, he's forcing me to compete only as a bat while everyone else got to compete in any way they wanted.

It's just not fair.

"Attention racers!" Hexum calls out. "When I say 'go,' an object will appear in the center of the gymnasium floor. The first one to bring it back to their side—by whatever means necessary—wins."

Um, what? Did he just say, 'by whatever means necessary?' He didn't say that for the other races.

Suddenly, there's a deep RUMBLE and I realize Blobby is laughing. You know, there's something really disturbing about a mountain of giggling flesh.

"You've got this, Bram!" Aura yells.

That's funny, I thought I did too. Right up until now.

"Ready!" Hexum calls out, raising his walking stick into the air. "Set! Go!"

Suddenly, a long, pointed piece of wood appears in

the center of the gym floor and I do a double take. Um, is that what I think it is? Because it sort of looks like a—

"Grab the stake, Bram!" Rage yells.

That is a stake! Like, a stake used to destroy vampires! And the last time I checked, I'm still a vampire. So, why would Hexum ask me to retrieve a—

"Less gawking and more flapping!" Aura yells.

Huh? Well, she's right about that. If I just hang here, we're guaranteed to lose. But I might be too late anyway because, despite Blobby's lack of legs, he's inching closer to the target!

I've got to move!

I figure my best bet is to just swoop down before Blobby gets there and pick up the stake with my feet. It sounds easy enough, but there's just one problem. I'm not so great at the 'swooping' part.

In fact, I'd say my flying skills are downright shaky.

Nevertheless, I have no choice but to go for it, so I angle my body towards the stake, and take off, flapping with all of my might. Within seconds I'm there, but so is Blobby, and he's completely covered the stake with his body, forming an enormous skin-shield.

I try slowing down, but apparently bats don't come with brakes! My head pushes into Blobby's sweaty flesh like I've jumped onto a trampoline, and then it recoils, slinging me skyward!

"I can't watch," I hear Rage say.

"Are you kidding?" InvisiBill says, "This is epic!"

Oh, when I get my fangs in that dufus…

I flap like crazy until I manage to right myself, and then I double back for another try. Except this time the stake is gone! Since Blobby is heading back to his side of the gym, he must be carrying the stake somewhere beneath his undulating body!

If he crosses the finish line, we'll lose!

I can't let that happen, but how can I stop him?

I mean, I'm just a bat.

And then it hits me.

I'm a bat!

That means I can do everything a bat can do—and that includes 'seeing' using sound. One of the more unique things about being a bat is being able to use sonic radar. When I'm flying (or at least, trying to fly) I can make high-frequency sounds that echo off of objects, allowing me to detect things I couldn't see as a regular human being, including the range, size, and shape of a target object.

Time for some radar love!

I sweep around Blobby and project sound waves all around him. Most of them hit his body and ping back, but some hit nothing—and bingo—I've found my opening!

Since Blobby is gelatinous, he's moving by using the folds of his skin to push himself along the ground. So that means at any given time, some parts of him aren't in contact with the floor. If I can slide into one of those pockets, maybe I can reach the stake and grab it from him.

I just need to time this right.

I hover at ground level, waiting for my chance, and when a large fold lifts, I act.

"Bram?" I hear Aura call out. "What are you—?"

But I don't wait for her to finish her sentence, because I dart beneath Blobby into a pocket of air. It's snug in here, and ugh, everything smells like armpit, but I've got a job to do!

Then, I locate my target.

Blobby has the stake beneath him alright, but it's wrapped in a ball of his flesh.

Nasty.

But I can't worry about that now. I just need to grab the stake and get out before my pocket closes. I spin around and latch onto an exposed part of the wood with my feet and attempt to fly out, but Blobby is holding it so tightly I can't pull away!

Then, I feel pressure all around my body. Blobby's skin is closing in on me! My left wing smushes against my side and suddenly I can't fly! Then, my feet slip off the stake! Hexum said to win by any means necessary and Blobby is taking him up on it!

He's trying to crush me!

I look up to see a wall of flesh closing in around my head. I've got to get out of here! I don't care what Hexum said about only competing as a bat!

I muster all of my concentration into one thought.

Be… a mist!

Suddenly, my limbs feel all tingly, and then my body is lighter than air. But as my molecules disperse, I realize I couldn't hold the stake in this form even if I wanted to, so there's no point staying trapped in here. Instead, I focus on pushing my molecules outward, squeezing through the microscopic gaps in Blobby's suffocating mass.

And then, I'm free!

I collect my molecules in the center of the gym floor and focus on becoming a kid again. As I rematerialize on my stomach, covered in flop sweat and breathing heavily, I can only watch as Blobby rumbles across his starting line and the Howlers jump for joy.

We lost. And it's all my fault.

Suddenly, I feel someone standing behind me. It's probably one of my teammates coming over to cheer me up. But when I roll over, all I see is Hexum.

"Your team is disqualified," Hexum says.

"What?" I say, confused. "Why?"

"I gave you strict instructions to compete as a bat," Hexum says. "And you violated those instructions."

"What are you talking about?" I say. "You said to win by whatever means necessary. If I stayed a bat, he would have pulverized me."

"*Your* instructions were to compete as a bat," Hexum says, scribbling on his pad. "And you could have won by whatever means were necessary—as a *bat.* The Monstrosities are disqualified from the tournament. Your team is eliminated from the Monster Cup."

"What?" Aura says, floating over. "But that's ridiculous! Bram was almost killed!"

"Was he?" Hexum says. "He seems fine to me. But I suppose you can view his survival as a positive outcome of your team's disqualification."

"Hardly," InvisiBill says.

"Shut it," Aura says. "This isn't fair. Not to mention that you made his object a stake. We all know that stakes kill vampires. What was that about?"

"I would call it an unfortunate coincidence," Hexum says. "The objects used in this competition are… randomly generated."

"Yeah," I say. "Sure they are."

"Congratulations, Howlers," Hexum says, exiting the gym. "You are moving on. The Monstrosities, however, will now have plenty of time for extra homework."

"This is so unfair," Rage says, crossing his arms.

"Nice try, Monstrosities!" Harpoon calls out as the Howlers leave the gym, giving each other high fives. "But don't feel bad you lost to us, because we're going to win the Monster Cup!"

"I'm sorry, guys," I say, turning to my team. But as I look around, I realize no one is looking back at me. Instead, they're all staring at their shoes. "I didn't try to break the rules."

"Well, that's what you did," InvisiBill says.

"Yeah," Hairball says. "Thanks for nothing."

As the two of them leave, I look over at Stanphibian who shakes his fishbowl-covered head and gives me two webbed thumbs down. Then, he follows them out.

Awesome.

I see Aura floating with her shoulders slumped and I feel awful. I know how much she wanted to win the Monster Cup. She really wanted to prove we were the best section. But thanks to me, now she won't get the chance.

"Hey," I say, as a thought crosses my mind. "Maybe we can appeal Hexum's ruling to Van Helsing? Maybe he'll let us back in the tournament?"

"Yeah," Aura mutters. "Maybe."

And then she turns and vanishes through the wall.

Well, that didn't go well.

"What about you?" I ask Rage. "Are you mad at me too?"

"What?" he says, looking glum. "Um, no."

"Great," I say. "Because—"

But he doesn't bother to hear the rest of my sentence, because he pushes through the gym door. And as it SLAMS shut behind him, the only person left to hear its echo is me.

VAN HELSING ACADEMY
THE MONSTROSITIES
CODENAME:
Aura
CATEGORY:
Spirit
TYPE:
Ghost
CODENAME:
Brampire
CATEGORY:
Undead
TYPE:
Vampire
CODENAME:
Hairball
CATEGORY:
Abnormal
TYPE:
Yeti
Got Monster?
CODENAME:
Invisi-Bill
CATEGORY:
Abnormal
TYPE:
Invisible
CODENAME:
Rage
CATEORY:
Abnormal
TYPE:
Jekyll/Hyde
CODENAME:
Stan-phibian
CATEGORY:
Abnormal
TYPE:
Gill-man
ROLL CALL SHEET

CHAPTER TWO

NEW BLOOD

I've never felt so alone.

And that's saying something considering all of the foster homes and group facilities I've passed through. Growing up I never bothered connecting with anyone because I knew I wouldn't be sticking around. But here I thought I found a place to call home.

I guess I was wrong.

Yes, I single-handedly ruined my team's chances for glory by getting us disqualified from the Monster Cup, but I didn't expect my friends to give me the cold shoulder like this. I mean, I already felt bad enough, but now I feel even worse because nobody came to my room to check up on me—including Rage, my roommate.

But it's probably for the best because I didn't want to see anyone anyway. I pretty much spent the entire afternoon fuming in bed, staring at the ceiling and wishing I was someone else.

Anyone else.

I did get up once to go see Van Helsing, but as soon

as I hit the foyer, I overheard someone saying he was locked in his office, talking to some strange man. That stopped me in my tracks. After all, I know Van Helsing and he doesn't like to be disturbed. So, I marched back upstairs for more fuming.

In fact, I was so upset I even skipped dinner, which I know is a major 'no-no' for a vampire like me. But even though I was hungry, I'd rather starve than see my 'so-called' friends' faces.

I bet they were talking about me anyway. After all, how many boneheaded things could one person do before they get kicked out of here? And I've done some pretty boneheaded things. You know, like resurrecting Count Dracula with my own blood.

I'm pretty sure no one can top that one.

I should probably just leave.

Suddenly, the door bursts open, scaring the bejesus out of me.

"You coming?" Rage asks, poking his head inside.

"Coming where?" I ask, not bothering to look his way. I guess I'm as mad at him as he is of me.

"To the auditorium," he says. "There was an announcement at dinner. Van Helsing called a mandatory assembly for all students and faculty in the auditorium. He expects everyone to be there, including you."

"Not me," I say. "I'll be right here."

"That's ridiculous," Rage says. "You have to go. Van Helsing never calls a mandatory assembly. Supposedly, this is the first time in years that's happened. Are you really going to miss it?"

"Yep," I say. "I don't need to hear anything else about the Monster Cup. It's pretty clear where we are in the standings, which is nowhere, all because of me."

"This assembly isn't about the Monster Cup," Rage says. "And besides, I'm not mad anymore. What happened wasn't your fault. You had a bad break, that's all. No one wanted you to die so we could win. Well, except for InvisiBill."

"Really?" I say, looking at him.

He's smiling and I can't help but smile back.

"What about Aura?" I ask.

"Don't worry about her," Rage says. "She'll get over it. Eventually. Now get up or we'll be late."

I hesitate for a second, but I am curious about why Van Helsing called this assembly. "Fine," I say, throwing my legs over the side of the bed. I grab my gray hoodie and follow Rage outside.

There's a full moon in the night sky as groups of kids make their way across the green towards the main building. Rage and I are the last to climb up the stone steps and push through the double doors. By the time we reach the auditorium, the room is abuzz—literally.

I duck just as a kid with dragon wings flies over me, nearly taking my head off. The place is packed and the volume level is deafening. Aside from the winged troublemakers divebombing their unsuspecting classmates, the rest of the kids are sitting with their sections. Through the crowd, I see the Juggernauts, the Freaks, and the Howlers, but I don't see our section.

"Over there," Rage says, pointing to the far side.

That's when I see a furry arm waving at us.

"There's Hairball," Rage says. "Let's go."

Well, here goes nothing.

I follow Rage through the crowd, and as I approach the Monstrosities I get a mixed reaction. Hairball and Stanphibian nod, but Aura crosses her arms and turns the other way. Wonderful.

I ignore her and take the empty seat beside her.

"Hey!" InvisiBill yells. "Get off of me!"

"Sorry," I say, moving over one.

As I settle in, I look up at the stage where the faculty is sitting. Professor Holmwood and Professor Morris are having an intense conversation, Professor Seward is flipping through a notebook, and Professor Hexum is staring straight ahead with his arms crossed and his walking stick across his lap.

As I look at him my blood boils, so I shift my attention to the large, black banner hanging above the stage. My eyes trace the bold, gothic letters that spell out the words: VAN HELSING ACADEMY. Then, I read the school's motto:

YOU MUST BELIEVE IN THINGS YOU CANNOT IMAGINE.

When I first arrived, I had no idea what that meant. But now, after everything I've been through, I totally understand it. The things I've discovered here still boggle my mind. I mean, before this I had no idea that monsters were real.

Or that I'm a vampire.

Suddenly, I get knocked in the ribs.

"Hey!" I say, rubbing my side. But when I look to my left there's no one sitting there.

"Stop daydreaming," InvisiBill says. "Van Helsing is getting on stage."

I want to sock InvisiBill, but when I look up, Van Helsing is walking up the stairs with a strange man in tow. As usual, Van Helsing looks like he's dressed for a winter storm, complete with a sweater, gloves, and a scarf.

But I don't recognize the man behind him.

He's wearing a pair of thick, black glasses that seem odd against his pasty complexion. He has white hair like Van Helsing and is dressed in a black turtleneck shirt with brown pants. As Van Helsing approaches the microphone, he invites the man to stand beside him and the man complies, smiling nervously.

The microphone SQUEALS as Van Helsing pulls it towards him, making everyone cover their ears.

Then, the room grows quiet.

"Students," Van Helsing says, looking up. "We will begin once you ground yourselves and take your seats."

Seconds later, all of the flyers have touched down.

"Thank you," he says. "I have called this assembly to introduce an old friend who will be temporarily joining our faculty. It is my privilege to introduce Dr. Eugene Renfield."

As Van Helsing turns to Dr. Renfield, the other professors applaud, except for Hexum whose arms are still crossed. Dr. Renfield nods in acknowledgment but looks like he'd rather be anywhere else.

"Dr. Renfield will add much-needed expertise to our staff," Van Helsing continues. "He is the preeminent expert in the field of monster psychology. Dr. Renfield has conducted extensive field studies across all categories of monsters, publishing papers on nearly every monster sub-type. His knowledge of monster behavior and monster motivations are unparalleled and he will be a tremendous asset in helping us to better understand our opponents and ourselves. I am beyond thrilled that he has agreed to join us this term and starting tomorrow all of you will begin a new class called Monster Mindset 101."

"Wait, what?" Hairball blurts out, a little too loudly.

Van Helsing raises an eyebrow, but Hairball merely expressed what everyone else was thinking, because suddenly the room erupts in a collective groan.

And I can see why. I mean, how can we possibly take on a fifth class? We're buried up to our eyeballs in homework from the classes we already have.

"Well, this is a disaster," InvisiBill whispers. "I'm

barely passing as it is."

"Do not dismay," Van Helsing says. "I understand this is an additional course of study, but it is not my intention to overload you. What Dr. Renfield will teach you is invaluable. Therefore, there will be no homework assigned in his class. However, you must be an active participant to get a passing grade."

"Yep," InvisiBill whispers, "I'm definitely flunking that one too."

This time there's a collective cheer as the kids high-five or high-paw one another. Well, that's certainly a relief. I don't think I could handle one more thing.

"You will find your adjusted course schedules in your mailboxes," Van Helsing continues. "I know you all will make Dr. Renfield feel at home here. Thank you for attending this brief announcement. You are dismissed."

Suddenly, the room is buzzing once more as the kids stand up to leave. But I have a different idea. This might be my only chance to catch Van Helsing and get my team reinstated for the Monster Cup.

But as I head towards the stage I freeze.

For some reason, Dr. Renfield is looking my way.

For a second, I'm confused, and I look over my shoulder to see if he's staring at someone standing behind me, but there's no one there. And when I look back, he's still staring at me.

Then, Hexum puts his hand on Dr. Renfield's shoulder and he turns. Well, that was weird.

Now Van Helsing is talking to both Dr. Renfield and Hexum. Do I really want to bring this up with Hexum standing right there?

Probably not a good idea.

"Let's go check our mailboxes," Aura says. "I'm curious to see if we're having Monster Mindset in the morning or afternoon."

Suddenly, I hear snickering, and when I turn I see Harpoon pointing at me and whispering to the other Howlers. Then, they all burst out laughing.

"Shut up!" Aura yells. "You won on a technicality. Next year you won't be so lucky."

"Why's that?" Harpoon asks. "Are you getting rid of the vampire kid before next year's Monster Cup?"

The Howlers bend over in laughter.

"Come on, guys," Aura says, floating past them.

As we follow her out, I can tell she's still seething, but there's nothing I can do. At least she stuck up for me.

I guess that's a good thing.

But as soon as we step outside, we're stopped by our very own half-man, half-spider.

"Hang on, Monstrosities," Crawler says, blocking us with two of his spider legs. "I've been waiting for you."

"For us?" Aura says. "Why? We didn't do anything wrong. We were just heading back to Monster House."

"Relax," Crawler says. "You're not in trouble. I need your help. For a little job off campus."

"Off campus?" Rage says. "Whoa, hold on there.

The last time we went off campus we got in really big trouble, remember? Like, we wrecked your jeep and nearly got eaten by zombies. Are you sure you're not looking for the Howlers?"

"Nope," Crawler says. "I'm looking for you guys."

"For what?" I ask. "And won't Van Helsing be mad at us for leaving school again?"

"Nope," Crawler says. "I'm following Van Helsing's orders."

"Really?" I say. "His orders for what?"

"For a mission," Crawler says.

"A mission, huh?" Hairball says, cracking his knuckles. "What kind of a mission?"

"Let's call it a search mission," Crawler says. "Follow me."

VAN HELSING ACADEMY

STUDENT ASSESSMENT

VITALS:
NAME: Bobby Rotunda
EYES: Brown
HAIR: None
HEIGHT: Unknown
WEIGHT: 1,000 lbs*
* Estimate

CODENAME: Blobby

NOTES: A boneless, shapeless pile of flesh who can contort and stretch his body in an endless variety of ways. Has a voracious appetite.

CLASSIFICATION TYPE:
Abnormal-Physical

SUPERNATURAL ASSESSMENT:

STRENGTH	●●●●○
AGILITY	●○○○○
FIGHTING	●●●○○
INTELLECT	●○○○○
CONTROL	●●●○○

TEACHABLE?	Yes	No
VAN HELSING	●	○
CRAWLER	●	○
HOLMWOOD	●	○
SEWARD	●	○
MORRIS	●	○
HEXUM	○	●
~~FAUSTIUS~~	~~○~~	~~○~~

RISK LEVEL: MEDIUM

CHAPTER THREE

GET ME OUT OF HERE

My gut is telling me this is a really, really bad idea.

After everything that's happened, the last thing I want to do is go on this little adventure. In fact, if I had it my way, I'd be back at Monster House lying in bed. But when Crawler 'volun-told' us that we were going with him on a "search mission"—whatever that means—everyone else jumped at the chance. So, I was forced to come along, whether I wanted to or not.

Of course, I could have backed out, but that would have irked the team even more. Right now, after blowing the team's shot at the Monster Cup, I need to do whatever it takes to mend fences. Especially with Aura, who still clearly hates me right now.

Like, really hates me right now.

She made that pretty obvious when we boarded the bus. I got on first and sat in the front. But Aura just floated past the empty seat next to me and went all the way to the back.

Message received.

Unfortunately, Stanphibian squeezed in next to me, so things are smelling rather fishy up here.

When it rains it pours.

Anyway, aside from my ghost-drama nobody even knows where the heck we're going because Crawler won't tell us. We've probably been on the road for half an hour and every time one of us asks if we're there yet, he just shakes his head and says, 'I'll tell you when we get there.'

I stare out the window at the passing trees when I suddenly remember something Crawler said when he roped us into this mission.

"Hey, Crawler," I say. "When you got us, you said you were following Van Helsing's orders. What exactly were his orders anyway?"

"He wants you guys to get more comfortable working together outside of the academy," Crawler says. "Let's just say your last two outings weren't exactly confidence builders."

Well, he's got that right.

The first time we left campus, we tried to stop a grave robbery and nearly got eaten by zombies and werewolves. That was totally scary, but it was relatively tame compared to my second time off campus.

That's when I got 'ported' through Professor Faustius' book into his secret lair and watched as he used my blood to bring Count Dracula back to life.

As much as I try, it's impossible to shake the fact that I've put the entire world in serious danger. I mean, no one talks about it around me, but I know everyone is nervous about how we'll stop Count Dracula—especially since Van Helsing said the only one who can actually do it is me.

Definitely not a confidence builder.

I mean, I know Count Dracula is out there somewhere gathering his strength. And now that he's back, I bet the Dark Ones' ranks are swelling right now. Apparently, evil is a magnet for demented people.

I look back out the window.

Then, I remember something else Crawler said and I shudder. It was right after he saved me from being demolished by Rage at the cemetery.

"Um, Crawler?" I call out. "Didn't you tell me we weren't safe once we left campus?"

"What, are you chicken now?" InvisiBill says from the seat behind me that I thought was empty. "We should call you Bawk-pire! Bawk, bawk!"

"I'm not a chicken, you goober," I say. "But after Crawler shot Rage with enough tranquilizers to put down a brontosaurus, he told me we weren't safe once we left the gates of the Van Helsing Academy. He said the school grounds are protected from evil by Supernatural artifacts, but we don't have that same protection once we leave campus. Isn't that right, Crawler?"

I catch Crawler looking at me wide-eyed in the rearview mirror. And when I turn around, the other kids are staring at me like I have two heads.

"Right, Crawler?" I say.

"Um, did I tell you that?" Crawler says.

"Yes," I say. "You did."

"Well, what do you know?" Crawler says, his voice rising. "I totally forgot about that."

"Great," Rage says, dropping his head into his hands. "Can we please turn around now?"

"But don't worry," Crawler says quickly. "This mission will be an easy one. And this time you're all under my supervision so it's cool. Hey, does anybody know some good road trip songs?"

"Hang on, Crawler," Aura says. "We're not just going to skip over this. How come no one told us the school has Supernatural protection?"

"Never came up?" Crawler offers.

"Spill it, Crawler," Hairball says. "What are these artifacts already?"

"Nothing, really," he says. "Oh my, look at that tree over there. Is that a squirrel?"

"Stop trying to change the subject," InvisiBill says.

"It's a big squirrel," Crawler says. "Look at its—"

"Spill it!" we all yell in unison.

"Okay, okay," Crawler says. "But I'm not supposed to talk about this. If I tell you, you can't repeat it to anyone—and I mean anyone. Do we have a deal?"

"Deal," we all agree.

"Alright," Crawler says, his eyes narrowing. "Legend has it that somewhere, hidden in the basement of the Van

Helsing Academy are three Supernatural objects—a bell, a book, and a candle—known as the Artifacts of Virtue. Now I've never seen them myself, but it's said that as long as they're aligned to form a triangle, they cast a shield of protection that blocks evil from breaking through their barrier."

"Hold on," InvisiBill says. "Are you saying the entire school is protected by a bell, a book, and a dinky candle?"

"Yep," Crawler says. "That's what I'm saying."

"Is it really true?" Aura asks.

"Ever seen any zombies in Monster House or werewolves on the quad?" Crawler says.

"Well, no," I say.

"I guess you have your answer then," Crawler says. "Now look alive because we're finally here. Thank goodness."

Here? Here where?

Out the window I see a battered blue sign:

MOREAU LABORATORIES

Moreau Laboratories? What's that?

But as I look up, I'm not sure I want to know the answer, because standing before us is a creepy office building that's seen way better days. It's three stories tall with a cracked brick facade and boarded-up windows. The overgrown bushes clearly haven't been trimmed in years and the chain-link fence surrounding the perimeter looks like it was run over by a tank.

"Were not going in there, are we?" Rage asks.

"Yes, we are," Crawler says.

"But it looks like the set of a horror movie," Rage says. "Like, a really scary horror movie."

"Well," Crawler says. "I guess it's a good thing we're monsters."

As we head down the driveway, I realize there aren't any streetlights. And as we get closer to the building, I notice empty guard towers and rolls of barbed wire stretched across the ground. Clearly, this was once a heavily fortified complex. But the question is why?

Crawler pulls into the parking lot and parks in the faded handicapped space right in front of the building. Normally, I'd tell him that's rude, but since it doesn't seem like anyone has parked here for decades, we're probably okay.

"Everyone out," Crawler says.

As we file out, it dawns on me that we can forget about the element of surprise. I mean, it's not like Crawler is trying to hide us.

"Okay," Crawler says, slapping two of his spider legs together. "Here's the deal. As you know, my spider network has eyes all over the world. Yesterday, one of my top scouts spotted strange activity here at Moreau Labs. For those of you who don't know what Moreau Labs is—which is pretty much all of you by the looks of it—let me give you a quick rundown. Moreau Labs was a government-backed research facility run by a man named Dr. Simon Moreau, a brilliant but misguided scientist who became infamous for conducting genetic experiments on regular people… and, well, monsters."

"Monsters?" Rage says. "Did you just say monsters?"

"Um, what kinds of experiments?" InvisiBill asks.

"Not good ones," Crawler says. "But don't worry, his lab has been shut down for a long, long time. The government didn't agree with whatever Moreau was doing, so they pulled his funding and came to arrest him. But Moreau escaped, went into hiding, and hasn't been seen since. His lab has been vacant for years. Until now, that is."

"Well, this just keeps getting better," I say. "What exactly does 'until now' mean?"

"It means my scout picked up movement inside the lab," Crawler says. "But it's nothing to be nervous about. According to her final report, the lab has been infiltrated by a couple of cats."

"Cats?" I say. "Like, kitty cats?"

"Exactly," Crawler says.

"So," I say. "what's the problem if cats are running around this old building?"

"Because we've been keeping our eyes on this facility ever since Dr. Moreau got away," Crawler says. "And this is the first activity we've picked up since he left. We just need to make sure everything checks out okay, that's all."

"Just one more question," Aura asks. "You said your

scout made her final report. What does 'final' mean?"

"It means I haven't heard from her since," Crawler says, his eyebrows rising with concern. "And she's not responding to any communication."

"Well, that's reassuring," I say. "Anything else you're not telling us?"

"Nope," Crawler says. "So, let's break up into smaller groups and sweep this building fast."

***

Well, so much for being under Crawler's direct supervision. Crawler split us into teams and we went our separate ways. Aura and Hairball got the first floor, Crawler, InvisiBill, and Stanphibian took the second floor, and Rage and I got the top floor. Not that I'm complaining. Believe me, I want to get this over with as quickly as possible.

The good news is that Crawler is keeping close tabs on InvisiBill and Stanphibian. If those two knuckleheads were left to their own devices, they'd definitely screw something up big time.

As Rage and I climb the last flight of stairs I notice him falling behind. I glance over my shoulder and see he's wincing, holding his head with one hand, and gripping the railing tight with the other.

"You okay?" I whisper.

"What?" Rage says, standing up straighter. "Yeah,

sorry. It's just… I'm fine."

Okay, I don't know what's wrong with him, but that's even more incentive to get this done fast. As I step onto the third-floor landing. I listen for the telltale sounds of cats, like purring, meowing, or the yakking of a hairball, but there's nothing. I guess this is where the 'search' part of the search mission comes in.

I peer around the corner of the stairwell down a long hallway. The square, overhead lights are out, the beige floor tiles run from end-to-end, and all of the doors along the hallway are closed.

Then, I notice something strange.

At the far end of the hallway is a smashed window with glass shards and a shattered wood panel scattered on the floor. Clearly, something busted its way inside. My first thought is the cats, but I don't think cats could climb three stories up the side of a building and smash through a boarded-up window.

"Here, kitty kitty," I call out.

"Shhh!" Rage whispers, coming up behind me. "What do you think you're doing?"

"Trying to find some cats," I say. "Do you want to be here all night?"

"Well, no," he says. "But I…"

The next thing I know, Rage wobbles, and I grab his arm, keeping him from falling over.

"Whoa," I say. "You okay?"

"Yeah," he says. "Just a little disoriented for some

reason."

"Okay," I say. "Lean against the wall here while I open these doors one by one. If any cats are up here, they'll probably be in one of these rooms."

I try every door, but they're all locked. And each one features a different plaque describing what's inside, like *Medical Supplies*, *Sanitation Chamber*, and *Disposal Room*.

We're halfway down the hall when I notice something else. Beneath the farthest door on the right is a faint sliver of light. Is someone in there?

I'm about to tell Rage when he suddenly says—

"I-I think I've been here before."

"What?" I say. But when I turn around, Rage is sliding down the wall, his eyes darting all over.

"I-I know this place," Rage says, breathing faster like he's hyperventilating.

"Hey, relax," I say. "Are you o—"

But before I can finish my sentence, his eyes roll back in his head and he crumples to the ground, hitting his head on a doorknob on the way down.

"Rage!" I yell, running over to him.

By the time I reach him he's out for the count. Fortunately, he's still breathing. I slap his face lightly to rouse him, but he won't wake up.

"Come on, Rage," I say, turning his head gently.

Then, I freeze.

There, on his left temple, is a thin trickle of blood.

It's not a lot, but it's dripping down the side of his

face. Suddenly, my stomach rumbles, and I remember I haven't eaten dinner. I lick my lips.

Boy, that red liquid sure looks good.

Wait, what?

I shake my head. I mean, what's happening? Where did that come from?

I… I don't drink blood.

Never.

I try putting it out of my mind and focus back on Rage. I don't know what happened to him but we can forget looking for these crazy cats. Rage needs help.

I've got to get him out of here, but how? He probably doesn't weigh a ton. So, should I try carrying him downstairs on my own or should I leave him here and go get the others?

Just then, I hear footsteps coming from behind me.

I breathe a sigh of relief.

"Crawler!" I say. "Thank goodness, Rage just passed out so maybe you can—"

But when I look up my heart stops.

Because I'm not staring at Crawler.

But rather a pair of red, luminous eyes.

CHAPTER FOUR

CAT FIGHT

I can't believe what I'm seeing.

Because standing over Rage and me, snarling in a low, rather unfriendly tone, is some kind of a half-boy, half-beast! His body looks completely normal, but his head is shaped like… a tiger?

My instincts tell me to run, but I can't just leave Rage lying here unconscious. I don't know who this tiger kid is or what he's doing here, but then it dawns on me. Could this be the cat Crawler's scout was referring to?

And if so, is he responsible for smashing through the boarded-up window at the end of the hallway? My eyes drift down to his sharp claws. Well, he certainly looks like he could climb up the side of a building.

Then, I realize something. We've been staring at each other for a good few seconds and he hasn't attacked us yet. Why hasn't he attacked us yet?

"Easy, fella," I say, rising slowly.

Tiger-boy growls and I freeze, my body stuck in a

crouched position. That's when I notice he doesn't seem much taller than I am. He's wearing jeans and a black t-shirt that says, "Rock On," and his arms are down by his sides which isn't exactly a threatening posture. In fact, I don't think he's planning on attacking us at all.

And then I hear him breathing. It sounds like he's wheezing—like he's struggling to catch his breath.

"Hey, it's okay," I say, putting my hands up. "I'm not here to fight you."

He tilts his head, his pointy ears pricking up.

I wonder if he understands me.

"My name is Bram," I say, pointing to my heart. "We just came here to find some cats. And, um, I'm thinking that might be you. Do you have a name?"

But when I point at him he jumps back to the window so fast it surprises me.

"It's okay," I say, reassuringly. "We're not here to hurt you." I look down at Rage who's still not stirring. "My friend needs help. Do you need help?"

Tiger-boy slowly moves in front of the last door on the right. That's the one with the light coming from beneath it. But then I notice the door is still closed. For a second I'm confused because I assumed he came through that door. But clearly, he didn't.

Suddenly, he turns the knob and pushes the door open. As it swings inward, more light pours into the hallway and I can see Tiger-boy even more clearly. For the first time, I notice he doesn't look so good. His orange fur is mangy and there are bald patches on one side of his head.

"Are you sick?" I ask. "If you come with me, I can help you. I have friends that can help you."

For a brief second, his eyes grow wide, like he wants to come with me more than anything, but then he nods towards the open doorway and growls. It's like he wants me to go in there. But before I can ask him what's inside, he rushes to the window with uncanny quickness and leaps outside!

"Wait!" I yell, running to the window.

But by the time I get there, he's long gone. I try spotting him in the underbrush but I can't. And all he's left behind is a shred of his t-shirt that's hanging off the windowpane. Man, he's powerful. I mean, we're three stories off the ground!

Ugh, now I'll never know who he is or what he was doing here. He looked like he was in some kind of serious trouble. Speaking of trouble, I've got to get back to Rage.

But as soon as I turn around, I hear moaning.

Rage is still out so that couldn't be him.

Am I hearing things?

Then, it comes again. It's a bit louder this time, and it's coming from inside the open room! I hesitate. Maybe I should call the others.

"Ohhh," comes a girl's voice.

This time I hear it clearly. Someone is definitely in there, and she sounds like she's hurt. There might not be time to get the others.

I approach the door cautiously and peer inside. The room looks like a patient recovery room, with a hospital bed and monitoring equipment. The first bed is empty, but there's a curtain drawn across the center of the room, blocking the second bed.

"Uhhhnnn," comes the voice again.

Okay, that came from behind the curtain!

I step inside softly, and as I get closer to the curtain I can see the shadow of someone lying on the bed.

I hold my breath, grab the curtain, and yank it back.

Then, I do a double take.

Because lying on the bed is a half-cat, half-girl!

***

"She's stable," Dr. Hagella says, "but barely. It's a good thing you found her when you did. She's malnourished and I'm not sure she would have survived another day in her state. I need to get more fluids. I'll be back in a few minutes."

As Dr. Hagella exits I breathe a sigh of relief. Cat-girl is resting comfortably in Dr. Hagella's infirmary, hooked up to monitors and an IV. Dr. Hagella cleaned her up a bit, and as I study her face it's interesting how different she looks from Tiger-boy.

While Tiger-boy was more like an animal than a human, Cat-girl is more human than animal. Yet, her cat features are clearly there. White, fuzzy ears protrude from her platinum-blond hair, and razor-thin whiskers extend beyond her cheeks. And it's hard not to notice her sharp fingernails, pointy teeth, and long, furry tail which is hanging off the bed.

Fortunately, Crawler and the others showed up right after I found her. And based on Crawler's reaction when he saw her, she wasn't the type of cat he was expecting to find either. On the ride back to Van Helsing Academy, I told the team about my encounter with Tiger-boy, but no one saw him but me.

I'm just glad we were able to get Cat-girl into Dr. Hagella's care when we did. Dr. Hagella is an expert in monster biology, and she seemed to know exactly what Cat-girl needed. Which is more than I can say for myself.

Honestly, this whole episode has left me more than a little freaked out. Our run-in with the cat-kids wasn't the only bizarre thing that happened. I mean, I nearly drank Rage's blood! I look over at poor Rage who is lying unconscious in the next bed.

Where did that crazy urge come from? I mean, I've never E-V-E-R had the desire to drink anyone's blood. I've been trying to put that near-disaster out of my mind, but I just can't shake it.

Maybe I should tell Van Helsing?

But if I do, what will he think of me? I mean, it only happened once. I'm sure it won't happen again. Right?

Well, it's a moot point for now anyway. As soon as

we brought Cat-girl back to school, Van Helsing took one look at her and informed us he had to leave immediately. I then overheard him whispering to Crawler about rounding up some of the other professors and heading back to Moreau Labs.

Then, they took off.

"Man," InvisiBill says from somewhere on the other side of the room. "I'm wiped. I'm gonna head back to Monster House for some shuteye. Anyone want to come?"

"I'm in," Hairball says, stretching into a big yawn. "There's nothing for us to do here. You coming, Aura?"

"No," she says. "I don't need sleep, remember? And besides, I want to stay until Rage wakes up."

"Suit yourself," Hairball says. "Night."

"I'm good," I say to no one in particular. "Thanks for asking."

As Hairball exits, Stanphibian waves a webbed hand and follows him out. I see a bunch of cords move on their own by the doorway which likely means InvisiBill is right behind them.

It's just Aura and me.

"Funny how we keep ending up together like this," I say.

But Aura doesn't respond. Instead, she crosses her arms and floats closer to check on Rage. Great, she's still mad at me. Talk about holding a grudge!

I'm about to apologize again for ruining the Monster

Cup when—

"Stop!" Rage yells, sitting up suddenly.

"Rage, relax," Aura says. "It's okay. You're back at school."

"What?" Rage says with panic in his eyes. "Where?"

"Back at school," Aura says. "At the Van Helsing Academy. You're home now. It's okay."

Rage looks around and then wipes his forehead which is covered in sweat.

"Are you okay?" I ask. "Do you remember anything before you passed out?"

"Y-Yeah," he says, looking confused. "We were at Moreau Labs, and suddenly everything came rushing back. I-I remembered… things."

Suddenly, the hairs on the back of my neck stand on end. When I first met Rage, he told me he had no memory of his past. In fact, he said his very first memory was waking up here at the Van Helsing Academy.

"What kinds of things?" Aura asks.

"I-I remember being wheeled down a hallway on a gurney," he says. "It was a long, narrow hallway just like the one we were in. And… and I remember the smell. It smelled… medical. Like… disinfectant. And…"

Rage opens his mouth but no words come out.

"And what?" Aura prods. "Come on, Rage. This could be important. You can do it."

"And then I remember being pushed into a room with a bright light overhead." Rage says. "Everything was kind of foggy but I could hear scraping. Like metal on metal. And the room was so cold I was shivering. And then, out of nowhere, I saw… him."

As Rage's voice trails off I can tell he's back there—back in that moment when his nightmare started.

"Who?" I say. "Who did you see?"

"A-A man," Rage says. "An older man, with white hair and… cold, gray eyes. And before he put his surgical mask on he smiled and said, 'Don't worry, this won't hurt—at least not too much.'"

Aura looks at me with sad eyes.

"I… I think that was him," Rage says.

"Who?" I ask.

"Moreau," Rage says. "I-I think Dr. Moreau did this to me. I think Dr. Moreau made me into a monster."

ROCK
ON

CHAPTER FIVE

TRANCE-SYLVANIA

Unfortunately, Van Helsing isn't back from Moreau Labs yet, so we have to sit tight on Rage's shocking news.

I feel bad for the kid. I mean, I can't even imagine the horrors he's reliving in his mind. And after he told us that he was one of Dr. Moreau's victims, another stress wave kicked in and he passed out again. Not that I can blame him.

And since Cat-girl hasn't woken up yet either, Dr. Hagella said there's no point in us just hanging around doing nothing. So, she sent us to class. Yippee. That's pretty much the last place I want to be right now.

Especially since it's our first day with super creepy Dr. Renfield.

"Welcome, students," Dr. Renfield says, standing at the front of the classroom with a pointer in his hand. "Please take out your notebooks. Today, I will be providing a comprehensive introduction to Monster Mindset 101, the fundamentals of monster psychology."

Great. Just what I need.

As I look around I realize I'm far from alone in my thinking. Stanphibian is doodling in his notebook, Hairball is half-asleep, and InvisiBill's chair appears empty because it probably is.

Then, there's Aura.

No surprise, she's sitting front and center at full attention. She loves learning new things, but even more impressively, she somehow retains it all. I bet she uses all of that time she's not sleeping to study.

Me? I could use a good snooze. Especially right now.

"Now," Dr. Renfield continues, "I am sure you are wondering what the exciting field of monster psychology is all about."

No, not really. But I am wondering if I'm going to survive this class. I mean, Dr. Renfield isn't the most dynamic teacher I've ever had. Hmmm, I wonder how long it would take me to count the ceiling tiles?

"As Headmaster Van Helsing explained," Dr. Renfield drones on. "It is frequently said that the human mind is one of nature's most astonishing creations. That may be true, but I can assure you that the mind of the monster is a wonder unlike anything produced in common nature. First, we will—"

"Pssst," comes a sharp whisper from behind.

I turn around to find Harpoon staring at me with her beady, yellow eyes. Then, she smirks and passes me a note. What could this be?

"I have psycho-analyzed every major classification of

monster," Dr. Renfield continues, completely oblivious to what's going on, "and nearly every sub-classification. I have dedicated my life to understanding the motivations of monsters. From shapeshifters to spirits. From the undead to the abnormal. Here, in this classroom, we will unlock the mysteries of the monster mind together. But this class will be more than lectures. It will also be quite hands-on. You see, most of my findings have been discovered through the science of hypnosis. Hypnosis is the—"

I tune Dr. Renfield out as I quietly unfold Harpoon's note under my desk. It reads:

I DARE U TO PASS THIS NOTE.
UNLESS U R A CHICKEN.

Seriously? And what's with the chicken thing?

I look back at Harpoon who mouths chicken noises. This is ridiculous. I'm not going to pass a note in the middle of class. I crumple it up.

"Pssst," comes another whisper, this time from over my left shoulder.

I turn to find Gnatalie and MinoTodd mouthing the same chicken noises. Okay, the last thing I need is for all of the Howlers to think I'm a chicken too. Especially after losing to them in the Monster Cup.

If passing this note will get them off my back, then I'll just pass the darn note.

But to who?

Hairball is closest, but he looks like he's sleeping. If I give it to him, I'll just have to be sure he won't make a scene. I wait for Dr. Renfield to write on the blackboard, and then whisper sharply—

"Hairball."

"Wha—?" he says, jolting upright, his big hairy arm slipping from his chin and banging on his desktop.

Oh jeez!

But thankfully, Dr. Renfield doesn't notice.

"Take this," I whisper, handing over the note.

But before Hairball can grab it—BOOM—it explodes into a ball of black smoke!

What happened?

"Who did that?" Dr. Renfield says, looking my way.

But when I turn around, all I see are the Howlers laughing to themselves, including Lucky and his cursed amulet. Suddenly, it all makes sense.

They set me up.

That note was cursed the whole time.

I'm such an idiot.

"You there," Dr. Renfield says, pointing at me. "Come to the front of the class."

Great. Here we go.

As I stand up, I debate whether I should tattle on the Howlers or not, but then decide against it. After all, what good would it do? I passed the note, so I'll just have to take my punishment like a man.

"Stand here," Dr. Renfield says, pointing to a spot in front of the whole class.

I dutifully take my mark and stand quietly, my hands fidgeting behind my back. I try to appear calm but my imagination is spinning. Why did he pull me up here? Why didn't he just send me to Van Helsing's office? At least I could set my own punishment then.

"You are Mr. Murray," Dr. Renfield says. "Is that correct?"

"Um, yeah," I say, surprised that he even knows my name. I mean, he didn't even take roll call when the class started. But then I remember him staring at me after the assembly.

"I thought so," Dr. Renfield says. "Mr. Murray, you will be our first volunteer."

"Um, volunteer for what?" I ask.

"For hypnosis, of course," Dr. Renfield says, as he reaches into his coat pocket and pulls out a gold pendulum. It's circular and hanging from a gold chain. "If you were listening, you would have learned that this is my primary method for uncovering the motivations of monsters."

"And what exactly does that mean?" I ask.

"There is nothing to fear," Dr. Renfield says. "Hypnosis is simply a technique that will put you in a very relaxed state of mind—a trance if you will—allowing you to reach a heightened state of awareness. How does that sound?"

"Weird," I answer, as the class laughs.

"Now, as I understand it, Mr. Murray, you are a vampire, a rare sub-species not seen for quite a long time. In fact, as far as I am aware, no psychologist has ever hypnotized a vampire before. This will be a first in the field of monster psychology."

"Um, okay," I say, not sure how to respond. But he seems rather excited.

"Now," Dr. Renfield says, swinging the pendulum in front of my face. "Try to relax as we begin."

"Um, hang on a sec," I say, swallowing hard. "Is this really a good idea?"

"I think it is an excellent idea," Dr. Renfield says. "Unless, of course, you are afraid?"

The class giggles again, and I look out at all of the faces staring at me. That's when Harpoon mouths more chicken noises.

"N-No," I say. "I'm not afraid. I'm good."

"I thought you would be," Dr. Renfield says. "After all, vampires are notorious for their courage. Now, I want you to relax and stare at the pendulum."

My eyes follow the gold pendulum as it swings back and forth from his fingers in a slow, regular rhythm. I don't know what he's getting at but I might as well play along. I'm sure this hypnotism thing only works in the movies.

"Notice how the pendulum moves as you breathe slowly," Dr. Renfield says. "And as you continue to watch, you may notice your eyelids becoming heavy as you start to relax."

Hmm, that's funny. My eyelids are getting heavier. In fact, I'm having a hard time keeping them open.

"You may notice as you continue to breathe you have the urge to blink," Dr. Renfield says. "That is completely normal. But, if you are ready, go ahead and close your eyes fully."

As my lids press down, I realize that even if I wanted to open my eyes, I couldn't.

In fact, I can't move a muscle.

"And as you continue to relax and breathe," Dr. Renfield says soothingly, "we shall begin…"

***

"… now wide awake," comes a voice.

SNAP!

My eyes pop open and I'm disoriented.

Where am I?

Then, as my vision readjusts, I realize I'm standing in front of the entire class! And they're all staring at me with big, goofy smiles on their faces. Suddenly, I feel my face go flush—or, at least as flush as it can go given my pale complexion.

What's going on? Why are they looking at me?

"How do you feel?" comes a voice to my right, surprising me.

I turn to find Dr. Renfield standing next to me. In his hand is that gold pendulum. Then, it dawns on me. He just hypnotized me!

"How do you feel, Mr. Murray?" Dr. Renfield repeats.

"Um, okay," I lie, crossing my arms. Truthfully, I feel kind of exposed right now. I mean, I don't remember anything that just happened.

Just then, the bell RINGS.

Class is over.

All of the students jump up in unison and begin to file past me and out the door.

"Well, that was… interesting," Hairball says, giving me a wink.

"You've got some pretty serious issues," I hear InvisiBill say. "You may want to see somebody about that."

"Wow," is all Stanphibian offers.

Now, panic sets in. I mean, what just happened?

What did he ask me?

What did I say?

Then, I see Aura with her eyebrows raised. Uh-oh.

"Were you really hypnotized?" she asks. "You weren't pretending, were you?"

"No," I say, exhaling. "Why, how bad was it?"

"Not too bad," she says. "Don't listen to those idiots. They're just messing with you. Dr. Renfield only asked you simple questions. Like, what's your favorite food, and what's your greatest fear."

"Wait, he asked me that?" I say, more panic setting in. I can't imagine how I answered that one. Hopefully, I didn't say clowns. Boy, do I hate clowns. Okay, I need to stay calm. "Um, so, what did I say?"

"Count Dracula," she says. "But don't worry. Pretty much everyone knew that already. I think it's pretty obvious given present circumstances."

"Yeah," I say, a little freaked out that I told everyone my greatest fear is the one person I'm destined to destroy.

"I wouldn't worry about it," she says. "Dr. Renfield was just demonstrating how the power of hypnosis can dig deep into the monster mind. It was actually interesting. You just went along with whatever he asked you to do. Who knew that hypnosis was such a powerful tool?"

"Well, isn't that just wonderful," I say, rubbing my head. "But I think I'm done volunteering for a while. I'm really not the Guinea pig-type. I'm just glad I didn't make too much of a fool of myself. Right?"

"Nope," she says. "You've pretty much done that already. See you later."

Then, she smiles and phases through the wall.

Right.

I'm the last kid in the room, so I go back to my desk to grab my stuff when I hear—

"How are you feeling, Mr. Murray?"

I freeze. It's Dr. Renfield.

"Oh, great," I say, lying through my teeth. "I'm fine. Well, I don't want to be late for my next class, so…"

"If you would allow me just one more moment, Mr. Murray," Dr. Renfield says, approaching me.

"Um, okay," I say reluctantly.

He stops in front of me and smiles.

"As I mentioned earlier," he says, "No psychologist has ever had the pleasure of delving into the mind of a vampire before. But it seems that fate has shined on both of us, because here we are, together at the famed Van Helsing Academy. Me, the world's leading monster psychologist, and you, one of the world's last remaining vampires. Wouldn't you agree that this is the opportunity of a lifetime?"

"Well, no," I say. "Not really."

"Together," he continues, "we can make scientific history. With just a few more sessions, we could easily reveal the inner workings of the vampire mind. Imagine the groundbreaking papers we could publish. Imagine the accolades we would receive."

"Wait," I say. "Are you asking to hypnotize me again? Like, a lot of times?"

"Oh, yes," he says. "I imagine the experience was painless for you, wasn't it? We would only need a few more sessions to do this properly. Of course, I would compile all of the findings and write all of the papers. You just need to show up."

Okay, this guy is nuts.

I'm not getting hypnotized again. Like, never again in my entire life. I've got to get out of here.

"Oh, that sounds like a generous offer," I say. "But I have to be honest. I'm really not interested. You see, I've got all of these other commitments, like class, and homework, and trying not to make a fool of myself everywhere I go. So, I've got to run along now."

"Are you sure?" he asks.

"Yeah," I say. "I'm sure. Rock-solid sure."

"Oh," he says, disappointed. "Of course. Perhaps we can revisit this topic at another time."

"Great," I say, moving around him for the door.

"Oh, one more thing Mr. Murray," Dr. Renfield says.

"Yeah?" I say, turning in the doorframe.

"You may experience some… lingering dizziness from the hypnosis," he says. "But don't worry, it's completely normal and you'll be just fine."

"Oh, okay," I say. "Thanks for letting me know."

Then, I take off as fast as I can.

CLASSIFIED

Person(s) of Interest

CODE NAME: NONE

REAL NAME: DR. EUGENE RENFIELD

BASE OF OPERATIONS: VAN HELSING ACADEMY

FACTS: Dr. Renfield is the preeminent expert in the field of monster psychology. Dr. Renfield has studied nearly every sub-type of monster and publishes his findings in scientific journals. He is currently working as an adjunct professor at the Van Helsing Academy.

Category: Natural

Sub-Type: Not Applicable

Height: 5'10"

Weight: 195 lbs

FIELD OBSERVATIONS:

- Expert in the science of hypnosis
- Highly intelligent
- Frequently travels for field research
- A former schoolmate of Lothar Van Helsing

STATUS: ACTIVE TARGET

DEPARTMENT OF SUPERNATURAL INVESTIGATIONS

CHAPTER SIX

FEVER DREAMS

We got quite a surprise before lights out.

There I was, brushing my teeth and thinking about my super-strange encounter with Dr. Renfield when Hairball barges through the bathroom door.

"Come downstairs," he says. "Van Helsing is back and wants to see us in the foyer."

I rinse quickly and spit. Van Helsing is back? And he's here in the Monster House foyer? I don't think I've ever seen Van Helsing in Monster House before. And since he was just out visiting Moreau Labs, he must be here on serious business.

For a split second, I debate getting dressed but given the seriousness of the situation, I prioritize speed over style and go downstairs in my pajamas.

When I reach the bottom, I find I'm not the only one. Hairball and Stanphibian are in their pj's too, while who knows what InvisiBill is wearing. Of course, Aura is a ghost, so she's always dressed the same.

And, just as Hairball promised, Van Helsing is here

waiting for us, but he's not alone. Crawler, Professor Morris, and Rage are with him too.

Boy, it's great seeing Rage on his feet again, and he's wearing a small bandage on his head where he got injured. He smiles when he sees me but based on the gloomy expressions on the adults' faces, it's clear they're not here for a celebration.

"Thank you all for joining us at this late hour," Van Helsing says. "Based on your trip to Moreau Labs, your discovery of the 'Cat-girl,' as you call her, and your concern for the wellbeing of your colleague, Rage, who has made a full recovery, I thought it would be best to update you all on what we have discovered."

"About time," InvisiBill says.

"As you know, I returned to Moreau Labs with Crawler and Professor Morris to examine the site," Van Helsing says. "The evidence we recovered is conclusive. Dr. Moreau is back in operation."

As soon as Van Helsing finishes his sentence, a chill runs down my spine.

"I'm guessing that's a bad thing," InvisiBill says.

"Yes," Van Helsing says. "Very bad. You see, before he was pursued by the government, Dr. Moreau conducted horrific experiments, bending the laws of nature for his own devious purposes. In particular, he was known for transforming innocent people into terrors known as 'Hybrids.'"

"Hybrids?" Aura says. "What's that?"

"A Hybrid is a term used to describe the combination of a human with an animal," Van Helsing says. "For example, a Goat-man or a—"

"—Cat-girl?" I say, finishing his sentence.

"Yes," Van Helsing says. "Dr. Moreau created many of these Hybrid creatures. He claimed that he was doing it for the good of all—that he was creating a new species of mankind that could serve humanity—but his experiments never survived for long. When Dr. Moreau went underground, we thought we were finally free of his evil ways. But sadly, he has returned."

I swallow hard.

My thoughts go back to Tiger-boy and Cat-girl. Based on what Van Helsing is saying, who knows how long they'll live? Tiger-boy looked sick, and Cat-girl is in pretty bad shape. Maybe she won't make it.

"I scanned the entire building with my DNA probe," Professor Morris says, holding up a silver device that looks like an eggbeater. "There was no evidence of Moreau anywhere, except for this."

As Professor Morris pulls out a piece of black cloth, my eyes go wide.

"The Tiger-boy was wearing that," I say. "It tore off his body when he jumped out the window."

"Well, guess what," Professor Morris says. "It's got Dr. Moreau's fingerprints on it. A perfect match."

"Wow," I say. "What about Cat-girl?"

"Glad to see you're thinking like a Supernatural

crime scene investigator," Professor Morris says. "Yes, she has the same prints on her clothing."

"Let's go talk to her," Aura says. "She has to know something."

"Unfortunately, she is still unconscious," Van Helsing says. "We will speak with her when she comes to, but we must do so delicately as she will likely be in a state of shock. I know I have provided you with a lot of information, but I ask that you keep it confidential. Tonight, your only job is to take care of your friend, Rage. He has recovered well, but he'll surely need your support."

"You can count on us," I say. "He's in good hands."

"I thought so," Van Helsing says. "Now, good night, Monstrosities. Sleep well."

"You too," Aura says.

Van Helsing nods at me and then exits, followed by Crawler and Professor Morris.

"Are you okay?" I ask Rage, putting my hand on his shoulder.

"Yeah," he says. "I don't know what happened. I was just overwhelmed being back in that building. It was just weird. What do they call it when it feels like you're reliving something you've experienced before?"

"Doggie-doo," InvisiBill says.

"No, you moron," Aura says. "It's called déjà vu."

"Oh, right," InvisiBill says. "Just kidding."

"Anyway," I say. "It's late. Maybe we should go

upstairs and finish getting ready for bed."

"Yeah, I'm pretty tired," Rage says, touching his bandage.

Suddenly, I feel an overwhelming sense of guilt. I mean, I nearly drank the poor guy's blood. What kind of a teammate am I?

"Let's head up," I say. "I'll help you pull your stuff together so you can go right to sleep."

"Thanks," Rage says, putting his arm around me. "You know, Bram, I'm lucky to have you as a friend."

***

I'm walking down a long, narrow hallway—except, it's not a hallway at all—it's a tunnel. The air is cold and musty, and as I walk, my arms brush against the rocky walls. Unlit torches hang from the wall every ten feet or so, but I don't need them to see. Strangely, a dribbling sound echoes through the tunnel, like running water, but I don't see a water source anywhere.

Occasionally, I need to stoop beneath the low, uneven ceiling to continue, and I suddenly feel claustrophobic, like the tunnel is closing in on me.

On the inside, I feel a burning desire to turn around, but my feet keep moving forward, step by step along the craggy floor. My entire body feels… odd. It's like I'm not in control of my movements.

I try calling for help. For Rage, or Aura, or Van

Helsing, but my lips won't form the words.

Then, the tunnel bends.

I follow it around, not that I have a choice. I'm like a passenger in an out-of-control car, but that car happens to be my own body.

Then, I see it.

The end of the tunnel, about twenty yards ahead.

And flush against the rock wall is an iron vault door.

Immediately, my alarm bells go off. There's something strange about this door. I mean, I don't know of any vault doors attached to rock walls. On the door itself is a small wheel that must be the locking mechanism. If I turn the wheel, the door will swing wide open.

I have an overwhelming desire to head back, but I can't. Instead, I walk over and stop in front of the door.

Suddenly, I notice it's deathly quiet. I don't hear the sound of water anymore. All I hear is the pounding of my own heart.

Then, there's a FLAPPING noise.

I don't see anything flying around me. In fact, if I didn't know better, I'd say that noise sounded like it came from the other side of the—

"Will you open the door?" a male voice asks.

I jump. Who was that?

"Will you open the door?" he repeats.

Okay, that definitely came from the other side of the door. And even though his voice sounded friendly, I feel like I've heard that deep, raspy tone before.

"Who are you?" I say, finding my voice again.

"A friend," he says. *"Will you please open the door?"*

"No," I say.

"Very well," he says. *"Then I will have to do it myself."*

Suddenly, my arms start moving towards the wheel.

No!

I focus everything I have on stopping myself, but my arms just won't listen.

What's happening?

"That's it," he says, his voice rising with excitement. *"Just turn the wheel. Trust me, you won't regret it."*

No! I… won't turn it! But despite my protests, my hands grip the cold, rusty wheel.

"Very good, Bram," he says. *"Now just turn it."*

I try screaming 'NO,' but instead, I feel the corners of my mouth expanding upwards, getting itself ready to say the word 'YES!'

NO!

NO!

N—

***

—O!"

"Bram?"

My eyes pop open, and I'm no longer standing in a tunnel, but rather sitting up in my bed. My skin feels clammy and I'm covered in sweat. How did I get here?

I lift my arms. They're back in my control.

"Bram?" comes Rage's voice.

Rage is standing next to me in his pajamas. What's he doing out of bed? I mean, the last thing I remember was helping him get into his bed. Then, I waited for him to fall asleep before I left the room to go for a walk.

So, what am I doing in my bed?

With my shoes on?

"Bram?" Rage says again. "Are you okay? You look kind of freaked out. It sounded like you had a bad dream or something?"

Was it a dream?

I guess it could have been. But everything felt so… real? And who was behind that door? Who wanted me to open the door so badly? And more importantly, why?

"Um, yeah," I say, trying to act natural. For some reason, I feel like I shouldn't tell him about it. I'll just tell him about one of my other dreams. "It's nothing. Now and then I have this weird nightmare where I'm a bat being chased by baseballs. Don't ask. Anyway, what are you doing up? I thought you were sound asleep?"

"I was," he says. "But InvisiBill woke me up."

"InvisiBill?" I say, looking around, not like I could see him even if he was here. "What for? What time is it?"

"After midnight," Rage says. "InvisiBill said we need to meet in the common room. He said the Howlers are waiting for us. He said they gave us a dare."

"A dare?" I ask. "What kind of a dare?"

"Well," Rage says. "Apparently, InvisiBill spilled the beans about the Artifacts of Virtue."

"WHAT?" I exclaim. "Crawler told us to keep that a secret. We weren't supposed to tell anyone."

"Yeah," Rage says. "Well, that didn't last long."

InvisiBill. You can't tell that big mouth anything.

"Just say he's lying," I say. "Tell them it's not true."

"It's too late," Rage says. "The Howlers already don't believe him."

"Great," I say. "Problem solved. See you in the morning."

"Well," Rage says, "it's not that simple. You see, they dared us to prove it."

"So?" I say. "Ignore them."

"Well, it doesn't quite work like that," Rage says. "You haven't been here for long so you probably haven't learned this yet, but there's an unwritten code of honor here at Monster House. If one team claims something and another team dares them to prove it, you have to prove it. Otherwise, the honor of your entire section is at stake."

"So?" I say. "Who cares?"

"You still don't get it," Rage says. "We have to answer the challenge, otherwise we'll be forced to serve the Howlers for the rest of the term. I don't know about you, but I really don't want to be bringing Blobby breakfast in bed every morning."

Well, I didn't know anything about that.

"And I'm not going to be the one to tell Aura we're not defending our honor," he adds. "The Monstrosities will be laughingstocks all over campus."

"Okay, okay," I say, getting out of bed. Honestly, the last thing I want to do is disappoint Aura again. Defending our honor sounds much easier. "So, what exactly do we have to do?"

"Well," Rage says. "That's the problem. We have to prove what InvisiBill said is true. We have to go into the forbidden basement and prove the Artifacts of Virtue are real."

VAN HELSING ACADEMY

STUDENT ASSESSMENT

VITALS:
NAME: Harper Gale
EYES: Yellow
HAIR: Black
HEIGHT: 4' 11"
WEIGHT: 88 lbs

CODENAME: Harpoon

NOTES: Half-human, half-bird with the wings of a vulture but the body of a girl. Bones are hollow and nails end in razor-sharp talons that can cut through metal.

CLASSIFICATION TYPE:
Abnormal – Harpy

SUPERNATURAL ASSESSMENT:

STRENGTH	●●○○○
AGILITY	●●●●○
FIGHTING	●●●○○
INTELLECT	●●●●●
CONTROL	●●●●○

TEACHABLE?	Yes	No
VAN HELSING	●	○
CRAWLER	●	○
HOLMWOOD	●	○
SEWARD	●	○
MORRIS	●	○
HEXUM	●	○
~~FAUSTIUS~~	~~○~~	~~○~~

RISK LEVEL: MEDIUM

CHAPTER SEVEN

THE FORBIDDEN BASEMENT

As Rage and I enter the common room, you could cut the tension with a knife.

The Monstrosities are standing on one side and the Howlers on the other. And smack dab in the middle are Aura and Harpoon, looking like they want to strangle one another.

I'd say this doesn't look good.

"Well, well," Harpoon says, glaring at me with her shifty, yellow eyes. "If it isn't old bat-brain himself. This is great news because if you put him in charge you'll definitely be doing my homework until the end of the term."

The Howlers cackle at my expense. Shocker.

"Where's InvisiBill?" I ask, ignoring them. "Because I'm going to throttle him."

"Take a number," Aura says, not taking her eyes off of Harpoon.

"InvisiBill isn't here anymore," InvisiBill says, his voice coming from somewhere behind us.

"Shut it," Aura and I say at the same time.

"What's going on here?" I ask.

"The Howlers don't believe what InvisiBill—now known as 'the Squealer'—said about the Artifacts of Virtue," Aura says. "And now they've dared us to prove it to them. So, per the Monster House code of honor, we need to cough up the evidence, otherwise, we'll essentially become their servants for life."

"Don't look so pale," Harpoon says with a smile. "Based on the company you're keeping; I'd consider it a major step up the social chain."

Aura crosses her arms and rolls her eyes.

"If they want us to prove it," I say to Aura. "Then let's just prove it."

"Bram," Aura says, shooting me daggers, "don't you remember? The Artifacts of Virtue are hidden in the basement. You know, the basement all students are forbidden to enter."

Oh, yeah.

When I first enrolled in the Van Helsing Academy, Vi Clops warned me never to go into the basement. She said it was 'off limits.' I think her exact words were something like, 'I'd hate for yer to become the second kid in Van Helsing Academy history that gets lost forever on some stupid dare.'

Maybe this is what she was talking about?

But according to Crawler, the Artifacts of Virtue are in the basement. So, if we're going to defend our honor, one or more of us are going to have to go down there.

"I don't care if we lose the dare," Hairball says. "I'm not stepping foot in that basement. I heard there's a monster down there. Like, a really big one."

"Same," Stanphibian says.

"I'm not going either," InvisiBill says.

"What?" Rage says. "But this was all your fault!"

"InvisiBill still isn't here," InvisiBill says.

Surprise, surprise. The three amigos have chickened out. Predictable.

"Fine," Rage says, standing up a bit taller. "I'll do it."

"No, Rage," Aura says firmly. "You're still recovering. I'll go."

"No," I say suddenly, surprising even myself. "I'll do it. I'll go into the basement."

"Whoohoo!" Harpoon yells, pumping her fist. "This is in the bag! Blobby, how do you like your bacon?"

Honestly, I don't want to go, but after everything I've screwed up, I need to prove myself all over again to my team.

"Bram," Aura says, staring at me with her bright, blue eyes. "You don't have to do this. Why don't you stay here and keep an eye on Rage? I've got this."

"No," I say. "I'm going to do it. It's my fault we're out of the Monster Cup in the first place, so I should be the one to go. Besides, it's right up my alley. I can see in the dark, remember? And believe me, you're the only person I trust to keep an eye on Rage tonight. Those were Van Helsing's orders."

"Hey!" Rage says. "I'm not a baby, you know?"

Aura stares at me, waiting for me to fold, but I don't.

"Okay," she finally relents. "It's settled. Bram will go. But only if he really wants to."

"So," I say, turning to Harpoon. "When I find one of these artifacts, how exactly am I supposed to prove to you that it exists? Based on their power, I'm certainly not bringing one back up with me."

"With this camera," Harpoon says, handing me a small, rectangular object. "After all, they say a picture is worth a thousand words."

"Great," I say, taking it from her. It's a small digital camera, about the size of my palm. I open the back cover just to make sure there are batteries inside and then tuck it into one of my hoodie pockets.

"You need to stay alert at all times," Aura says. "It's going to be dangerous."

"That's alright," I say with a wink. "Danger is my middle name."

"Really?" InvisiBill says. "That's funny, for some reason I always thought it was 'Carl.'"

***

Now that it's settled, my first task is to get into the basement. Since I don't know where it is, I'll need Hairball to take me there. And to do that, we'll have to get past Vi Clops—our super-scary cyclops in charge of Monster House. Since Aura has to keep an eye on Rage, I enlist the help of Hairball, Stanphibian, and InvisiBill.

I guess I'll never learn.

The plan is simple. While Stanphibian preoccupies Vi Clops by telling her that he feels sick, InvisiBill will cause a distraction on the other side of the foyer. Then, when Vi Clops goes to investigate, Stanphibian will give a thumbs up when it's all clear, and I'll follow Hairball down the stairs, past Vi Clops' office, and straight to the forbidden basement.

It was foolproof.

Unless, of course, you're working with fools.

"Is InvisiBill in place?" I whisper to Hairball, tapping the staircase banister. I survey the foyer but don't see signs of him anywhere. "He was going to give us a signal when he was in place."

"No clue," Hairball whispers back.

Stanphibian is standing outside Vi Clops' office. He smiles and gives me a thumbs up.

Wait, why is he giving me a thumbs up? I look to the other side for InvisiBill. Did he give a signal?

"Uh-oh," Hairball says.

Uh-oh? Uh-oh, what?

But when I look back down at Stanphibian, I see him entering Vi Clops' office!

"Stan, wait!" Hairball whispers firmly, but Stanphibian has already gone inside.

"What are yer doin' here?" comes Vi Clops' deep, rumbling voice.

Stay calm, Bram. Stanphibian is just going to have to talk for a while until InvisiBill shows up.

Then, I smack my hand into my forehead.

Stanphibian barely ever talks! We're doomed!

Suddenly, someone pushes past me from behind, nearly knocking me down the stairs.

"Sorry," InvisiBill whispers. "Had to make a potty."

"Seriously?" Hairball says.

"Sorry, young one," I hear Vi Clops say. "But I ain't understandin' yer. I'm takin' yer back upstairs to bed."

Oh no! She's coming this way! I try to find

somewhere to hide but my only option is to duck behind Hairball—which isn't an option at all!

Suddenly, I see Vi Clops' large foot in the doorway.

"Follow me," Vi Clops says.

The next thing I know she's standing in the foyer! All twenty feet of her!

CRASH!

The sound of glass shattering echoes through the foyer, and when I look over I see one of the hanging pictures smashed on the floor. The frame is busted and glass is everywhere.

Holy cow! InvisiBill destroyed school property to make a distraction. That's not good.

"What's goin' on?" Vi Clops says, her giant eye darting to the other side of the room. Then, she STOMPS past the stairwell.

Thank goodness! She didn't see us!

I glance back down to find Stanphibian waving at us with his webbed hand. I nod, and Hairball and I race down the stairs and dash under the stairwell through a maze of corridors.

The last time I came this way was when we snuck out of Monster House to stop that grave robbery. I sure hope things work out better this time. I stick close to Hairball as he navigates his way through the seemingly endless twists and turns. Fortunately, he knows this place like the back of his furry hand.

After what feels like hours, we make a final turn, and Hairball stops short in front of a door that would look pretty ordinary if it weren't for the yellow caution tape, multiple locks, and 'DANGER! DO NOT OPEN

UNDER ANY CIRCUMSTANCES!' sign.

"We're here," Hairball says. "You know, in case you didn't notice."

"Oh, I noticed," I say, counting all of the locks. There are five in total.

"Let me break those for you," he says.

But as soon as he reaches for one, I stop him.

"Hold on," I say. "You remember Faustius' door, don't you? I bet these locks are cursed."

"Right," he says. pulling his hand back. "Good call. So, how are you going to get down there then?"

"The vampire way," I say. "Wish me luck."

"You'll need more than luck," Hairball says. "Look, I don't want to freak you out, but I've heard a three-headed monster lives down there. And there is that story about a kid who went down there and was never seen again."

"You know," I say. "I'd appreciate it if you stopped talking now."

"Sorry," he says. "Just want you to be prepared."

"I'm sure it's just an urban legend," I say. But in the pit of my stomach, I'm not so sure. I mean, I've encountered some crazy stuff over the last few months.

"I hope so," Hairball says. "For your sake."

"Gee, thanks," I say. "See you soon."

Then, I focus on becoming a mist. I envision myself as a vapor cloud, flowing seamlessly through the cracks of the door. I hold that vision in my mind, focusing only on that goal, and suddenly, I feel tingly all over.

The next thing I know, my body feels light, like it's pulling itself apart. And then I flow through the cracks of the basement door and collect myself on the other side.

Once I'm pulled together, I focus again on becoming a kid, and when I transform, I'm standing on the top step of an old stone staircase. Well, that was easy. Now I just need to take care of business. But when I look down the staircase, I realize I can't see a thing. It's pitch dark and my eyes don't seem to be adjusting.

Hmmm. That's weird. I blink my eyes a few times and then open them wide, but my vision doesn't change.

What's going on here?

Then, a lightbulb goes off.

If I thought the door was cursed, then I bet the darkness may be a curse too. I bet Van Helsing did that to deter visitors who managed to get past the door. Well, if that's the case, then this is going to be way creepier than I imagined. I sure hope the camera has a powerful flash setting.

Suddenly, my heart drops to my toes.

The camera!

I feel inside my pocket to make sure it's still there and it is. Whew! I didn't realize I could transport objects with me when I went into mist-form, but I guess that's why my clothes stay on my body when I go back to kid-form. I don't understand how that works, but it sure beats standing here naked.

Then, my head bumps into something high against the wall. I lean over and feel it with my hand. It's a lantern. Perfect! I grab it off the hook and turn the dial, and it lights up the space around me. Well, that's helpful. Now I can see a few feet in every direction.

Okay, here goes nothing. I take a deep breath and make my way down the twisting staircase. Judging by the stone walls and dusty floor, this place is really, really old. And about halfway down I notice a hanging wooden sign that reads:

DANGER!
TURN BACK NOW!

Well, that's comforting.

Believe me, I'd love nothing more than to heed that warning, but I know I can't. After all, I don't want to let my team down again. All I need to do is find one of the Artifacts of Virtue hidden somewhere down here and snap a photo. How hard could that be?

It's not until I hit the bottom of the staircase that I have my answer, because I'm standing in the center of a large chamber surrounded by a dozen corridors.

Are you kidding me? Which way am I supposed to go? I turn aimlessly in a circle as a million thoughts fly through my brain at once. Which corridor should I pick first? What if I pick the wrong one? What if I get lost down here forever? What if I die of starvation?

Speaking of starvation, I haven't eaten anything since dinner. Normally, I'd be fine until breakfast, but what if I'm stuck here past breakfast? And if I use my super-speed, I may get through some of these corridors quicker, but I'll just end up making myself weaker.

And that wouldn't be good if there really is a three-headed monster down here.

Okay, get it together. There's no science to this. I'm just going to have to pick a corridor and go for it. I raise my lantern, searching for any clues as to which way to go, but the corridors all look the same.

So, I pick the one straight ahead.

As I move forward, I realize I'm walking through a cold and musty tunnel that looks strangely familiar. Unlit torches hang from the rock walls every ten feet or so and I hear the sound of running water overhead.

That's when it hits me.

This was the tunnel I saw in my dream!

I stoop beneath the low ceiling when my lantern reveals something that makes my heart stop.

Footprints.

Heading in the same direction I'm going.

Someone is down here.

"H-Hello?" I call out, my voice echoing through the tunnel.

Then, I wonder why I did that. I might as well have doused myself in ketchup and told the three-headed monster it was snack time! At this point I could turn back—I probably should turn back—but then I would have failed Aura and the others. So, I take another breath and follow the footprints.

My pace quickens as I weave my way through the tunnel. But it's not until I step directly on one of the footprints that I notice something else.

The footprints match my shoe size.

I shake my head in disbelief. Something is not right, but I can't stop. I need to see where this goes, so I follow the tunnel to the end.

And that's when I see the iron vault door.

And it's wide open.

CLASSIFIED

Person(s) of Interest

CODE NAME: NONE

REAL NAME: VIOLET CLOPS

BASE OF OPERATIONS: VAN HELSING ACADEMY

D.S.I.

FACTS: Violet Clops (a.k.a. 'Vi Clops') is the Residence Hall Manager of Monster House – the living quarters for students of the Van Helsing Academy. She is responsible for ensuring the safety of students on campus. Her origin and relationship with Van Helsing is unknown.

Category:	Supernatural
Sub-Type:	Cyclops
Height:	20'4"
Weight:	535 lbs

FIELD OBSERVATIONS:

- Angers easily
- Incredibly strong
- Requires an extreme number of daily calories
- Falls asleep after consuming large meals

STATUS: ACTIVE TARGET

DEPARTMENT OF SUPERNATURAL INVESTIGATIONS

CHAPTER EIGHT

RATS AGAIN!

I'm in total shock.

The vault door is… open?

And the footprints that led me here match my shoe size exactly! My mind is working on overdrive. I mean, I can't help but put two and two together.

I thought it was all just a bad dream. Yet, the evidence in front of me is telling me something else. I clearly remember walking down this very same tunnel and grabbing the wheel that opens the vault door. I couldn't stop myself. And now that I'm standing here in person, there's no denying it.

It wasn't a dream at all.

Somehow, I must have come down here after helping Rage go to bed. And when he woke me up, I had no clue where I was, yet I was lying in my bed with my shoes on. But how did I even get here? I had no idea where the basement door was even located. I needed Hairball to take me there.

Then, something else makes me shudder.

The voice.

That cold, raspy voice who was trying to convince me to open the door.

The hairs on the back of my neck stand on end.

I-I know that voice.

It-It couldn't be him. But then I remember that flapping sound. And the fact that he called me by my first name. But that's impossible, right?

I mean, if it was him, he was… in my head?

Count Dracula was in my head!

No, it couldn't be. The last time I saw him, he was a shell of himself. His spirit had just been revived inside a mish-mashed skeleton of dead people. He was skin and bones and whiter than a ghost. But it's been months since then. He could be stronger by now. Much stronger.

But why would he come here?

Van Helsing is his greatest enemy. He'd be risking his own life coming to the Van Helsing Academy. But then I remember looking into his red, evil eyes, and watching his mouth curl into a sinister smile as he told me: 'Until next time.'

Does that mean he's coming for me?

I try wiping the thought from my mind, but it won't go away. Suddenly, a burst of cold air blows through the tunnel and I shiver. That's when I notice the vault door swaying on its hinges. Maybe I'm just being paranoid. I mean, I never actually saw Dracula in my dream. Maybe it wasn't him? Maybe my mind is playing tricks on me?

But as I stare into the darkness beyond the open doorframe I get a curious thought.

What's on the other side?

I step towards the dark opening but stop myself. This is all strange enough, do I really need to see what's through the door too? Probably not, but as soon as I take a step backward, my curiosity gets the best of me and I lunge forward, extending the lantern through the doorframe.

SCREEEEECCCHHHH!

Suddenly, a million tiny creatures scatter up and away before my eyes!

I jump back, my heart pumping like crazy, and I barely manage to hang on to the lantern. Those were bugs. Like, lots of bugs. But what were they doing there?

And that's when I notice the door opens into a hollow tree trunk. And in the middle of the tree trunk is an iron ladder, climbing straight up the inside of the twisted, hollowed-out tree!

At first, I'm confused. Then, it clicks.

This hollow tree must be a secret entrance from the outside—right into the basement of the Van Helsing Academy!

I'm shocked. I mean, I didn't know this entrance existed. But someone did. And whoever knew, must have passed that information to Count Dracula!

Okay, I think I've seen enough. So, I step back inside, slam the door closed, and lock the vault door.

Well, I know one thing, no one else is getting in.

But the question is, will I ever get out?

SSSNNAAARRRLLL!

The growl echoes through the tunnel and I spin around, but there's nothing there.

Two thoughts flash through my mind. One, there really is a three-headed monster. And two, the last kid who came down here never made it back.

I feel like I'm gonna puke.

Okay, I didn't want to use my super-speed, but given present circumstances, I may need to rethink my plan. I'm just here to snap a picture of one of the Artifacts of Virtue. I don't care if it's the bell, book, or candle.

But then again, maybe I should just abandon this little dare and get the heck out of here? After all, I'm not interested in becoming someone's lunch. I think the team would forgive me. They wouldn't respect me, but they'd probably forgive me.

Of course, if I did use my super-speed, I could jet through these corridors until I found one of the artifacts and take the stupid picture. But if I run into whatever made that noise, I might not have the strength to fight back. I don't know what to do, but I do know one thing, I can't just stand here.

Just then, I hear pitter-patter noises behind me, like clawed feet walking across a hard surface, followed by—

"...dangerous me said."

"Hear you me do but see if it made it, we must. Then

reward we collect."

I lift my lantern high, and my jaw hits the floor. To my astonishment, I see a tall, thin rat squeezing through a crack in the stone wall. And then I see a second one who is smaller and fatter than the first.

Now, I'm no expert in rat identification, but these two look very, very familiar. And if they are who I think they are, then they owe me big time.

"Done is job," the thin one says. "Me food reward now me want, not danger."

"Well, too bad, that is," I say, speaking in my best Rat. "Because danger you found."

The fat one turns around and his eyes bulge out. "The pink one!" he yells. "Run!"

The fat one takes off, but I'm too fast for the thin one, grabbing him before he knows what hit him.

"Let go!" he yells, trying to sink his claws in my hand.

"Knock it off," I say, tightening my grip. "Or squeeze I will and gone you be."

"Help!" the thin rat yells.

But the fat one just stands there.

"Help me you will," I say. "Or friend goes bye-bye."

"So?" the fat rat says, shrugging his shoulders.

"So!" the thin one says outraged, pointing down at his friend. "Save me you must!"

"Must me?" the fat rat says. "Care me don't. Food more for me."

"What?" the thin rat yells.

But I'm not fooled. These two are partners in crime. According to Van Helsing, they were the ones who sold me out to the Dark Ones after I was dumped into that kid dungeon at the New England School for Troubled Boys. It's funny how long ago that seems now.

Then, I realize something.

If these two are walking around here so casually, they must know about the secret entrance. In fact, I bet they're the ones who sold that information to Count Dracula! And come to think of it, I bet they've also been down here a million times, which means they probably know where other things are located.

Like the Artifacts of Virtue!

But I know they won't just tell me. These guys are mercenaries. If I'm going to get them to take me there, I'm going to have to negotiate a deal—even if I don't intend to hold up my end of the bargain.

"Okay," I say. "No care for life of friend me see. But me have other things you may be interested in, like secrets."

"Secrets?" the fat one repeats, his little ears perking up. "Of secrets what kind?"

"Important secrets," I say. "Secrets worth much food. Much, much, much food. But me no tell. Secrets too important."

"Much, much, much food?" the fat rat says, his voice rising with excitement. "Me your secrets tell?"

"Play you not," the thin one says. "Pink one me bite now."

But as he opens his mouth, the fat rat and I both yell "No!"

"Fool!" the fat one yells. "No bite Pink One! Pink One has secrets worth much, much, much food. Secrets me want to hear."

"Fine," the thin one says, crossing his arms. "Me want much, much, much food also."

"Tell you me will," I say. "But first me you help."

The fat rat doesn't respond and instead puts his hands on his hips. He looks like a furry teacup, but I can tell his tiny mind is churning. I need to be careful with this guy.

"Okay," he says finally. "Me help you. But then secrets tell you will."

"And me release!" the thin one says. "Me release!"

"Deal," I say. "And me release only after you help."

"Okay," the fat one says. "What you want?"

"Me want you to lead me to bell, book, or candle," I say. "Me know you know where they are."

The two rats look at one another and break out into squeaky laughter.

"What?" I say.

"Nothing," the fat rat says suspiciously. "Show you we will. Hurry but you must."

I nod, and the fat rat takes off like a mini rocket, heading back towards the tunnel entrance. I try to keep up, but the floor is uneven and I don't want to drop the thin rat or the lantern. Plus, I'm keeping a lookout for whatever made that growling noise.

For some reason, heading back seems to take even longer, but then, we suddenly exit the tunnel and I'm back in the main chamber. I'm more than relieved to see the stairwell leading upstairs again, and nearly talk myself into taking it, but I just can't do it. Like it or not, I'm committed to seeing this through.

"Left we go!" yells the thin rat.

"No!" the fat one yells back. "Right it is."

"Right is taken," the thin rat complains.

"Shut your snout," the fat one yells. "Me lead."

"Ohhh," the thin one finally says.

"Um, what's wrong?" I ask the thin rat.

"Oh, nothing," he says casually. "All good."

The fat rat enters the corridor diagonally to the right and I follow, but I can't help but think that something is not 'all good.' The thin one made it sound like we're going the wrong way. And what did he mean by 'it is taken?'

I know I can't trust these rats, but it's not like I've got a choice. Right now, I just have to go with the flow and hope my fake secrets pay off.

As we run through the tunnel, I realize how eerily similar it is to the one we just came out of. I mean, if you weren't keeping track of where you've been, it would be impossible to tell one tunnel from the next. Nevertheless, we travel for what seems like an eternity until we hit a feature that stops us cold—a rock wall blocking our path.

"We here," the fat one says, pointing to the wall. "What seek you be through there."

"But that wall be rock?" I say confused.

"No, Pink One," he says. "Touch."

Since my hands are full, I lift my right leg, but when I try making contact with the rock, my leg passes right through. There's nothing there. It's an illusion!

Of course it is.

This basement has more tricks than a magic shop.

"Now, tell secret," the fat one says.

"And me release," the thin one says.

"Um, no," I say. "Me know not what is back there. You come me with, then me tell secret."

The rats shoot each other another look.

Something is up.

"Very well," the fat one says. "Follow." Then, he darts straight through the imaginary rock wall.

I'm about to grill the thin one but he turns the other way. Okay, he's not giving up any info. Well, here goes nothing. I take a deep breath and then step through the rock wall.

When we come out the other side I do a double take, because we're no longer standing in a narrow tunnel, but rather in a large, stone chamber. And in the center of the chamber is a white pedestal, which is holding a green, glowing object.

"The Bell of Virtue!" I exclaim.

I-I can't believe it. It's real!

It's shaped like an upside-down cup, with an ornate handle that looks like a serpent wrapped around a pole. And the whole thing is surrounded by a translucent green glow. I can't take my eyes off of it.

"Now secret!" the fat rat demands.

"Right," I say, snapping back to reality.

Well, to my surprise, the rats delivered on their promise. Unfortunately, I've got nothing for them. I guess they can consider it payback for what they did to me. All I need to do now is get a picture.

I bend over and put down the thin rat and the lantern. He immediately runs over to the fat one and bops him on the head.

"Hate you me do!" he says.

"Ow!" the fat one says, rubbing his noggin. "Now secret!" he demands.

"Sorry," I say, fishing in my pocket for my camera, "but there is no secret. Thanks for bringing me here. Now run along while you still have the chance."

"No secret!" they yell.

"Surprising not." the thin one says with a chuckle. "Pink One think he fool us. But me fool him." And then he pulls out a camera from behind his back.

Huh? Wait a second.

I reach into my pockets again, but my camera is gone! That rat stole my camera!

The rats start cackling again.

"You fool," the thin one says. "Now you fight for life."

Fight for my life? What's he talking about?

GRRRRRRRRR!

Then, something leaps over my head and lands in a crouched position in front of the pedestal!

"Luck good!" the fat one yells.

"No, luck bad!" the thin one yells. "Luck very bad!"

And as the rats scamper off with my camera, the creature in front of me rises and fixes me with its red, luminous eyes.

I stumble backward in shock.

I-I can't believe it.

It's… Tiger-boy?

CHAPTER NINE

FOR WHOM THE BELL TOLLS

I don't know what's worse, facing an angry tiger-kid or being outwitted by a pair of rats!

Well, I've got to hand it to them, those annoying vermin got me again. They knew Tiger-boy was hanging out in this chamber, and now they've run off with my camera, ending my chance to prove the Artifacts of Virtue are real.

Awesome.

After all of this effort, I'll have absolutely nothing to show for it when I get back. Of course, there's still the open question if I'll even make it back. After all, Tiger-boy is standing between me and the Bell of Virtue, looking none too pleased to see me.

What I can't figure out is what he's doing here in the first place? Did he come through the vault door? And if so, why?

"You know," I say, "we've got to stop meeting like this."

"GRRRRR," he responds.

"Okay, okay," I say, raising my hands and taking a step back. "No need to get testy."

But then I realize something.

Crawler said the Artifacts of Virtue guard the academy from evil. He said that nothing evil at heart could step inside their protective barrier. So, if the Bell of Virtue hasn't moved from its pedestal, and the Tiger-boy is standing here, then maybe he's not evil at all?

I mean, he's not attacking me now, and he didn't attack me at Moreau Labs either. The only thing he did there was point me to Cat-girl.

So, if he's not evil, then maybe he's good?

I stare into his red-eyes and flash a friendly smile.

"I just want you to know," I say, "that we are taking good care of your friend."

His eyes widen, and that's when I notice he actually looks worse than before. His wheezing seems louder, and he's got more bare patches in his fur.

"We brought her here," I continue. "To the school up above. She's getting cared for by one of the best doctors in the world. She's doing much better."

Tiger-boy opens his mouth to speak, but only a small growl comes out.

"We can help you too," I offer, stepping closer to him. "If you want."

"SNARRRRLLL!" he growls.

I freeze. Well, clearly he doesn't want our help.

"Okay," I say. "No problem. Can you at least tell me

who you are? Or what you're even doing here? If you want to see your friend I can take you to her."

I wait for some kind of response, but he just stares at me. And as I look into his eyes, I feel like he's trying to tell me something. I just don't know what. Maybe I'll try again.

"Are you sure you don't want help?" I ask, slowly stepping towards him. "I have friends that can help you. Like Headmaster Van Helsing. He'll be happy to—"

RRROOOAAARRR!

I cover my ears but his growl is deafening, echoing through the chamber. And then, to my surprise, he snatches the Bell of Virtue from the pedestal!

"Wait!" I yell. "What are you—"

But before I can finish my sentence, he jumps over my head and bounds through the rock wall illusion! For a nano-second I'm stunned, and then realization sets in. He just swiped the Bell of Virtue!

Without the bell, the school will lose its Supernatural protection from evil. I've got to stop him!

I turn on super-speed mode and dash after him, but he's nowhere to be seen. I mean, I'm fast but he seems to be even faster! And as I race through the tunnel, the only thing going through my mind is that I blew it.

I'm the one who left the vault door open. I'm the one who failed to stop Tiger-boy. I'm the one who put the whole school in danger.

Suddenly, I exit the tunnel back into the central

chamber. I see the stairwell leading upstairs and the eleven other corridors. I spin around, searching for some clue as to which way he went. I scan the floor for footprints, pawprints, any prints, but I don't see anything! And I'm so turned around I can't even figure out which tunnel leads back to the vault door. Suddenly, I hear—

SCREECH!

SLAM!

And after the echo subsides, there's nothing.

Tiger-boy went out the vault door!

He escaped.

And now there's nothing left to do but go upstairs and face the music.

***

Van Helsing's face hasn't moved a muscle.

I mean, I just spent the last thirty minutes telling him all about the Howlers' dare, my venture into the forbidden basement, and how Tiger-boy ran off with the Bell of Virtue—and all he did was stare at me.

Honestly, I don't even know if Van Helsing is still breathing, but now that I've finished my tale, he hasn't said a word. Instead, we're all just sitting in his office in awkward silence. The Monstrosities are here, along with Crawler, and all I want to do is jump into Van Helsing's raging fire.

And while Van Helsing's face is a study in stone,

Crawler's eyes are practically bugging out of his head. I already felt guilty enough, but now I feel even worse since I'll probably get Crawler in trouble for telling us about the Artifacts of Virtue in the first place.

I try reading Van Helsing's steely expression to guess what he's thinking. The last time we got in major trouble he let us set our own punishments. Something tells me he might think differently this time. Especially after listening to what I had to say.

I mean, I pretty much told him everything, including being tricked by those rats, which I admit wasn't one of my finer moments.

But there were a few things I left out.

With everyone standing here, I couldn't find the courage to tell him about my 'dream' that wasn't really a dream at all. And I sort of left out the part about me being the one who opened the vault door. I couldn't even imagine my team's reaction if I dropped that stink bomb.

I mean, what would they think of me then?

Honestly, I'm not even sure what I think of me right now. Between this blunder and nearly drinking Rage's blood, I feel like I'm totally losing control of myself.

And I'm scared.

I rub my eyes with my palms.

I don't know what to do next.

"We are all in grave danger," Van Helsing says suddenly, snapping me back to attention.

"Here we go," InvisiBill says.

"The Artifacts of Virtue only work as a unit," Van Helsing continues. "Removing one negates the power of all. They were passed down to me from my grandfather, Abraham Van Helsing, who stumbled across their legend in ancient texts while researching methods to defeat Count Dracula. My grandfather had to overcome great personal danger to recover each artifact, which had been scattered across the globe."

"I'm so sorry," I say.

"It is not your fault," Van Helsing says. "Clearly, Count Dracula learned the Supernatural objects were here, protecting the academy from his influence, and he executed a plan to remove this barrier."

But Van Helsing doesn't understand. It was my fault. And according to what he just said that voice on the other side of the door must have been Count Dracula after all!

I feel like I'm gonna puke.

"Wait," Rage says. "Are you saying that Count Dracula could now come on campus?"

"Yes," Van Helsing says. "He is free to walk the grounds, but there is one limit to his reach. As long as you remain indoors, you may be safe, for a vampire must be invited inside a building to gain entry. But that rule does not apply to his minions."

Well, there's something else I just learned. I didn't realize a vampire needed an invitation just to enter a building. But I guess that doesn't apply to me because I'm half-human. I have no problem going in and out of places.

"But here's something I don't get," Aura says. "How did that tiger-dude get in the basement anyway? If the Artifacts of Virtue were doing their job, then I thought evil couldn't step foot on school grounds?"

"An excellent question," Van Helsing says. "But I believe there is only one possible explanation. The perpetrator was likely not evil at heart. Only truly dark souls cannot breach the Artifacts' protective barrier. Those who are not evil, but merely misguided, are not impeded."

So, I was right. Tiger-boy isn't evil.

"Wait," Hairball says. "I don't understand. If the tiger-kid isn't a bad guy, then why did he steal the bell?"

"Count Dracula is a master of manipulation," Van Helsing says. "Who knows what he promised the child in exchange for the Bell of Virtue? But whatever it was, clearly it was motivation enough. We may never know the answer."

"Well, I know how to get some answers," Aura says. "Let's go wake up Cat-girl. I bet she knows what's going on. Come to think of it, I bet she's the one who opened the vault door in the first place."

"Yeah!" Stanphibian says unexpectedly.

"No," Van Helsing says. "We will not subject that poor child to additional trauma. She is still recovering from her time in Dr. Moreau's clutches. When she comes to, we will gain more answers if she has them. But until then, we will continue to operate under our mission as a sanctuary for monster children. Is that understood?"

"Yes," Aura mutters, reluctantly.

As Van Helsing looks us in the eyes, I feel relief. I mean, I wouldn't want that girl to be blamed for something I did. And if Van Helsing hadn't stepped in, I'd be forced to tell everyone that I was the one who opened the door. I know I'll tell them eventually, but first I need to figure some things out.

Like, what's wrong with me?

"Monstrosities," Van Helsing says, "I would like to thank you all for bringing this situation to my attention. We will discuss your punishment when I return."

"Punishment?" InvisiBill says. "But we told you everything."

"As I expect you would," Van Helsing says, tightening his scarf. "But we cannot forget your actions violated our rules. Therefore, we will discuss the consequences at another time. At the moment, we have a bell to recover."

"We'll come too," Aura says, clenching her fists.

"No," Van Helsing says. "All of you will be going back to Monster House to await instructions from Professor Hexum. I will be leading a small team in pursuit of the tiger boy. Based on Bram's account of his agility, he is likely far away by now. But we should be able to pick up his trail and track him to his destination."

"Um, didn't you say it's not safe here anymore?" Hairball asks.

"That is true," Van Helsing says. "But it is much safer if you are all together under the watchful eye of our faculty. Crawler, can you please collect Professor Morris and get ready for our journey? And please ask Professor Hexum to wait outside my office."

"Yes, Headmaster," Crawler says, heading out, but not before shooting me a disappointed look.

"As for the rest of you," Van Helsing says. "I will notify Professor Holmwood, Professor Seward, Mrs. Clops, and Dr. Renfield to collect you and your fellow students at Monster House. I expect all of you to follow their instructions without exception. You are all dismissed. Except for Bram."

As I watch the others file out with their heads hanging low, I shift nervously in my chair. This is not going to be good. I mean, I crossed the line the most by actually going into the forbidden basement. Van Helsing has to be royally upset with me.

It's only after the door to his office finally shuts that he looks at me and says—

"Your life is at risk."

"W-What?" I say, swallowing hard. Of all the things I thought he'd say, I certainly wasn't expecting that.

"Your life is at risk," he repeats. "With the removal of the Bell of Virtue, the academy is no longer a safe haven for you. Now, nothing is stopping Count Dracula and his minions from coming onto campus and attacking you."

My stomach drops.

"So," I say, "are you telling me Count Dracula had the bell stolen just to… kill me?"

"Possibly," Van Helsing says. "After all, you are the only thing standing between him and immortality. Remember, only a vampire can truly kill another vampire. A fatal blow from one vampire to another will not only destroy his mortal body, but his spirit as well, and that is the only way he will forever cease to exist. And as far as I am aware, you are the only two vampires left in existence."

"B-But," I stammer, "won't he make more vampires? Isn't that what vampires do?"

"Dracula is many things," Van Helsing says, "but he is no fool. Since his reemergence, I have monitored the globe for reports of new vampires. But to my surprise, there has been nothing. That tells me he has finally learned his lesson."

"Lesson?" I say. "What lesson?"

"That creating more vampires merely creates more enemies who could destroy him," Van Helsing says. "Dracula is still weak, and he will not compromise his existence. I believe he is living off of animal blood for the time being, but that does not make you any safer."

"Well," I say, feeling more panicked by the second, "if I'm not safe here, where should I go?"

"Nowhere," Van Helsing says, rising from his chair and picking up his Crossbow of Purity.

"Um, really?" I say. "But you just said I'm not safe here?"

"You are not safe anywhere," he says. "But you also cannot afford to waste time traveling from town to town like a nomad. Here you can continue your training immediately under the supervision of Professor Hexum and Dr. Renfield. They will be by your side at all times, helping you to become both physically and mentally stronger for a possible encounter with Count Dracula."

"O-Okay," I mutter.

I can't believe this.

"Now I must go," Van Helsing says, putting his hand on my shoulder. "To protect us all, we must find the Bell of Virtue as quickly as possible. Do you understand everything I have told you?"

"Y-Yes," I stammer.

"Very well," he says. "Professor Hexum will be waiting outside my door for you. You must focus day and night on becoming the most powerful vampire you can be. Good luck, Bram."

"Y-Yeah," I manage to say. "You too."

But as he exits, my mind is focused on only one terrible image.

Count Dracula.

CHAPTER TEN

THAT'S JUST FANGTASTIC

"He will destroy you!"

I hear Hexum's voice in the distance, but I don't want to listen. I'm in full bat-form, gliding through the air without the greatest of ease. He's been putting me through death-defying drills for hours, and quite frankly I'm exhausted. But he promised me this is the last one, so I'm gonna go with that.

I turn the corner and swoop down over the target, a yellow number 2 pencil. All I have to do is pick it up with my little bat feet and fly back to Hexum before the timer runs out.

It sounds easy.

Unless, of course, someone is firing arrows at you.

THWIP!

I flap hard, lifting myself up just as the arrow zips by, its feathers brushing my derriere. Whew! That was way too close for comfort. I can't believe Van Helsing left me in the care of this psycho.

This time, Hexum is training me to sharpen my

radar—and I can tell you it's working on overdrive! I send my signals out again.

THWIP! THWIP!

Two more arrows! Heading straight for my wings!

I rotate sideways and suck in my gut as the arrows whizz past on each side. Thank goodness I had a light lunch. But this guy is nuts!

His training is going to kill me!

I set myself over the pencil and drop down, wrapping my feet around its hexagonal barrel. Then, I pull up into the air.

Time to end my torture once and for all.

I spot Hexum at the far end of the gymnasium. He's leaning on his walking stick and looking at his watch. I had one minute to get the job done and based on all of the time I used dodging killer arrows, I'm pretty sure I'm right on the bubble. But now I should be in the clear.

I'm going to make it.

I pulse out my radar one last time but nothing pings back, except for a strange reading from the pencil I'm carrying. It seems… bigger? And when I look down, I'm no longer holding a yellow pencil, but a dark green snake with yellow bands running down its body!

It's a King Cobra!

SSSSSSSSSS!

AAAAHHH!

I open my toes and the snake plummets. But right before it hits the floor it turns back into a pencil!

"Time!" Hexum barks, as I fly over his head.

What happened? I land on the ground and focus on becoming a kid again, transforming back to my normal self. Then, I look at Hexum's smug face and I realize he's tricked me again. That pencil was never a snake. And those arrows weren't real either. Hexum put all of those things in my mind.

"You failed, Mr. Murray," Hexum says. "When will you learn that your mind is your weakest instrument. If you are easily tricked, you will be easily defeated."

"What can I say? You got me," I admit.

"I did," Hexum says. "But luckily for you, I am only your teacher. Count Dracula is your enemy. His powers of deception are legendary, and he will show you no mercy. If you are going to defeat him, you will need to harden your mind to see beyond the obvious. Shall we try again?"

"No!" I say, with more passion than I intended. "I mean, sorry, but I'm just… tired. And you promised that was the last one. Can't we take a break? Please?"

Hexum stares at me for a few seconds, drumming his fingers on the silver cap of his walking stick.

"Very well," he says. "It appears to be Dr. Renfield's shift anyway. I guess time does fly when you're having fun. Good evening, Mr. Murray. And good luck."

Good luck? What's that supposed to mean.

But I guess I won't have to wait long to find out, because as soon as Hexum leaves, Dr. Renfield enters the gymnasium. He smiles when he sees me and I instantly get a case of the heebie-jeebies.

I don't know why this guy creeps me out so much. Maybe it's because he put me in a trance and embarrassed me in front of the whole class. Or maybe it's because he seemed so excited to study me like I was some kind of a lab animal. I don't know what it is, but there's something strange about him.

"You must be tired, Mr. Murray," he says, walking towards me. "But don't worry, we won't be doing anything physical this evening. That is Professor Hexum's area of expertise. Headmaster Van Helsing has tasked me with helping you to better understand yourself."

"Can't I just hang out with my friends?" I ask. "I haven't seen them in a while and I just want to relax."

"Unfortunately, no," he says. "It is a dangerous time, Mr. Murray. And right now, relaxation is a luxury you cannot afford."

"So, you think Dracula is coming for me also, don't you?" I ask, my voice rising. "Hexum is convinced he is."

"Shall we sit?" Dr. Renfield suggests.

Why not? I guess I'm gonna be here a while, so I nod and plop myself down on the gym floor. Dr. Renfield follows, positioning himself directly across from me.

"Now, to answer your question," he says. "Yes, I do believe it is likely. But I also know there are other things here at the Van Helsing Academy that are of great interest to him. However, if you are his true target, then you must be prepared to defend yourself. Now, shall we begin?"

"Hang on," I say. "Are you saying I might not be his target? That there are other things here that interest him more? Like, what kinds of things?"

"Oh, I do not think that is very important right now," Dr. Renfield says dismissively. "We should use our time more wisely."

"No," I insist. "I think I have a right to know."

Dr. Renfield looks hesitant to tell me, but right now I'll take any reason for why Dracula wants to invade the school as long as it isn't me.

"Very well," Dr. Renfield says. "But after this, we will have to begin."

"Okay," I say. "Sounds fair."

"How should I start?" he asks. "Well, you are aware that Headmaster Van Helsing is a collector of Supernatural lore. After all, you have seen his Crossbow of Purity and, of course, the Bell of Virtue. But it is rumored that Van Helsing also possesses many other Supernatural artifacts—one of which is of particular interest to Count Dracula."

"Really?" I say, my curiosity peaked. "What is it?"

Dr. Renfield peers over his shoulder to ensure the coast is clear, and then he looks back at me. I lean forward, eager for him to tell me, but I can see he's not quite sure if he should say anything. I need to convince him.

"I swear," I say, putting my hand over my heart. "I

won't tell anybody. I'll keep it to myself."

"Very well," Dr. Renfield says. "It is an object of great power. An object known as the Spear of Darkness."

The Spear of Darkness?

Why does that sound so familiar? Then, it clicks. I vaguely remember Professor Seward talking about it in his Supernatural History class.

"Based on your expression," Dr. Renfield says, "it looks like you have heard of it?"

"Yes," I say. "I mean, I've heard its name mentioned before in class. What does it do?"

"According to ancient scriptures," he says, "the Spear of Darkness gives the one wielding it the power to blanket the sky in a shroud of darkness, blotting out the sun."

"Blotting out the sun?" I say. "You mean, like, getting rid of daylight?"

"That is correct," Dr. Renfield says. "As you know all too well, sunlight is the enemy of the vampire. When vampires are directly exposed to sunlight for an extended period, their mortal bodies will be destroyed by the light. That is why Count Dracula operates only at night. Now, imagine a world without daylight? There will be nothing stopping Count Dracula from terrorizing the innocent at all hours, day and night. He will grow stronger faster, quickly becoming unstoppable."

I swallow hard.

I mean, I know exactly what he's talking about. My

skin burns easily when I'm exposed to sunlight, but I never imagined that anything could blot out the sun. I guess it would solve my sunburn problems, but that's just being selfish. There's no way I'd ever want Count Dracula roaming around uninhibited.

"You can see why obtaining the Spear of Darkness would be so valuable to Count Dracula," Dr. Renfield says. "But unfortunately, I do not know if it is truly here at the Van Helsing Academy or not. I was unable to ask Headmaster Van Helsing about it before he left, but if it is here, it will be up to us to protect it from Count Dracula and his minions, just as we need to protect you."

"Yeah," I say. "I would think so."

"If we only knew where it is hiding…" Dr. Renfield says, his voice trailing off. "Did Van Helsing ever discuss the Spear of Darkness with you—even as just a passing comment?"

"No," I say, wracking my brain, but I don't remember anything. "He's never mentioned it."

"Are you sure?" Dr. Renfield presses. "After all, this is very important. I'm sure he must have mentioned it at least one time. You just have to think harder."

"Um, okay," I say. I mean, I know finding the Spear of Darkness is important and all, but it's not like my answer is going to change.

But as I look into Dr. Renfield's eyes I realize I might have been wrong about him. After all, Van Helsing clearly trusts him, and it seems like he wants to stop

Count Dracula as badly as I do. So, maybe my first impression was wrong? Maybe I can put my trust in him?

"Dr. Renfield," I say. "I know you're an expert in what makes monsters tick, so I was wondering if you could, well, help me out. You see, some strange things have been happening to me lately. But I don't want to do the hypnosis thing, like, ever again."

"Of course, Mr. Murray," Dr. Renfield says, his eyebrows rising. "We don't have to use hypnosis. Why don't we just talk?" Then, he reaches into his shirt pocket and pulls out a tiny pad and a pen. "Please, tell me."

I consider telling him about my weird 'dream' but change my mind. Instead, I decide to tell him about the other thing that's been bothering me.

"Well," I say, "there was a situation where one of my friends was injured, and he was bleeding, and…"

I stop. This is just so embarrassing.

"Yes," Dr. Renfield says, encouraging me. "Please, go on. Do not worry. I have heard it all. I will not judge you."

"Well, okay," I say, feeling a little better about sharing. "I-I had this incredible urge to drink his blood. I-I didn't, but it was kind of hard not to. But it worries me. A lot."

"Worries you in what way?" Dr. Renfield asks, his voice sounding calm and even, like what I'm telling him isn't something to be worried about at all.

"Well," I say, "I-I've never wanted to drink anyone's

blood before. I mean, I only eat red food, but never blood. I-I just hope I'm not turning into a… a…"

"Vampire?" Dr. Renfield says, finishing my sentence for me. "But you are a vampire, Mr. Murray."

"No," I say. "I'm a half-vampire. My father was a vampire but my mother was human."

"Yes, of course," he says. "But as you get older, your father's vampire genes will likely try to dominate over your mother's human genes. This is not unusual when it comes to monster biology. In fact, it has been scientifically proven that Supernatural cells divide far more quickly than Natural cells. And as your Natural cells die through damage or aging, they are replaced by more and more Supernatural cells. Thus, over time, the molecular structure of your body will become less Natural and more Supernatural. And this transition will gradually impact your thoughts and behaviors."

Um, what?

My jaw is hanging open, because based on what he just said, my desire to drink Rage's blood wasn't a fluke at all, but rather a result of me becoming more and more of a vampire every single day!

I'm totally speechless.

"I know this is shocking information to absorb," Dr. Renfield says. "But based on what you have described, it appears to fit your situation. Do not despair. Not all half-breeds end up fully embracing their Supernatural side. A handful that I have studied were able to control their monster instincts and live relatively normal lives."

"That's great for them," I say. "But didn't you tell me you've never studied a vampire before?"

"Well," he says. "That is a fair point."

My mind is totally spinning right now.

Because now I not only have to stop Count Dracula, but I may need to stop myself!

I mean, I can't become a full-fledged vampire!

BOOM!

Suddenly, the gym doors fly open and Rage is standing in the doorway with a bizarre look on his face. It's great to see him, but what's he doing here? I thought he was being watched by the other professors with the rest of the kids in the auditorium.

"Bram! Dr. Renfield!" he yells. "Come quick!"

"Why?" I ask. "What's going on?"

"You've got to hurry!" he yells back. "Cat-girl finally woke up!"

CLASSIFIED

Person(s) of Interest

CODE NAME: None

REAL NAME: ALASTAIR HEXUM

BASE OF OPERATIONS: VAN HELSING ACADEMY

D.S.I.

FACTS: Alastair Hexum is the tenured Professor of Survival Skills at the Van Helsing Academy. He is a powerful mentalist with the unique ability to tap into a person's mind and alter their sense of reality. He is considered extremely dangerous and should not be confronted alone.

Category: Unknown

Sub-Type: Unknown

Height: 6'2"

Weight: 213 lbs

FIELD OBSERVATIONS:

- Sustained an unknown leg injury requiring use of a walking stick
- Extremely clever and highly observant
- Unpopular among his colleagues and students due to his abrasive personality

STATUS: ACTIVE TARGET

DEPARTMENT OF SUPERNATURAL INVESTIGATIONS

CHAPTER ELEVEN

THE TRUTH HURTS

By the time we reach the infirmary, I'm ready to check myself into the psychiatric ward.

I mean, Dr. Renfield basically told me the reason I wanted to suck Rage's blood is because my body is attacking itself! He said the vampire cells inside of me are slowly taking over the human cells inside of me. And if it continues at this pace, it'll only be a matter of time before I'm a full-fledged vampire!

The very thought makes me shudder.

I mean, what if I can't control myself?

"Through here," Rage says, entering the infirmary.

I follow him inside when it hits me. What if I become the vampire version of Rage? I mean, Rage loses all control when he turns into a purple monster. He has absolutely no clue where he's been or what he's done. If I become a full vampire and that happens to me, then no one around me is safe.

And what's even scarier is that I have no clue when this might happen. Who knows? It could take years or it could happen in a few hours. It's not like some alarm clock is going to go off telling me time's up. I could slip at any moment, but I know one thing, I will never put innocent lives in danger. No matter what.

"Over here," Rage says, snapping me back to reality.

As he passes through the reception area into the medical wing, I hold the door open for Dr. Renfield, who arrives huffing and puffing behind us from the long run over. Once he gets to the door, I catch up to Rage.

I've never seen the infirmary this empty before. But other than Rage, I guess all of the other kids are still in the auditorium. Well, all except for one, because floating inside one of the patient rooms is a very angry-looking ghost girl.

"It's about time you got here," Aura says. "Because I was just about to ask her the tough questions."

I look down at the infirmary bed to find the subject of Aura's interrogation staring back at me. It's Cat-girl, and she's awake! For the first time, I see her green, cat-like eyes, and it's clear she'd rather be anywhere else than here.

"Not so fast," Dr. Hagella says, entering the room with Dr. Renfield. "No one gave you permission to be in here. And now that our new friend has just woken up, she'll need some space to recover."

"Recover?" Aura says. "The only thing we should be trying to 'recover' right now is the Bell of Virtue her tiger-buddy stole."

"Tiger-buddy?" Cat-girl says, sitting up. "Peter? Is he here? Where is he?"

"Peter?" Aura says. "Who's Peter?"

"Then, he's not here," Cat-girl says, slumping back down into the bed.

"Um, sorry," Aura says. "But what are you even talking about?"

"Aura, please," Dr. Renfield says, holding up his right hand. "Give her a moment. I know we all would like answers, but she has been through quite a difficult experience." Then, he looks at Cat-girl and says, "Why don't we start with something simple? Can you tell us your name?"

"My… name?" she says. "Yes, I-I'm Katherine, but you can call me Kat. Or at least I was before all of this happened." Then, she runs her hand through her whiskers.

"Do you remember what happened?" I ask. "I mean if it isn't too hard to talk about."

"I… I remember some of it," Kat says, her brow furrowed. "But there are… gaps."

"That is quite alright," Dr. Renfield says, soothingly. "Just tell us what you can remember. Take as much time as you need."

Take as much time as you need? At first, I want to argue that we're running out of time. But then I remember Dr. Renfield is an expert in this area. If this is the pace he wants her to go at, it's probably for a good reason. But when I look over at Aura, she's tapping her foot impatiently.

"Okay," Kat says. "I'll… tell you what I remember. You see, we've always struggled. The 'we' being my twin brother and me. His name is Peter. Well, our dad died when we were young, and our mom held down three jobs just to make ends meet. Peter and I tried to help out where we could, but it was never enough. And then our mom met a new man. He wasn't a nice guy and treated us badly. Peter tried to stand up to him, but they had a big fight. And then…"

As her voice falls off, tears well up in her eyes.

"Do not worry," Dr. Renfield says, putting his hand on her arm. "You are doing just fine. Please continue."

"Well, after that, Peter said he was going to run away. He said he'd rather live on the streets than live in our house. I tried changing his mind, but I couldn't. He was set on leaving, but I couldn't let him go alone. I mean, he's like my other half. We've done everything together our whole lives. So, I knew I had to go with him, and later that night we left."

I swallow hard. Hearing her story reminds me so much of my own. There were so many foster homes I left in the middle of the night because I wasn't being treated right. Except, I was alone. At least they had each other.

"We went as far away as we could go," she says. "But we're just kids. We didn't have any money. We spent all of our time looking for food and finding safe places to sleep. I remember one time we even saw our faces on a 'Missing Persons' flier. I told him that maybe we should go back, but Peter just laughed and said, 'Are you kidding? Look, we're famous!'"

"Maybe we were, but we were also scared. But I couldn't just leave him out there. He's my brother, and I was going to protect him no matter what. And then, one night when we were in some back-alley looking for loose change, he… found us."

"Who?" Rage blurts out, totally enraptured by her story. "Who found you?"

"A man," she says. "He was dressed in all white, from his hat to his suit to his shoes. And parked behind him was an expensive-looking car with its own driver. Clearly, the man was rich, and at first, I wasn't sure he was even talking to us, but we were the only ones in the alley. He had gray eyes and a kind smile. He said we needed help, and he would be willing to help us if we would help him with a special project he was working on. He offered to feed us and let us stay in his home for as long as we wanted. It sounded great, but there was something about him I didn't trust. But Peter was so hungry he accepted the man's offer on the spot."

"You mean, you went with him?" Aura asks.

"Yeah," Kat says, lowering her head, "and it was the worst mistake of our lives. The man took us to his home way up at the top of a mountain. At first, he was very kind. He said we should call him 'Doctor,' and his staff served us a feast. I thought it was strange that their faces were covered except for their eyes, but I didn't dwell on it. Peter ate until he felt like his stomach would burst, but I only ate a little. And then the Doctor showed us to our room and we slept for what seemed like days. But when we woke up everything… changed."

"Please continue," Dr. Renfield says. "I know this is difficult for you, but you are doing great."

"O-Okay," she says. "Well, when I woke up, I was in a cage. Of course, I thought I was dreaming. I mean, what would I be doing inside a cage? But then I noticed another cage across the way, and inside was a large cat. At first, I could only see its head and I thought it was a tiger. That is, until the animal moved and I realized it wasn't a tiger at all because it had the body of a boy. I was horrified and convinced myself I was having a nightmare. But when the boy rolled over and I saw what he was wearing, I knew instantly it wasn't a nightmare at all. It was Peter."

As I listen to the emotion in her voice, the hairs on the back of my neck stand on end.

"Suddenly, I felt sick," she says. "And when I looked down at my own body, my arms and legs were covered in white fur, and I had a tail. Then, I caught my reflection and saw my whiskers. Somehow, I was also part-cat, but not as extreme as Peter. I called out to him, and he heard me, gripping the bars of his cage with his paws. But when he called back, his voice was nothing but a howl. And that's when I knew what had happened."

By now, tears are running down her cheeks so I grab a tissue and hand it to her.

"Thanks," she says, wiping her eyes. "The 'Doctor' had used us for his 'special project.' He tainted the food he fed us with something that transformed us into… this. Because Peter ate more than me, his transformation was more complete. I still looked partly human. I could still speak with words. But Peter was gone—except for his heart. I could tell he was still in there somewhere, fighting to get out."

"I'm so sorry," I say. "But this 'Doctor,' did you ever find out his real name?"

"Yes," she says. "His name was Moreau."

My heart skips a beat.

"Moreau?" Rage says. "That animal!"

"Everyone stay calm," Dr. Renfield says. "Let her tell the rest of her story."

"I-I don't remember it all," she says. "But I do remember Dr. Moreau telling us that he was proud of us. He said we had been the only ones who had gone through this type of transformation and had survived, but it was unlikely we would live for long. He said our bodies would give out under the stress of our new forms. But he could help us. He said he had an antidote."

"An antidote?" Rage says. "What's that?"

"It is a way to reverse a process," Dr. Renfield says. "A way to change them back to their human forms. Did

Dr. Moreau show you this antidote?"

"Yes," she says. "He held it up. It was a red liquid in some kind of vial. There wasn't much of it, and I begged him to give it to Peter, but he just laughed at me. He said he couldn't just give it to us, he said we had to earn it."

"What?" I say. "Earn it, how?"

"By retrieving one of three objects," she says. "hidden in the basement of a school."

"The Artifacts of Virtue!" I blurt out.

"Yes," she says. "That's what he called them. He said if we brought one of them back, he would give us the antidote. Then, he showed us a map. He circled the location of the school as well as an abandoned building where he said we could sleep for the night. After that, he released us into the wild. Things started fine. But after a while, I was having difficulty keeping up. I felt so tired I just needed to sleep. And then I remember feeling dizzy, and that's all I remember up until right now."

"Well, that explains a lot," Aura says.

I nod in agreement, but deep inside I know it doesn't explain everything. Like, what happened in my dream for instance.

"Where am I?" Kat asks, looking around.

"You are at the Van Helsing Academy," Dr. Renfield says. "The same school that Dr. Moreau identified on his map."

"Yeah," Aura says suspiciously. "And your brother stole the Bell of Virtue."

"He did?" Kat says, her eyes lighting up. "That means he'll get the antidote!"

"That's great for him," Aura says. "But he's also put everyone on campus in danger."

"What?" Kat says. "What are you talking about? Peter would never put anyone in danger. He's not like that."

"I hear what you're saying," Aura says. "But we don't know your brother. Or you for that matter."

"Aura, chill," I interject. "I believe what she's saying. If her brother had bad intentions, he would have attacked me down in the basement. But he didn't."

"Wait," Kat says, looking at me. "You saw him? You saw Peter?"

"Yes," I say. "Twice actually. In the basement, and before that at Moreau Labs where we found you. Actually, your brother wanted us to find you. That's when you blacked out. I guess Peter knew we could help you."

"Or," Aura says, her eyes narrowing, "her brother knew we went to the Van Helsing Academy. And this was one big set-up to get little Miss Cat-girl here inside the gates so she could open the vault door for him."

"I didn't think of that!" Rage says.

"What vault door?" Kat asks.

"Don't play dumb," Aura says, pressing harder. "Come on! Admit it! You set us up!"

"No!" I say, surprising even myself. I mean, I didn't want to tell them about the vault door yet, but I can't just stand here and let Kat take the blame for something I did. "She didn't do it. I was the one who opened the vault door."

"What?" Aura and Rage say in unison.

"I did it," I say. "It was me. At first, I thought it was just a strange dream. But as I was walking through that tunnel I realized it wasn't a dream at all. Somehow, I had come down that tunnel before and opened the vault door."

"Mr. Murray?" Dr. Renfield says, his eyebrows raised in surprise. "Are you certain?"

"Yes," I say. "Very certain."

I look up ashamed. Everyone is staring at me and the room is so quiet you could hear a pin drop. I blink and my eyelashes feel damp. Great, now I'm gonna cry.

"Bram," Dr. Hagella says, reaching for my arm, but I pull away. I just want to get out of here.

"AAAAAHHHHH!"

"Um, what was that?" Rage asks.

"A scream," Aura says. "From outside. Hold on."

Then, she phases through the infirmary wall, and when she returns, her face is whiter than her normal ghostly self.

"Aura?" I ask. "What's wrong?"

"Z-Zombies," she says with a shaky voice. "There are Zombies all over campus."

CHAPTER TWELVE

ZOMBIEPOCALYPSE

Zombies?

There are Zombies on campus?

Then what Van Helsing said must be true. The Artifacts of Virtue do have Supernatural powers to ward off evil. And with the Bell of Virtue gone, we're sitting ducks!

My shoulders slump under my sense of guilt. After all, I was the one who opened the door that let Peter—Tiger-boy—inside the academy. If anyone gets hurt, it's all my fault.

I feel sick to my stomach.

"We've got to get out of here!" Aura says. "And we should take Cat-girl with us. I still don't believe she's as innocent as she claims."

"I believe her," I say. "If she and her brother were evil, they wouldn't have been able to step foot on school grounds in the first place because the Artifacts of Virtue would have kept them out. And based on her story, Dr.

Moreau didn't give them a choice. If they didn't steal one of the Artifacts of Virtue, they wouldn't get the antidote that could save their lives."

Aura and I stare each other down. I can tell she's thinking about what I said, but she's still not convinced.

"And by the way," Aura says. "I'm also questioning what side you're on."

For a second, her comment catches me off guard.

But then I realize I shouldn't be so surprised. I mean, I just admitted to committing an act of treason! But I couldn't let Kat take the blame for opening the vault door. I'm about to respond, when—

THOOM!

Suddenly, a green hand smashes through the wall!

"Zombies!" Rage yells.

"Take the girl and run!" Dr. Hagella commands, slamming the hand back through the wall with a fire extinguisher. "This is a sanctuary for the sick and injured, and if those zombies think they can destroy what we've built then they've got another thing coming."

Then, Dr. Hagella unhooks Kat from her IV and Rage and I help her to her feet. As she stands up, our eyes meet and I realize that underneath the whiskers and cat ears, she's really pretty.

"Um," I stammer. "Do you think you can run?"

"Like the wind," she says.

"Great," Rage says. "Let's go!"

"Students, get behind me," Dr. Renfield says,

bursting out the infirmary door onto the school grounds.

We follow close behind, and when I finally get outside, my eyes grow wide with horror, because there are dozens of zombies lumbering across campus. Their red eyes shine brightly through the night as they limp along aimlessly in packs of three of four.

"Don't let them bite you!" Aura calls out. "They'll turn you into a zombie!"

Roger that. I'm having enough trouble just being a vampire. The last thing I need is to become a vampire-zombie!

"Dr. Renfield!" Rage yells.

At the sound of his voice, I spin around to see two zombies grab Dr. Renfield's arms. But just as one opens his mouth, he's engulfed in a giant fireball and releases Dr. Renfield's arm! Then, Dr. Renfield kicks the other zombie in the midsection and pulls free just as that zombie goes up in flames.

Huh? How'd that happen?

But as the two zombies collapse to the ground I have my answer. Because Professor Hexum is standing behind them with his walking stick in one hand and a torch in the other.

"Thank you, Dr. Renfield, but I will take it from here," Hexum says. "I need you to go back to the auditorium immediately and help Professor Holmwood, Professor Seward, and Mrs. Clops relocate the other students. Mr. Murray's safety is now my concern."

Hexum's comments surprise me. I mean, why is he coming back here for me when so many other kids are in danger?

"B-But…" Dr. Renfield stammers, looking at me and then back at Hexum.

"Dr. Renfield," Hexum says firmly, "the Headmaster gave me full authority in his absence. Please go to the auditorium and help the others. That is an order and not a request."

"Of course," Dr. Renfield says finally. Then, he looks at me and says, "Take care of yourself, Mr. Murray. Hopefully, we will meet again."

I smile weakly as he heads off, but for some reason, his words strike me oddly.

"Let's go!" Hexum barks, grabbing my hoodie and pulling me forward.

"But, my friends," I say, digging my feet in to stop his momentum. "I can't just leave them."

Hexum turns to Aura, Rage, and Kat.

"Very well," he sighs, "come along."

"Yes!" Rage says, pumping his fist.

"Now move!" Hexum orders.

"Where are we going?" I ask.

But before Hexum can answer, we're suddenly surrounded by six more zombies!

"Get close to me!" Hexum commands.

But as we circle Hexum, even more zombies close in. Hexum waves his torch around us and in the blazing light

I can see the zombies' decaying faces. But Hexum's flame does its job, keeping the creatures at bay. If I wasn't about to die right now, I'd probably throw up.

"W-What now?" Rage asks.

That's when I notice he's breathing heavier.

Oh no.

If Rage loses control and turns into a purple sledgehammer, we'll have an entirely different problem on our hands. I need to keep him calm.

"Relax, buddy," I say, putting my hand on his shoulder. "We've got this. Don't we, Professor Hexum? Um, Professor Hexum?"

But when I look up, I notice his eyes are closed! He's focusing on something.

FWOOOMMM!

Suddenly, a giant ring of fire erupts all around us!

"Move forward!" Hexum barks.

At first, I resist. I mean, I don't want to walk straight into a raging fire. But Hexum pushes me forward, right into the zombies' path! But instead of getting burned, the ring of fire moves with us—keeping us safely in the center of its fiery circle!

As we charge ahead, the zombie crowd falls back, afraid of the fire blazing around us. And that's when I realize something else—there's no heat! If we were surrounded by an actual fire, we'd be incinerated instantly!

So, that can only mean one thing—it's an illusion!

Hexum must be using his mental powers to trick the simple-minded zombies into thinking this is a real fire—and I guess my simple mind as well. Within seconds, we've cleared a path through the zombie brigade and made our way off of school grounds through a hole in the busted perimeter wall. Then, Hexum turns and waves his arm, causing a massive wall of fire to flare up behind us.

There's no way they'll try crossing that.

Kat looks shell-shocked.

"W-What's happening?" she asks.

"Jedi mind tricks," I say.

"What now?" Aura asks. "What about our friends? Shouldn't we go back and save them?"

"No, it is too dangerous," Hexum says. "Besides, they are in good hands with the other teachers. There is an underground escape route from the auditorium that will take them safely off campus. But Mr. Murray is no longer safe here."

"So, where are we going to go?" Rage asks.

"Wait," Kat says sniffing the air. "It's Peter. I… I think I've picked up his scent. He went straight ahead. Through those woods."

"Excellent," Hexum says. "We can follow the trail."

"Hold on," Aura says. "Do you actually trust her? What if it's a trap?"

"I certainly hope it's a trap," Hexum says with a wicked smile. Then, he turns for the woods. "Let's go."

Aura frowns at me and then floats after Hexum.

Rage shrugs his shoulders and takes Kat by the arm, helping her along. But before I follow, I take one last look at our zombie-infested academy.

I can't imagine things getting worse, but deep down inside I have the dreadful feeling it will.

"Mr. Murray!" Hexum calls out.

"Coming!" I call back. Then, I flip my hood over my head and get moving.

***

It seems like we've been walking for hours. Every now and then, we cross a road or some train tracks, but other than that, it's been all woods all of the time. Hexum is still leading the way, which is pretty impressive since he needs a walking stick. Other than Aura, the rest of us look like we could collapse at any second.

Kat and I are a few paces behind Hexum. Once Rage tired out, I stepped in to help her over the rough terrain, but for a girl who just got out of a hospital bed, she's doing really well on her own. In fact, she seems to have no problem scampering over anything in our path.

"You're pretty agile," I say.

"Oh, thanks," she says, smiling at me. "I guess it's one of the perks of being part-cat. The tail not-so-much. I know I look freaky, but what's the story with your friends? I mean, that doctor had green skin like a witch. And if I didn't know better, I'd say that girl who doesn't like me is a ghost. And you look, well, sort of like—"

"—a vampire?" I say, finishing her sentence for her. "Yeah, well, that's because I am a vampire. Well, half-vampire anyway."

"And what about the blond kid?" she asks.

"You don't want to know," I say. "But I guess we all seem strange from your point of view. We didn't exactly explain things to you back in the infirmary. You see, our school is a school for monster kids."

"Monster kids?" she says.

"Yeah," I say. "That's us."

"Well, okay then," she says. "I guess that explains a lot. And by the way, thanks for stepping in about that vault door thing. Honestly, I didn't know what your friend was accusing me of."

"Oh, that's just Aura," I say. "Trust me, she's okay. Just give her some time. I'm sure she'll turn around. Well, I hope she'll turn around. Anyway, I'm sorry about what happened to you and your brother. It sounds like you've been through a lot."

"Yeah, thanks," she says. "He's a good person. I just wish he wasn't so impulsive all the time. That's why I feel like I need to keep an eye on him. I never know what he's going to get into—AH!"

Suddenly, Kat stops and doubles over. Based on her expression, it looks like she's in pain.

"Are you okay?" I ask, grabbing her shoulders so she doesn't topple over. "Professor Hexum, stop!"

"Y-Yes," she says, straightening up and leaning back. "Just got a sharp pain in my side."

"That's not good," Rage says, catching up to us. "Maybe you should sit down for a minute."

"N-No," she says, breathing heavily. "I don't want to lose Peter's scent. He's close. I can smell it. Let's just keep moving."

"Are you sure?" Hexum asks.

"Yes," she says.

Rage and I stand next to Kat and put one of her arms over each of our shoulders. As we start up again, I'm surprised by how light her body seems. It's like her bones are hollow or something.

"You know," Rage says. "the thing I can't figure out is why the Dark Ones would send zombies onto campus? I mean, if you wanted to destroy stuff, wouldn't you send werewolves?"

"That's simple," Aura says, floating beside me. "Most people think zombies are brainless, but in truth, they're just single-minded. If you give a zombie a goal, it will pursue that goal until it's destroyed. I think you need to brush up on your Monsterology."

"That makes sense," I say. "Remember when we went to the graveyard and those zombies were digging up those bones? I didn't think of it then, but I guess that's what they were told to do."

"Exactly," Aura says.

"Okay," Rage says, "so what do you think they were

looking for when they invaded our campus?"

"Bram, probably," Aura says. "Hexum said he wasn't safe there anymore."

"Great," I say, but just then something else pops into my head.

"What's wrong, Bram?" Aura asks. "Now you look like you've seen a ghost."

"What? Nothing." I say, "Except, Dr. Renfield told me there was something else on campus that Count Dracula was searching for. Something called the Spear of Darkness."

"Nonsense!" Hexum blurts out suddenly.

What's his problem? I didn't even realize he was listening to our conversation.

"That blowhard doesn't know what he's babbling about," Hexum continues. "The Spear of Darkness is not on campus and we will not discuss it any further."

Rage, Aura, and I exchange glances.

What's got him so riled up?

"What's the Spear of Darkness?" Rage mouths.

"Tell you later," I mouth back.

"Halt," Hexum says, blocking us with his walking stick.

Suddenly, I realize we're standing on the edge of a cliff. With all of the thick underbrush, I didn't even see the ground drop off. One wrong step from here and we could have tumbled hundreds of feet to our doom. Well, I guess this is a dead end. I start to turn back, when—

"There," Kat says, pointing across the way.

Huh? There? There where?

But when I follow her arm, I see an oddly shaped structure in the distance, peeking out from behind a tall mountain. It's not a rock formation or anything natural.

In fact, it kind of looks like… a tower?

"He's in there," Kat says. "My brother is in there."

CHAPTER THIRTEEN

DID YOU MIST ME?

As we stand at the cliff's edge, looking up at the dark tower randomly jutting out from the top of the mountain, there's only one thought running through my mind:

Nothing good ever happens in a dark tower.

And this one certainly fits the bill. It's tall and thin, rising from the mountainside like a twisted spire, its tip cutting through the full moon hanging behind it in the night sky. And as I scan the mountain itself, there's no obvious way to get up to the tower, other than scaling the mountain itself.

"Um, what is that thing?" Rage asks.

"Moreau's headquarters," Kat says. "That's where he took Peter and me. That's where he turned us… into this."

"M-Moreau?" Rage says with a shaky voice. "He's… in there?"

"Yes," Kat says. "I can smell his putrid cologne from here. He's in there. And so is my brother."

"Okay," I say. "Everyone stay calm for a minute.

Let's take Kat's word for it that they're both up there. That tower has a three-hundred-and-sixty-degree view of everything around it. I bet they can see for miles. There's no way anyone could sneak up on them."

"No," Hexum says. "But we are not just anyone. Students, please huddle."

"Alright," Aura says, rubbing her palms together. "I feel a plan coming on."

As Aura, Rage, and I circle Hexum, Kat stands on the cliff's edge.

"Now listen closely," Hexum says, gathering us all in with his walking stick. "If Katherine believes her brother is in that tower, then the Bell of Virtue is there as well. It must be retrieved to restore the academy's Supernatural protection from evil. But Moreau is a brutal adversary. He will not spare you simply because you are children. Therefore, this task is far too dangerous for your skill level. You will all wait here until I return."

"What?" Aura and I blurt out at the same time.

"Stop!" Rage adds, pointing at Hexum.

"Excuse me?" Hexum says, his eyebrows raised.

"No," Rage says, moving around Hexum and pointing down the cliff. "Stop her!"

Stop her? Stop who?

But when I turn around, Kat is gone! And that's when I see her climbing down the side of the cliff! While Hexum was talking to us, she took off on her own!

Is she crazy! Dr. Moreau will see her coming.

I've got to stop her!

Without a second thought, I picture myself as a bat and transform instantly. Then, I take flight.

"Bram, wait!" Aura yells, but I'm already soaring through the air.

"Mr. Murray, get back here at—!" Hexum yells, his voice fading in the distance.

I don't want to disobey him, but Kat is in real danger. At first, I don't see her, but then I pick her up using radar. She's already made it down to the base of the cliff and is bounding across the rocky surface towards the mountain. She's fast—maybe even faster than me—but I've got to catch her before we get—

AROOOOOOOOOOOOO!

—spotted.

Uh oh. That sounded like a horn—otherwise known as an alarm—and it came from the top of the mountain! I glance back up at the cliff and Hexum, Rage, and Aura are gone. Hopefully, they're hiding back in the woods.

But that's more than I can say for Kat, because alarm or no alarm, she's not stopping. In fact, she's reached the bottom of the mountain and is starting to climb up! It's a long way to the top so this might be my only chance to stop her before Moreau sends who knows what army down to fight us.

But just as I swoop in, I hear—

FWOOP. FWOOP. FWOOP.

What's that?

Suddenly, I pick up something massive coming right at me through the air! Out of the corner of my eye, I catch a pair of giant wings, and I dart down just as it zooms over me, generating so much wind force it sends me into a tailspin! I flap my wings hard, pulling myself up before I crash onto the rocks below.

What the heck was that?

I loop around, but I don't see it anywhere. And what's even worse is I don't see Kat either! Did that thing get her?

"Psssst!" comes a voice. "Up here! Quick!"

I scan the mountain until I pick up a white speck waving at me from inside a cave. It's Kat! She's found a hideout in the side of the mountain! I've got to get to her and then get us out of here before—

SQUAWK!

I flap left as the creature nosedives past me!

Okay, that was way too close for comfort! But when I look down, I do a double take, because what's circling me is like nothing I've ever seen before. It's absolutely huge, with the head and wings of an eagle and the body of a lion! It's like some crazy person decided to stick two animals together just for laughs.

Except, in this case, the crazy person happens to be Dr. Moreau. But as it soars around me, I remember studying a beast like this in Monsterology class. I think it's called a griffin, and it's like facing two predators in one!

"Don't just sit there!" Kat yells. "Move!"

Well, I don't need to be told twice. The only problem is that the griffin isn't just going to just let me go. I beat my wings as hard as I can, heading for Kat, but there's no way I'm going to outrun this thing. I mean, its wingspan is like twenty feet long! I'm a bat snack!

It's coming!

Please, please somehow miss me.

Wait a second. 'Miss' me? 'Mist' me?

Suddenly, a lightbulb goes off.

I focus my concentration on becoming a mist.

But it's right behind me!

It's ten feet away.

Can't lose focus.

Five feet.

C'mon!

One foot.

Please.

Suddenly, my body feels weightless, and as the griffin flies through me, my molecules scatter everywhere.

Yes! I did it!

WAAAAAK!

I guess birdbrain is annoyed, but tough noogies, because I'm alive! All I need to do now is collect myself near Kat. It takes some doing in the open air, but I manage to gather my atoms over the ledge and transform back to a kid. As I hit the ground by her feet, I'm absolutely exhausted.

"Bram, move it!" Kat yells, running into a cave.

SQUUUAAAWWWKKK!

As the griffin's shadow covers the ledge, I follow her, squeezing through the narrow cave entrance. We go back as far as we can until we hit a dead end. Both of us lean against the rock wall, breathing heavily.

"Thanks for spotting me," I manage to say.

"I picked up your scent behind me," she says, her eyes wide. "But it took me a second to realize you were a bat. How did you do that?"

"Vampire, remember?" I say. "It's what we do. But enough about that. Do you think this cave opening is small enough?"

"For what?" she asks.

SQUAWK!

"That!" I say, pulling Kat back against the rock wall.

Just then, giant talons burst through the cave and claw around recklessly. But fortunately, the entrance is narrow enough to keep the griffin out. The beast pushes its shoulder against the opening to extend its reach, but it simply can't fit its body through.

"We're trapped," I say. "There's no way out."

"No," Kat says, sniffing into the air. "The smell."

"Sorry," I say. "I didn't exactly have time to put on deodorant."

"Not you," she says. "I've picked up Peter's scent again. He came this way. Follow me."

Then, she turns and climbs straight up the rock wall!

Where's she going now? I mean, I thought this was

literally a dead end. But to my surprise, Kat disappears through a hole in the rock ceiling.

"Come on!" she says, popping her head down through the hole. "There's a tunnel up here."

A tunnel?

I hate tunnels.

SQUAWK!

But as I look back at the cave opening, the griffin stretches its arm as far as it can and nearly shish kebobs me. Well, I haven't had the best of luck with tunnels, but it's got to be better than this.

"Coming!" I say, carefully scaling the rock wall.

When I reach the top, I pull myself through the opening and find Kat crouched low inside a narrow tunnel. That's strange. It seems to cut diagonally upwards through the mountain itself.

"Peter went this way," Kat says, heading through the tunnel.

I get to my feet and lean against the wall to catch my breath. I can't believe what's happened. I mean, just a little while ago we were all safe and sound at the Van Helsing Academy. Now I'm running through the mountain headquarters of a mad scientist.

I sure hope Rage and Aura got away before that griffin got them. And speaking of getting away, I've got to get moving to keep up with Kat, except I'm completely drained. I'd love to rest, but I can't let Kat face Moreau on her own. He's simply too dangerous.

"Come," a man's voice echoes through the cave.

Huh? Where'd that come from?

But when I look around, there's no one here but me.

"Come, Bram," he says.

That's when I realize the voice isn't echoing through the cave, it's echoing through my head! And what's worse is that I know who the voice belongs to.

Count Dracula!

I wait for him to speak again, but the only sound I hear is the beating of my own heart. Suddenly, I get chills. What exactly did he mean when he said 'come?' Is he here? Is he waiting to attack me?

I don't want to die.

"Bram?" Kat says, walking back towards me looking concerned. "Are you coming? I was calling you."

Suddenly, I'm confused.

Was that Kat calling me? But it didn't sound like her?

I want to tell her 'no,' I'm not coming. In fact, I'd rather take my chances with that hideous eagle-lion thing, but deep down I know I can't do that. She's not going to back down. I mean, her twin brother is in trouble. Plus, I'm responsible for what happened to the Van Helsing Academy. I'm the one who needs to find the Bell of Virtue or the school will be toast.

My mind must be playing tricks on me.

"Yeah," I say, pushing myself forward. "I'm coming. Sorry, I just needed a breather."

"It's okay," she says. "You've been through a lot.

Listen, I scouted ahead a bit and this tunnel just keeps going up and up. I think we're in some kind of a secret entrance to the tower."

"Dandy," I say. "Well, then, let's go for it."

She's about to turn, but then stops and freezes me with her bright, green eyes.

"I… I just want to say thanks again," she says. "I know we don't know each other that well, but I'm really glad you're here."

"Hey, no problem," I say, feeling my cheeks go flush. "I guess charging into highly terrifying situations is just what new friends do for each other."

She giggles and turns, brushing me with her tail, and then she takes off.

Well, here goes nothing.

I try keeping up with her, but it's difficult to match her agility navigating the twists and turns inside the tunnel. Considering that she could barely walk on her own when we left the infirmary, her cat-like adrenaline must be off the charts.

I hope she also has nine lives.

As we continue to weave our way along, my mind turns to other thoughts. Like, what happened to Van Helsing, Crawler, and Professor Morris? I mean, they went looking for Peter long before we started. And why was Dr. Renfield so reluctant to leave me when Hexum ordered him to go? And speaking of Hexum, why did he have such a big reaction when I mentioned the Spear of

Darkness?

Suddenly, I slam into Kat.

"Sorry," I say. "Why'd you stop?"

"Shhh," she whispers, her finger over her lips. "Look straight up."

And that's when I see it. I was so in my head I didn't even notice. We're crouched beneath a hatch door and there's light coming through the edges.

Dr. Moreau could be standing right over our heads!

"Okay," I whisper. "We need a plan. Let's—"

SMASH!

I flinch and shield my face as Kat bursts upwards through the hatch door!

And then I make a mental note:

Kat is not much of a planner.

MONSTEROLOGY 101 FIELD GUIDE

GRIFFIN

CLASSIFICATION:

Type: Abnormal
Sub-Type: Hybrid
Height: Variable
Weight: Variable
Eye Color: Red
Hair Color: Variable

KNOWN ABILITIES:

- Has the head, wings, and forelegs of an eagle and the hind-quarters of a lion
- Incredible strength, speed, and vision
- Large talons are razor-sharp

KNOWN WEAKNESSES:

- Lacks body armor
- Large size makes them easy to spot in the air
- Not intelligent

DANGER LEVEL:

HIGH

TIPS TO AVOID AN UNWANTED ENCOUNTER:

- Stay out of the air
- If outside, remain hidden under trees or beneath covered structures
- Avoid mountainous areas

CHAPTER FOURTEEN

PURE EVIL

And Kat said her brother is the impulsive one?

As I shield my body from the falling debris of the shattered hatch door, I realize I have no choice but to follow Kat into the mysterious room. This isn't how I would have approached the situation, but it's too late now. So, I stand up and pull myself through the opening.

And then I wish I hadn't done that.

We're standing in the center of a large, circular room with stone walls, large glass windows, and a high ceiling. Based on the sweeping three-hundred-and-sixty-degree view of the surrounding landscape, it's actually pretty cool up here. You know, if it weren't for the guy dressed in all white pointing the gun at us.

"Welcome," the man says. "Truthfully, I wasn't expecting you to survive my pet griffin, yet here you are."

Kat and I look at each other and freeze. Based on the terror in her eyes and her description from earlier, the guy doesn't need an introduction.

It's Dr. Moreau!

He's a bit older than I imagined, with white, slicked-back hair and deep wrinkles around his cold, gray eyes. His white, three-piece suit is pressed and pristine, and he's wearing a black tie and shiny, black shoes. But it's not his appearance that has my attention—not by a long shot. It's what he's holding in his left hand.

The Bell of Virtue!

"Looking for this?" he asks.

Well, yes. I want to tell him to hand it over, but the odds of him listening to me are zero to none. So, I hold my tongue. At least, for now.

"Where is Peter?" Kat demands. "You got what you wanted, now where is my brother?"

"Ah, yes," Dr. Moreau says. "They say twins have a special connection, don't they? Although you really don't look anything like twins anymore. A shame. I was so hoping you would evolve to be more like your brother."

"Where is he?" Kat repeats. "Tell me, you monster!"

"Insistent, aren't you?" Dr. Moreau says, placing the Bell of Virtue on a nearby table. "Have no fear, your savage brother is right here."

Then, he steps back and pulls a black cloth off a large box sitting behind him, revealing an iron cage with Peter inside! Peter is lying on his back, his stomach barely moving up and down.

"Peter!" Kat yells.

But just as she takes a step towards them, Dr. Moreau points his gun at the cage—right at Peter.

Kat stops cold.

"I suggest you stay there," he says. "After all, I would hate to waste a silver bullet on your poor brother. Especially since he is dying anyway."

Just then, Peter erupts in a deep coughing fit.

That's when I remember what Kat said. Dr. Moreau told them that neither of them had long to live. That they were the only ones who had even survived this type of transformation. But based on how bad Peter looks, I'm concerned his time could be running out.

"Give him the antidote!" Kat demands. "You promised that if we got you one of those Artifacts of Virtue, you'd give us the antidote. You have your stupid bell, now give it to him!"

"Ah, yes. The antidote," Dr. Moreau says, picking up a glass vial filled with a red liquid. "The only means of changing him back to natural form. Was this the antidote you were referring to?"

"Yes!" Kat says, her eyes growing wide. "That's it! Now give it to him! Please!"

But Dr. Moreau smiles.

And then he drinks it down in one gulp.

"No!" Kat yells.

"Foolish girl," Dr. Moreau says, wiping his mouth with his sleeve and putting the empty vial back on the table. "There is no antidote for your condition. There never was."

"Nooo!" Kat cries, dropping to her knees. "W-Why?

Why did you do this to us?"

"For this, of course," Dr. Moreau says, picking up the Bell of Virtue again. "With the Artifacts of Virtue in place, there was no way I could infiltrate the Van Helsing Academy myself. Instead, I needed to send in an agent. Someone with an innocent heart and a desperate mind who could pass through the school's magical protection, as long as they were properly motivated, of course. And when I discovered you and your brother digging for scraps in that back alley, I knew I had found my recruits."

"No," Kat says, as tears stream down her cheeks.

"But I still don't get it," I say. "You used them, but why? Why do you want to remove the school's magical protection in the first place?"

"For science," he says smugly.

"Um, what?" I say. "Sorry, but that makes no sense."

"It does to me," Dr. Moreau says. "You see, my brand of science has been deemed 'unacceptable' by mankind. And as a result, they have stripped me of my resources—my grants, my research, my laboratory. They took everything from me. And why? Because they are afraid of my genius."

Well, yeah, I can see why.

This guy is no genius. He's insane!

"It is human nature to fear what you do not understand," he continues. "And my former 'peers' failed to understand what I was striving to achieve. They said I was mad. They said it was morally wrong to create an entirely new species of Hybrid creatures merely to do the bidding of mankind. They said it couldn't be done, it shouldn't be done. Yet, I found a way to do it—to become the ultimate creator right here on earth."

Okay, this is going downhill fast.

"Despite all of their objections," Dr. Moreau continues, "all of their obstacles, I continued my work. However, they never accepted my arguments that a few must be sacrificed for the good of all. They tried to silence me, to cut me off, but I have persevered."

"Kat," I whisper, but she doesn't respond. She's just staring straight ahead, completely oblivious to everything happening around us.

"You see," he continues, "I am not like them. I am not limited by things like 'morals' or 'ethics.' Those beliefs only serve to restrain creativity. But I will not be stopped. And once I deliver my side of the bargain, I will be given all of the subjects I need to continue my genetic experiments, however, and wherever I please. I will have an army of Hybrids to follow my every command. And then I will show all of my adversaries what madness looks like."

Is that what this is all about? He's creating all of these Hybrid creatures, hurting all of these innocent people, just to serve his own ego? But then I remember something he said.

"Um, you mentioned something about a bargain," I say. "What are you talking about?"

"Observe," Dr. Moreau says.

Just then, a door on the far side of the room opens and two large men enter the room, except they're not men at all. They both have muscular, human bodies but animal heads! One has the head of an ox and the other the head of a bear, and I wonder if Dr. Moreau tricked them in the same way he tricked Kat and Peter?

But then I realize they're wheeling in two more covered boxes behind them, and the boxes are the same size as the one Peter is stuck in. Then, Dr. Moreau nods, and the beast-men whip off the cloth covers.

My jaw hits the floor.

It's Rage and Hexum!

Moreau's beast-men must have captured them after Kat and I took off. Poor Rage is gripping the iron bars and looking around with panic in his eyes. Hexum, however, is lying face down and not moving at all.

"Rage," I call out, "are you okay?"

"I-I think so," he answers.

"Professor?" I call out. "Are you okay?"

But Hexum doesn't answer.

"Do not worry," Dr. Moreau says. "He will be fine once he regains consciousness. At the moment he is enjoying a deep sleep."

I breathe a sigh of relief, but then I realize someone is missing. Where's Aura? I look around the room but don't see her anywhere.

"Let them go," I say firmly. "Now."

"I don't think so," Dr. Moreau says. "Professor Hexum's reputation precedes him and I really don't want to deal with his mind games. The boy, however, will make a fine specimen for one of my future experiments."

"W-What?" Rage says, his voice cracking. "B-But… you already experimented on me. Don't you remember?"

"I did?" Dr. Moreau says, studying Rage's face. "Funny, I don't remember you."

"B-But," Rage says meekly, looking stunned, "y-you ruined my life. And you don't even remember…"

"Please, child," Dr. Moreau says, shrugging his shoulders. "I experiment on dozens of specimens every day. It simply isn't important for me to remember them all. But enough of this. It is time to deliver what I promised. And then there will be no limit to my science."

I look over at Rage who is curling into a ball.

"Bring me the walking stick!" Dr. Moreau demands.

Wait, did he just say, 'walking stick?'

Like, as in Hexum's walking stick?

I'm totally confused as I watch the ox-man reach into Hexum's cage and yank out his walking stick. I mean, what does Dr. Moreau want with Hexum's walking stick? But as the burly beast-man hands it over to Dr. Moreau, the evil scientist breaks into a disturbing smile.

"My ploy worked brilliantly," he says, looking at the walking stick. "Truthfully, I never expected it to be this easy. But as luck would have it, my plan drove you from your academy and brought the prize right to my front door. I should probably thank you for your ignorance."

"What are you talking about?" I ask.

But Dr. Moreau doesn't answer me.

Instead, he walks over to a set of large windows and throws open the panes. Then, he raises the walking stick over his head.

"Come, my Dark Lord," he yells out the window. "Come to my tower and claim your bounty. For it is I, your most loyal servant, who will finally deliver what you have long been seeking. I willingly invite you to come inside, my King of Darkness!"

Um, did he just say, King… of Darkness?

A chill runs through my body.

"We've got to get everybody out of here!" I whisper to Kat, shaking her shoulders. "Now!"

"What?" she says finally. "What's happening?"

But before I can answer, a black mist flows through the open window and I know it's too late. It swirls around the room, passing over our heads, and then collects itself next to Dr. Moreau.

Holy cow! There's no mistaking it now!

"Yes, my Dark Lord," Dr. Moreau says, his face beaming.

I've got to stop this, but I'm pretty much on my own. I mean, Hexum and Rage are stuck in cages, Kat looks like a shell of herself, and Peter is dying. But I have to act. Lives are in danger!

I go with my best bet.

"Get up," I whisper to Kat, helping her to her feet. "We've got to work together."

But as soon as she stands up, things go from bad to worse, because the dark mist transforms into the one person I'd least like to invite to my birthday party.

Count Dracula!

"Um, is that…?" Kat whispers.

"Yep," I say. "The end of the world."

As I take him in, I'm shocked. He's incredibly tall, just like I remembered, but this time he looks… different. I mean, the last time I saw him he was struggling to breathe. But now, as he towers over Dr. Moreau, he looks, well, way healthier. His pale skin isn't paper-thin anymore and his black hair is thick and full. And when he sees me his red eyes flicker and he smiles—his white, pointed teeth gleaming inside his bright, red lips.

For some reason, I can't take my eyes off of him.

"Bram?" Kat whispers, nudging me in the arm. "Snap out of it."

I shake my head. She's right. That was weird. It almost felt like he had me in some kind of a spell.

"Got to… stay calm," I hear Rage mutter from inside his cage. "Need to… stay calm."

"My Dark Lord," Dr. Moreau says, presenting him with Hexum's walking stick, "here is the object you have long desired. Just as I have promised you."

"Thank you, my loyal servant," Count Dracula says, his voice much deeper than I expected. He takes the walking stick from Dr. Moreau and holds it out in front of him.

But I don't get it. What does Count Dracula want with Hexum's walking stick?

"You still don't see it, do you, young one?"

Wait, what?

That voice inside my head.

That sounded like… Count Dracula!

"You are seeing only what he wants you to see, but not what is truly here."

"What are you talking about?" I answer. *"And get out of my head!"*

"Your blood gave me life," he says. *"We are now bonded in ways you cannot even imagine. Forever."*

"No!"

"It is true," he says. *"But I see that you have not yet learned to use your powers to their full potential. Allow me to assist you. For your power to see the truth is not limited to when you are in bat-form. Try it now."*

My power to see the truth is not limited to when I'm in bat-form?

What's he talking about?

But then I get what he's saying. When I'm a bat, I can use radar to see things my human eyes can't detect.

But can I also do that when I'm not a bat?

I've never tried it before.

I focus in on Hexum's walking stick and activate my radar, sending high-frequency sounds at the object in

Count Dracula's hands.

And when it bounces back I'm stunned!

I mean, I had no clue I could use radar in human-form. That's incredible! But what's pinging back is even more incredible. Because according to my radar, the walking stick is much bigger than it looks. And one side ends in a long, sharp… point?

Suddenly, it hits me.

I-I can't believe it.

Hexum tricked us!

He never needed a walking stick.

In fact, his walking stick was never really a walking stick at all!

It's the Spear of Darkness!

CLASSIFIED

Person(s) of Interest

CODE NAME: NONE

REAL NAME: DR. SIMON MOREAU

BASE OF OPERATIONS: UNKNOWN

D.S.I.

FACTS: Dr. Moreau is a brilliant biologist renowned for pushing the boundaries of science. Lost all government funding when his experiments on people went beyond the scope of human morality. Escaped before his arrest and now his whereabouts are unknown.

Category:	Natural
Sub-Type:	None
Height:	5'11"
Weight:	192 lbs

FIELD OBSERVATIONS:

- Lacks morals and ethics
- Typically armed
- His "creations" usually die within days
- Observed meeting with known operatives of the Dark Ones organization

STATUS: ACTIVE TARGET

DEPARTMENT OF SUPERNATURAL INVESTIGATIONS

CHAPTER FIFTEEN

EVERYTHING GOES CRAZY

I'm speechless.

I mean, Hexum's walking stick wasn't ever a walking stick at all. It was the Spear of Darkness!

Hexum was fooling us with his mind powers this entire time. Now I understand why he flipped out when I mentioned the Spear of Darkness in the first place. Dr. Renfield was right, the Spear of Darkness was at the Van Helsing Academy, but it was hidden in plain sight!

And now that I've used my radar to expose the truth, I don't even see the walking stick anymore. Instead, I see a long, black spear with a sharp, black blade shimmering with the twinkling of a hundred tiny stars.

It's amazing to look at, but there's one problem.

It's in the hands of the one person everyone was trying to keep it away from.

"You see it now, don't you?" Count Dracula's voice says inside my mind. *"I can see it on your face."*

"We've got to get that away from him," I whisper to

Kat. "And fast."

But the question is how? I take a quick scan of my options. I've got Kat, but Peter is still in his cage looking worse for wear. Moreau isn't going to help us. Hexum is still knocked out. And Rage…

"B-Butterflies and puppies…" Rage says, breathing heavily inside his cage. "Just think of butterflies and puppies."

That's it!

"I need you to create a distraction," I whisper to Kat, "It's our only chance."

"Um, okay," she whispers back. "What kind of a distraction?"

"A big one," I whisper. "But be careful."

"Yeah, yeah," she whispers.

"Are you pleased, my Dark Lord?" Dr. Moreau asks.

"Yes, my loyal servant," Count Dracula answers, turning the spear in admiration. "I have searched for the Spear of Darkness for centuries, and now it is finally in my possession, where it belongs. According to ancient legend, once I throw the spear at the first rays of the morning sun, it will blanket the sky in eternal darkness, blocking all sunlight. Then, I will be free to walk the—"

"Yoohoo!"

"Who dares?" Count Dracula says, turning his head.

"Just furry little me," Kat says, running at incredible speed straight towards them. "You see, the old guy and I have some unfinished business."

Well, I have to give her credit, she certainly knows how to create a distraction. But I can't just stand here gawking, I've got a job to do. Mustering up my own super-speed, I rush over to Rage's cage before the beast-men can react.

"Butterflies," Rage mutters, his face bright red. "Stay calm. Gotta… stay calm."

I feel guilty for what I'm about to do, but I know I have no choice. For everyone's sake.

"Dude," I whisper. "This isn't stay calm time. This is crush the butterflies and puppies time. I mean, you heard what Dr. Moreau said. He doesn't even remember you. He has no recollection of what he did to you. But you can make him remember. You can show him what happens when you get angry. Just let yourself go."

"A-Angry?" Rage says, his breathing quickening. "Make him… remember me? Let myself… go?"

"Yes," I say. "Show him what you've become. Show him what he did to you."

"I-I'll show him," Rage says, the veins popping out of his neck. "C-Crush butterflies. C-Crush puppies."

"Back off!" Dr. Moreau yells.

His scream grabs my attention, and that's when I see Kat jumping on top of Moreau! Uh-oh. I told her to be careful. I mean, Moreau's got a—

BLAM!

There's a blinding flash of white light.

"Aaahhh!" Kat yells.

And when she hits the ground she rolls over in pain, holding her right arm! She's been shot!

"GRRRRRAAARRR!" Peter growls from his cage.

I've got to stop the bleeding! But just as I start to move, the two beast-men pull me back!

"Get off of me!" I yell. "Let! Me! G—"

RRRIIIPPP! CCCLLLAAANNNGGG!

Suddenly, metal bars fly past my head, and something slams into Ox-man with such force that he knocks us all to the ground. As we hit the deck I narrowly avoid being crushed by the bear-headed guy when everything darkens around us.

And when I look up, my jaw drops.

Because standing over us is a seven-foot, purple monster with blond hair, ginormous muscles, and a really, really angry expression.

Yes!

It worked! Rage became a monster!

But, oh no!

If I can't control him, he'll destroy everyone in this chamber—including the good guys!

"Rage?" I call out.

Rage looks around the room and then spots me lying by his feet.

Uh oh.

"RRROOOAAARRRR!"

My hair blows straight back, and I just manage to roll out of the way as Rage reaches down and picks up Ox-man who howls in protest. But Rage ignores his pleas and throws him hard against the wall. Ox-man flops onto the floor and doesn't get back up.

"Is that purple monster one of your creations, Moreau?" Count Dracula asks. "Stop it. Before it ruins everything."

"I-I can't believe it," Dr. Moreau stammers, staring at Rage. "It can't be…."

"Moreau?" Count Dracula says. "Do something!"

Moreau! That's right!

"Rage, over there!" I yell, pointing at Dr. Moreau. "He's the one you want! He's the one who did this to you! He's the one who turned you into a monster!"

Rage studies me for a moment and then looks over at Dr. Moreau who raises his gun.

BLAM!

I turn away as the bullet whizzes past me and ricochets off of Rage's chest, lodging into the rafters.

"RRROOOAAARRR!!!" Rage yells.

Then, with surprising speed, Rage picks up Bear-man and hurls him right at Dr. Moreau.

BLAM!

The gun goes off again as they tumble to the floor.

"Aargh!" Count Dracula yells, dropping the Spear of Darkness to the ground. He's shaking his left hand, which is smoking, but there's no blood. "You careless fool!"

He's hit! This is my chance!

I turn on my super-speed, scoop up the Spear of

Darkness, and race over to Kat. When I reach her, she's lying on her side, wincing in pain.

"Kat, are you okay?"

"I-I think so," she says. "Just stings. And losing blood. Need… a doctor."

She's right. Her arm is bleeding—a lot—and for a second I freeze. I mean, her blood could reenergize me.

Wait, no! What am I thinking?

That's not me talking. I've got to snap out of it. I've got to help her. I pull off my hoodie and wrap it tightly around her forearm. That might help stop the bleeding for a while.

Now, if I can just get her out of here before—

STOMP!

Rage's footstep bounces us in the air like popcorn kernels, and when I look up I see him heading our way!

His brow is furrowed and he's focused on one target.

Dr. Moreau.

"No!" Dr. Moreau says, scrambling to find his gun. "Stop him! My Dark Lord, please, save me!"

"I am afraid this is your affair," Count Dracula says, wrapping himself in his cloak and disappearing into a black mist.

"You!" Dr. Moreau says desperately, turning to Peter. "Help me!" Then, he reaches inside his jacket pocket, pulls out a key, and fumbles to unlock Peter's cage. "Destroy that monster and I'll give you the real antidote. I promise you."

"GRRRRRR," Peter snarls, limping out of his cage. But he doesn't look fit enough to fight anybody. His whole head is nearly bald and he's leaning hard to his right like he's going to fall over.

"RRRAAARRRGGGHHH!" Rage roars, towering over Peter.

Oh, jeez. Rage is gonna pummel Peter!

"N-No, Peter!" Kat yells from her position. "D-Don't listen to Moreau! He lied to us! S-Save yourself!"

"Ignore her, Tiger-child," Dr. Moreau says, backing up behind Peter towards the open window. "You're dying. Without me, you won't last until morning. I have the real antidote. I can save you… and your sister too. Don't you want to save her?"

But then Dr. Moreau bends over.

And that's when I see it.

"The gun!" I yell. "He's going for his gun!"

Suddenly, Peter wheels around and lunges at Dr. Moreau. They grapple for a second before Peter lifts the evil scientist into the air and over his shoulder.

"Release me!" Dr. Moreau yells.

But Peter jumps onto the windowsill with Dr. Moreau in his arms. Then, he looks out the window.

"Peter, no!" Kat yells.

Peter turns and stares at his sister for a second, his eyes wide. And then he falls backward out the window, taking the squirming Dr. Moreau with him.

"Noooooo!" Dr. Moreau yells, his voice fading in

the distance.

"No!" Kat yells. "Peter!"

I race over to the window and look down, but they're gone. We must be a hundred feet in the air! I-I can't believe it. Peter pulled Dr. Moreau down to his death. He sacrificed himself for us.

"RRRROOOOAAARRRR!"

Speaking of death…

I turn around slowly to find Rage standing over me, looking out the window himself. What is he doing? And that's when I realize what's happening. Peter robbed Rage of his chance for revenge. Rage wanted a shot at Dr. Moreau, but now he'll never get it.

"GGGRRRRAAAARRRR!" Rage yells.

Um, oh boy.

"MMAAKKE! HHIIMM! RREMMEMMBBERR!"

"Mr. Murray!" comes a familiar voice. "Move!"

I dive out of the way just as Rage jumps out of the window, taking half of the wall down with him!

"Rage!" I yell. "No!"

"Do not worry," the voice says. "He will be fine. He is nearly indestructible."

At first, I'm confused as to who's talking to me. But when I turn around I see Hexum moving inside of his cage. He's awake!

"Look out!" Hexum yells, pointing up high.

Suddenly, a huge bat drops from the rafters and latches onto the Spear of Darkness! It's Count Dracula!

With everything going on, I forgot all about him! How could I be so dumb!

I hold onto the spear with everything I've got, but I'm not strong enough, and Dracula flaps his mighty wings, ripping it clean from my grasp.

No!

But before I can stop him, he flies out the window!

I can't let him get away! The world is in danger!

Out of the corner of my eye, I spot the Bell of Virtue. In all of the commotion, it's been forgotten. But I guess it was only a means to an end anyway. Count Dracula has what he wanted all along.

"Kat," I say quickly. "I know you're hurting right now, but you've got to let Professor Hexum out of his cage. He can help you. And Professor, don't forget to bring the Bell of Virtue back to the school! The other kids will be safe."

"Mr. Murray—Bram—wait!" Hexum yells. "It is too dangerous!"

Hearing Hexum use my first name stops me cold, and I look into his concerned eyes. He's right, it is dangerous, but it's my responsibility to stop Count Dracula.

So, I focus my mind on one thought—becoming a bat—and then I transform. My arms shrink and then expand into wings, my legs retract into my body, and my senses explode.

And then I fly out the window.

CHAPTER SIXTEEN

TWO BATS OF A FEATHER

I spot Count Dracula against the purple sky.

Fortunately, given his sheer size, he's pretty hard to miss. He's flying away from the tower, still holding the Spear of Darkness in his feet. But there's something strange about how he's flying. He's tilted a little to the left like he's wounded.

At this point, I'm absolutely exhausted, but I can't stop now. Dracula may be faster and stronger, but I can't let him get away with the Spear of Darkness. I need to give it my all to stop him, even if it costs me my life.

I put everything I've got into flapping, but my wingspan is no match for his. I mean, his wings must be seven feet wide when fully extended! But if I can't out-flap him, maybe I can outsmart him.

Changing my trajectory, I go for height over distance, reaching an altitude higher than he's flying at. Then, I tuck in my wings and use gravity to my advantage, dive-bombing right at him.

As the wind whips across my bat-face, I realize I

don't exactly have a plan when I reach him. Should I try knocking him out or should I go for the Spear of Darkness? And what happens if I miss? I mean, we're hundreds of feet above the ground, so if I mess up it could be a long way down.

Decisions, decisions.

He's five feet away!

Since all I see is his back, I know what I've got to do.

Three feet!

I aim for his spine.

One foot!

I brace for impact, but just when I expect to make contact, there's nothing. What happened? But I'll have to figure that out later because I'm hurtling straight down.

I'm gonna crash!

I start flapping as hard as I can and pull myself up, my toes scraping the top of the rocks below. Whew! That was a close one. But as I pull back up, I find Count Dracula hovering above me.

"*Why are you fighting me?*" Count Dracula asks, his voice echoing in my brain. *"After all, we are the only two vampires on the planet. Why not join me instead?"*

"Um, what?" I say in my mind.

"Once the sun rises," he says, *"and I use the Spear of Darkness to put out its light forever, the Earth will be shrouded in eternal darkness. I will be unstoppable."*

"No!" I yell back. *"I won't let that happen!"*

"You cannot stop me," Count Dracula says. *"It is bad*

enough that you do not know how to harness the full extent of your power, but your greatest weakness lies in your naivete."

"What are you talking about?"

"You may think you are safe under the house of Van Helsing," he says, *"but you are wrong. The Van Helsing bloodline carries one goal and one goal only—the complete and utter destruction of all vampires. Think into the future. Once he is finished using you to destroy me, what fate will befall you as the last remaining vampire?"*

As I stare into his red eyes, I feel like I've been punched in the gut. I mean, what if he's right? What if Van Helsing is only using me to destroy Count Dracula? If I'm the last vampire left, what will Van Helsing do with me after that?

"Abraham Murray, you are what you are for a reason," he says. *"You may try to fight it, but your vampire tendencies are slowly taking over your body—taking over your soul. You can only fight it for so long before you will have to give in."*

H-How does he know that?

"Join me," he continues, *"and I will show you what it means to be a vampire. Join me and fulfill your true destiny. Join me and we will rule over mankind."*

Strangely, I-I feel myself being pulled to him. But then the faces of my friends flash through my mind.

Aura. Rage. Stanphibian. Hairball. InvisiBill—not that I can even see his face.

"No!" I yell, snapping back to reality. *"I-I'm not like*

you! I'll never be like you."

"A pity," he says. *"Because that means I must destroy you."*

Then, he rotates the Spear of Darkness with his feet, pointing the sharp blade right at me! And that's when I notice his left wing is smoking! That was the spot where Dr. Moreau accidentally shot him. He must have used a silver bullet. No wonder he was flying off-kilter.

But silver bullets will only wound a vampire's mortal body They won't destroy its spirit. According to Van Helsing, only a vampire can truly kill another vampire—spirit and all.

"Farewell," Count Dracula says, coming towards me.

Holy cow! I start flapping backward, but he's coming too fast. I'm a goner!

SSSQQQUUUAAAKKK!

Suddenly, a giant winged creature swoops past my field of vision, taking Count Dracula with it!

The force of the wind gust propels me backward, and I flap like crazy to stop my momentum before I hit the rocks below.

After righting myself, I look up into the sky to find the griffin soaring above, with Count Dracula in its mouth! But that doesn't last for long, because one second later the beast is chomping on nothing but a dark cloud.

Count Dracula escaped!

But then I see something else.

The Spear of Darkness is falling to earth!

I've got to grab it! Then, a lightbulb goes off. Dracula said I didn't know the full potential of my power. So, if I can use my radar power in human form, then maybe I can use my super speed in bat form?

I concentrate and then flap, turning on the jets, and the next thing I know, I'm off like a rocket! I grab the spear in mid-air and circle. Now I've got to get out of here before I get killed, or even worse, eaten! But as I try to use my speed again, I can't. I'm plum out of gas!

Just then, I sense I giant object flying over me. It's the griffin! And out of the corner of my eye, I see a large bat heading my way!

At this pace, we're all gonna collide into each other!

Where's an air-traffic controller when you need one?

I try flapping but it's no use. I've got nothing left in the tank and I'm losing altitude. There's no way I can outrun them. My only option is to turn into a mist—if I can even do that. But if I do, I may have to release the Spear of Darkness! I don't know if I'll be able to carry something so large in mist form.

I don't know what to do.

They're almost on me!

I feel like I'm gonna pass out.

I close my eyes.

THWIP!

SSSQQQUUUAAAKKK!!!

Huh? What was that ear-piercing scream?

But when I look up I see a silver arrow sticking out

of the griffin's chest, and then it plummets down, barreling into Count Dracula on its way!

Where'd that arrow come from?

"Bram!" a girl's voice calls.

What? Who?

But as I scan the ground below, I find a transparent girl floating off the ground. And next to her are three men, one of whom has spider legs, and another is pointing a crossbow my way.

It's Aura! And that's Van Helsing, Crawler, and Professor Morris! They found us!

Just then, the griffin CRASHES to the ground, kicking up a giant pile of feathers.

But there's no sign of Count Dracula.

Suddenly, the sky brightens and my body feels warm. It's the sun! It's coming up! And that's when I realize that if I stay up here, I'll get a really, really bad sunburn.

Not that I can maintain this height anyway. I'm wiped, and the Spear of Darkness is getting heavier by the second. Everything is getting dizzy.

And then I drop like an anchor.

"Bram!" I hear Aura yell. "Turn into a mist!"

Yeah.

Good idea.

Is that the ground?

Why is it spinning like that?

"Bram, drop the spear!"

Spear? Right. I open my toes.

"—mist!" Aura yells.

What was that?

Mist.

Right.

***

"Bram?"

I hear a voice, but it's so dark.

"Bram, wake up."

I try opening my eyes, but they feel super sticky.

"Bram?"

"Trying," I say.

And then, with what seems like Herculean effort, I manage to pry my eyes open. There's a bright light overhead, and a smiling, blue-eyed girl hovering over me.

"Am I dead?" I ask, squinting in the light.

"Almost," Aura says. "I'd say you tried really hard. But no, you're not dead."

"Oh," I say. I try sitting up, but my whole body hurts. "Where am I?"

"In the infirmary," Aura says. "You're back home."

Home? I look down at my arm and there's an IV stuck in it running red fluids into my body. It feels amazing. But I can't quite figure out how I got here in the first place. I remember something about a spear. And a bell. And—

"Rage!" I say, popping up, causing the monitors to

go bonkers. "And Kat! Where are they? Count Dracula is on the loose and—"

"Relax, Bram," Aura says. "Settle down. Rage is just fine. And Kat is too. They're getting care also. Everything is okay. Well, mostly okay."

"Glad to see he's alert," Dr. Hagella says, entering the room and quieting the monitors. "There are a few visitors here who are waiting to see you."

That's when I notice the infirmary has a bunch of holes in the wall. And then I remember the zombie attack. Dr. Hagella must have held them at bay after all.

Boy, she is one tough lady.

"W-What happened?" I ask. "The last thing I remember is stealing the Spear of Darkness from Count Dracula and freefalling. After that, it's pretty much a blank."

"Well," Aura says, "it's kind of a long story."

"I can handle it from here," comes a familiar voice from the doorway. "Can you give us some time alone?"

It's Van Helsing! I remember him saving me with the Crossbow of Purity. I'm happy to see him, yet something inside of me is telling me to be wary. Like I can't fully trust him.

"Of course, Headmaster," Aura says. "Feel better, Bram." And then she smiles at me and phases through the wall.

"You are lucky to have such a caring friend," Van Helsing says, sitting on the edge of my bed.

"Yeah," I say. "She's pretty awesome."

"Yes, in more ways than one," Van Helsing says. "Once Rage and Professor Hexum were captured, she went in search of us and found us on the far end of the forest. Fortunately, we got to you in the nick of time."

"No wonder she wasn't around," I say.

"Indeed," Van Helsing says. "How do you feel?"

"Like I've been run over by a truck," I answer.

"You have had quite an adventure," Van Helsing says. "Much of which seemed outside of your control."

What's he talking about? And then I realize he's referring to the episode in the tunnel. We never did resolve my punishment for that. Is that why he's here now?

"Tell me, Bram," he says, "were there other moments you have felt out of control? Is there anything you are not telling me?"

His question catches me off guard. I open my mouth to speak, but nothing comes out. I mean, I still haven't told him about nearly sucking Rage's blood at Moreau Labs. And then there was the situation with Kat's wound. I want to tell him about it, but then my conversation with Count Dracula comes flooding back.

No wonder I feel on edge. What if Count Dracula was right? What if Van Helsing is only using me?

"Um, no," I say, rather unconvincingly. "You know everything I know."

"Are you sure?" Van Helsing asks, raising his

eyebrows. "For example, I only recently learned from your peers that you were hypnotized by Dr. Renfield. Do you remember that?"

Dr. Renfield? That's funny. With everything going on, I totally forgot about him. He was the one who brought up the Spear of Darkness in the first place.

"Yes," I say. "But he was just making an example of me because I passed a note in his class."

"It may have seemed that way at the time," Van Helsing says, "but I believe he was doing much more than that. And now he is nowhere to be found."

"What?" I say. "You mean, he's gone?"

"Yes," Van Helsing says. "He never met up with the others in the auditorium."

"So," I say, trying to put the pieces together, "what exactly are you telling me?"

"What I am saying is that I made a mistake," Van Helsing says. "I believe Dr. Renfield did more than just hypnotize you that day. I believe he put subtle instructions inside your mind to sneak into the forbidden basement and open that vault door. You see, I now believe Dr. Renfield is working for the Dark Ones. He was looking for the Spear of Darkness."

"Excuse me?" I blurt out.

"I know it is shocking to hear," Van Helsing says. "But I put it all together once Professor Hexum told me about Dr. Renfield's comments regarding the Spear of Darkness. As a master of hypnosis, it was easy for him to execute once he had you in a trance. Although it appeared he was asking you simple questions, he was actually implanting detailed instructions deep in your mind. And none of the other students were any the wiser. That is why you have little memory of going into the forbidden basement and opening the vault door. You were in an unconscious state, almost like sleepwalking. And you followed his instructions perfectly."

Now I'm in total shock. I feel like such a fool. But it's no wonder I did what I did. I was manipulated!

"After Crawler subdued Rage," Van Helsing says, "I sent him after Dr. Renfield. But it is likely too late."

"And what happened to the Spear of Darkness?" I ask. "Does Count Dracula have it?"

"No, it is safe," Van Helsing says, "thanks to you. Professor Hexum did a good job disguising it for a long, long time. But now that its hiding place has been discovered, I have taken it back into my possession. I am the only person who knows where it is."

"And the Bell of Virtue?" I ask.

"It has also been returned to its proper place," Van Helsing says. "Professor Hexum and Katherine brought it back from the tower. The school is safe once again under the protection of the Artifacts of Virtue. And I have removed all known hidden entrances to the academy. The vault door and basement entry are gone."

Well, that's a relief.

But that's not the only thing I'm worried about.

"But what about Count Dracula?" I ask. "He got away, didn't he?"

"He did," Van Helsing says. "He escaped before sunrise. If we had only kept him exposed to the sunlight for a while longer, we at least would have destroyed his mortal body. But alas, it was not meant to be."

Well, that would have been great. I'd take destroying Count Dracula's mortal body any day of the week. At least it would buy me some time before I had to deal with his spirit.

"Your friends are excited to see you," Van Helsing says. "But I have one last question. When we arrived on the scene, I noticed that you and Count Dracula faced each other in bat-form for a long while without fighting. What was happening?"

Suddenly, my mind starts spinning. I mean, what am I supposed to say? Should I tell him that Dracula wanted me on his side? Or that he told me not to trust Van Helsing? I mean, what if Count Dracula was right? What if Van Helsing doesn't want any vampires alive at the end of all of this.

"Um, nothing much," I say finally. "He was just crowing about how powerful he was and that he wanted me dead. You know, the usual stuff."

Van Helsing squints and smiles at me.

He doesn't believe me for a second.

"Very well," he says, patting my arm. "You have done well, Bram. I am proud of you."

"Thanks," I say.

"Now let me bring in your friends," Van Helsing says. "They have some news to share."

"Okay," I say, as Van Helsing stands up and exits.

Then, Aura returns, with Hairball, Stanphibian, and InvisiBill in tow—or at least I think InvisiBill is in tow.

"Hey, Brampire," Hairball says. "Are you okay?"

"Yeah," I say, lying through my teeth. "I'm great."

"Awesome," InvisiBill says, his voice booming from the foot of my bed. "Because you'll never guess what Professor Hexum just did."

EPILOGUE

STARTING OVER

"Are you sure you're ready for this?" Rage asks.

"I was born ready," I answer with a smile, looking at all of the teams gathered in the gymnasium. It's been a few weeks since the incident at Moreau's tower, and I'm feeling much better.

"I never thought we'd get back in the Monster Cup," Rage says. "I thought we were done for good."

Honestly, so was I. But I was thrilled when the team told me that Professor Hexum reversed his disqualification ruling. I mean, I know how much the team wanted to win the cup.

Heck, I kind of wanted to win it too.

And now we'll actually have the chance.

With everything that happened after the Bell of Virtue was stolen, the competition never got off the ground, so Van Helsing decided to restart the entire tournament once the school was patched up. For the first time, as a signal of school solidarity, he's having all of the teams compete in each event at the same time.

And the first race is about to begin!

"Listen, Bram," Aura says. "We're all sorry for the way we treated you when we got kicked out of the Monster Cup. And we're not just saying that because we're back in the competition. Can you ever forgive us?"

"Can I forgive you guys?" I say. "Of course I can. I mean, after everything I did, I'm wondering if you can forgive me?"

"You're totally forgiven," Aura says.

"Not so fast," InvisiBill says. "Let's see if he wins his heat first."

"Shut it, InvisiBill," Hairball says.

"Break a wing," Stanphibian grunts.

"Thanks," I say. "I will."

We all put our hands in a circle and on the count of three yell, "Monstrosities!"

It feels great having the gang back together. And I'm so relieved I'll have the chance to make it up to them. But before my race begins, I need to check on one more person.

"Is everything ready?" I whisper to Aura.

"Yep," she whispers. "Would you like to do the honors?"

I nod and then walk over to the bleachers where I find Kat sitting with her arm in a cast.

"How are you doing?" I ask.

"Okay," she says. "Except for this, of course. Dr. Hagella said the bullet shattered my radius bone. I guess the good news is that I should heal pretty fast due to my cat anatomy."

"Well, that's great news," I say. "Kat, I'm so sorry about your brother. You were right, he had a good heart."

"Thanks, Bram," she says, looking down and wiping away a tear. "I'll miss him forever."

"He did a brave thing," I say. "And he did it to protect you."

"Yeah, I know," she says. "He was the best."

"So," I say, "Van Helsing told us he invited you to stay here at the academy."

"Yeah," she says. "It was nice of him to offer. I mean, I don't exactly have anywhere else to go, especially looking like this. So, I guess I'm stuck with you guys now."

"Well, I'd be thrilled if you stayed," I say. "We could use someone with your skills. You're an animal out there. Literally."

We both look at each other and laugh.

"Well, what about your friends?" she says. "I don't know if they want me here. Especially your ghost friend."

"Don't worry," Aura says, appearing behind her. "Of course I want you here. You've more than proven yourself to me, and we need all the help we can get."

"Really?" Kat says.

"Really," Aura says. "Fish-face, give her the gear."

Just then, Stanphibian walks up and hands her a black sweater and a silver badge.

"Welcome to the Monstrosities," Aura says.

"Are you serious?" Kat asks, breaking into a big smile. Then, she picks up the badge, turns it over, and reads the name engraved in its center. "WildKat?"

"That's your new code name," I say. "And after seeing the way you fight, it's well earned."

"Thanks," she says, holding the badge against her heart. "You know, you guys are great."

"Racers, please report to the starting line!" Hexum calls into a megaphone.

"Well, that's me," I say.

"Good luck, Bram," Kat says.

"You've got this," Rage says.

"If you lose, you're still a moron!" InvisiBill adds.

Yep, it's good to see things are back to normal.

As I approach the starting line, I notice Professor Hexum is no longer pretending to use a walking stick. Now that Van Helsing has the Spear of Darkness, I guess there's no reason to keep up the charade.

"Mr. Murray," Hexum says, casually acknowledging my presence like the whole crazy tower episode never even happened.

"Professor," I say, acknowledging him back. "Before we start, I want to thank you for allowing us to compete."

"Kindness will not earn you any extra advantages,"

Hexum says. "You will win or lose based on your own merits."

Yep, things are definitely back to normal.

"Get ready to eat my dust, loser," Harpoon says, lining up next to me.

"The only thing I'll be eating is victory cake," I answer back with a wink.

"We'll see about that," she grumbles.

Well, I know one thing. This isn't going to be easy. I mean, all of the best flyers are in this race. But if I use what Count Dracula taught me about combining my abilities, I should give them all a run for their money.

"Racers, on your mark!" Hexum calls out.

Aura and Kat give me a thumbs up.

"Get set!"

Then, I catch Van Helsing staring at me from the stands. He nods and I wonder if he still trusts me.

But what's even worse is that I'm starting to wonder if I trust myself.

"Go!"

For a split second, I hesitate as everyone else takes off. And then I transform into a bat and take flight.

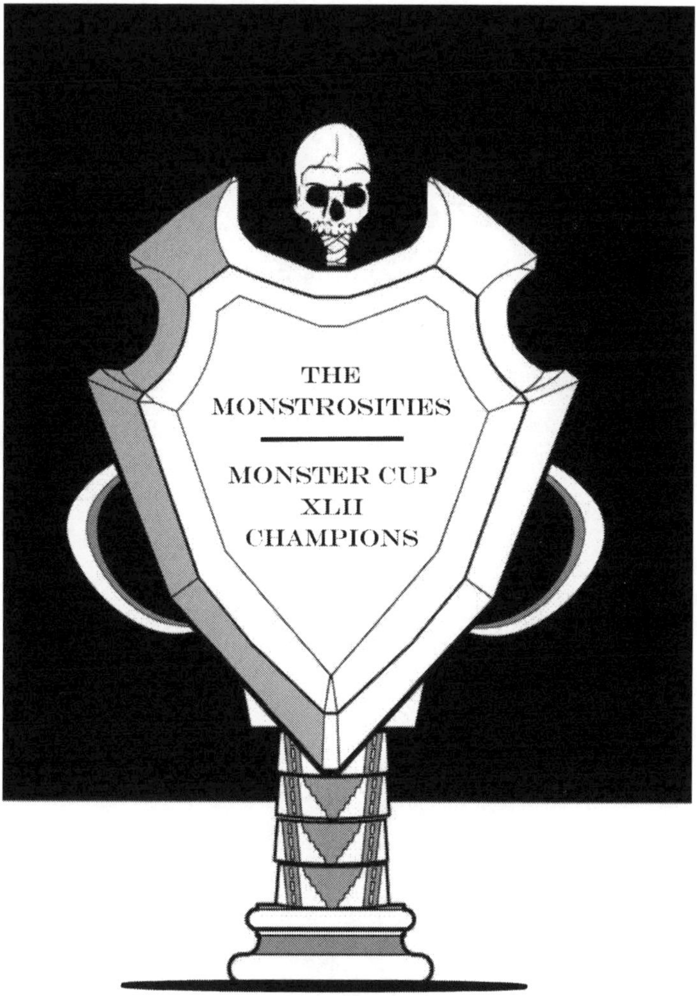
THE
MONSTROSITIES
MONSTER CUP
XLII
CHAMPIONS

Monster Problems 3: Prince of Dorkness

CHAPTER ONE

BLOOD HUNT

I'm in bat-form, soaring high above the city.

It's well after midnight and a full moon hangs in the night sky. I don't remember how I got here, but the cool air feels good against my skin. It's peaceful among the clouds and I spread my wings, riding the air currents to a higher altitude.

From my vantage point, the city below looks abandoned, absent of any signs of life. Other than the streetlamps lining the roads, there isn't a light to be found inside the many homes and apartments. Yet, despite how empty the city looks, I know it's filled with people.

Sleeping people.

And I'm ravenously hungry.

My stomach rumbles and churns like I haven't eaten for days. Of course, I know that isn't true, but despite what my head is telling me, the longing in my stomach is only growing stronger.

It feels like a craving.

A craving I must satisfy.

With each flap of my wings, I feel my strength slipping away. If I don't feed soon I'll lose energy. I pulse my radar across the sprawling, concrete landscape, looking for my best opportunity. Finding an open window would make things a whole lot easier, and there are literally hundreds of windows to choose from.

But which one should I pick?

Then, I spot it.

There's a three-story brownstone with a brick stairway out front. For some reason, this particular building is calling to me, but I don't know why. I scan the windows which are shut except for one on the third floor.

I zero in and land on the windowsill.

The room inside is pitch black, but that's not an issue for me. As I look around the tiny room, I notice the minimal accommodations. There's a bed, a dresser, a desk, and little else. Not that it matters, because I'm not here for the décor, but rather for what's lying in the bed.

As I stare at the figure snuggled in the blankets, I suddenly feel an overwhelming sense of guilt. I mean, this is crazy. Am I really going to do this?

Am I really going to suck someone's blood?

Suddenly, I have a change of heart. I back up to fly away when my stomach grumbles again. Ugh. I'm so hungry and regular food just won't satisfy my craving.

Maybe I'll move a little closer.

I hop off the windowsill onto the cold floor and concentrate on becoming a kid again. Seconds later, I'm back in human-form standing over a curly-haired boy who looks about my age. His head is resting on his pillow and he's snoring lightly, the nape of his neck exposed.

I lick my lips and lean forward.

And then I stop myself.

I mean, I've never actually done this before. But I won't take a lot of blood, just enough to get rid of this crazy hunger. And if I'm gentle enough maybe he won't even wake up. Then, I'll fly out of here and he'll never know the difference.

It seems easy enough.

But suddenly, I feel a wave of disgust. What am I doing? The last time I checked, I wasn't a full-fledged vampire. But if that's true, what am I doing here?

I think back to my conversation with Dr. Renfield at the Van Helsing Academy. He said it was only a matter of time before my father's vampire genes took over my mother's human genes. And once that happens, the molecular structure of my body will become less Natural and more Supernatural, impacting my thoughts and behaviors.

In other words, I'll be a true vampire.

Is that why I'm here?

Has it already happened?

I've got to get out of here!

I take a step back and land on something round! My foot rolls and I SMACK hard into the wall behind me. Fortunately, I manage to grab the windowsill before toppling over.

Great job, Bram. Could I be any clumsier? And when I look down I see a baseball lying next to my foot.

Awesome. I just hope I didn't wake—

"Hey!" the boy says, sitting up. "Who are you?"

"Um, no one," I say, getting back to my feet. "You're just having a dream. Don't worry, I'll be going now."

"Bram?" the boy says. "Is that you?"

Bram?

How'd he know my name?

But as I look closer at his face, my jaw drops, because I can't believe my eyes. That curly hair! It's Johnny! My orphan friend!

But how?

Now I know why everything seems so familiar. Without even realizing it, I flew back to the New England Home for Troubled Boys! And I was about to drink Johnny's blood!

Suddenly, I feel sick to my stomach.

"Bram?" he says, looking closer. "It is you! I'd recognize those ears anywhere. What are you doing here?" Then, his eyes go wide as he grabs his throat. "Were you trying to hurt me?"

"N-No," I stammer.

"I-I don't believe you," he says. "You came through my window! You were going to suck my blood!"

"No!" I insist.

"Br—"

***

"—am?"

"No!" I yell, sitting up, sweat pouring from my forehead.

"Bram?" Rage repeats, staring down at me with a puzzled look on his face. "Um, are you okay?"

"What?" I say, looking around. Where am I? What happened to Johnny?

Then, I realize I'm lying in my bed at the Van Helsing Academy.

I glance at our shut window and realize it was all a dream. I was never at the New England Home for Troubled Boys. I never tried to drink Johnny's blood. I flop down on my pillow relieved.

"Are you okay?" Rage asks. "You look kind of pale, even for you."

"Yeah," I say, catching my breath. "I'm good. Just had a really bad dream."

"Should I get Van Helsing?" Rage asks. "The last time you had a really bad dream you kind of endangered the whole school, remember?"

Van Helsing?

"Oh, no," I say quickly. "It wasn't anything like that. I'm good. Really."

I try looking calm, but I'm totally freaked out right now. And truthfully, Van Helsing is the last person I want to share my dream with because I'm not exactly sure I can trust him.

When I fought Count Dracula at Dr. Moreau's tower, he opened my eyes to Van Helsing. Now, I know Count Dracula isn't the most reliable source of information, but he said a few things that rang true. He reminded me that Van Helsing descends from generations of vampire hunters who dedicated their lives to the complete extermination of all vampires. And since only a vampire can kill another vampire, Count Dracula said Van Helsing is just using me to get rid of him.

And then, I'll be next.

I don't want to believe him, but Van Helsing has withheld things from me before. And strangely, it was Count Dracula who gave me tips on how to use my powers better. But that wasn't all Count Dracula had to offer.

He asked me to join him.

He said I am what I am for a reason. He said I could try fighting my destiny but it wouldn't work because my vampire tendencies will slowly take over my soul.

I tried to ignore him, but based on my dream, I'm afraid he might be right. And I'm scared.

"Big day today," Rage says, grabbing his backpack from his bed. "Are you ready?"

"Ready?" I say. "Ready for what?"

"For end of term exams," Rage says, looking at me like I'm nuts. "You know, the thing we've been studying like crazy for over the last few weeks? On second thought, maybe I should get Van Helsing to look at you."

End of term exams? That's right!

I rub my eyes and exhale. Right now, the last thing I want to do is take exams.

"No, I'm good," I say, swinging my legs out of bed. "They just slipped my mind for a second. Wishful thinking, I guess."

"I guess," Rage says. "Well, just to remind you, our exams are today. And in case you also forgot, you have to pass them to move on with our section."

"I know, I know," I say, standing up and stretching. "I'm not planning on failing. But I am worried about InvisiBill. You think he knows his stuff?"

"He'd better," Rage says. "Aura's been grilling him non-stop for days. If he fails he'll not only have to repeat the coursework, but he'll have to answer to her too."

"Then he'd better pass," I say.

Just then, my stomach rumbles.

"I think you need breakfast," Rage says. "I heard that from here."

"Sorry," I say, holding my stomach. Well, I guess one part of my dream was true. I put on my gray hoodie and grab my backpack. "Let's go. We can quiz each other while we eat."

By the time we get to the cafeteria, it's an absolute madhouse. Usually, most kids skip breakfast, but clearly, the whole school decided to fuel up before facing their exams. We scan the room but can't find our section through the throng of students stuffing their faces and flipping through their textbooks.

"There they are," Rage says, nodding towards the back.

We weave through the crowd until we find the rest of the Monstrosities in various degrees of distress. Kat and Stanphibian look like they don't have a care in the world, Hairball is rapidly paging through his notes, and Aura has her nose in her Monsterology book, barking questions at a seemingly empty seat across from her.

"What type of metal injures vampires?" she asks.

"Excuse me?" I say, putting my backpack on the table.

"Relax, Bram," Aura says. "I'm quizzing InvisiBill. Questions like this are sure to be on Professor Holmwood's exam. Right, InvisiBill?"

"Um, right," InvisiBill says, his voice coming from the empty seat. "That's an easy one. It's copper."

"No, InvisiBill," Aura says, clearly annoyed. "We already went over this three times. It's not copper, it's silver. Don't you remember? Weapons made of one hundred percent pure silver can mortally injure a vampire by purifying the vampiric virus within their cells. Now, how many types of doppelgangers are there?"

"Uh, one," he answers.

"Nope," Aura says, furrowing her eyebrows. "Didn't you do any of the extra reading I recommended? You've gotten every question wrong."

"I studied," he says. "Some."

"How about you, Bram?" Aura asks, closing her book in frustration. "Did you study?"

"Of course," I say, "but probably not as much as you."

"No one studies more than she does," Hairball says. "It's like a disease."

"Very funny," Aura says. "I strive to do my best. Is there anything wrong with that?"

"Not at all," Kat says, lapping up some milk. "I wish I'd been here long enough to take the exams. Studying makes me feel like a normal kid. But instead, I'm stuck at Monster House while you guys take your exams."

"What's wrong with girls anyway?" Hairball asks.

"We're just smarter," Aura says. "Isn't it obvious?"

"I'm not touching that one," I say. "I'm gonna get some food. I'm starving."

As I make my way over to the buffet, I grab a plate and start loading it with red food, like tomatoes, red peppers, and beets. Just then, a cafeteria imp flutters by and offers me a plate of Swedish Fish.

"Gee, thanks," I say, popping one into my mouth.

But as soon as I chew it, the imp giggles, and I realize it tastes nothing like Swedish Fish. In fact, it sort of tastes like… liver? Gross!

But as I spit it into the trash, I hear—

"Good luck today, Fang Face."

I turn around to find Harpoon and the other Howlers standing behind me. Blobby squeezes his head beneath the buffet sneeze guard and starts swallowing all of the hamburger patties. Well, that's utterly disgusting.

"Um, thanks," I say. "You too."

"You know," Harpoon says, with a sly smile, "I overheard Professor Hexum telling Professor Morris that he has a special test just for you."

"Um, what?" I say, my head spinning.

Is she serious? Why would Hexum be giving me a 'special' test? What does that even mean? Is she messing with me? I wouldn't put it past her.

"You heard me," Harpoon says. "Enjoy your Survival Skills exam. I know we'll enjoy watching you. C'mon, Howlers. Let's go."

As the Howlers walk away cackling, Blobby scarfs down a whole tray of prepackaged jelly cups, forms into a big ball of flesh, and rolls after them. Meanwhile, I've pretty much lost my appetite.

I find my way back to our table and sit down.

No matter how hard I try, I can't get Harpoon's comment out of my head. I mean, Hexum is a mentalist. He could embarrass me a million ways to Sunday.

Ugh, what's he going to do to me?

"You okay?" Kat asks. "You're not eating anything and you look a little shell-shocked."

"I'm fine," I say, lying through my teeth.

"Great," Aura says, standing up. "Because our first

exam starts in ten minutes."

Awesome.

I can't wait.

CLASSIFIED
Person(s) of Interest
CODE NAME: THE MONSTROSITIES
BASE OF OPERATIONS: VAN HELSING ACADEMY
D.S.I
TARGET: Rage
TARGET: Aura
TARGET: WildKat
TARGET: Brampire
TARGET: Hairball
TARGET: Stanphibian
Got Monster?
TARGET: InvisiBill
DEPARTMENT OF SUPERNATURAL INVESTIGATIONS

CHAPTER TWO

SCHOOL DAZE

My mind is totally muddled.

I mean, between my nightmare about Johnny and Harpoon's breakfast bombshell about my 'special' test with Hexum, I'm totally off my game.

My first exam disaster is in Professor Holmwood's Monsterology class. I worked hard all semester to learn the various monster categories and characteristics so the test should have been a breeze. But instead, I'm struggling to remember the difference between a chimera and a chupacabra and a kelpie versus a kobold.

Time seems to stand still and I find myself staring off into space when, all of a sudden, the bell rings ending class. While the other kids hand in their exams with big smiles on their faces, I'm feeling depressed. And I'm not the only one disappointed with my submission.

"Bram, is everything okay?" Professor Holmwood asks, looking at both sides of my paper. "The second page of your exam is completely blank."

"What?" I say, peering over. "Oh, well, look at that. I

didn't even know there was a second page. Sorry, I-I guess it was harder than I thought."

"I would say so," she says, reviewing the page I did manage to fill out. "This is very unlike you, Bram. You're one of my strongest students and know this material inside and out. Tell me, what's a wraith?"

"A wraith?" I say. "That's easy. A wraith is a type of spirit who still has business in the mortal realm."

"That is correct," Professor Holmwood says. "Yet, here you mistook a wraith for a wight."

"I did?" I say, looking at my paper. "Oh, wow, I don't know what I was thinking."

"This is your final exam, Bram," she says. "It's a big part of your overall grade. I suggest you focus harder on your remaining exams. I don't think you want to be left behind."

She's right about that.

But things just go downhill from there.

My next class is Supernatural History 101 with Professor Seward who is notorious for asking impossible essay questions. Sadly, he lives up to his reputation and asks us to answer this doozy: Throughout history, monsters have been persecuted by man. In no less than ten pages, describe five time periods in history where man sought to stamp out the existence of monsters.

Um, no less than—gulp—ten pages?

As soon as Seward says 'begin,' it's like a cannon is shot off in our classroom because everyone starts writing at a frantic pace. I put pen to paper but find myself moving way slower than my classmates. In fact, I'm having a hard time concentrating at all.

I remember the Werewolf Inquisition of the 1200s, but that's about it. I write as much as I can recall about that period and then find myself counting the blank lines in my essay book until the bell once again puts me out of my misery.

Fortunately, we hand in our booklets closed so Professor Seward can't see how little I've written. I'm pretty sure I gutted out three pages but that's all I could manage. No matter how hard I try, I can't stop thinking about Johnny's face in my dream and what Hexum has in store for me.

Thankfully, it's time for lunch.

"How did you guys do on Professor Holmwood's exam?" Aura asks, looking at her Paranormal Science textbook. Since she doesn't need to eat I guess she's doing some extra studying. Not that she needs it.

"Okay," Hairball says, cutting into a thick, raw steak. "At first, the abnormals section threw me off, but then I got into a groove. How'd you do Stan?"

"So-so," Stanphibian says, sipping a bowl of green algae through a straw.

"Great," Aura asks. "Now for the big question. InvisiBill, how did you do?"

"Oh, I blew chunks on that one," InvisiBill says from the empty seat across from her. "Major chunks."

I turn away as he takes a big bite of his hamburger and starts chewing it up. So disgusting.

"I hope you did better than that," Aura says. "Do you really want to take Holmwood's class over again?"

"Yes," Stanphibian answers for him.

"Shut it, Stan," InvisiBill says.

"Crush on teacher," Stanphibian adds.

"I said shut it!" InvisiBill repeats.

"Well, I think I did well on that one," Rage says, talking with a mouth full of meatball. "I finished with enough time to double-check my answers. What about you, Bram? I bet you killed it."

"Next question," I say.

"Seriously?" Rage says. "What happened?"

But instead of answering, I look up to see the Howlers staring at me from a few tables over. Harpoon waves at me with her fork.

"No comment," I say, biting my cheese-less pizza.

"I'm sure you did better than you think," he says.

"Professor Seward's exam was like running a marathon," Aura says. "I started writing from the second he handed out the booklets to the second the bell rang."

"My paw still hurts," Hairball says, shaking his furry wrist. "I thought I was gonna run out of ink."

"What did you write about?" Rage asks Aura.

"I gave seven examples of monsters being persecuted through the ages," Aura says casually.

"Seven?" InvisiBill says. "That's funny, I did the

same thing. Minus five."

Great. Even InvisiBill did better than me.

"You know," Aura says, "as I was writing, I thought it was ironic how humans have always tried to get rid of monsters, yet here we are being trained to save humankind. Kind of makes you wonder who the real monsters are?"

"Hey, guys," Kat says, sliding into our table with a tray full of fish. "How are the exams going?"

"Painfully," InvisiBill says.

"I sure wish I was with you," Kat says. "I've been twiddling my tail and watching TV all morning."

"The horror!" InvisiBill says sarcastically.

"It's boring," she says. "Believe me, I'd rather be challenging myself with the tests you guys are taking."

Just then, the bell rings ending lunch. I take a deep breath and exhale. Our next exam is Paranormal Science, and then we see Hexum.

Harpoon smiles as she exits and my stomach drops.

"Time to go," Aura says, floating from the bench.

"Good luck," Kat says, waving from the table.

I have a distinct feeling I'm gonna need more than luck, and boy am I right. For our Paranormal Science exam, Professor Morris asks us to solve a super-complicated case study about a bank robbery involving a gang of Supernatural suspects.

As part of the exam, we're handed a huge packet of information about the crime, including pages of statements from eyewitnesses. Then, we're supposed to write all the steps we would take to conduct a proper Supernatural crime scene investigation and our conclusion as to who committed the crime. It's interesting but there's so much evidence to sort through it's taking forever.

After a while, I get a headache so I take a look around. Aura is reading, Rage is writing intensely, Hairball is pulling his hair out, Stanphibian is staring into space, and there are dozens of crumpled up papers near InvisiBill's seat. Then, my eyes meet Harpoon's and she makes a throat-cutting signal with her pencil.

Lovely.

I get back to work, but by the time I've narrowed it down to three possible suspects, the bell goes off again! I quickly scribble down my guess as to who did it and then hand in my work. It's not until we head out that I realize how wrong I was.

"Well, that was easy," Aura says. "The troll was the culprit. The giant footprints inside the bank vault were a dead giveaway."

"Yeah," Rage says. "I had the troll also. The footprints were too obvious. What about you, Bram?"

"Wait, there were footprints?" I say. "Well, um, I must have missed that part. I thought the ghost did it."

"The ghost?" Aura says, looking at me like I have three heads. "Bram, how could the ghost have done it? I'm a ghost. Do you see me leaving footprints all over the place?"

"Well, um," I stammer. "No. Not really."

"Exactly," she says. "I don't know what's wrong with you, but there's only one exam left this term. You better nail it."

Right. Except the odds of me nailing anything related to Hexum are pretty much zero to none. Hexum's class is called Survival Skills for a reason. It's all about thinking and acting—the quicker the better. And if you're not quick enough, well, you'll be lucky to get out alive.

As we enter the gymnasium everyone goes silent. We place our backpacks against the wall and fan out shoulder-to-shoulder. Hexum stands in the center of the gym, staring us down with his arms behind his back.

It's strange seeing him without his walking stick, but I'm still shocked it was really the Spear of Darkness all along. I've got to hand it to Hexum, he kept it hidden in plain sight for years. I'm just glad Van Helsing tucked it away so we don't have to think about it again.

I'd say no one embodies the Van Helsing Academy motto of 'You Must Believe in Things You Cannot Imagine' better than Hexum. So, needless to say, there's no telling what's about to happen.

And that's what worries me.

"Welcome, students," Hexum says, sounding unusually chipper as he walks down the line. "Welcome to the most joyous day of the year. Because today you will either prove that you have learned all of the material we have studied, or you will fail miserably. The rules for the exam are simple. Rule number one, do your best. Anything less will result in failure. Rule number two, no exam will be alike. Each of you will experience an exam personally tailored to you. Rule number three, everyone will take their exam simultaneously. And finally, rule number four, be prepared, because this exam will push you to the edge."

Then, he stops in front of me.

"And some of you will break."

I swallow hard.

What's that supposed to mean?

"Please ensure there is ample space between you and the students to either side of you," Hexum says.

I look right to find Rage, who slides over with a nervous smile. Then, I turn left to find a pair of yellow eyes staring back at me. It's Harpoon!

"I wanted to get close enough to hear you scream," she whispers.

"How thoughtful," I whisper back.

"Silence, Mr. Murray!" Hexum barks.

I look at Harpoon who sticks out her tongue.

Nice.

"Now, close your eyes," Hexum says. "You are to keep them closed for the duration of the class, even if your exam ends prematurely."

I close my eyes.

"Your exam will begin now," Hexum says, his voice

echoing inside my head.

Suddenly, I'm standing in the middle of a dark chamber with stone walls, a low ceiling, and no windows. I don't know what I'm doing here, but when I breathe in the air tastes stale and musty.

Just then, a large object appears.

It's a black, wooden box, tapered at both ends and covered with a lid.

My heart skips a beat.

It's… a coffin!

As my mind jumps to what might be lying inside I have an overwhelming feeling of dread. Could it be a dead body? A zombie? I scan the chamber for a way out, but I don't see a door anywhere. I'm trapped!

CRRREEEAAAK!

What's that noise?

Then, I see the lid of the coffin opening!

The next thing I know, a pale hand emerges and latches onto the side of the coffin! I jump back as shivers shoot down my spine. What is that thing?

And then it hits me.

I-I know whose hand that is!

Holy cow!

It's Count Dracula!

And there's nowhere to run!

I'm gonna have to fight him! B-But I'm not ready!

He's going to kill me!

STOP!

What?

That was a girl's voice! I look around to see where it came from, and as the background of the chamber suddenly shifts back to the gymnasium, I see Kat standing there with panic in her eyes.

"What are you doing here?" Hexum yells, striding up to her with his arms crossed.

"I-I'm sorry, Professor," she says. "But something terrible just happened."

"What is it, child?" Hexum demands, looming over her. "What could be so terrible you needed to interrupt my exam?"

"I-It's the Dark Ones," Kat says. "I-I was watching the news, and the Dark Ones just attacked New York City! They're… turning people into evil monsters!"

CLASSIFIED

Person(s) of Interest

CODE NAME: NONE

REAL NAME: LUCY HOLMWOOD

BASE OF OPERATIONS: VAN HELSING ACADEMY

FACTS: Lucy Holmwood is the tenured professor of Monsterology at the Van Helsing Academy. She is a multiple award-winning biologist and is widely considered to be the leading expert in the field of Monster Species Classification. She is a trusted confidante of Lothar Van Helsing.

FIELD OBSERVATIONS:

- Highly intelligent
- Dedicated to her students
- Use extreme caution when tracking as she is quick to notice new patterns or unusual behaviors

Category: Natural

Sub-Type: None

Height: 5'5"

Weight: 145 lbs

STATUS: ACTIVE TARGET

DEPARTMENT OF SUPERNATURAL INVESTIGATIONS

CHAPTER THREE

MONSTERS UNLEASHED

I would have taken any excuse to get out of Hexum's exam, but not this.

I mean, the Dark Ones are attacking New York City! After Kat crashed class, Hexum postponed his exam and immediately went to find Van Helsing. Once he left the gymnasium, the rest of us dashed over to Monster House to catch the news on TV. There's probably thirty of us smushed in the common room.

"Ugh, what's that?" Hairball complains.

"It smells like rotten fish sticks," InvisiBill says.

"Sorry," Stanphibian says.

"Quiet!" Aura shouts. "Turn on the TV."

"On it," Kat says, grabbing the remote control.

Just then, the TV flicks on and my jaw drops because I can't believe what I'm seeing. Monsters are all over the city! Werewolves are prowling the subway system, zombies are lumbering through Times Square, and winged creatures are flying around the Empire State Building!

"What are those things?" InvisiBill asks.

"Gargoyles," Rage says. "You really did flunk Professor Holmwood's exam, didn't you?"

"Shush!" Aura orders. "Turn up the volume. Everyone be quiet!"

Well, she doesn't have to worry about me because I'm absolutely speechless right now. I've never seen so many monsters in public before. There must be hundreds of them and watching them attack innocent civilians is horrifying.

Those poor people. One minute they were going about their day, and the next they're running for their lives. They don't stand a chance against these evil monsters.

"… city is in ruins," a female news anchor says, as the volume increases and the screen flips from one horrible scene to the next. "There is nowhere to run. Nowhere to hide. The police are doing their best to mount a response, but they are simply not equipped to deal with this… this barrage of terror. We remind you again to stay indoors. Bar your doors and windows. Do not, I repeat, do not let a werewolf or zombie bite you. The President has declared a state of emergency and the military is on their way. But will it be enough to—. Wait. Please hold on, this just in… I'm now being handed a letter, written… in blood? It's from Count Dracula himself. The letter is addressed to all world leaders, and it says…"

"Turn it off," comes a voice from the back of the room, startling everyone.

Kat immediately clicks off the TV, and when we turn around we find Van Helsing standing in the doorway with Crawler, Professor Morris, and Professor Hexum behind him. And Van Helsing is holding a letter of his own.

"I will read you the correspondence myself," Van Helsing says, snapping the paper taut. "To all Naturals. Be warned, for what is happening in New York City is a small demonstration of my power. For far too long your kind has hunted my kind to the brink of extinction. But now it is your turn to experience what it is like to be hunted. I have returned to fulfill my destiny and lead my army of Dark Ones to destroy you. Prepare yourselves… if you can. Your Master, Count Dracula."

"Um, what's that supposed to mean?" Hairball asks.

"It means the war has finally begun," Van Helsing says. "The war between monsters and men."

Suddenly, a chill runs down my spine.

"Students," Van Helsing continues. "we are facing the most dangerous foe in the history of the human race. Count Dracula intends to rule over the entire population of Earth, and he has never been so bold. Billions of lives are at stake, and if Count Dracula succeeds those lives will not only perish, but their undead souls will join the ranks of the Dark Ones."

"We've got to stop him!" Aura says.

"No," Van Helsing says. "There is no 'we.' It is far

too dangerous and you are not ready for a threat of this magnitude. All of you will remain here under the Supernatural protection of the Artifacts of Virtue. No one is to leave campus for any reason. Is that clear?"

"Yes," we respond in unison.

"Very good," he says. "But as an added precaution, I have called upon Mrs. Clops to look after you—some of you more than others."

Not surprisingly, he's staring at our section.

"I must travel to New York City to put an end to this madness," he says, raising his Crossbow of Purity. "Several of the professors will be joining me on this mission, but Professor Seward and Dr. Hagella will join Mrs. Clops and remain here at the academy. I am relying on all of you to keep your word. It is extremely dangerous out there, and if you venture beyond these gates there is no telling what may happen to you."

I swallow hard.

Van Helsing stares everyone down, ending on me.

"Please, I implore you," he says. "Heed my warning."

And then he turns and exits the common room, followed by Crawler, Morris, and Hexum.

Once he's gone, we all look at each other wide-eyed, but nobody says a word.

***

What's happening in New York City is bad enough,

but not being able to do anything about it feels even worse. Especially since we've been stuck in the common room for hours under the watchful eye of Vi Clops, our resident cyclops, and Monster House manager.

"This is so frustrating," I whisper to Hairball.

"Yeah," he whispers back. "Everything is going nuts out there and we're not even allowed to fight."

"Quiet yer selves down," Vi Clops grunts, her giant eyeball shifting between Hairball and me. She's sitting on the floor with her back against the doorframe, forming a twenty-foot tall barricade. "No one is leavin' here unless yer bein' carried out on a stretcher."

Well, that's pleasant.

After another ten minutes or so of silence, Vi Clops rubs her eye and Kat leans over.

"I still don't understand why she's babysitting us," Kat whispers. "How come the Howlers aren't being forced to sit here until Van Helsing gets back?"

"Because they haven't snuck off of campus before," I whisper back. "I know you're new here but our team has a reputation for leaving school grounds without permission. Van Helsing doesn't trust us to listen to him and actually stay put."

"I wouldn't trust us either," Hairball says, stretching out in his tiny chair. "I wouldn't trust us at all."

"Same," Stanphibian adds.

"No talkin'!" Vi Clops snipes.

Everyone clams up.

Then, Aura floats a little closer to me.

"We've got to get out of here," she whispers.

"No kidding," I whisper back.

"No, I mean we've really got to get out of here," she whispers more urgently. "A while ago I received an alert from the spirit network. A cargo ship just arrived at the port."

"Um, okay," I whisper, totally confused. "Don't ships arrive at the port all the time?"

"No," she whispers. "You don't get it. This ship is unusual. It came from Romania and is carrying cargo from Bucharest."

"So?" I whisper.

"So," she whispers. "Don't you know your geography? Bucharest is the capital of Romania, and it's located in a region called Wallachia."

Wallachia?

Why does that name sound so familiar?

"Do I really have to spell it out for you?" she whispers. "Wallachia was Vlad Dracul's kingdom. Count Dracula is from Wallachia."

"Quiet!" Vi Clops barks.

Holy cow! She's right!

I look at Aura, my eyes bugging out, and she nods in acknowledgment. Now I remember. Wallachia is where Vlad Dracul's men used the original Blood Grail to turn him into Count Dracula. So, if a ship is coming from Wallachia, it could be carrying supplies from Count

Dracula's homeland. Supplies he'll use to take over the world!

I wait for Vi Clops to look away, and then whisper—

"We've got to get to that ship."

"Ya' think, dummy?" Aura whispers back. "But don't worry, I'm on it. I already put InvisiBill on the case."

"InvisiBill?" I whisper. "Are you nuts?"

"Probably," she whispers. "But he's the only one who can get in and out of here without being seen."

Well, she's right about that. And come to think of it, I haven't heard his annoying voice in a while. I wonder what he's been—

"Delivery!"

Huh? That came from the hall.

Suddenly, a dozen pizza boxes stacked sky-high march through the common room door. But the thing is, there's no one carrying them.! That's when everything clicks. It's InvisiBill, and he ordered pizza.

My stomach rumbles as the delicious smell wafts through the common room. But why is InvisiBill bringing in pizza? Then, it clicks. Aura is a genius.

"What's this?" Vi Clops says, licking her chops.

"Dinner," InvisiBill says, placing the stack of boxes in front of her. "You looked hungry so I took the liberty of ordering you a few snacks."

"Yer violatin' the rules," Vi Clops says, looking around for InvisiBill. "But I am hungry. We'll talk later."

She rips the top off the first box, grabs the entire

pizza with one giant hand, and woofs it down in one bite. Then, she moves on to the next box.

"Um, what's going on?" Kat asks. "Because I really can't unsee this."

"Vi Clops is a cyclops," I whisper. "And all cyclops pass out after they've eaten a big meal. So, it's just a matter of time before we're outta here."

"Well, then," Kat says, positioning her chair to face Vi Clops. "I guess this is worth watching after all."

A minute later, Vi Clops has finished eating.

"Just what I needed," she says, her big eye closing slowly. "Yer all jus' stay here."

"Shame to miss out on all that pizza," Hairball says. "But it was for a good cause."

"I guess I could have saved a pie for you guys," InvisiBill says.

"Yeah," Rage says. "That would have been nice."

"Sorry," InvisiBill says. "Well, at least I had one before I came in."

"What?" Rage says.

"Shhh!" Aura whispers. "Look, she's going down."

Just then, Vi Clops' eyelid closes and her head tilts to the side. Then, she starts snoring like a buzz saw.

"Okay, let's go," Hairball whispers. "But walk softly."

We carefully squeeze past Vi Clops one-by-one. Of course, Stanphibian trips and nearly falls on top of her, but thanks to Kat's catlike reflexes, she catches him just in time. Then, we book down the stairs into the foyer.

Fortunately, no one else is around.

"It sure is dark," Rage says, looking out the window. "It feels like we were trapped in there forever."

"What now?" Kat asks.

"Now we've got a ship to catch," Aura says. "We need to see what cargo came on that boat."

"Do you really think that's a good idea?" Rage asks. "You heard Van Helsing. He told us not to leave campus. Besides, every time we go off school grounds someone nearly eats it."

"Look, I know it's scary," Aura says, "but Count Dracula is attacking New York City. We've got to do whatever we can to help. Right, Bram?"

I open my mouth to answer but nothing comes out.

I mean, they're both right. Every time we leave campus something bad happens. But if we don't see what's on that boat, we may let Count Dracula get exactly what he needs to win his war against humanity.

And the worst part is it's all my fault.

Count Dracula only exists because of me.

If Professor Faustius didn't use me as the Blood Grail this whole nightmare never would have happened.

"Bram?" Aura repeats.

"Um, yeah," I say finally. "Aura's right. We've got to see what's on that boat. It might be important to stop Count Dracula."

"Okay," Kat says. "I'm always ready to mix it up. But

how will we get to this port anyway? It's not like any of us are old enough to drive."

"Don't sweat it," Hairball says. "I'll drive us there."

"Oh," Kat says, "do you have a driver's license?"

"Nope," he says, smoothing his hairy mustache. "I just look the part. Let's roll."

"Oh, no," Rage says, his head in his hands. "This might be worse than facing Count Dracula."

CLASSIFIED

Person(s) of Interest

CODE NAME: NONE

REAL NAME: QUINCY MORRIS IV

BASE OF OPERATIONS: VAN HELSING ACADEMY

FACTS: Quincy Morris IV is the tenured professor of Paranormal Science at the Van Helsing Academy. He is a former Sergeant with the Texas Rangers and is the leading expert in the field of Supernatural Crime Scene Investigations. He is a trusted advisor of Lothar Van Helsing.

Category: Natural

Sub-Type: None

Height: 6'2"

Weight: 193 lbs

FIELD OBSERVATIONS:

- High technical acumen
- Patented new technology to track Supernatural criminals
- Uses 'unorthodox' techniques to solve difficult cases
- Armed and Dangerous

STATUS: ACTIVE TARGET

DEPARTMENT OF SUPERNATURAL INVESTIGATIONS

CHAPTER FOUR

GIVE ME THE DIRT

Remind me to never, ever, E-V-E-R get into a vehicle Hairball's driving again.

This time we swiped Crawler's bus from the garage, and even though Hairball managed not to turn us into roadkill, he certainly did his darndest to try. First, he nearly smashed through the front gates of the academy. Then, he almost caused a twelve-car pileup on the highway. And last, but not least, he flew by a cop going way over the speed limit.

So, yeah, I'm done with that.

And I'm not the only one.

"Stop the bus!" Rage calls out. "I've gotta puke."

"Seriously?" Hairball says, pulling to the side of the road. "Did you eat something that didn't agree with you?"

"No, you idiot," Rage says, running down the aisle holding his stomach. "Your stupid driving doesn't agree with me. Now open the door."

"Backseat driver," Hairball says, opening the folding door. "There's always a backseat driver."

Rage hops out and tosses his cookies in the bushes.

"I know how he feels," Kat says, looking green herself. "Someone should ban Hairball from ever driving again."

"Well, this is actually a good place to stop," Aura says, looking out the windshield. "The port is a few miles up the road. Hairball, turn off the engine and kill the headlights. We don't want anyone to know we're here."

"Yes, sir," Hairball says, shutting off the engine.

"What now?" I ask.

"Now we need to find the cargo ship," Aura says. "It's dark and foggy which should help us stay hidden, but we need to get the lay of the land."

"Leave it to me," I say, stepping off the bus. "Dark and foggy is my specialty. See you in a few minutes. Feel better, Rage."

Rage is still bent over but manages to wave goodbye.

I concentrate on one thought—become a bat—and then transform and take flight. I figure the best way to see everything is from up high. But Aura is right, the fog is so thick I need to stay focused. The last thing I need is to screw up my sonar and crash into the side of a ship.

I reach a comfortable altitude and take in the scene. The port itself is massive, serving as a transportation hub between land and sea. On land, there are a bunch of large warehouses that all look the same—long and low with trucks parked in the loading zones. On the sea, several wooden piers jut into the water for ships to dock.

It's an impressive complex, but I'm not here for a grand tour of the place. We need to find Count Dracula's cargo, but I notice a few problems that will make that easier said than done.

For instance, there are actually three ships docked here, so we'll need to figure out which one came from Wallachia. There are also a bunch of armed guards patrolling the place, so this isn't going to be a cakewalk. I just don't see how we'll get everyone inside the port without being seen. Especially with knuckleheads like Stanphibian and Hairball.

I think I've got all the intel I need, so I head back. When I reach the bus, I see Rage still crouched near the bushes, so I touch down next to him.

"Ahh!" Rage screams, startled. "What's wrong with you? You scared me half to death."

"Sorry," I say, turning back to kid-form. "Are you done yakking?"

"Yeah," he says, wiping his chin. "I think so. Although I considered saving some for Hairball."

"Shhh!" Aura whispers, phasing through the side of the bus. "Do you want to get us discovered?"

"No," I say. "But we're going to need a plan so we don't get shot."

I run the team through everything I saw and after much debate, we come up with a plan. Finding the cargo will require stealth so we can't take everybody. Based on our abilities, we eventually decide that Aura, InvisiBill, and I are best suited for the job. Each of us will sneak into the port on our own and explore one of the ships.

Aura will take the ship farthest away, I'll take the one in the middle, and InvisiBill will take the one closest to the entrance. I'm a little nervous about giving InvisiBill such a big responsibility, but it's not like we have better options.

"Don't worry," he says. "I've got it."

"You better," Aura says. "Now the rest of you stay put or you'll answer to me. Is that clear?"

"Crystal," Rage says, swallowing hard.

"Okay," she says. "Let's do this."

I go back to bat-form, but as soon as I take off, I hear—

"Oof!" Stanphibian yelps.

"What happened?" Kat asks.

"Stan slipped," Hairball says. "Yuck, what's on the bottom of his flipper?"

"My barf," Rage says.

I shake my head. I'll be amazed if those bozos manage not to get caught. Anyway, I can't worry about them now, I have my own issues to deal with. I flap my way into the fog and glide over the port entrance. Looking down, I see two armed guards talking to one another. Fortunately, they have no idea I'm up here.

I keep flying until I'm directly over my target docked at the center pier. For the first time, I realize the ship is really big. From here it looks like it's half the size of a football field, with a tall bridge, and a bunch of crates stacked on the rear deck.

Well, that must be the cargo.

I circle and do a quick count. There must be twenty crates in total. I need to figure out what's inside, but how?

Just then, I see two deckhands heading my way. This could be my chance to get some info. But as I descend towards them, I'm not sure I'm in the best form for stealth mode. After all, I don't want them to freak out if they see a bat hanging over their shoulder. So, I transform into a mist, blending into the fog over their heads.

As the wind picks up, I realize I need to concentrate just to keep my molecules together. Then, the men show up and start removing the ropes that fasten the crates to the deck. One of them has dark hair and the other is wearing a gray, knit cap.

"Worst job we've ever had," the dark-haired man says, untying a knot. "Now I know why 'ole Sam refused to do the second run. I nearly broke my back lifting those crates."

"Nearly?" the man with the cap says. "I think Tommy broke his. The poor guy can't even get out of bed. To think, we got all of those things on the ship and now we have to get 'em off."

"We need equipment to get these off," the dark-haired man says. "I don't care how much that guy paid us, it took six of us to carry one crate and I've never lifted anythin' so heavy in my life."

"The guy gave me the creeps, too," the man with the cap says. "Barely said a word. And you couldn't see his eyes beneath the shadows of his hat. I don't trust people who don't look you in the eyes. And there was somethin' else. I didn't want to say nothin' at the time, but I swear he carried ten of these crates all by himself. One second they were sittin' on the dock, and the next thing I know they're sittin' on the ship. Did you see that?"

"I did," the dark-haired man says. "But I thought I was crazy. I don't know about you, but if I never see that guy again I'll be just fine."

"Wouldn't it be nice to know what we were carryin' though?" the man with the cap asks. "What do you think is inside these boxes?"

"I don't know and I don't care," the dark-haired man says. "To me, it smells like somethin's rotting in there. I just want to get 'em off our ship and be done with the whole thing. But I do know one thing. I'm never takin' a job from Romania again."

"I agree with that," the man with the knit cap says.

Romania?

That's it! This is the ship!

The two men untie the ropes on the last crate and head back towards the other end of the ship. If I'm going to find out what's inside this might be my only chance! I wait a few minutes to make sure they're gone and then transform back into a kid. Even though we're docked I need to steady my feet as the ship rocks back and forth on the water.

I wish Aura was here to help, but I'll just have to finish my investigation and head back to the bus to share what I've learned.

If I heard the deckhands right, this is actually the second delivery from Romania. If that's the case, then Count Dracula may already have some of what he needs from his homeland. And when they were talking about that creepy guy, I realized there's only one person who fits that description—Count Dracula himself!

I peer around the crate to make sure the coast is clear and then get to work. The crate itself is big and rectangular. It's a few feet taller than me and probably seven feet wide. I can see why it would take six men to lift one of these things. Just for fun, I try lifting it but it doesn't budge.

Note to self: I may be half-vampire but I don't have even half of Count Dracula's strength.

Now, how do I get this thing open?

I look around the outside of the crate and realize it's bolted shut by metal clips. To get inside I'll need a tool to pry those clips off. Then, I spot a crowbar leaning against one of the crates.

Bingo!

I grab the crowbar and move to the crate on the end. I shove the crowbar beneath one of the metal clips and push down, putting all of my weight behind it. After a good struggle, the clip pops off. I repeat this process all the way around until the entire panel is loose, and then I remove it.

To my surprise, inside the crate is another large, wooden box. Suddenly, my nostrils are flooded by a horrible stench! Man, that guy wasn't kidding. Whatever's inside that box smells like it's well past its due date!

In fact, the smell is so noxious it's making me lightheaded. But I'm too close to stop now. I need to find out what's inside this box. So, I grab my crowbar and explore the outside of the wooden box.

This time there aren't any metal clips to deal with, but there are plenty of wood planks. So, I brace myself for the smell and push the crowbar into a seam. I pull down hard, popping a plank from the end of the box, and the smell hits me full force.

I stumble back, feeling kind of woozy when—

"Hey," comes a girl's voice from behind me.

I jump out of my skin, somehow managing not to scream my lungs out. And when I turn around, Aura is phasing up through the deck of the ship.

"Didn't you just yell at me for freaking out Rage?" I whisper. "You could've blown the whole thing."

"Sorry," she whispers, covering her mouth. "I guess I'm not perfect either. My ship wasn't the one we're looking for. What do you have here?"

"This is it," I whisper. "This ship just arrived from Romania. And according to the men on board, Count Dracula himself helped them load these smelly crates onto the vessel. The smell is actually making me dizzy."

"Really? I can't smell anything," Aura says. "It's one of the drawbacks of being a ghost. What's it smell like?"

"Death," I whisper. "Now can you stop talking so we can look inside?"

"Yeah," she says. "Let's do it."

I pinch my nose and we both lean forward, poking our heads through the opening. But when I see what's inside my jaw drops because it doesn't make any sense.

"It's just… dirt?" Aura says. "Lots and lots of dirt."

"Foul-smelling dirt," I say.

Then, I see little white specks wiggling around inside.

"Oh, yuck," I say. "It's filled with maggots."

"Thank goodness I can't throw up," Aura says, backing out of the crate. "Because that's really, really disgusting."

"Yeah," I say, pulling my head out. I don't think I could take a second more. "But I don't get it. Why is Count Dracula shipping boxes of dirt from Romania to America? There's dirt here too."

"But it's not just from Romania," Aura says. "It's from Wallachia. His kingdom."

"Yep," I say. "And the men said all the crates are like this one."

"This is so weird," Aura says. "We should probably go back and tell the others. And speaking of others, where's InvisiBill? That moron better not have been—"

"FREEZE!" squawks a loud voice from overhead.

What?

Suddenly, I hear FWOOP FWOOP noises, and when I look up there's a squad of helicopters flying in the sky, shining spotlights on us!

Then, I notice the initials 'D.S.I.' painted in black on the side of one of the helicopters.

"What's going on?" I say.

Just then, the helicopter above us lowers a long, black tube attached to a big, brown bag.

"Bram, run!" Aura says.

But before I can move, there's a loud SUCKING noise, and the next thing I know, Aura is vacuumed into the tube!

"Aura!" I yell.

"DON'T MOVE, MONSTER!"

Monster?

I've got to get out of here!

But just as I take a step, a clear tube drops from the sky, trapping me inside! And then a pink mist fills the tube, making me gag!

What is this stuff? It smells like sulfur!

I try pushing the tube over but it won't budge.

And suddenly, I feel… super tired.

I try… keeping my eyes open but I can't.

And then everything goes dark.

CHAPTER FIVE

AGENT M

I wake up in a haze.

I'm lying on a cold floor and my limbs feel like they weigh a thousand pounds each. There's drool running down my chin and it takes everything I have just to wipe it away with my sleeve. I don't know what that pink stuff was that knocked me out, but boy it's powerful stuff.

I blink my eyes a few times until my vision clears, and that's when I realize I'm in a small, concrete room that looks like it belongs in a dungeon. And apparently, I'm still trapped inside that giant, glass tube those helicopters dropped on me at the port.

Well, this certainly isn't the Holiday Inn.

Where the heck am I anyway? I press my hand against the glass and pull myself up to my feet. Okay, I guess it doesn't matter where I am. The real question is, how am I going to get out of here?

Suddenly, a loud CLICK echoes through the room, and when I spin around I'm blinded by a bright light! I shield my eyes when I realize it's not only bright but incredibly hot.

It's burning my skin!

"Good evening, 'Brampire,'" comes a woman's voice.

"Who are you?" I ask.

I try focusing on her face, but it's impossible to see through the intense light. Besides, I have to cover my face with the hoodie so I don't burn to death! I don't know how much more I can take!

"P-Please," I plead. "Turn it off!"

Then, the light clicks off and I feel immediate relief. I look at the back of my hands and they're bright red.

"Sorry, Brampire," the woman says. "Just taking some precautions."

"H-How do you know my name?" I ask, but when I look her way I'm still seeing spots.

"Well, it is written right there on your shiny badge," she says. "But we didn't need the help because we've been watching you for quite a while."

Just then, the light goes on again and I flinch, but this time it's way less glaring and there's no heat.

"I'll introduce myself," she continues, and when she steps forward I can finally see her face, but she doesn't look anything like I expect. She's super tall, with red, spikey hair, a square jaw, and piercing blue eyes. She's wearing a crisp, black suit with a matching tie, and she's holding up some kind of a device that looks like a high-tech flashlight, complete with blinking lights.

"You can call me Agent M," she continues. "And I

work for DSI, also known as the Department of Supernatural Investigations."

The Department of Supernatural Investigations?

Suddenly, I remember seeing the initials 'DSI' on one of the helicopters.

"Are you, like, part of the Dark Ones?" I ask.

"The Dark Ones?" she repeats. "Oh, no, no, no, my dear. We work for the government. In fact, you're now part of a very exclusive club who know we even exist. When monsters come crawling out of their holes, we get the call. So, I guess you can call us the good guys."

The good guys? Suddenly, I feel much better.

"That's great news," I say. "Because this is all a big misunderstanding. See, we're good guys, too."

"Right," she says. "You must think I just fell off the back of a turnip truck. Let's get this straight, kid. You're a monster. That makes you a bad guy."

"What?" I say. "No, I'm on your side."

"Oh, really?" she says, breaking into a smile. "Well, let's do the good guy test then. Are you a vampire?"

"Well," I say. "Technically, yes. But I'm only half—"

"Were you on Count Dracula's ship?" she presses on, not waiting for my answer.

"Well, yes," I say, and suddenly I feel like I'm being interrogated.

"So, let's summarize," she says. "You're a vampire who was captured aboard Count Dracula's ship? I have news for you, kid. You just aced the bad guy test."

"Hold on," I say, "maybe we can have a do-over?"

"A do-over?" she says. "That's cute. Listen, kid, I don't think you understand what's going on here. You see, the Department of Supernatural Investigations was formed way back in the 1930s for one purpose—to protect the United States of America from monsters. You can think of us as government-employed monster hunters. We spend our entire professional lives hauling in monsters just like you. Of course, we wouldn't want to frighten innocent people so we keep it all undercover. But now that Count Dracula attacked New York City, the secret is out and my phone won't stop ringing."

Wow, for all of the Supernatural History we covered in Professor Seward's class, he never mentioned the Department of Supernatural Investigations. It must be so secret he doesn't even know about it.

"So, let's look at the facts here," Agent M continues, pacing back and forth. "Count Dracula's minions have attacked New York City, with an estimated population of—"

"Hang on," I say. "If your job is to protect the United States from monsters, then why aren't you in New York City right now? Wouldn't stopping Count Dracula be a better use of your time than grilling me?"

"Don't you worry," Agent M says. "My agents are all over the crisis in New York City. But believe it or not, Count Dracula isn't even there, so you've jumped to my number one priority. See, we were monitoring that cargo ship for a reason. We thought we'd catch Count Dracula red-handed when he came to claim his cargo. And while we didn't nab Count Dracula, we got the next best thing, his protégé, who also happens to be the only other vampire on the planet."

His protégé? Who's that?

Wait a second. She's talking about me!

"So, tell me," Agent M says. "Why do you need twenty boxes of dirt from Romania?"

"What?" I say. "I-I don't need them. I already told you, I'm not working with Count Dracula!"

"Uh-huh," she says. "Look, kid, we know this is the second shipment from Romania. What was in the first shipment? More boxes of dirt?"

"I've got no clue," I say.

"Come on," she says. "We're already tracking down where that first shipment went, so you might as well come clean. What are you and the Dark Ones up to?"

"I don't know," I say firmly. "Look, I'm not with the Dark Ones. I'm just a student at the Van Helsing Academy."

"The Van Helsing Academy," she says, rolling over a stool and sitting down. "We know all about the Van Helsing Academy. The school's charter says it's an accredited private academy dedicated to the education of extremely 'gifted' children. What it doesn't say, however, is that it's a secret organization for the next generation of Supernatural terrorists."

"What?" I say. "That's not true."

"No?" Agent M says, her left eyebrow raised. "Then I'm guessing your infamous Headmaster doesn't talk about what happens to his graduates."

"What are you talking about?" I say.

"You mean, you don't know?" she says. "Tell me, haven't you ever wondered what will happen to you when you 'graduate' from the prestigious Van Helsing Academy?"

Well, come to think of it, I haven't.

And now that she's mentioned it, it's actually a great question. I mean, other than my father, I haven't heard Van Helsing talk about anyone who's left the school before. But my dad didn't even graduate, he just took off on his own.

"Um, no," I say.

"Well, let me clue you in," she says, leaning forward. "You're not going to make it. You see, Van Helsing is just setting you up for failure. He's not teaching you how to blend into society, and when monsters like you get out into the real world and struggle to fit in, well, you tend to go berserk. And do you know whose job it is to put you back in your place?"

"Um, yours?" I offer.

"See, now we're getting somewhere," Agent M says. "That's right. My agents remove dangerous monsters like you from society so ordinary citizens can live in peace."

"But then you release them, right?" I ask.

"Oh no," she says, shaking her head. "We never release monsters back into the world. That's not what we're about. Our job is to protect the public, and once we capture a monster it's for keeps. That's when the real fun begins. That's when we find out what their weaknesses are. What scares them. What makes them scream. And sometimes, what makes them die."

"Wait, what?" I say.

"You heard me," she says, lifting her flashlight. "That's how we develop things like the solar beam I'm holding here or the weapons we used to capture you and your friends at the port. We test and test and test on different monsters until we find the most effective tools to bring them down."

Holy cow! That's crazy. She's using monsters as guinea pigs to take down other monsters! But what she's saying must be true because they nabbed Aura and me in a matter of seconds.

Suddenly, I realize I have no clue where Aura is.

Or the rest of the Monstrosities.

"Where are my friends?" I demand.

"Don't worry," she says. "We've got them all. The ghost girl, the fish boy, the hairy kid, the cat girl, the little guy with glasses, even the invisible boy."

Suddenly, panic sets in. I mean, based on what she just said, she could be torturing them right now!

"Let them go," I say. "I promise, I'll do whatever you want if you just let them go."

"Impressive," she says, her eyebrows raised. "A monster with character. I think that's a first. Unfortunately, I can't let your friends go. After all, we don't want anyone else getting hurt out there."

"I told you we're good monsters," I say.

"That's right," she says, tapping her index finger on her chin. "But is there really such a thing as a 'good monster?' I'm going with a 'hard no.'"

"Let me out of here!" I demand, pounding on the glass tube.

"Now there's the monster I was expecting to see," she says. "Relax, you're not going anywhere. I'm honored to have you here. We've never captured a bona fide vampire before. But here's the good news. Whatever we learn from studying you will be used to capture and destroy your leader, the King of Darkness himself. Just you wait. We're going to have all sorts of fun together."

I open my mouth to speak but stop myself. She won't believe me anyway. I've got to get out of here.

Agent M stands up and kicks her stool away.

"Listen, this has been a great conversation," she says. "But I need real answers. So, I'll give you a choice. You can either tell me the truth about your plans, or I'll bring in your friends one-by-one, and we'll see how much pain they can take."

"But…," I say, dropping to my knees. "I am telling you the truth."

"Uh-huh," Agent M says. "Sure, kid. Tell you what,

I'll give you one hour to think about what you want to do and then I'll be back. Maybe I'll bring in your ghost friend first. We've had lots of ghosts here at DSI, and I've got a pretty good idea of what makes them squeal. See you in an hour."

Then, Agent M smiles and exits the room.

I press my back against the glass and slide down until I'm sitting on the floor.

Great.

I have one hour.

And I don't know what to do.

CLASSIFIED

AGENT PERSONNEL PROFILE

AGENT DETAILS:

ROLE: DSI SUPERVISOR

REAL NAME: [redacted]

AGENT NAME: AGENT M

HEIGHT: 6’ 2”

HAIR COLOR: RED

EYE COLOR: GREEN

YRS OF SERVICE: 13

SPECIALTY: MONSTER HUNTING

TRAINING:

- Monster Biology
- Monster Psychology
- Monster Capture
- Firearms
- Law Enforcement

SKILLS:

- Leadership
- Risk/Threat Assessment
- Operation Planning
- Counter-Intelligence
- Effective Communication

DEPARTMENT OF SUPERNATURAL INVESTIGATIONS

CHAPTER SIX

THE GREAT ESCAPE

I'm running out of time before Agent M comes back, and I don't know what to do.

She thinks I'm in cahoots with Count Dracula, and if I don't tell her what she wants to hear she'll torture my friends one by one! The thing is, I already told her the truth and it wasn't good enough. So, at this point I'm clueless.

Ever since she left I've been walking in circles inside my glass prison, waiting for the answer to magically appear. Unfortunately, no miracles have arrived, so I guess that leaves me with two choices. Either I try pleading my case again or I start telling lies.

But the thing is, even if I do lie and tell her I'm working for Count Dracula—which I'm not—I'm sure she'll torture my friends anyway. After all, she said putting monsters in their place was her job. And she seems to really love her job.

So, that takes me to option number three. I need to bust out of here and free my friends before she gets back.

I put my hands on the glass tube and push with all of my might but it doesn't budge. I pound on the glass but it's way too thick. I swipe my palm along the surface looking for a crack to mist out of, but it's perfectly smooth. Well, so much for that.

I take a deep breath and exhale. They thought of everything. In other words, it's a perfect vampire trap.

You know, I bet they were planning to put Count Dracula in here, but instead I'm the lucky one.

Awesome.

If only Van Helsing knew where we were. He'd come to rescue us. Of course, after he rescued us he'd probably kill us for sneaking off again, but he'd rescue us first.

At least, I think he would.

But who am I kidding? Van Helsing isn't coming and there's nothing I can do to save my friends. I sit down on the floor and try not to think of what's to come.

Then, something catches my eye.

There's some sort of a faint, grayish mist circling the top of the tube. It's moving incredibly fast, so fast I can barely track it as it goes around and around. I stand up to take a closer look.

What is that?

Suddenly, my alarm bells go off. I mean, what if it's one of Agent M's weapons? What if she sent this thing in to scare me into talking? What if—

But before I can finish my thought, a section of the gray mist branches off from the rest, forms a big ball, and

SLAMS into the glass tube!

The impact rocks the tube hard, knocking me off balance, and I smash my shoulder against the far side of the glass. Then, the tube teeter-totters back and forth a few times until it finally settles back down on the ground.

What just happened?

But when I look back up the gray mist is gone!

I don't see it anywhere. Was it even real?

My shoulder is still throbbing so I don't think I imagined it. But then again, I can't explain it either. I look to the spot where the mist made contact and see a crack in the glass. Well, there's the evidence.

So, I guess it was—

Wait a second!

The glass is cracked!

That means I can get out of here! I don't know who sent that mist in here but I'll have to find out later. Because right now I've got to escape before Agent M comes back. Without wasting a second, I transform into a mist and flow out of my prison.

It feels great to be free, but there's no time for a picnic. After all, who knows what DSI is doing to my friends. I've got to find them and fast!

I stay a mist and pass through the doorframe into a narrow, dingy hallway. Well, I guess DSI doesn't care for uplifting work environments. But the drab décor is the last thing on my mind because I spot three more doors with armed guards posted outside.

I'm guessing my friends are behind those doors, so as long as I stay in mist-form I should be able to enter unnoticed. I cling to the ceiling, staying high above the guards' heads until I reach the first door, and then I slip inside.

I'm in a room identical to the one that held me, but instead of a glass tube there's a large, brown sack hanging from the ceiling—and it looks eerily similar to the one that sucked up Aura! And next to that is a metal table with wrist and ankle shackles.

I circle the bag but don't hear anything coming from inside. Since time is of the essence I should probably move on, yet something tells me the bag isn't empty. I don't see an opening so if I'm going to check inside I'll need something to cut it open with.

Now, where can I find something sharp?

Then, it hits me.

Duh! I've got something sharp built-in!

I transform from a mist to a bat and rip into the sack with my razor-sharp fangs. The material is super tough, so it takes a few bites before I tear a decent-sized hole.

And then a ghost flies out!

"Bram?" Aura says, looking around confused. "Is that you?"

I drop to the ground and go to kid-form.

"Shhh!" I whisper, putting my finger to my lips. "There are guards outside the door."

"Guards?" she whispers, looking at the bolted door.

"Where are we anyway? After I got sucked into that stupid vacuum bag I couldn't phase through it no matter what I tried. I don't know what that thing is made of."

"We're at DSI," I whisper. "They've created special weapons to capture monsters, including ghosts."

"DSI?" she asks. "What's that?"

Well, if Aura hasn't heard of them, then nobody has.

"I'll explain later," I whisper. "But we're in danger. We've got to find the others and get out of here as quickly as we can. Follow me."

But just as we start to move, we hear—

"B-Bram?"

Huh? Where's that voice coming from?

"Bram?" it repeats, sounding strangely familiar. "Are you here?"

"InvisiBill?" I whisper, looking around. "Is that you? Where are you?"

"Shackled to the table," he says.

Ah-ha. No wonder the table looked empty. And that's when I notice the shackles are closed. They must be locked around his wrists and ankles.

"The key is dangling off the side of the table," he says. "Ever-so-cruelly out of my reach."

"I've got you," I whisper. "But then again, maybe we're better off leaving you here."

"Not funny," InvisiBill whispers.

I use the key to get him free and now I've got two of my teammates back. Four more to go.

"Listen," I say, "There are two other rooms to search and I'm guessing the others are split into pairs like you guys. This place is crawling with guards so you should wait here so you don't get caught."

"Get caught?" InvisiBill whispers. "She's a ghost and I'm invisible. Who's gonna catch us?"

"Dude," I whisper, "up until two seconds ago you were shackled to a table."

"Right," he says. "Sorry. Bad short-term memory."

"New plan," Aura says, "You said we needed to move fast so here's what we're gonna do. InvisiBill and I will take one room and you take the other. We'll be done twice as fast."

"That's not the plan," I say.

"Plans change," Aura says, folding her arms.

I stare into her blue eyes, reluctant to give in. I mean, she has no idea how brutal Agent M and DSI can be. But I also know she's not going to stay put.

"Fine," I say. "I'll search the room across the way and you do the one next door. But be careful. These guys are professional monster hunters and they can take you down easily. Uh-oh."

"What?" she whispers.

"The rest of the team aren't ghosts, mists, or invisible," I whisper. "How are we going to sneak them out of here?"

"We're not," she whispers. "A kid like Hairball is impossible to hide. After you get your group free, listen for my signal and we'll all rush the guards in the hall."

"Now there's a great plan," I whisper sarcastically.

"You got a better one?" she asks.

"Not really," I say.

"Then we'll see you in the hall," she says with a wink. "Come on, InvisiBill."

I roll my eyes as I go to mist-form. Even though Aura is as stubborn as an ox, I'm glad I found her first. No matter how tough the situation, she always finds a way to figure things out.

InvisiBill on the other hand…

This time I stay low, snaking my way across the hall, and when I enter my designated room I find two more of my friends imprisoned. Hairball is locked inside a cage like an animal while Stanphibian is chained beneath a giant heat lamp.

"Shhh!" I whisper, as I float next to Stanphibian and assume kid-form. His skin is all cracked and dried out.

"H-Help," Stanphibian stammers.

"I got you," I whisper.

Wow, this heat lamp is super-hot! Thank goodness he still has his fishbowl helmet on or he would have died from heat exhaustion. I quickly find the power switch and turn the lamp off, but the chain around his leg is too strong for me to break and I can't find the key.

"Thanks," he says, as I help him to his feet.

"Quiet," I whisper. "Let me free Hairball and he'll deal with your chain."

But as I approach the cage, I find Hairball sitting cross-legged in the center, his fur sticking straight out all over his body.

"Careful," Hairball whispers. "The bars are electric."

"Clearly," I say. I look around until I find the key hanging on the wall. Then, I avoid the bars, pop the lock, and carefully open the door. "Can you bust Stan's chain? But do it quietly."

"No problem," Hairball whispers, and then he grabs Stanphibian's chain and breaks it off his leg without making a noise.

"Great job," I whisper.

"Thanks," Hairball says, casually tossing the chain over his shoulder.

"Hairball, no!" I whisper, but it's too late.

The chain CLANKS loudly on the cement floor.

"What's that?" comes a voice from outside.

"Seriously, Hairball?" I say.

"Sorry," Hairball says, cracking his knuckles. "Well, maybe you should stand back while I handle this."

Suddenly, the door swings open and a guard appears.

"Batter up!" Hairball yells.

And then he punches the man so hard he flies backward and breaks down the door across the hall. The next thing I know, I'm staring at Aura, Rage, and Kat through the broken down doorway!

"I thought I was giving the signal?" Aura says.

"Plans change," I say, shrugging my shoulders. "Let's

go!"

We rush into the hall and Hairball and Kat make short work of the remaining guards.

"This way!" I call out, leading the team around the corner and down a super long hallway.

"Do you know where you're going?" Aura asks.

"Nope," I say. "Just look for a way out."

"Hold on," Kat calls out. "I smell people up ahead. Lots of people. I think we should turn back. Like, now!"

We all skid to a stop, crashing into one another.

"Let's go back!" InvisiBill yells.

"We can't!" I say. "It's a dead-end!"

"Get them!" comes a woman's voice.

My heart races as I look down the hall to see an army of agents heading our way.

And leading the charge is Agent M!

"What now?" InvisiBill says.

I look around but there's nowhere to go. We're trapped in this hallway, unless…

"Hairball," I say. "Bust through that wall!"

"Got it," he says. And then he cocks back his giant fist and punches the wall. There's a massive BOOM but little else. "Ow!" he yells, shaking his hand.

Holy cow! There's barely a dent! What's that wall made of?

"We're doomed!" Rage says, breathing heavily.

"It's okay," I say, trying to sound calm even though I'm panicking inside. But the last thing we need is Rage flying off the handle.

But then again, maybe that's exactly what we need.

"Freeze!" Agent M orders.

"Rage!" I say, shaking his shoulders. "You've got to help us! You've got to become the beast!"

"W-What?" he says, looking at me confused.

"You need to become Monster Rage!" I say, shaking him harder. "You can easily bust through this wall. It's our only way out or we'll all die!"

"D-Die?" he says, his eyes getting bigger. "I-I don't want to die? B-But I can't control the monster."

"Dispose of them!" Agent M commands, her voice getting closer. "Except for the vampire! He's mine!"

"That's not true," I say. "You can control it. But we need you to do it now."

"N-Now?" he says.

"Yes," I say. "I know you can. When we were at Moreau's tower, I saw something different in you. I believe in you."

"They're closing in!" Aura yells. "Get ready!"

And when I look up I realize she's right. The agents have gotten a lot closer, and they're drawing their weapons!

"Rage!" I say.

But when I look back, his pupils have gone from blue to red. Holy cow! He's… doing it!

"Look out!" I warn the others.

Suddenly, Rage arches his back, and his entire body

expands! His shirt rips down the middle and his muscles balloon to ridiculous proportions! I back up, tripping over Hairball's leg. And when I look up, I'm staring at a seven-foot, purple monster with blond hair!

"What is that thing?" an agent yells.

"Who cares?" Agent M says. "Just kill it!"

Suddenly, bullets start flying and we duck behind Rage's huge body.

"RRRRAAAARRRRGGHHH!" Rage cries, as the bullets bounce off his chest and ricochet off the walls.

"Take it down!" Agent M orders. "Now!"

"Rage!" I call out. "Forget them! We need you to smash the wall! Get us out of here so we don't die!"

Rage looks down at me, his eyes seething with anger.

Uh-oh. I hope I didn't get this wrong.

"It's me, Bram!" I yell. "You can control this! I know you can!"

Suddenly, his eyebrows raise. Yes, he hears me!

"Now bust through this wall," I say. "Help us get out of here. Help us get to safety!"

"SSSAAAFFFEEETTTYYY!" Rage says.

And then he drives his powerful arms straight through the wall and pulls back a huge slab.

"Stop them!" Agent M yells. "They're getting away!"

But before the agents can get any closer, Rage lifts the massive chunk of wall over his head and throws it down the hallway, completely blocking their path.

"Let's go!" Aura says. "Everybody out!"

The team streams through the hole, except for one.

"Rage!" I yell. "Let's go!"

"GGGRRRAAARRR!" Rage growls as he stares down the hall at our pursuers, his muscles twitching.

"Rage, no!" I say, stepping halfway through the opening to freedom. "You're part of our team! You're one of the Monstrosities! You belong with us!"

Rage looks at me and then back down the hall.

And then he comes thundering through the opening behind me.

D.S.I. CLASSIFIED PHOTOGRAPH

Rage Monster - Extremely Dangerous!!

CHAPTER SEVEN

MONSTERS ON THE RUN

We're running for our lives.

As soon as we busted out of DSI headquarters we hit the nearby woods and took off. The problem is, DSI clearly doesn't want to let us go.

Somehow, we manage to dodge dozens of helicopters, tanks, and foot soldiers as we make our way through the underbrush. We've been lucky so far, but who knows how long that'll last. DSI is getting closer and closer but we can't give up.

Our lives are in the balance!

The only good news is Rage transformed back to a kid again. As soon as we got out of DSI, he took two lumbering steps before his eyes rolled back in his head and he passed out. Hairball is carrying Rage now but we need to make good on all of his hard work.

I'm so proud of him for mastering his monster side. He came through when we needed him most and now we need to get him—and all of us—to safety. I don't ever want to see the initials 'D.S.I.' again.

"Everybody down!" Aura whispers, and we huddle

beneath a large tree as a helicopter hovers overhead, its searchlight beaming through the branches.

"Stan, hide your head!" I whisper. "The light will reflect off your fishbowl."

Stanphibian burrows his noggin beneath Hairball's shaggy armpit, making me gag.

Seconds later the helicopter flutters away.

"That was close," InvisiBill says. "What do we do now?"

"Can someone tell me who's chasing us first?" Hairball asks. "I have no clue what's going on right now."

"They're called DSI," I say. "That's short for the Department of Supernatural Investigations, a secret government agency that protects the public from monsters. I met their leader, a woman named Agent M. She thinks we're working with Count Dracula and the Dark Ones."

"What?" Kat says. "That's ridiculous!"

"I agree," I say. "But she didn't believe me. She thinks all monsters are evil, so we must be evil too. And she was going to torture you unless I told her what she wanted to hear. Luckily, I escaped and now here we are."

"Wow," Hairball says. "How'd you manage to escape anyway? The rest of us were pretty well contained."

I open my mouth to answer but stop myself. For some reason, I'm hesitant to tell them about that strange, gray mist. I mean, first of all, I have no clue what it was. And secondly, they'll probably think I'm nuts.

"Who cares," InvisiBill says. "The important thing is he got out."

"True," Hairball says. "So, where do we go now?"

"Home," Aura says. "Back to school. We just need to figure out where we are right now. We need a map."

"No," Kat says, her whiskers bouncing as she sniffs the air. "We don't need a map. I think I can get us there."

"With just your schnoz?" Hairball asks.

"Yep," Kat says, still sniffing. "Our school has a very distinct scent, and I think I've picked it up. It's faint, but it's there. Follow me but keep up because I don't want to lose the trail."

Then, she takes off, her tail flowing behind her.

"Great," InvisiBill says. "Now we're chasing a cat."

"Do you want to live?" Aura asks.

"Chasing now," InvisiBill says, as a pile of leaves kick up behind his feet.

As I follow the team, I think back to my conversation with Agent M. I still haven't told the team everything, and if Agent M is right we'll all have trouble adjusting to the real world once school ends. Sadly, I can kind of see what she's talking about. I mean, Van Helsing isn't teaching us anything about fitting into society. Our days are spent studying monster history and honing our monster abilities. We're not being taught anything about how to adapt to the real world after school is over.

If there even is an 'after.'

Now that Count Dracula is on the attack, society will look very different if we don't get our act together. And boy did we stumble out of the gate with this mission. If we keep this up, there's no way we'll stop Count Dracula.

Speaking of stopping Count Dracula, at some point I'm going to have to face him. Just the thought of being alone with him terrifies me. The fact that I nearly passed out when he was coming out of his coffin in my Survival Skills exam tells me I'm not ready.

And I'm not sure I ever will be.

"Take cover!" Kat whispers, snapping me back to reality. She's up ahead, waving for us to get down.

I stay low and make my way to her position. We've reached the end of the woods, and just up ahead is a small town—or rather, a small town in ruins.

It looks like a nuclear bomb went off. Plumes of black smoke rise into the sky, buildings are demolished, and vehicles are turned upside down. Yet, despite all of the destruction, there's an eerie silence.

And that's when I realize something.

There aren't any people.

"Look at that sign," Aura says, nodding to her left.

There's a bent, green highway sign leaning against a crushed dumpster bin. It reads:

WELCOME TO SMILEVILLE
POPULATION 3,575

"Smileville?" InvisiBill says. "I doubt anyone is smiling now."

"What happened to this place?" Hairball asks.

"I'm guessing the Dark Ones marched through here on their way to New York City," Aura says. "It's totally destroyed."

"Shhh!" Kat whispers, her ears pricking up. "I hear something coming."

"Wonderful," InvisiBill says.

I brace myself, but when I look back at the town, I

see a small, blond-haired girl with pigtails standing on the street corner. She's facing the other way, wearing a blue dress, and holding a teddy bear by the leg. She doesn't look older than six, and she's all alone.

"We've got to help her," I say, standing up. "She might be the only survivor!"

My instincts take over and I run out of the brush.

"Bram, wait!" I hear Aura yell.

But I can't wait. I mean, this poor girl's life has been wrecked because of me. Everything that's happened to her, everything that's happened to all of these innocent people, is all my fault.

I wish none of this ever happened.

I wish I wasn't the Blood Grail.

I wish I wasn't a vampire.

Running feels good right now. And even though I haven't eaten in a while, I crank on my super-speed to get to her as fast as I can. I couldn't forgive myself if something happened before I got there.

I mean, haven't I done enough?

But I have a decision to make. Do I just pick her up and keep running, scaring her half to death, or should I stop and talk her into coming with me? While a big part of me thinks scooping her up is the right thing to do, I figure the kid's been through enough trauma for one day.

I stop behind her and get down on one knee.

Better to connect at her level.

"Hey," I say gently, putting my hand on her shoulder. "I know you're probably scared right now, but why don't you come with me and my friends? I promise we'll take you to safety."

I smile, hoping to make her feel as comfortable as possible, but as she turns I recoil in horror. Because instead of talking to a sweet, wide-eyed little girl, I'm staring at a green, slack-jawed creature with red eyes, peeled skin, and rotting teeth!

I-I'm too late!

The little girl is… a zombie!

Suddenly, she grabs my hoodie!

Holy cow! If she bites me, I'll turn into a zombie too!

I push her away, but when I do her hand grips my hoodie tight and her arm detaches from her body!

I scream!

I yank her appendage from my hoodie when I realize it's still moving!

GROSS!

But as I throw the arm as far away as possible, I hear MOANING coming from both sides of me. That's when I see dozens of zombies lumbering my way, and even more are popping out all over town!

I'm totally outnumbered!

I start panicking, and then I remember I'm not alone.

I'm about to call for help, when—

POW!

"Dude," Hairball says, punching the lights out of three zombies with one blow. "Please don't run away all bat-crazy again."

"Yeah," Stanphibian adds, picking up one zombie and throwing it at a group of others.

Seconds later, the other Monstrosities join in and we're quickly in the middle of a monster battle royale! Aura stands guard over a still-unconscious Rage while the rest of us do everything we can to keep the zombies away. But no matter how many we knock down, more just keep showing up!

"There's too many of them!" Kat yells as she kicks a zombie right between the eyes.

She's right! Hundreds of zombies are swarming our way! I could turn into a bat and save myself, but other than Aura, the rest of the team would be overwhelmed. I could never leave them behind, but how can I get us out of this mess?

Just then, a ten-foot wall of fire flares up in my face and I jump back! Where'd that come from? But then I realize the flames aren't just in front of me, they're circling the whole team, separating us from the zombie onslaught!

But strangely, there's no heat.

And that's when I realize what's happening.

We're being rescued!

"Get back you vile creatures!" comes a familiar voice.

It's Hexum!

The flames grow larger and the zombies back away in fear. Then, a pair of hairy, spider legs wrap around my body and lift me into the air. Seconds later, I'm face-to-face with Crawler.

"Thanks!" I say. "But grab Rage next. He needs the most help."

"On it," Crawler says.

A minute later, he's leg-lifted the rest of the team to safety. Once Aura floats over, Hexum erects a massive fire barrier behind us and we head for Crawler's jeep.

"How did you find us?" Aura asks.

"Actually, by tracking you," Crawler says, holding up his arm to reveal a familiar-looking Spirit Sensor around his wrist. "Professor Morris still has it programmed to read your ghost-signal. He never reprogrammed it, and based on how often we need to track you guys down, he probably never will. What happened to Rage?"

"He saved us by turning into the monster," I say. "But then he passed out."

"Really?" Crawler says, placing Rage gently in the jeep. "Well, we nearly passed out when we got back from New York City and discovered you were gone."

"Enough small talk," Hexum barks. "Everyone in the jeep. Now!"

Uh-oh. Hexum is clearly agitated.

As I hop inside, Hairball and Stanphibian squeeze in beside me, but honestly, their stink is the last thing on my mind. I'm thrilled Crawler and Hexum saved us, but I suspect whatever we've just been through will pale in comparison to what Van Helsing has in store for us.

Crawler turns on the engine, and as we hit the road I look back at the absolute disaster we've left behind. No matter what I do, I can't shake that little girl's zombie face from my mind.

"My, what a lovely drive," InvisiBill says, breaking the awkward silence. "So, does anybody have any plans for the weekend? I know I'm—"

"Quiet!" Hexum orders, holding his forehead. "I simply do not have the mental capacity for your senseless drivel. Now please, do not utter another word for the rest of the trip."

"Right," InvisiBill says. Then, I get a whiff of his bad

breath as he leans across Hairball and whispers, "In case you need a translation, that means we're in really big trouble."

CHAPTER EIGHT

AN UNEXPECTED GUEST

Van Helsing is not a happy camper.

I could tell from the second we walked into his office that this was going to be ugly. Unfortunately, we'll have to wait until we finish explaining ourselves to see how ugly. But at least we have a plan this time.

Before we entered Van Helsing's office we agreed that Aura and I would do all of the talking. Everyone else would stay quiet, especially InvisiBill. The only one lucky enough to be spared from this ordeal is Rage since Crawler took him to the infirmary.

Aura kicks things off, and I have to say, she's doing a great job. The way she's explaining it, we had no choice but to investigate that cargo ship. In her words, we were 'morally obligated' to defy Van Helsing's orders once we found out about Count Dracula's ship. Anything less would have been irresponsible.

By the time it's my turn I'm pumped up. I pick up right where she left off, covering our discovery of the dirt boxes, being captured by DSI, and our escape from their death trap. I end things by stating the obvious, we were just at the right place at the wrong time.

Then, I nod and flash a big smile. I feel pretty good about what I told them. But I didn't tell them everything.

For one, I left out what Agent M said about Van Helsing. I mean, why poke the bear? Oh, and I also left out the part about the mysterious gray mist. I'll mention that later. Like, after we're out of hot water.

Once I wrap up, I expect loads of questions from Van Helsing and Hexum, but instead, all I get is silence. Long, awkward, uncomfortable silence. I swallow hard and shift my gaze from Van Helsing's penetrating stare.

After a while, I'm sweating. And then—

"I know you think your actions are justified," Van Helsing says, "but you do not realize how fortunate you are not to be dead—or worse, undead."

His words strike me funny. I mean, it never dawned on me that we could have ended up as part of Count Dracula's undead army. The thought of a Hairball-zombie or Stanphibian-zombie makes me shiver.

"If we are operating from a place of 'moral obligation,'" he continues, "then as Headmaster, it is my moral obligation to provide you with the consequences of your actions."

I glance at Hexum who's sporting a sly smile. I bet he's loving this. My pain is his joy.

Then, I jump as a hand lands on my shoulder.

"Get ready," InvisiBill mutters under his breath.

I shrug him off and brace myself. Given the magnitude of what we've done, I'm expecting Van Helsing to nail us this time. If this isn't the last straw then I don't know what is. It wouldn't surprise me if he expelled the whole lot of us.

Aura and I meet eyes and I take a deep breath.

"Therefore," Van Helsing says, "I have decided that you have suffered enough for your actions."

"What?" Hexum and InvisiBill blurt out simultaneously.

"Your continued disobedience is a signal I can no longer ignore," Van Helsing says. "You have demonstrated that you are eager and ready to join this fight, and I will no longer stand in your way."

There's a collective gasp.

"Wait," Hairball says. "Are you serious?"

"Yes," Van Helsing says. "The horrors of New York City and Smileville will be the reality across the globe unless we stop Count Dracula once and for all."

As he utters those words I can't help but notice he's staring at me.

"From this point forward," Van Helsing continues, "you will no longer be students, but soldiers. Your primary duty as soldiers is to prepare yourselves, both physically and mentally, for the difficult road ahead. Because once you receive the call to battle you must answer. Are those consequences satisfactory?"

"Oh, yeah!" Hairball says, pumping his fist. "We

finally get to fight!"

"Hold on," InvisiBill says. "Does that mean our exams don't count?"

"That is correct," Van Helsing says.

"Woohoo!" InvisiBill screams, right in my ear.

"Now I suggest you get to work," Van Helsing says. "Your time will come sooner than you think. You are all dismissed. Except for you, Bram. I would like to speak with you further."

Great.

All of my excitement fades as I watch the team high fiving one another as they exit. Then, I notice one person who isn't celebrating with the others. It's Aura, and she shoots me a worried look before floating away.

"Professor Hexum," Van Helsing says. "You are also dismissed."

"Yes, Headmaster," he says and then glares at me before he exits.

Well, so much for his exam. I guess I'll never know the full extent of what he had planned for me.

"Bram," Van Helsing says, rising from his chair. "Walk with me."

"Um, okay," I say.

That's strange, he's never asked me to walk with him before, but I follow him out of his cluttered office. Even though my friends are long gone, I can still hear InvisiBill whooping it up in the distance. Van Helsing walks slowly down the hallway with his hands clasped behind his back.

I'm not sure what he wants to talk to me about, but I'm guessing it's not good. We walk silently for a while, making our way through the building into the grand entrance hall. It's late, so no kids are rushing to make their classes before the bell goes off.

Finally, as we cross to the wing on the other side, Van Helsing says—

"Tell me more about your conversation with Agent M. We have quite a history together."

I look at him surprised. Well, I wasn't expecting that. I mean, I didn't think he knew who she was. But as I start to open my mouth, I debate if I should tell him what she said about the kids who graduate from here. But now that we're alone I figure I might as well go for it.

"Um, there's not much to tell," I say, nervously. "Except that, well, she did mention she's rounded up lots of monsters who graduated from here. She said they don't fit into the real world and become menaces to society."

"I see," Van Helsing says, raising a bushy eyebrow. "And do you believe her?"

"D-Do I believe her?" I stammer. "Well, I mean…"

"Did she tell you how many monsters DSI has captured?"

"No," I say. "I-I don't think she told me that."

"Interesting," Van Helsing says. "Bram, do you know how many students have graduated from our academy?"

"Um, no," I say.

"One thousand, five hundred, and twenty-seven," Van Helsing says. "And do you know how many of our graduates have been captured by DSI?"

"No," I say.

"Three," Van Helsing says. "That is far less than one percent. The rest of DSI's victims never attended our school."

"Really?" I say.

"Really," Van Helsing says, looking me in the eyes. "You could say DSI is one of the reasons I founded this school in the first place. It is my life's mission to provide a sanctuary for Supernatural children. Here they can learn to control their gifts without fearing for their lives. Here they can avoid persecution at the hands of monster-hunting organizations like DSI. I have known of Agent M for many years and she is not to be trusted."

Wow. Well, I guess I was wrong to believe her. But why would she tell me that stuff in the first place? Maybe she was trying to get me to spill information?

"But we have more to fear than DSI," Van Helsing continues. "We must stop Count Dracula before it is too late. And our task will only get more difficult."

"What's that supposed to mean?" I ask.

"Follow me," he says, leading me down a hallway I've never stepped foot in before. A sign on the wall reads:

FACULTY LOUNGE

Hmmm, maybe he's taking me for a late-night snack? But as we approach the double doors to the kitchen he walks right by. Disappointed, I look through the window and see Professor Seward eating a sandwich. My stomach grumbles loudly but Van Helsing ignores it and leads me to the end of the hallway, stopping in front of an old grandfather clock.

I have no clue what we're doing here. I mean, it's a nice clock and all, made of mahogany and standing several feet taller than Van Helsing, but if he needed to know the time we passed a million other clocks on the way over here.

"Um, are we waiting here for a reason?" I ask.

"We have an appointment," Van Helsing says.

"We do?" I say.

"Indeed," he says. "In approximately one minute."

One minute? I look at the clock and notice it's 11:59 p.m. I follow the second hand as it ticks around the face of the clock until it finally strikes midnight.

There's a loud DONG, and suddenly, the front panels of the clock open wide revealing a long hallway! I lean forward to take a closer look and do a double take. Nope, I'm definitely not seeing things. There's actually a hallway inside this clock!

"Follow me," Van Helsing says, stepping inside.

"You mean, inside the clock?" I ask, my mind still refusing to believe there's an actual hallway inside a clock.

"Yes," Van Helsing says. "You will be safe."

"Um, okay," I say, bending down and stepping cautiously inside. But as I straighten up, I look around in disbelief at the mahogany hallway.

"It takes some getting used to," Van Helsing says. "We call it a 'pocket clock.' Professor Holmwood discovered it on one of her many adventures. At the time it was being used to store biscuits, but we use it to hold 'other' things.'"

Other things? Like what?

But I soon get my answer, because as we reach the end of the hallway there's a prison cell! And sitting inside is a blindfolded man!

At first, I'm taken aback. I mean, this was the last thing I was expecting. But as I study his face more closely I realize I know this man!

"Dr. Renfield!" I exclaim.

Suddenly, my heart starts racing. The last time I saw him, he hypnotized and manipulated me. But before we could do anything about it he escaped.

"Mr. Murray?" Dr. Renfield says, perking up. "Is that you? What a surprise. How have you been?"

"What's he doing here?" I ask Van Helsing. "And why is he blindfolded?"

"He is my guest," Van Helsing says. "And if you will allow, I will answer your second question momentarily."

"Where did you find him?" I ask.

"In New York City," Van Helsing says. "One of Crawler's scouts reported that he was in the area. But do not worry, he cannot escape and he cannot lie. Professor Morris put him under the influence of a truth serum."

A truth serum?

"Tell us, Renfield," Van Helsing says. "Do you have anything you would like to say to Mr. Murray?"

"Why, yes," Dr. Renfield says, standing up. "I am so sorry for controlling you against your will. But I hope you understand it was not my choice. You see, at times I am not in control of my own mind."

"Huh?" I say. "What does that mean?"

"Go ahead, Renfield," Van Helsing says. "Show him."

"Show me?" I say. "Show me what?"

Then, Dr. Renfield reaches for his neck and rolls down the fabric of his black, turtleneck shirt, revealing two pink puncture marks.

Holy cow! That's a legit vampire bite!

"It is Count Dracula's signature," Van Helsing says. "The vampire bite itself does not always result in death. Sometimes it has another purpose, as blood contact forges an unbreakable mental bond between Count Dracula and his victim, providing Count Dracula great influence over the victim's mind. This is what happened to Dr. Renfield, and that also answers your other question. We blindfolded Dr. Renfield so he cannot share what he sees with Count Dracula."

Hold on a second. If Count Dracula can form a mental bond just by drinking blood, then maybe that's why I hear him in my head sometimes. I mean, the blood coursing through Count Dracula's veins comes from my body! That's crazy scary.

And speaking of crazy scary…

"But isn't it dangerous even having him here?" I ask. "Won't he give our plans away to Count Dracula?"

"Thanks to the truth serum, Dr. Renfield will inform us if Count Dracula reaches out to him," Van Helsing says. "Thus far, there has been no contact. However, also thanks to the truth serum, Dr. Renfield has been very helpful in sharing Count Dracula's plans with us. Renfield, would you mind sharing Count Dracula's plans with Mr. Murray?"

"Certainly," Dr. Renfield says. "While Count Dracula's primary objective is to rule over mankind, it is not his only goal. You see, despite all of his power, his biggest fear is true death. And with the existence of another vampire who could destroy him once and for all, Count Dracula wants to ensure that he lives forever. Therefore, he has tasked the Dark Ones with finding the one artifact that could resurrect his body and spirit, even if he is destroyed by another vampire."

Dr. Renfield's words make me shudder.

Resurrect? As in, come back to life?

"W-What artifact does that?" I ask.

"It is called the Crown of Souls," Dr. Renfield says.

The Crown of Souls?

I've never even heard of it.

But before I can ask about it, Van Helsing stops me

by putting his hand on my arm and his finger to his lips.

"Thank you, Renfield," Van Helsing says. "That will be all for now. Good night."

Then, Van Helsing nods at me to follow him out.

"Good night?" Renfield says, pressing against the cell bars and shouting after us. "Van Helsing, wait! Won't you release me? I promise I won't hurt anyone! Mr. Murray? Please, release me! Mr. Murray?"

But Van Helsing doesn't stop. I hate hearing Dr. Renfield's cries of desperation, but it's not like he can be trusted. Especially if Count Dracula has so much influence over him.

When we're well out of earshot, Van Helsing says—

"I hope that was not too disturbing for you?"

"A little," I say. "But I don't understand. What is the Crown of Souls?"

"It is a Supernatural artifact with tremendous power," Van Helsing says. "According to legend, if you are wearing the Crown of Souls when you are slain, it will resurrect your body and spirit, even if you are a vampire."

"So, wait a minute," I say. "Are you saying that even if I destroy Count Dracula, if he's wearing this Crown of Souls thing he'll come back to life again?"

"Precisely," Van Helsing says.

My stomach drops. I mean, let's say I do somehow manage to destroy him—and I don't even know how that could happen—the thought of him coming back to life is absolutely terrifying. All of that effort would be for nothing!

"Then, we can't let him get it!" I say.

"I agree," Van Helsing says. "I did not want us to discuss it openly in front of Dr. Renfield, but we must recover the Crown of Souls before Count Dracula does."

"Wait," I say, stopping short. "Did you say 'we.'"

"I did," Van Helsing says. "I suggest you get some rest. I have some preparation to do and then we will depart in a few hours. Oh, and there is one more thing. You must tell no one."

I feel my eyebrows rising with surprise as I take in what Van Helsing just said. I mean, why is he asking me not to tell anyone about something so important?

"Um, sure," I say. "But why not?"

"The Dark Ones have many secret operatives," Van Helsing says. "We simply cannot risk the possibility of anyone revealing our whereabouts. Do you understand?"

"Yeah," I say. "I understand."

"Very good," he says. "Rest up. We will regroup shortly."

CLASSIFIED

Person(s) of Interest

CODE NAME: NONE

REAL NAME: LAWRENCE SEWARD

BASE OF OPERATIONS: VAN HELSING ACADEMY

D.S.I.

FACTS: Lawrence Seward is the tenured professor of Supernatural History at the Van Helsing Academy. He is also a notable archeologist specializing in the identification and recovery of Supernatural artifacts. He is a trusted advisor of Lothar Van Helsing.

FIELD OBSERVATIONS:

- Highly observant
- Travels often for archeological fieldwork
- Is deceptively quick on his feet
- Is armed at all times so approach with caution

Category: Natural

Sub-Type: None

Height: 6'0"

Weight: 285 lbs

STATUS: ACTIVE TARGET

DEPARTMENT OF SUPERNATURAL INVESTIGATIONS

CHAPTER NINE

TOO LITTLE TOO LATE

I open the door to find a ghost in my room.

"Aura?" I say. "What are you doing here?"

"We need to talk," she says.

She's sitting on the edge of Rage's bed with her arms crossed, which is never a good sign. Rage, of course, is still in the infirmary.

"Um, okay," I say, entering the room and closing the door behind me. I take off my hoodie and notice there's a giant hole in the right pocket. "Great. This must be from that zombie girl. Well, it's not like I didn't deserve it."

"What do you mean?" Aura asks.

"I mean this whole nightmare is my fault," I say, sitting on my bed and poking my finger through the hole. "If I never got captured by Faustius, Count Dracula would still be a spirit instead of the flesh-and-blood monster he is today. And then everyone's lives would be normal."

I toss the hoodie on my desk chair.

"Your fault?" Aura says, her eyebrows raised. "Bram,

this isn't your fault. If anything, it's my fault. The only reason you were in Faustius' lair was because of me, remember? My stupid curiosity has gotten us into more trouble than we can count. So, if we're going to go down that road you should blame me for everything."

"What?" I say. "That's ridiculous. I would never do that. It's not your fault."

"Okay," she says, "then it's not yours either."

We stare at each other for a while.

"Look," Aura says finally breaking the silence, "wallowing in self-pity won't change the past. All we can do now is save the future."

She's right about that, but the question is how? Saving the future is going to be difficult, especially if Count Dracula gets the Crown of Souls. But Van Helsing had me swear not to tell anyone about that. Time to change the subject.

"So," I say half-smiling. "Is that what you came to tell me, oh wise one?"

"No," she says. "I wanted to talk about what happened in Van Helsing's office. We're not ready."

"Ready?" I ask. "Ready for what?"

"To fight," she says, standing up. "To be soldiers. To take on Count Dracula and the Dark Ones. Do you honestly think Hairball and Stanphibian are ready to fight hordes of evil monsters? And what about Rage who can barely control himself? Or InvisiBill who can't follow simple directions? Or Kat who just got here and hasn't even been properly trained? If they go into battle they'll be slaughtered. Something is wrong with Van Helsing."

"What?" I say, surprised. "What do you mean?"

"I mean he's off his rocker," Aura says. "I get it that the war has started, but until today he would never put innocent kids on the front lines. Someone needs to talk to him about it, and I think that someone is you?"

"Me?" I say.

"Yes, you," she says. "You have a special relationship with him. He talks to you all the time. Maybe you can tell him we're not ready to be soldiers? Maybe you can get him to change his mind?"

The concern in her blue eyes tugs at my heartstrings, but I seriously doubt I can convince Van Helsing of anything. But I know she's right. If Crawler and Hexum hadn't shown up in Smileville we would have been overrun by zombies.

"Okay, okay," I say. "I'll talk to him. But he might not listen."

"Thank you, Bram!" she says.

And before I can respond, she leans over and gives me a big hug, but her arms go right through my body, sending chills down my spine.

"Sorry," she says, pulling back awkwardly.

"N-No," I say. "It's okay. Really."

She smiles nervously, her arms behind her back. Boy, if ghosts could blush her cheeks would be fire engine red.

"So, um, what did Van Helsing say after we left?" she

asks, quickly changing the subject.

Uh-oh. What am I going to tell her? I don't want to lie to her, but I have to stick to what I promised Van Helsing.

"Bram?" she asks. "Are you okay?"

"What? Yeah," I say. "He just wanted some more info about Agent M and DSI. So, I filled him in on some of those details."

There, that wasn't a lie.

"Oh, okay," she says. "Speaking of more info, I'm still trying to track down the cargo that arrived on that first ship from Romania."

"Really?" I say. "Um, here's a newsflash, but didn't you just tell me your curiosity has gotten us into more trouble than we can count?"

"Good point," she says, "but I know there's something there. I mean, why is Count Dracula shipping dirt from Romania to America? And according to those sailors you overheard, this was the second shipment. So, where did that first shipment go after it got here?"

"Great question," I say. "No clue."

"Exactly," she says, with a suspicious look in her eyes. "It's a mystery, and I love a good mystery."

"Then maybe you should stick to detective novels," I say. "They'll be less dangerous for everyone."

"Ha," she says. "Anyway, I've got things to do. Thanks for, well, listening to me. And thanks for talking to Van Helsing."

"Yeah," I say. "No problem."

"Have a good night," she says, and then phases through my door.

I kick off my shoes and lie down on my bed.

Well, I know I'll be seeing Van Helsing later, but I'm pretty sure I won't be having a good night.

***

After my talk with Aura, my stomach reminds me I'm starving! I put my shoes and hoodie back on and head down to the cafeteria. I know it's not open at this hour, but luckily I find some imps playing dice games out back and they let me in.

I raid the pantry, gobbling down anything red I can find while politely declining anything the imps offer me. After all, now isn't the time for unnecessary risks. When I'm finished I thank them and head back to my room.

And then I wait.

Crawler comes for me an hour later.

"Ready?" he asks.

"I guess so," I say, standing up.

We meet up with Van Helsing and Hexum at the garage. Barely a word is spoken as we load into Crawler's jeep and take off. Van Helsing and I are sitting in the back, giving me the perfect opportunity to have that conversation I promised Aura. But for some reason, now doesn't seem like the right time.

Van Helsing is staring out the window, and I can only imagine what he's thinking. I mean, this is a major mission. He's probably running through millions of scenarios about how we'll get the Crown of Souls before Count Dracula.

But then I notice his eyes are closed.

I lean forward and take a closer look when I realize he's sleeping. That's funny, I've never actually seen Van Helsing sleep before. I guess he has our plan all set.

Well, I don't know how long it will take to get to wherever we're going, and I'm actually feeling sleepy myself. So, I close my eyes and drift off.

***

"Bram," comes a voice. "It is time."

Huh?

I open my eyes, and for a split second, I have no idea where I am. I look out the window and see trees and mountains, and when I look the other way I see Van Helsing staring at me.

"We have arrived," he says. "It is time."

"Right," I say, rubbing my eyes.

Van Helsing steps out of the jeep and reaches back inside, pulling out a black crossbow. Something's off but I don't know what. Then, it hits me.

What's he doing with a black crossbow? Normally, he has the Crossbow of Purity, which is silver.

"Headmaster?" I say. "What happened to the Crossbow of Purity?"

"Oh, it is broken," he says. "But this one is a worthy substitute."

Um, okay. I didn't even know the Crossbow of Purity could break. I step out of the jeep and a chilly breeze makes me shiver. I pull my hood over my head and take a look around. We're parked on a dirt road that ends at the base of a sweeping mountain range.

"Where are we?" I ask.

"According to my research," Van Helsing says, "the Crown of Souls should be located here."

"You mean, up in the mountains?" I ask.

"No," Van Helsing says, loading a bolt into his crossbow, "down inside the cavern."

I swallow hard. Did he just say 'cavern?'

Why do I have a bad feeling about this?

"Let's go," Crawler says.

I follow the three men as they make their way across the rocky terrain towards the largest mountain. At first, my eyes can't help but drift up to the mountain's soaring peak. But as we climb over a ridge, I spot an ominous cave burrowing deep into the mountain itself.

Two dark, slanted stones protrude above the entrance like watchful eyes, while jagged rocks hang into the opening like sharp fangs. If I didn't know better, I'd say we were walking straight into the mouth of a monster!

Van Helsing gathers us outside the cave.

"The artifact we seek should be inside," Van Helsing says.

"Should be?" Hexum says. "What does that mean?"

"It means the research has led us here, but we may be in the wrong place," Van Helsing says.

"To that point," Crawler says, "it's also a cavern. So, don't be surprised if there are bats in there."

"Bats?" I say, my voice cracking nervously.

They all look at me funny and I feel embarrassed.

"Um, sorry," I say quickly. "I mean, I love bats."

"According to my records," Van Helsing says, "the cavern will descend gradually for three hundred feet before opening into a large chamber. The Crown of Souls should be inside that chamber, but that is not all. According to legend, the artifact is protected by a guardian."

"A guardian?" Crawler says. "What kind of guardian?"

"A mummy," Van Helsing says. "Supposedly, it will come to life if anyone attempts to steal the Crown of Souls."

A mummy? Seriously?

"Got it," Crawler whispers, his voice not wavering in the least. "Let's get this show on the road."

Crawler and Hexum head for the cave entrance, but for some reason, my feet don't want to move.

"Come, Bram," Van Helsing says. "Do not worry, I will be right behind you."

"Right," I say, trying to look brave.

I fall in line behind Hexum, and Van Helsing brings up the rear. The cave is cold so I pull my hands into my sleeves to keep them warm. I can see clearly in the dark, but the others need flashlights, and the rock walls sparkle as they shine their lights around.

Strangely, for a guy who can transform into a bat, I've never actually been in a cavern before. I have to say, it's pretty incredible. With the dripstone formations and reflective pools of water, it feels like you're walking on another planet. The ever-changing landscape, from ten-foot stalactites to thirty-foot stalagmites, is truly amazing.

One day I'd love to bring the team down here but under entirely different circumstances.

SKREEEE!

"Get down!" Crawler whispers.

I duck just as a colony of bats zooms over our heads. Holy cow! There must be hundreds of them! I stay low until the last one clears, my heart pumping fast. That was close, but then I realize something.

We've lost the element of surprise.

"Come on," Crawler whispers.

As we continue, I remember my conversation with Aura. She's right, maybe none of us are ready for this, including me. I mean, I have no idea why I'm even here. Van Helsing has never included me on his missions before, so why did he rope me into this one? I'm pretty sure they could have handled it without me. I'd love to ask him about it but it's kind of late now.

"Up here," Crawler whispers, waving us ahead.

And when we reach his position, we're standing on a rocky ledge looking into a circular chamber with a high ceiling and multiple levels, each with its own tunnel. And there, sitting in the center of the floor is a gray tomb!

That's it!

The Crown of Souls must be in there!

"Let's go," Crawler says, using his spider legs to gracefully climb down a crude rock stairway.

We follow him far less gracefully, congregating around the dusty, stone tomb. As I study it, it's hard not to notice its large size, perfect for holding a kid-eating mummy.

"Open it," Hexum says to Crawler. "But slowly."

Crawler nods and slides his spider legs beneath the lid. Well, if there's really a mummy in there then I'm probably standing a little too close. But when I step back I nearly jump out of my skin as a hand clamps down on my shoulder.

"Stay right here," Van Helsing orders.

Um, okay. What's wrong with him?

But as Crawler lifts the lid, the tomb is empty!

There's no mummy inside, and more importantly, no Crown of Souls!

"What foul trick is this?" Hexum says, looking at me and Van Helsing.

But then his eyes go wide.

And when I glance over, I see Van Helsing's crossbow pointed right at Hexum's chest!

"I'd say a good one," Van Helsing says.

HA! HA! HA!

Maniacal laughter echoes through the chamber, and suddenly, four werewolves pop out of the tunnels above!

"Well done, 'Headmaster,'" comes a familiar, evil voice from somewhere up high. "Well done indeed."

And that's when I see him, standing on the highest ledge with a round, wooden object in his hand.

It's Count Dracula!

And he's got the Crown of Souls!

CHAPTER TEN

BAD BLOOD

I'm floored right now.

I mean, in the blink of an eye everything just went bonkers! Count Dracula has the Crown of Souls, we're surrounded by werewolves, and Van Helsing is pointing his crossbow right at Hexum's chest!

I don't know what's going on, and Van Helsing is gripping my shoulder so tight I can't pull away!

"Headmaster," Crawler says, "are you okay? You do realize you're pointing your crossbow at Professor Hexum, right?"

"I know where my crossbow is pointed," Van Helsing says. "And I am perfectly fine, thank you very much."

"Yes, he is perfect isn't he?" Count Dracula says from high on his ledge. "Nearly perfect in every way."

"What are you talking about?" Crawler says.

"I know exactly what he is talking about," Hexum says, staring into Van Helsing's eyes. "You aren't Van Helsing, are you?"

"No," Van Helsing says, flashing an evil grin. "Not

exactly."

Huh? What's going on?

Suddenly, I feel something strange spreading across my shoulder, and when I look over Van Helsing's fingers aren't fingers, but flesh-colored tendrils expanding down my hoodie! And when I look up I don't see Van Helsing anymore, but a creature with a distorted head and folds of skin shifting across his face!

"A doppelganger!" Hexum says.

A… doppelganger? Suddenly, I remember Professor Holmwood talking about doppelgangers in our Monsterology class. They're shapeshifters who can duplicate the physical and vocal characteristics of someone else! And they're pure evil!

"Indeed," the doppelganger says. "But I'm no ordinary doppelganger."

Suddenly, everything clicks into place. No wonder Aura thought Van Helsing was off his rocker. It was never Van Helsing at all!

But wait a second, how could a doppelganger even step foot on campus? I mean, the Artifacts of Virtue are supposed to protect the school from evil.

"I'm known as a doppelganger-superior," the creature continues. "The best mercenary-for-hire around. Unlike my weaker kin, with a simple touch, I not only mimic the surface characteristics of my victims but their thoughts and desires as well. As long as I stay in character, I'm as good as the real thing."

"So," I say, "you weren't the real Van Helsing when we talked to Dr. Renfield?"

"Nope," the doppelganger-superior says. "I've been pretending to be your sappy headmaster since New York City. I knew you and your 'mentor' had a rocky relationship, so bringing you to see Renfield was a simple ploy to earn your trust. And that's how I got you here without you suspecting a thing."

As his words sink in, I feel like such a fool.

"It was a trap from the start," Hexum says, disgusted. "Congratulations on fooling us and the Artifacts of Virtue. Now, where is the real Van Helsing?"

"Do not worry about your beloved Headmaster," Count Dracula says, floating down to ground level, his cape billowing behind him. "He is in good hands. Rest assured that he is enjoying his 'special' accommodations."

Seeing Count Dracula up close shocks me. Somehow, he looks even younger than when I saw him last at Dr. Moreau's tower. His cheeks are fuller, and I can see his muscular shoulders through his cape. It's like he's aging backward, which can only mean one thing.

He must be drinking human blood again.

"Wait until I get my legs on you," Crawler says, stepping towards Count Dracula, but the four werewolves jump down to block his path.

"Crawler, wait," Hexum says, putting his arm out. Then, he looks at the Crown of Souls in Count Dracula's hand and says, "You have what you want, now let us go."

"I do," Count Dracula says, putting the artifact on his head. "But this is not the only thing I came for."

For the first time, I get a good look at the Crown of Souls, a collection of intertwining twigs woven into a circular crown. All I know is that if I destroy Count Dracula while he's wearing it, he'll come back to life. And that's not a good thing.

"What do you want?" Hexum asks.

"Is it not obvious?" Count Dracula says, turning towards me. "I want the boy."

What? I try pulling away, but the doppelganger-superior still has me in his powerful grasp.

"Retrieving the Crown of Souls before you was easy," Count Dracula says. "But getting you to deliver the child was far more difficult. Fortunately, I have plenty of operatives at my disposal."

"I just want my pay," the doppelganger-superior says.

"And you will receive it," Count Dracula says.

"I assume your list of operatives includes Renfield?" Hexum says. "I must admit, you used him perfectly to set your trap. I thought it was an odd coincidence to find him in New York City where you also unleashed your attack, but now it makes sense. Well played, but unfortunately, the child is not yours for the taking."

"And who will stop me?" Count Dracula says.

Hexum opens his mouth but thinks better of it.

I look at Count Dracula and shudder. I can't believe it. All of this trickery was to get me here. Now I know why Van Helsing invited me on this mission. It was all to bring me to Count Dracula!

"Hello, Bram," Count Dracula says. "Have you reconsidered my offer?"

"Your offer?" I repeat. "You mean, the one to join you and rule the world?"

"Yes," he says. "Why should we fight and risk one of us dying? After all, we are the last of our kind. The last of a magnificent and superior race feared and envied by all of humankind. Imagine how much I could teach you. Envision how we could rule together. I, the King of Darkness, and you, the Prince of Darkness."

As his lips curl into a menacing smile I feel disgusted. I mean, I'm not evil. I don't want to be a bloodsucking vampire like him. I'll do anything to stop myself from getting to that point. And I mean anything.

"Open your pointy ears," I say, "because I want you to get this through your thick skull. I will NEVER, EVER join you! Got it?"

"That is a shame," Count Dracula says, his smile fading. "Because that means I have no use for you." And then he opens his mouth wide, revealing razor-sharp fangs!

"Bram, go!" Crawler yells. He tries pushing past the werewolves but they wrestle him to the ground.

I try to run, but the stupid doppelganger-superior still has me by the shoulder! I'm about to mist, when—

RRRAAUURRRGGGHHH!

Everyone freezes.

What's that noise?

Just then, the tomb's lid CLANGS onto the floor and two bony hands emerge from inside, gripping the sides.

"What?" Count Dracula says, turning.

Suddenly, a bandaged figure with dried-out skin, cracked lips, and yellow eyes leaps out of the tomb and attacks Count Dracula!

I can't believe it! It's… the mummy!

And it's trying to take back the Crown of Souls!

"Get him off me you fools!" Count Dracula yells, holding the mummy's wrists.

The werewolves release Crawler to help their master, but the mummy is too strong. As they tussle on the ground, Hexum shoots Crawler a look, and the spider-man nods back.

"But that's impossible," the doppelganger-superior mutters, watching the action. "It can't be real. I made up the story about the mummy just for fun."

"Shoot it, you imbecile!" Count Dracula yells, as he finally flips the mummy over his head into the rock wall.

The doppelganger-superior finally lets me go and aims his crossbow at the mummy.

THWIP!

The arrow pierces the mummy's chest, knocking it down for a moment. But then it gets back up.

"Time to leave," Crawler says, grabbing me with his spider legs and throwing me over his shoulder like a sack of potatoes. "This is our chance."

"But the Crown of Souls?" I say. "We can't just let Count Dracula have—"

"It's too late, kid," Crawler says, cutting me off. "We need to get you out alive."

"But what about Hexum?" I say.

"I am behind you, Mr. Murray," Hexum calls out.

As Crawler scales the stairs with ease, I see Hexum behind us, struggling to make his way up the rocky incline.

"Stop!" a voice echoes through the chamber.

But this time it isn't Count Dracula, but the doppelganger-superior! And he's raising his crossbow!

"Speaking of foul tricks," the doppelganger-superior says, aiming his crossbow at Hexum. "I should have known. You're using mind tricks to make us believe there's a mummy. But it's not real."

"Hexum, look out!" I yell.

THWIP!

"Arrrgh!" Hexum yells as the arrow strikes him square in the back.

"Crawler!" I yell. "Hexum was shot! We have to go back!"

"N-No!" Hexum barks, his voice cracking. "Go! Get him out of here! N-Now!"

"I'm sorry, kid," Crawler says. "Orders are orders."

"No!" I cry as Crawler pulls me up into the tunnel.

The last thing I see are Hexum's eyes.

His sad, green eyes.

"Fools!" Count Dracula yells. "Get the boy!"

AWWWOOOO!

Werewolves!

The werewolves are coming!

Seconds later, the first one enters the tunnel, followed by three more! We can't outrun them! But then—

YELP!

The werewolves scream and jump back frightened as a ball of fire erupts in front of the pack! But I know the truth. Hexum is helping us escape!

Crawler picks up his pace and the diversion gives us enough time to cover some serious distance. And then, just as quickly as the fire came, I hear Hexum SCREAM, and the flame flickers out.

And that's when I know.

He's dead.

Hexum is… dead.

He sacrificed himself… so I could live.

I choke back tears and flinch as sunlight hits my eyes. We're outside the cave now and Crawler keeps on moving, crossing the rocky plains in no time flat. Then, he puts me in the jeep.

"Buckle up," he says, getting into the driver's seat.

And then he pounds the gas and we're off.

MONSTEROLOGY 101 FIELD GUIDE

DOPPELGANGER

CLASSIFICATION:

Type: Shapeshifter
Sub-Type: Superior
Height: Variable
Weight: Variable
Eye Color: Variable
Hair Color: Variable

KNOWN ABILITIES:

- A rare subtype of doppelganger
- With one touch, can replicate the surface characteristics of a victim, including their thoughts and inner-most desires

KNOWN WEAKNESSES:

- Cannot mimic the special abilities of a victim
- Can only change into human forms, unable to take the form of animals or objects

DANGER LEVEL:
EXTREME

TIPS TO AVOID AN UNWANTED ENCOUNTER:

- It is nearly impossible to identify a Doppelganger-Superior
- If an individual is exhibiting slightly uncharacteristic behavior, they may have been replaced by a Doppelganger-Superior

CHAPTER ELEVEN

RAISING THE STAKES

As we pull into the academy, all I feel is numb.

Professor Hexum is dead.

Because of me.

His final scream keeps replaying in my head, haunting me. I'm still having a hard time processing it all. I mean, despite everything we've been through, in the end, he sacrificed his life to save mine.

Honestly, I don't think I've ever been such a terrible judge of character. Hexum said I didn't have to like him, but his job was to make me stronger so I could defeat Count Dracula. He told me that's why he's harder on me than the other kids. He was always on my side, but I just couldn't see it.

And now I hate myself for it.

Crawler had little to say on the ride home, but as he pulls around the circular driveway, he finally says—

"Listen, Bram. I know things are difficult right now, but we need to get everyone together to tell them what happened. Why don't you head up to the auditorium and

I'll meet you there? Can you do that?"

"Yeah," I say, staring absently out the windshield.

"Great," Crawler says. "I'll round everyone up and bring them to the auditorium. But don't worry, I'll do all of the talking, okay?"

"Yeah," I hear myself say. "Okay."

"See you soon," he says, and then he gets out of the jeep and slams the door behind him.

As I step out of the car it feels like I'm having an out of body experience. It's morning and the sun is shining but I don't care if I get burned. I don't care about anything right now. Strangely, I barely feel my feet walking across campus. Instead, it's like I'm floating across the quad.

As I climb up the front stairs and enter the building, I see the school banner hanging up high. It reads:

YOU MUST BELIEVE IN THINGS YOU CANNOT IMAGINE

Isn't that the truth.

It's crazy how much has happened that I couldn't imagine. Like, the last time I walked through this entranceway I was with Van Helsing. Or at least I thought it was Van Helsing. Now I'm kicking myself for not realizing he was a doppelganger. I should have been more aware. I should have figured it out.

But I didn't.

And now the real Van Helsing is in Count Dracula's evil hands. Just thinking about what he must be going through makes me shudder. And I feel like such a fool for even considering the things Count Dracula said to me.

Why did I let him mess with my head? Count Dracula said Van Helsing was using me. That Van Helsing would destroy me once he was finished with me. But I don't believe him anymore.

After all, Van Helsing took me in when no one else would. Sure, we've had some trust issues, but every relationship has bumps in the road. Van Helsing was just trying to protect me, and now I know what I've got to do.

I've got to rescue Van Helsing.

I've got to destroy Count Dracula once and for all.

I open the doors to the empty auditorium and my mind flashes back to the last time I was here. It was when Van Helsing introduced Dr. Renfield as our new professor of Monster Mindset. I can still see him staring at me from the stage.

Then, as I step inside the auditorium, a realization hits me like a ton of bricks.

Dr. Renfield!

He's probably still here! Inside that crazy clock!

I've got to talk to him!

But as soon as I exit the auditorium, a wave of students are coming my way. Crawler must have sent them to hear the news about Van Helsing and Hexum. I'd love to stay here and support Crawler, but I need answers.

I push my way through the crowd when I hear—

"Bram?"

Then, I see Aura and Rage. Rage smiles when he sees me and I'm relieved he's back on his feet again, but I can't afford to stop and chit-chat.

"Hey," I say. "I'd love to join you guys, but I can't talk right now. I've got somewhere I've gotta be."

"Why do you look so stressed out?" Aura asks, looking at me funny. "And do you know why Crawler called this assembly?"

"Yeah," I say, "and it's horrible news. Look, when you said Van Helsing was off his rocker you weren't kidding."

"What does that mean?" she says.

Just then, Blobby bumps into me on his way to the auditorium and the rest of the Howler's laugh.

"Look," I say, ignoring them as I head for the stairs. "Just go inside. Crawler will tell you everything. If he asks where I am just tell him I had to go to the bathroom."

But instead of going to the auditorium, Aura and Rage follow me to the stairs.

"Okay," Aura says, floating beside me. "Clearly, you know what's going on, so save us Crawler's sugarcoated explanation and tell us what's really happening."

As we head downstairs I debate if I should give them the whole story. But as I look at their determined faces I realize the two of them have been by my side the entire time. I couldn't ask for better friends. So, I might as well give them the unfiltered truth.

"Here's the scoop," I say, stopping on the landing. "And it's really bad, so get ready."

"Okay," they say in unison.

"Alright," I say, taking a deep breath. "Here it is. Last night, after you left, Van Helsing took Crawler, Hexum, and I to a cavern to recover a Supernatural object called the Crown of Souls before Count Dracula could get it. But it was a trap because Van Helsing wasn't Van Helsing at all, but rather a creature called a doppelganger-superior who led us right into the hands of Count Dracula and his minions. Count Dracula got the Crown of Souls first and would have killed me if it weren't for Hexum who created an illusion of a mummy that allowed Crawler and I to escape. But Hexum got shot by the doppelganger-superior and now… now he's dead."

Tears flood down my cheeks as I finish.

"What?" Rage says. "A-Are you serious?"

"Oh no," Aura says. "I'm so sorry, Bram."

"I can't believe it," Rage says, still stunned. "Are you sure Hexum is dead?"

"Yeah," I say. "And it's all my fault. Again."

"Bram, you can't take the blame for this," Aura says. "There's no way you could have known. I mean, that explains why Van Helsing was acting so out of character, but a doppelganger-superior? We studied those in

Holmwood's class. It replicates a person's physical characteristics and what they think and feel. It could fool anyone, and I guess that includes the Artifacts of Virtue."

"Yeah," I say. "That's clear now."

"What's the Crown of Souls?" Rage asks.

"It's an artifact that can resurrect you if you die," I say. "Your body and spirit."

"And Count Dracula has the Crown of Souls?" Aura says. "That's, like, bad news."

"You're telling me," I say.

"So, where are you going now?" Rage asks.

"To see Dr. Renfield," I answer.

"Renfield?" they say, looking at one another.

"Yeah," I say. "I know it sounds crazy but he's here, at the school. He's the one who told us about the Crown of Souls. He and that fake Van Helsing set me up, and now I want answers."

"Okay, then," Aura says. "Lead the way."

We finish going downstairs and then scoot across the entranceway into the faculty lounge wing. I lead them down the hall, past the kitchen, and stop in front of the grandfather clock. That's when I realize we may have a problem. When the fake Van Helsing took me here, the clock only opened up when it struck—

"Um, what are you doing?" Rage asks.

"Moving the minute hand to one minute before midnight," I say, standing on my tippy toes.

"Why?" he asks. "It's the middle of the morning."

"You'll see," I say, stepping back.

We stare at the second-hand ticking around the face of the clock, until… DONG!

Suddenly, the front doors of the clock spring open.

"Whoa!" Rage says. "That's wild."

"You ain't seen nothing yet," I say, stepping inside.

Rage and Aura look awestruck as they follow me down the clock hallway until we reach the prison cell at the end. But their amazement quickly turns to shock when they spot the blindfolded Renfield inside.

"You weren't kidding," Rage whispers.

"Dr. Renfield," I say. "Are you surprised to hear my voice?"

"Bram?" he says, standing up and looking around. "Is that you? And was that Mr. Rage I heard as well?"

"Hi," Rage says.

"It is nice to hear your voice," Dr. Renfield says, feeling his way over to the barred door. "Should I assume Ms. Aura is here as well?"

"Check," Aura says.

"The three musketeers," Dr. Renfield says. "It is such a pleasure to be with you all again."

"Knock it off," I say. "You know you set us up. Count Dracula nearly killed me and Professor Hexum is dead because of you."

"Dead?" Dr. Renfield says, his eyebrows raised. "That was never my intention when I provided you with that information. I certainly hope you are okay and I am so sorry for your loss. I never liked Alastair Hexum, but I certainly never wished him dead. He was such a passionate teacher."

"What's with him?" Rage whispers.

He is acting weird, but then I remember why.

"Last night Professor Morris gave him a truth serum," I whisper. "Maybe it's still in his system."

"Well," Aura whispers. "test him."

Right. I try to think of something to ask him, and then I remember our conversation in the gymnasium when he was still a teacher here.

"Dr. Renfield," I say, "when you asked me if I knew where the Spear of Darkness was, were you working for Count Dracula?"

"Yes, I was," Dr. Renfield says without hesitation. "I was completely under his influence."

Aura and Rage look at each other.

"I thought so," I say. "But it's good to hear you admit it. Here's another one. Were you aware that Van Helsing was a doppelganger-superior?"

"A doppelganger-superior?" Dr. Renfield says, looking genuinely surprised. "No, I was not aware of that nor did I suspect it was even a possibility."

"Interesting," I say. "So, you're saying you had no idea Van Helsing was a fake when you told us about the Crown of Souls?"

"No," Dr. Renfield says. "None at all."

Well, that's interesting. I guess he was as clueless

about the trap as we were.

"I've got one," Aura says. "Do you know where Count Dracula is hiding out? Where his base of operations is located?"

"No, I'm afraid not," Dr. Renfield says. "Count Dracula always visited me, usually in the middle of the night. I never visited him."

"Drat," Aura says.

"Well," Rage says. "This is useless. Let's go."

But as I think back to the conversation Dr. Renfield and I had about the Spear of Darkness, I also remember him saying that Van Helsing had other Supernatural objects here at the academy. And that gives me an idea.

"Hang on," I say. "Did Van Helsing ever tell you if he had any other Supernatural artifacts in his possession that could help us defeat Count Dracula?"

"Why yes," Dr. Renfield says. "He did."

The three of us look at one another.

"Really?" I say. "Like what?"

"Well, I recall him telling me once about another artifact," Dr. Renfield says. "He called it… the Eternal Stake. He said it was whittled from the Tree of Life itself, and if it struck a vampire it could destroy their mortal body with just one blow."

The Eternal Stake?

For a second, I'm flabbergasted. I mean, Van Helsing never mentioned anything about an Eternal Stake. Then, I get a frightening thought. Did he keep it from me because he was planning to use it on me?

"Interesting," Aura says. "I've never heard of it. Did he tell you where he kept this 'Eternal Stake?'"

"No," Dr. Renfield says. "Except he did say he was keeping it warm, just in case he needed to use it."

Keeping it warm? What's that supposed to mean?

"Is there, um, anything else you think we should know?" I ask. "You know, like any other secret vampire-destroying weapons Van Helsing was hiding?"

"No," Dr. Renfield says. "That was all. But now that I have helped you, maybe you can help me? Can you let me out of this cage?"

"Um, no," I say. "Sorry."

"I understand," he says sadly, slinking down to the ground. "I wouldn't let myself out either. But perhaps you would be willing to do me a favor. I'm quite hungry. Would you be able to get me a sandwich?"

"Sure," I say. "No problem. Thanks for your help."

"It was my pleasure," Dr. Renfield says. "Good luck. It was great speaking with all of you."

As we make our way back down the clock hallway, no one says a word. Then, we reenter the main building.

"Well, that was unexpected," Aura says finally.

"Yeah," I say. "You're telling me. But strangely, despite everything Dr. Renfield's done, I believe him."

"What's the Tree of Life anyway?" Rage asks.

"The Tree of Life is a mythical tree known throughout ancient cultures," Aura says. "Different civilizations might call it different things, but they all see it as the source of spiritual and physical life."

"Right," Rage says. "So, what do we do now?"

"Duh," Aura says. "We find the Eternal Stake. I bet it's here somewhere, just like the Spear of Darkness was. Something tells me Van Helsing would want to keep something that powerful close at hand. What do you think, Bram?"

I hear Aura talking, but I'm lost in thought. I just can't shake the feeling Van Helsing didn't tell me about the Eternal Stake for a reason. But what was the reason?

"Bram?" Aura says. "Don't you think we should find the Eternal Stake?"

"Um, yeah," I say. "Totally. We need to get right on that. But first I've got to take care of this."

I push through the doors of the faculty kitchen.

"Where are you going?" Rage asks.

"To find a cafeteria imp," I say. "I promised Dr. Renfield a sandwich."

CHAPTER TWELVE

RELATIVELY SPEAKING

The Eternal Stake.

I still don't understand why Van Helsing never told me about it. I mean, having a weapon that can destroy the mortal body of a vampire with one blow seems like something he'd want to share. Unless, of course, he was planning to use it on me.

I inhale deeply and breathe out.

I don't know what to think anymore.

Whatever Van Helsing's intentions were, Rage, Aura, and I turned the academy upside down searching for the Eternal Stake. But there was so much ground to cover we had to split up. Rage searched Monster House, Aura covered the faculty residences, and I scoured the main building.

But no one found it.

Now Rage and I are back in our room exhausted while Aura is still out there looking. I wish I had the stamina of a ghost, but my feet are throbbing and it wouldn't surprise me if they fell off.

I was so confident I was going to find the Eternal Stake in Van Helsing's office but it didn't happen. Not that I'm surprised. There's so much clutter in there it's hard to move around, let alone find an Eternal Stake in a proverbial haystack. Between the mountains of books, half-finished inventions, and medieval weaponry it was probably a lost cause from the start.

Speaking of lost causes, I was pretty much an emotional wreck as soon as I entered Van Helsing's office. But I really lost it when I saw his empty chair by the fireplace. I remembered all the times I sat across from him, soaking in his wisdom as he fed logs into the fire.

But now his fire is out.

So, I didn't find the Eternal Stake. It probably didn't help that I have no idea what it looks like. I mean, a stake is a stake, right?

Unless, of course, it's not.

As I've come to learn when you're dealing with the Supernatural, nothing is as it seems. I mean, who would have thought that Van Helsing wasn't actually Van Helsing but a doppelganger-superior? Or that Hexum's walking stick was really the Spear of Darkness?

Every time I think of Hexum I feel incredible guilt. He sacrificed himself to save me, and what am I doing to honor his sacrifice? Sitting on my bed like a useless lump.

Some hero I turned out to be.

I look at Rage's innocent face. I don't think I could live with myself if something happened to him or Aura or my other friends. This all started because of me and I'm the one who's going to have to finish it.

Alone.

"Um, Bram," Rage says, sitting up in his bed.

"Yeah," I say. "What is it?"

"Well," he says, "remember when I told you I checked Monster House from top to bottom?"

"Yeah," I say.

"Well, I didn't check the 'real' bottom," Rage says.

The 'real' bottom? For a second I'm confused, but then it dawns on me what he's talking about.

"You mean, the forbidden basement?" I say.

"Yeah, that bottom," he says.

Just thinking about the forbidden basement sends a chill down my spine. I went down there to prove that the Artifacts of Virtue existed, and I barely made it out alive. Could Van Helsing have hidden the Eternal Stake in the basement?

I guess it's possible, but I do remember it being pretty cold down there. Didn't Dr. Renfield say Van Helsing liked to keep the Eternal Stake warm, in case he needed to—

Warm?

Holy cow!

I know where it is! I can't believe I missed it!

"Don't be mad at me," Rage continues. "I-I didn't really forget to look down there, but I didn't want to go down there alone. And I don't want to go down n—"

"Don't worry about it," I say, hopping off my bed. "The Eternal Stake isn't down there. But I think I know where it is."

"You do?" Rage says. "Where?"

"I've got to go," I say, grabbing my hoodie. "You stay here."

"Stay here?" Rage says, jumping off his bed. "Forget it. I'm coming with you. And shouldn't we get Aura?"

But I don't answer him. Instead, I turn on my super-speed and bolt down the stairs, leaving him in the dust. I feel bad not bringing him along, but I've hurt enough people. Going forward, I need to handle this on my own.

Within seconds, I'm outside the main building.

And that's when I run into Crawler.

"Bram?" he says, exiting through the double doors.

Uh-oh. I'm sure he's upset with me for missing his assembly but I can't let him know what I'm up to.

"Where are you off to at top speed?" he says. "I'm sure you heard that I suspended all classes for the time being. The main building is closed."

"Closed?" I say. Well, I guess I missed out on that little tidbit when I skipped the assembly. But I have to get inside. "Right, but I um, think I left my backpack in the gymnasium when we had exams. So, I thought I'd check and see if it's there. I'll be quick."

"No problem," Crawler says. "But I'm glad we ran into each other. I intended to speak with you after the assembly but couldn't find you."

"Yeah," I say. "Sorry about that."

"Hey, it's okay," Crawler says. "I just want to make sure you're okay. That battle in the cavern was… intense, and you've been through a lot."

"Yeah," I say. "You could say that."

"I know," he says, patting me on the shoulder with one of his spider legs. "But, well, now that Van Helsing isn't here, we need to talk about the future."

"The future?" I say.

"Yes," he says. "The professors and I were talking, and you're going to need more guidance now than ever before. No one here expects you to pick up the pieces and figure out what to do on your own. We're fighting a war, and we need to fight it together. So, the professors and I are going to band together to counsel you."

"Oh," I say, with obvious surprise in my voice.

I mean, I appreciate what he's trying to do, but I've already decided that enough is enough. Once I find the Eternal Stake, it'll be time to do what I do best, which is go solo. So, it's time to get out of this conversation.

"That sounds great," I say.

"I'm glad to hear you say that," Crawler says with a smile. "We'll get through this, Bram. Now go see if your backpack is there, and then I'll meet you over at Monster House in about a half-hour. Deal?"

"Deal," I say, faking a smile.

As Crawler walks away I breathe a sigh of relief. For a second there I thought he was going to stop me for good.

As soon as I enter the building I take off again. I have to say it does feel weird that no one is around. At this late hour, you'd usually see kids coming and going from their extracurricular activities. But now the place is empty.

That is, until I hit the faculty wing.

"P-Professor Seward!" I say, screeching to a halt.

The portly professor is standing in the hallway locking his door. And under his arm is a stack of exam booklets.

"Mr. Murray," he says, clearly surprised to see me. "What are you doing here? The main building is closed."

Not again.

"Yes," I say, scrambling for a good answer. I mean, it's not like I can tell him the same story I just told Crawler. I'm nowhere near the gym. "I know. I'm, um, just making sure there are no students left in the building. Trying to help out in any way I can."

"I see," Professor Seward says. "Well, I am looking forward to reading your exam essay this evening."

"My exam essay?" I say, surprised.

"Why yes, Mr. Murray, your exam essay," he says, holding up the exam booklets. "We may be in a war, but we must ensure we are delivering upon our high academic standards."

"Right," I say, kind of shocked he's even bringing this up right now. "Of course. Well, I, um, hope you enjoy it. Mine might be a little brief, but it's very profound."

"Excellent," he says. "Well then, I have a busy night ahead of me. Good evening Mr. Murray."

"Yes, good evening," I say.

As I watch Seward disappear around the corner I realize he'd be one of my counselors, and that just solidifies why I can't stick around. I wait until his footsteps fade away and then get down to business.

I approach Van Helsing's office and put my hand on the door. It's usually warm to the touch but not tonight. I peer over my shoulder to make sure I'm alone and then mist through the crevices of the doorframe.

Once inside I float over Van Helsing's mess until I reach the large room in the back. I collect my molecules near the fireplace and transform back to kid-form. I can't believe I missed it the first time, but now I've put all the clues together.

Renfield said Van Helsing kept the Eternal Stake 'warm' in case he needed to use it. Well, there's nowhere on campus warmer than his fireplace, and since he would only use the Eternal Stake on a vampire it all fits together. Van Helsing must have kept the Eternal Stake close at hand for our fireside chats just in case he needed to use it—on me!

Just thinking about it makes me sick.

And if I'm right, I guess it answers the question once and for all if Van Helsing ever trusted me. Not that I could blame him if he didn't. I mean, maybe he was just trying to protect himself. After all, I could become a bloodsucking vampire at any moment.

Now I just need to find it.

I get on my hands and knees and look under his chair but don't see anything. Then, I stick my head in the unlit fireplace and look around but still nothing. Come on, where would I find a wooden—

Wooden?

Man, am I a dufus or what?

What's wooden and near a fireplace?

Logs!

I inspect the log holder next to the fireplace. There are a bunch of jagged, axe-cut logs stacked inside an iron holder, but they all look the same. Then, I notice one log on the very bottom that looks quite different. Unlike the others, this one has a round, smooth bottom.

I pull it and it slides out easily, like it wasn't part of the pile at all but sitting inside a separate holder. And as I turn it in my hands, it's smooth, brown, and has a sharp point on one end.

It's a stake!

But it looks kind of ordinary.

Is it a stake, or is it the Eternal Stake?

Then, I notice Van Helsing's chair is right next to the log holder. All he would need to do is reach back with his right arm and grab it. I never would have seen it coming.

Well, this has to be it, so it's time to get moving. But as I start to head out something catches my eye. There's a folder lying on the floor next to Van Helsing's desk. I must have knocked it off when I was going through his stuff earlier.

I reach down to pick it up when I see the corner of a yellowed paper sticking out. Curious, I open the folder and see an old student assessment profile from years earlier. And attached to it is a black and white photograph of a boy who is a little older than me. He has dark hair, dark eyes, pointy ears, and… fangs?

And then I read his name and my heart stops.

GABRIEL MURRAY

G-Gabriel Murray? But that's… my dad?

I blink hard and look at the photo again. I mean, I've never actually seen a picture of my dad before. I put the profile on the desk and trace his features with my index finger. I-I can't believe how much I look like him.

Then, I read through his profile. We're about the same height and weight, and according to these scores, no one other than Van Helsing thought he was a good candidate for the academy.

I wonder why Van Helsing never showed this to me. And why was he looking at my father's profile in the first place? He must have pulled it out before he went to New York City.

"Bram?"

"Ahh!" I scream!

My heart is pounding, and when I look up I see Aura floating there. I close the folder.

"How did you get in here?" I ask.

"Seriously?" she says. "I'm a ghost, remember? Rage told me you took off like a lunatic to find the Eternal Stake. So, I figured you probably came here." Then, she sees the stake in my hand. "Is that it?"

"I think so," I say, holding it up. "It was in the log holder next to the fireplace."

"Keeping it 'warm,'" Aura says. "Just like Renfield said. That's great news. And I have some good news myself."

"Really?" I say, "what's that?"

"Well," she says. "I tapped into the spirit network and we finally figured out where that first shipment from Romania went. Sleepy Hollow, New York."

"Sleepy Hollow?" I say. "As in, the Legend of Sleepy Hollow? As in, the creepy story with the Headless Horseman? That's a real place?"

"Yep," she says. "As real as you and I. The cargo was delivered from the port to an abandoned estate in Sleepy Hollow, and I'm guessing that's where we'll find Count Dracula."

"Great job," I say. "Just give me the address and I'll get going."

"You'll get going?" Aura says, crossing her arms. "Bram, what are you talking about? The rest of the team are outside and we're going with you. We have to save Van Helsing."

"No," I say. "It's too dangerous. I… I won't let anyone else I care about get hurt. I'm going alone."

"Don't be stupid, Bram," she says. "This is Count Dracula and the Dark Ones we're talking about. You're going to need help. Look, I know you're upset about Hexum and Van Helsing. We all are. But it doesn't mean you should run off and do something stupid. Look, we may not be ready, but we're a team and we stick together. Besides, I'm the one who knows where we're going, remember?"

Well, she's got me there.

We stare at each other in silence. Unfortunately, she's probably right. Taking on Count Dracula and the Dark Ones alone would be suicide. And it would be nice to have their company. But I can't let anyone else get hurt. So, once we get where we need to go, I'll do my thing.

"Fine," I say. "But only because you're holding the location hostage."

"Perfect," she says. "Now get ready, because Hairball is driving again."

"Wonderful," I say. "I'll grab my barf bag."

And as she turns to leave, I take my dad's profile out of the folder, fold it in half, and slip it into my hoodie pocket.

Gabriel Murray
- Spring

CHAPTER THIRTEEN

ALMOST THERE

"We're here," Aura says. "Slow down, Hairball."

Thank goodness because I'm not feeling so hot.

At first, I thought it was Hairball's typically terrible driving, but now I'm not so sure. Unlike the other roller coaster rides he's taken us on, the problem this time isn't my stomach but my head, which is pounding. I'd love to just lay down and chill but there's no room in the back of this cramped jeep. Besides, there's no time for rest.

It's showtime.

I turn the Eternal Stake in my hands. I sure hope it's ready because I know I'm not. After all, everybody here thinks our mission is to rescue Van Helsing. I'd like that too, but I also have another more personal mission.

I'm going to destroy Count Dracula.

"Um, is that the place?" Rage asks, pressing into my arm as he leans forward to look out the front windshield. "Because it's, like, super creepy."

"Yep, that's the place," Aura says, checking her map. "Right in the heart of Sleepy Hollow. Hairball, stop driving, and pull over already. I said we're here."

"Okay, okay," Hairball says. "No need to get sassy."

As Hairball steers us to the side of the road and parks, I look out the passenger-side window. We're high on an empty mountain road overlooking a massive estate. But as I take it all in, I think Rage undersold the place because it's way more than super creepy, it's downright frightening.

The estate has acres of greenery surrounding a stately old manor, which would have been lovely if the greenery weren't swampland and the manor wasn't falling down. In fact, with the black vines clawing the exterior, plywood covering the windows, and grotesque statues weighing down the roof, I'm not sure how the manor is still standing. The whole vibe feels dark and empty, just like the evil vampire living inside.

"My, what a charming home," InvisiBill says. "Now how about we keep driving until we find a pizza place?"

"That's enough, you cowards," Aura says. "Everybody out of the jeep. Our headmaster is in trouble and we're going to get him out of there. Now stop complaining."

"But I love complaining," InvisiBill says.

"Shut it." Aura responds.

"Message received," InvisiBill says.

As we step out of the jeep, Kat sniffs the air and says, "That's weird, it smells like gas."

"Sorry," Stanphibian says.

"What?" Kat says. "No, not that kind of gas, but yuck. No, it smells like—"

CLICK!

Suddenly, we're blinded by a massive spotlight!

I turn away, shielding my eyes, but the light is so intense it's making my headache worse!

"Hello, monsters," comes a familiar female voice. "Long time no see."

"Agent M?" I say, and when I squint I see a tall, thin silhouette coming towards us. "What are you doing here?"

"Funny, I was going to ask you the same thing," she says, stopping several feet away. "We've been tracking your vehicle since you left the Van Helsing Academy, and let me tell you, your driving is horrific. But let's get to the point. You monsters did a heck of a job damaging our headquarters. My boss is even threatening to cut my budget to make the repairs. So guess what? It's payback time. But before things get ugly for you, I'm curious why you pulled over in the middle of nowhere."

"Turn off the light and I'll tell you," I say.

There are a few seconds of silence, and then—

"Cut the spotlight!" Agent M commands.

The spotlight CLICKS off and it takes a few seconds to stop seeing stars, but that's not my biggest problem right now. I wasn't expecting Agent M and her agents to show up and I can't let her stop me from getting inside that manor. I mean, they could take us down quickly.

This is so annoying.

I'm so close to Count Dracula, but I might never get to him because of DSI. But then again, maybe that's the answer. If she thinks I'm as bad as Count Dracula then I'll give her exactly what she wants. I'll show her what a real vampire can do.

Wait, what?

That wasn't me thinking those thoughts, was it?

"You have one minute," Agent M says, looking at her watch. "One minute to explain yourselves before I unleash a world of hurt."

"Bram?" Aura says. "Are you okay?"

"Yeah," I say, rubbing my forehead. Where did those thoughts even come from?

"Forty seconds," Agent M says, tapping her watch.

"Look," I say. "I-I know we didn't get off on the right foot the first time, but please hear me out because it was all a big misunderstanding. We want to stop Count Dracula as badly as you do. And based on our detective work we've determined he's inside that manor over there, and he's holding our headmaster prisoner."

"Count Dracula?" Agent M says, looking over at the estate. "You're saying he's in that abandoned building?"

"Yep," Aura says. "The first cargo shipment from Romania was delivered to that address."

"Really?" Agent M says skeptically. "And how did you figure that out? We have the best agents in the world and they couldn't trace the cargo."

"I'm guessing your agents aren't ghosts," Aura says, flipping her hair.

"I see," Agent M says, looking down at her watch. "Well, time's up. Hit the spotlight, boys!"

CLICK!

The spotlight flashes again, and as I turn away from the light I see something moving on the roof of the manor. In fact, lots of large, gray things are moving on the rooftop. And that's when it hits me.

Those grotesque statues!

They were never statues at all!

They're… gargoyles!

Just then, one unfurls its stony wings and looks our way. Holy cow! It's the spotlight! It's like a homing signal!

"Turn off the light!" I yell, pointing towards the manor. "It's attracting the gargoyles!"

"Gargoyles?" Agent M says with a laugh, looking at the manor. "Nice try, kid, but… Uh-oh."

"Monstrosities, move out!" I yell.

"DSI!" Agent M yells. "Get ready to rumble!"

Rage, Aura, and I cluster together and bolt down the side of the mountain as the rest of the team scampers the other way. We stumble down the rocky landscape until we hit the bottom and duck into the woods. Looking up, I see a gigantic shape fly above the trees, and then—

KABOOM! KABOOM!

Massive explosions erupt overhead as artillery shrapnel rains down from the sky.

"We've got to get to the manor!" I yell.

We slog our way through the murky swamp, but it's so deep I'm soaked up to my thighs. I cover my ears as more explosions go off overhead.

"What's happening?" Rage says, struggling to move through the swamp which is up to his waist.

"DSI is fighting the gargoyles," Aura says, floating above the swamp surface. "I hope the others got away."

I do too, but it's not like we can stop and check.

Count Dracula definitely knows we're coming now.

I grip the Eternal Stake tight. I can't afford to lose this baby. And then I remember what's inside my pocket. I reach into my hoodie and feel the folded paper inside. Whew, it's still there. I don't know why, but it feels good to have my dad with me, even if it's just his old school profile.

"Bram!" Aura yells, pointing up. "Look out!"

Just then, I hear SNAPPING from overhead as thick branches come crashing to the ground, followed by a massive figure splashing down in front of us! Suddenly, I'm drenched in dirty swamp water.

I wipe my eyes with my sleeve and when my vision clears, I'm staring at a ten-foot-tall, winged gargoyle. He fixes me with his bulging eyes and flexes his gigantic stone muscles!

"Scatter!" I yell.

The gargoyle leaps at me and I dive out of the way as he plows into a massive tree behind me, knocking it over like it was a bowling pin. But as I pull myself out of the swamp, he gets back up.

"We've got to stop him!" Aura yells. "All this noise will bring more gargoyles!"

She's right about that. But the question is how? And then I realize I don't see Rage. Where'd he go?

POW!

There's an explosion of rock, and the gargoyle goes flying back into another tree! And when I look over to see who punched him, I find myself staring at another ten-foot monster, but this one has blonde hair and purple skin!

It's Rage!

"RRRAAAGGGEEE FFFIIIGGGHHHTTT!"

I-I can't believe it! Rage turned himself into Monster Rage to protect us!

The gargoyle rolls over and there's a massive hole in his chest. Honestly, with a wound like that, I can't believe he's still moving. But then he arches his back and SCREECHES into the night air.

"Stop him!" Aura yells. "He's calling for help!"

Rage marches over, raises his big foot, and STOMPS.

The screeching ends.

But it's too late.

We hear more branches SNAPPING from above, and two more gargoyles drop from the sky!

This is not good.

"GO!" Rage barks at us. "RRAAGGEE

FFIIGGHHTT!"

"Are you crazy?" I say. "We can't leave you!"

"Bram, let's go!" Aura yells, waving me on. "He's got this! We've got to save Van Helsing."

I hesitate for a second, but as Rage socks another gargoyle I realize Aura is right. I'm so proud of him. He's got this whole situation under control. He's finally mastered the beast inside.

The question is, can I do the same thing?

As we get closer to the manor we find ourselves engulfed in a thick fog. I stick close to Aura so I don't lose her, but when I look at the manor in the distance, I see something else coming through the fog—a furry, hunched figure with long arms and pointy ears. And then I spot another. And another. And another.

Werewolves!

I scan the horizon and see a whole army of them!

"Aura!" I yell. "Werewolves coming fast!"

"Got it," Aura says, stopping. "This one is mine."

"What?" I say. "There's like, twenty of them."

"And none of them can touch me," she says. "Look, let's make this simple. You go to mist-form and blend into the fog while I create a distraction to pull them away from you. Then, you go rescue Van Helsing. Got it?"

"You're kidding right?" I say. But when I look at the manor the werewolves have gotten much closer. I turn back to object to Aura's grand plan but she's gone!

"OVER HERE, SUCKERS!" comes Aura's voice

from far away. "CATCH ME IF YOU CAN!"

ARRRROOOOO!

That was a howl! I go to mist-form and see the werewolves gathering only twenty feet away. One of them SNARLS and the pack takes off in hot pursuit. Once they're gone I go back to kid-form. I've got to hand it to Aura, she might be the bravest monster I know.

I start for the manor when something tackles me from the side! We tumble into the swamp and I kick up my leg, using our momentum to flip my attacker over my body. Then, I get to my feet, spitting swamp water out of my mouth. And that's when I realize my hands are empty.

The Eternal Stake! It's gone!

That's bad, but I've got an even bigger problem right now because I'm staring at a soaking wet werewolf. Clearly, Aura didn't fool this one and I curse myself for not staying in mist-form. But I don't have time for fun and games right now.

Suddenly, I spot a sharp, wooden object floating in the swamp between us. It's the Eternal Stake!

Unfortunately, the werewolf tracks my eyes and sees it too. It's gonna be a foot race. We both jump for it at the same time, but I turn on my super-speed and beat the werewolf to the spot. I grab the Eternal Stake and clear out as the werewolf dives headfirst into the swamp.

Okay, it's time to get back on track. I concentrate hard and go back to mist-form. The werewolf resurfaces and looks around for me, but I'm not planning on telling him where I went. That was too close for comfort and the last mistake I can afford.

Fooling a werewolf is one thing but fooling Count Dracula won't be so easy. As I drift away towards the manor, I hear the werewolf HOWLING in frustration.

From this point forward, I can't let anything stop me from completing my mission. I can't let anything stop me from destroying Count Dracula.

MONSTEROLOGY 101
FIELD GUIDE

GARGOYLE

CLASSIFICATION:

Type: Abnormal
Sub-Type: Demon
Height: Variable
Weight: Variable
Eye Color: Gray
Hair Color: None

KNOWN ABILITIES:

- Transform from stone statues
- Stony hide makes them nearly indestructable
- Deceptively agile when flying in the air

KNOWN WEAKNESSES:

- Not intelligent
- Large size makes them easy to spot in the air
- Some only come alive at night

DANGER LEVEL:

HIGH

TIPS TO AVOID AN UNWANTED ENCOUNTER:

- Avoid buildings typically decorated with gargoyle-like statues
- If in a city environment, remain indoors as much as possible

CHAPTER FOURTEEN

DOUBLE CROSS

I stay in mist-form until I reach the manor.

I breeze past a few more werewolf sentries and then flow through the cracks of a boarded-up window. It's unnaturally dark inside but I can see everything clearly. Based on the ornate molding and antique furniture, I'd say the place must have been pretty swanky back in its day. Unfortunately, in its present condition, it should probably be condemned.

The wood floors are buckled, the staircase has fallen, and hundreds of rats are living in every conceivable nook and cranny. Other than the vermin, I'd guess no one's lived here for decades.

At least, until now.

As I drift through the various rooms, I think back to my first day at the Van Helsing Academy. There was so much I didn't know about monsters, and so much I didn't know about myself. And now I'm here, about to realize the destiny I didn't even know I had.

I hear Van Helsing's voice in my head, *'Only a*

vampire can kill another vampire.'

I see the faces of all the people counting on me.

Aura, Rage, Van Helsing, even Johnny.

I can't let them down.

I won't let them down.

Count Dracula is here and I need to find him.

I look for signs of life as I float through the once-grand ballrooms and spacious hallways but don't see anything. There's not even a dish in the kitchen sink. Hmmm? If I were a vampire where would I be hiding?

Oh yeah, I am a vampire.

Then, I approach a room with a plaque that reads, 'Butler's Pantry,' and flow inside. That's when I spot something interesting. There's a closed door in the corner. In all of the rooms I've explored, this is the first closed door I've found. I hover beside it and listen but don't hear any noises coming from the other side.

In my gut, I'm sure this door leads to a dark and creepy basement, and nothing good ever happens in a dark and creepy basement. Truthfully, I'm terrified, but I push past the fear. After all, I've got a job to do.

So, I move through the crevices and find a stairway going—yep—straight down. I knew it! I hesitate over the top stair for a few seconds to gather my courage and then drift down the steep stairway.

It's darker down here than upstairs, and when I reach the bottom I'm in a large, stone chamber staring at a long, narrow box made of wood that makes my jaw drop.

It's a coffin!

My misty heart starts racing.

I've seen enough horror movies to know that a coffin like that is for one person and one person only—Count Dracula! Now's my chance! But the lid is closed so I don't know if he's in there or not.

I-I can't believe it. This is the moment I've been waiting for—and the moment I've been dreading the most. If Count Dracula is inside, then I'll have a chance to finish this once and for all.

Unless, of course, he finishes me first.

I can't be a mist for what I need to do next, so I move to ground level and transform back into a kid. But as soon as I rematerialize, my nostrils are flooded with a foul stench that makes me gag.

Yuck! Where have I smelled that before?

I try ignoring it but it's just so strong. Then, I remember the Eternal Stake! Whew, even though I traveled a long way in mist-form it rematerialized with me. I sure hope it works as advertised because if not, I'm in serious trouble.

Well, there's no turning back now. I take a deep breath and tiptoe cautiously over to the coffin, sweat pouring down my forehead. With every step, I keep expecting the lid to spring open and Count Dracula to pop out and attack me.

But I can't stop now. Strangely, the closer I get, the dizzier I feel. I don't know if it's the stench or my headache but both seem to be getting worse. Suddenly, the room feels like it's spinning. It takes all of my willpower to finally reach the coffin, but when I do I place one hand on the lid and raise the Eternal Stake with the other.

Ready or not, here I am.

I brace myself and throw open the lid, hoping to find Count Dracula lying peacefully inside, but instead all I see is dirt! But not just any dirt, the coffin is filled with the same maggot-infested dirt we found on the ship! Aura was right, this is where the cargo was delivered. And now I know where that horrible smell is coming from.

But where is—

"Welcome, Bram," comes a deep voice that sends shivers down my spine.

I spin around to find Count Dracula hanging upside down from the ceiling like a bat! I back away from the coffin and raise the Eternal Stake, but for some reason, I'm seeing double right now. I wouldn't know which Count Dracula to strike even if I tried.

"I see you are experiencing some dizziness," Count Dracula says. "Do not be alarmed, it is an expected reaction when you are first exposed to our homeland."

"Homeland?" I say. "What are you talking about?"

"The dirt inside my coffin," Count Dracula says calmly, dropping to the ground feet-first, his cape flowing behind him. "It is native soil from our homeland of Wallachia. It is essential for rest. Connecting with its energy greatly renews my strength. It can be overwhelming at first, but soon enough it will become a great source of comfort to you. Now, you have had quite a challenging day. Perhaps you would like to rest in it?"

Rest in it? I glance over at the coffin. Strangely, other than the maggots and stench, it does look kind of comfortable. Almost like a dirt mattress. I bet it's pretty soft too.

Wait! What am I talking about? I shake my head. I-I don't know what I'm thinking right now. I'm dizzy and I feel myself getting… angrier.

"No way!" I yell, raising the Eternal Stake higher over my head. "I'm good. And Wallachia is NOT my homeland! Never was. Never will be."

"A pity," Count Dracula says shaking his head. "I see you have the Eternal Stake in your possession. I assume you are expecting to use it against me."

"You've got that right," I say. "Your evil ends now."

"You must be confident in its abilities," he says.

"Yeah," I say. "I am, but if you want to test it out come on over."

"You are either very brave or very foolish," Count Dracula says. And then he reaches into his cape and pulls out the Crown of Souls! As he puts it on his head, he says, "There, I believe we are even now. You with your artifact of destruction and me with my artifact of resurrection. We can fight if you wish, but it will end poorly for you."

I swallow hard. He's probably right about that. Either he'll destroy me or I'll destroy him, only to watch him get resurrected. And then I'll have to do it all over again. I'd call this a lose-lose situation!

What am I going to do? I need to stall. I've got to throw him off his game.

"You know, everyone thinks you're this big, bad guy," I say, "but deep down you're a coward at heart, aren't you?"

"What are you driveling on about?" Count Dracula sneers.

"You're a coward and you know it," I say. "You just hide in the shadows, manipulating the weak to get what you want. Remember Faustius, or Moreau, or Renfield? They were weak-minded and easy to control. And what about your war against mankind? You didn't even go to New York City to start your own war. You don't stick your neck out for anything because you're afraid to die, aren't you?"

"You know nothing about me," he says.

"I know a lot," I say. "And that's why you wanted the Crown of Souls, isn't it? You're afraid to die. And your quest for power is nothing more than you trying to save your own pitiful existence."

"Enough," Count Dracula says. "You know neither me nor your own mind! Here you stand, a monster in your own right, betraying your kind! Do you think humans will let you walk the streets in freedom when this is over? If you do you are a fool! They are, and always will be, afraid of what they cannot control, including you. They will hunt you down and destroy you, just as they have done to monsters like us for centuries."

I-I don't want to listen to what he's saying, but deep down I know he's right. I mean, I learned all about monster persecution in Seward's Supernatural history class. And Agent M and DSI are legitimate monster hunters who want nothing more than to capture me! I hadn't thought about it, but even if I win the battle against Count Dracula, no Naturals are going to throw us a parade. They'll just take us down next.

"Monsters can only stand with monsters," Count Dracula continues. "And your beloved headmaster is no exception. He will just as readily destroy you as he would me. I already know you question his motives."

I open my mouth to argue but nothing comes out.

He's right. I do question Van Helsing's motives. I mean, he never told me about the Eternal Stake in case he needed to use it against me.

Speaking of Van Helsing…

"Where is he?" I ask. "Where are you keeping him?"

"Still such blind loyalty?" Count Dracula says. "Well, you need not worry. He is here. Would you like to see him now? He has been waiting anxiously to see you."

"Yes," I say. But his sarcastic tone raises my alarm bells. What does he mean that Van Helsing has been waiting anxiously to see me?

"Very well," Count Dracula says, clasping his hands together. "Van Helsing, enter!"

The next thing I know, one of the doors opens and Van Helsing comes walking into the chamber! The good news is that he looks like he's okay, but the bad news is that he's aiming his Crossbow of Purity right at me!

"Headmaster?" I say. "What are you doing?"

"He is doing what I command," Count Dracula says.

"What?" I say. "What are you talking about?"

"Show him," Count Dracula says to Van Helsing.

Then, Van Helsing removes one hand from his crossbow and unwinds his scarf. And that's when I see two puncture wounds on the side of his neck!

Holy cow! Dracula bit him!

"Van Helsing is fully under my control," Count Dracula says, tapping his fingertips together. "Now, this will be most entertaining. Which of you will kill the other first?"

CHAPTER FIFTEEN

THE LAST AT BAT

I never expected this.

My eyes drift to the two puncture wounds on Van Helsing's neck. There's no doubt about it, that's a vampire bite, just like the one I saw on Renfield's neck.

And that can only mean one thing.

Count Dracula is controlling Van Helsing!

Staring down the barrel of Van Helsing's Crossbow of Purity puts everything in perspective. This whole mission was doomed from the start. There's no way I can defeat Count Dracula, especially since he has the Crown of Souls. And now he's gonna get the last laugh by watching me die at the hands of my mentor.

Nice going, Bram.

But I promised myself I wouldn't give up, no matter how dire the circumstances. If I don't figure something out right now then it's game over for me and mankind. So, let's take this one step at a time. And first up is breaking Count Dracula's influence over Van Helsing.

"Headmaster," I say calmly. "Please, don't shoot. It's

me, Bram. You remember me, don't you? Well, in case you forgot, I'm one of your students. You run an amazing academy that teaches monster kids how to be good so we can fight evil threats like Count Dracula over there. You are a kind and good man. You need to focus right now. You need to remember who you are."

Just then, Van Helsing's bushy eyebrows quiver.

"Fool," Count Dracula says, his lips curling into a menacing smile. "Your words have no meaning. Van Helsing is under my control now. Hear me, Van Helsing. Your ancestors have dedicated their pathetic lives to exterminating vampires, and now you have one in your sights. Destroy the child, Van Helsing! Make your ancestors proud!"

Van Helsing furrows his brow and lines up his crossbow to shoot me right through the heart. I-I can't believe it. I've lost him… and everything else.

"Shoot!" Count Dracula barks. "Get rid of our pest!"

"Yes, master," Van Helsing says robotically. "I will."

I brace myself for impact as Van Helsing's trigger finger twitches, but suddenly he wheels on Count Dracula and fires!

The villain's eyes light up and he disappears in a cloud of black mist! The silver arrow passes through harmlessly, scattering wisps everywhere.

"Devil!" Van Helsing shouts into the air. "You never controlled me and you never will! Bram, raise the Eternal Stake. It is time to end this."

A wave of adrenaline rushes through me as I realize that somehow Van Helsing is back—and he's on my side! But as Van Helsing reloads, the King of Darkness rematerializes right behind him.

"Headmaster!" I call out.

But it's too late.

"Yes, we will end this," Count Dracula says, lifting a surprised Van Helsing over his head like he weighs nothing. "Starting with you!"

Then, Count Dracula slams Van Helsing onto the stone floor. Van Helsing lands with a sickening thud and his arms flail across his body like a rag doll, sending the Crossbow of Purity clattering across the room.

"No!" I cry, rushing to Van Helsing's side.

His eyes are closed and there's a trickle of blood flowing from the corner of his mouth, but thankfully he's still breathing—barely.

"Monster!" I yell.

"Yes, I am," Count Dracula says, dusting off his cape, "and so are you. As you can see, nothing will stand in my way, including you. But I am feeling generous, so I will give you one last chance. Will you continue to be subservient to Naturals or will you embrace your true destiny? The world's greatest vampire-hunter is at your feet. Finish him and show me you have chosen wisely."

"What?" I say, getting to my feet. "Are you nuts? The only person I'm gonna finish is you!"

"Very well," Count Dracula says with a smirk. "Your

choice is made and your life must end. Though I must admit, I am curious to see how men taught a monster to fight."

As we circle each other, my heart is pounding out of my chest. I can't believe this moment I've been thinking about non-stop for months is actually happening. All of my fears are being realized.

And only one of us will come out alive.

Whoever wins will destroy the other's body and spirit for all of eternity!

Except I'm at a serious disadvantage. Not only is Count Dracula wearing the Crown of Souls, but he's also stronger, faster, and several-hundred-years more experienced than I am. I swallow hard. This shouldn't even be close.

Yet, he hasn't attacked me.

And that's when I realize I have something he's afraid of—something that's keeping him at bay.

The Eternal Stake.

Then, I remember what Renfield told me. Even though he's got the Crown of Souls, he's afraid of dying again. I mean, it took centuries for him to come back the first time and I'm guessing you don't forget something like that too easily.

Then, it dawns on me.

Just like I don't know if this Eternal Stake will work, he probably doesn't trust what's sitting on his head either? So maybe I can use that to my advantage.

"Boy, I sure hope the Crown of Souls is real," I say, "because wouldn't it stink to die again, but this time forever?"

"I think you should be the one concerned with dying," he says.

"I'm good," I say. "Because I've got this!"

I lunge at him with the Eternal Stake, but when I strike he easily sidesteps me and I get a face full of cape.

Okay, this isn't going to be easy. But maybe he's right. If I'm going to defeat him, it won't be by using what men taught me. Maybe I need to use what he taught me.

It's time to go vampire-ninja!

I turn into a mist, kick on my super-speed, and race behind him, but as soon as I rematerialize he goes into mist-form and dissipates before I strike. When he reappears, I turn into a bat and divebomb him, but he goes into bat-form and glides to the other side of the room as I crash into the wall.

"I am impressed," he says, buffing his black nails. "Your skills have improved, but this could take all evening."

"I've got time," I say, turning back to kid-form.

But while he doesn't look like he's even broken a sweat, I'm totally exhausted. If I don't get a lucky strike sometime soon I'm going to run out of energy.

And then I'll be easy pickings.

"Unfortunately," Count Dracula says, "I do not have that kind of time to spare. You see, I have a world to conquer, and once it is mine I will have an endless supply of blood to sustain me. So, I am afraid we will need to bring this to a tidy conclusion immediately."

Um, immediately?

But before I can react he becomes a blur, and the next thing I know, he's by my side, wrestling for control of the Eternal Stake! His fingers are like iron rods, digging into my wrists to pry the weapon free from my grasp! I try knocking him back with my thigh but he's too strong!

His face is so close I can smell his hot, putrid breath. If I can just angle the point of the Eternal Stake towards him, I might be able to jam it into his stomach. But he's so strong he's turning it towards me! I'm barely managing to hold him off, but I don't know for how long!

"Release the stake!" Count Dracula commands.

"N-Never!" I say.

Then, he unhinges his jaw, opens his mouth wide, and bites me in the left shoulder!

"AAAGGGHHH!" I yell as intense pain shoots through my body.

I react instinctively, SLAMMING my head into his. I scream again as his fangs release from my skin and we both fall to the ground disoriented. I sit up as soon as I land and grab my burning shoulder, only to feel a warm, wet liquid streaming down my arm. Holy cow! He bit all the way through! I'm bleeding all over the place!

Suddenly, my entire body feels hot and achy, like a fever is taking over. Yet, despite all of that, I'm somehow still holding the Eternal Stake. And when I look over at Count Dracula he's back on his feet, adjusting the Crown of Souls and licking his lips.

"There," he says, his voice echoing inside my head. *"Now I will take complete control and this will finally be over."*

N-No! He's in my head. And then I realize, with that bite he's bonded to me even more!

"Be a good boy and hand me the Eternal Stake," he says, walking towards me. *"I will be merciful when I end your life. Or not."*

N-No!

Yet, despite my protest, my arm is rising like it isn't even part of my body. Holy cow! This is what happened in the forbidden basement when he made me open that vault door! But this feels ten times more intense. I-I can't stop it!

"Yes," he says, inside my head.

And before I know it, my arm is fully extended, my palm is opening, and I'm offering him the Eternal Stake like it's on a silver platter!

"Thank you," Count Dracula says, reaching for it. "I will make your end quick and painful."

But then something catches my eye.

There's… a gray mist, swirling behind Count Dracula.

W-What is that?

And just as Count Dracula is about to wrap his hand around the Eternal Stake, the gray mist circles rapidly and knocks the Crown of Souls clear off his head!

"What?" Count Dracula exclaims, reaching up with both hands.

But before he can pick it up, the gray mist engulfs the Crown of Souls inside a mini cyclone, breaking it into a thousand pieces!

"No!" Count Dracula yells.

"Bram!" comes a familiar voice. "Strike now!"

I look over to find Van Helsing crawling across the floor, and I realize what he's saying.

Count Dracula is distracted.

Despite the pain coursing through my body, I muster all of my willpower and spring up. And then I drive the Eternal Stake straight into Count Dracula's back!

"AAAAAHHHHHHHH!" he screams, his voice echoing through the chamber and inside my brain.

Suddenly, the Eternal Stake gets too hot to hold and I release it just as it turns bright yellow! Smoke pours out of Count Dracula's back as he stumbles to his knees. I step back in horror as Count Dracula looks at me, his eyes wide with surprise. And as he opens his mouth to speak, his fangs gleam, and then his entire body explodes in a blinding flash of yellow light!

I turn away, shielding my eyes, and when I look back, there's nothing left but a black scorch mark on the stone floor.

I drop to my knees and look for any trace of black mist, any trace of Count Dracula's spirit getting away, escaping to fight another day. But… there's nothing.

And… that gray mist? It's gone too.

What was that?

For some reason, I remember the picture inside my hoodie pocket. I reach inside and touch it, but it's deteriorated into pulp. It must have gotten drenched when I was fighting in the swamp.

"Bram," I hear Van Helsing say. "You did it!"

I… did it? I mean, he's right, I just destroyed Count Dracula, once and for all. But instead of feeling elated, I feel… down. And my shoulder hurts so bad.

I touch it again and wince in pain. Suddenly, I don't feel… like myself. In fact, all I feel is hunger. I'm ravenous. I need food. But all I want… is blood.

"Bram," Van Helsing says, blood still trickling down his face. "That is a big wound. How do you feel?"

"N-Not good," I say, my vision hazy. But for some reason, I can't stop looking at the blood dribbling down his chin. It looks so… good.

"Bram?" Van Helsing says.

Suddenly, he's blocked the blood with something, and when my focus comes back I notice he's sitting up, and he's pointing his Crossbow of Purity at me!

"Tell me," Van Helsing says. "Can you feel Count Dracula's venom coursing through your veins?"

"Y-Yeah," I say.

My insides are… burning.

And that's when I realize my worst fears have come

true.

"H-Headmaster," I say.

"Yes, Bram," Van Helsing says, studying me closely.

"I-I think it's too late for me. I-I think you need to… destroy me. At least… my mortal body. Hopefully, I… I won't come back."

"Bram…" he says.

"N-No," I say. "Y-You don't understand. The h-hunger is so strong. This time, I won't be able to c-control it. I-I know you've wanted to… do this for a long time. I… I guess that's why you didn't tell me about the E-Eternal Stake, right?"

"No, Bram," he says. "That is not true."

"I-It doesn't m-matter," I say. "Look, th-thanks for helping me when no one else would. I-I think of you like a father. Always wanted to… please you. B-But I need you to help me now. I-I promised myself I… wouldn't become a full v-vampire. P-Please, destroy me. And tell the t-team I… I'll miss them. Especially Rage… and… and Aura."

Tears stream down my face as I think of their faces.

I'm going to miss them. But I just can't hurt anyone else. It's time.

"P-Please," I repeat. "H-Help me."

"Bram," Van Helsing says. "I am so sorry for what I am about to do."

I see him raise the Crossbow of Purity.

"P-Please…"

THWIP!
I feel something pierce my body.
And then everything goes black.

EPILOGUE

THE AFTERMATH

I hear beeping.

Why is there beeping? I try opening my eyes but my eyelids feel stuck together. After a few failed attempts, I finally manage to pry them open, only to discover I'm lying in a familiar white room with tubes sticking out of my arm.

I'm in the infirmary.

And then I notice I'm not alone.

"How long have I been here?" I ask.

"Three weeks," Van Helsing says, sliding his chair closer to my bed.

"Am I dead?" I ask.

"No," Van Helsing says. "But you were in a coma. Your injury was quite severe. We are very lucky you are alive."

"Yeah, but my body doesn't feel so lucky," I say,

rubbing my eyes. I try sitting up but a dull pain shoots through my right leg. And when I look down my thigh is wrapped in a heavy bandage. "What happened?"

"Please, try to relax," Van Helsing says. "It will take time for you to fully heal. After you destroyed Count Dracula, his venom was rapidly taking over your body, accelerating the multiplication of your own vampiric cells. To stop this infection, I was forced to shoot you in the leg with the Crossbow of Purity."

"Really?" I say, vaguely remembering Van Helsing aiming his weapon at me. "And that worked?"

"Fortunately, yes," he says. "The Crossbow of Purity is a Supernatural artifact that enhances the power of one hundred percent pure silver, the only substance known to purify a vampiric virus. If I did not shoot you immediately, the virus would have taken over and you would have become a full vampire."

"Oh," I say, totally shocked. "But does that mean I'm no longer a vampire?"

"No," Van Helsing says. "Once the crossbow bolt was removed, your DNA took over again. You are still a vampire. Or rather, half-vampire. But you will likely retain some of the purifying effects of the Crossbow of Purity in your bloodstream, which should prevent you from ever becoming a full vampire in the future."

"Really?" I say. Suddenly, it feels like the weight of the world is lifted from my shoulders. I-I can't believe it. I won't ever have to worry about losing control again.

Just being half-vampire never felt so good.

But as I look at Van Helsing, another thought crosses my mind. "You know, I… I thought you were going to kill me."

"Bram," he says, putting his hand on my arm. "I told you I would stand by you from the beginning, and I am a man of my word. Taking your life was never an option."

I look into his determined eyes and wonder why I ever doubted him. But there were so many red flags. So many question marks, like—

"But what about the Eternal Stake?" I say. "Why didn't you tell me about it?"

"I intended to," Van Helsing says, "when the time was right. However, if I told you before you were ready, I feared you would run off with it in pursuit of Count Dracula. After all, you and your friends do have a habit of breaking the rules."

"My friends!" I say, sitting up, the pain returning.

"They are fine," Van Helsing reassures me. "All of them. And they have visited you frequently."

I lie back down relieved. Thank goodness they're okay. If anything happened to them because of me…

Then, I realize Van Helsing is wearing his scarf.

"Headmaster?" I say. "Count Dracula bit you, but somehow you resisted him?"

"Yes," Van Helsing says, removing his jacket and rolling up his sleeve. And that's when I see a bandage covering his entire forearm. "Suspecting his motives before I traveled to New York City, I inserted a sliver of the Crossbow of Purity directly into my arm. His venom never affected me."

"Wow," I say. "That sounds painful but smart. Now that Count Dracula is gone, what happens next?"

"The Dark Ones have crawled back into their holes," Van Helsing says. "Without a leader, I do not think we will be hearing from them anytime soon. But darkness will always try to blot out the light."

I think about what he said and he's right. But now I know I'll always be there to stop them, no matter what.

And speaking of darkness…

"What about Dr. Renfield?" I ask. "What happened to him?"

"I let him go," Van Helsing says.

"He was innocent in all of this, wasn't he?" I say.

"Yes," Van Helsing says. "Dr. Renfield is a good man who was an unwitting victim of Count Dracula, just like you and me. And with Count Dracula gone for good, Dr. Renfield is finally free."

I hope Dr. Renfield is able to move on with his life. What he did wasn't his fault and he deserves a second chance. Then, I see my gray hoodie hanging on the back of the door and it triggers another memory.

"The gray mist!" I say, sitting up again. "Did you see it? I-I didn't tell you about it the first time, but it saved me from DSI. And then it saved me again from Count Dracula. But I… I don't know what it is."

"Are you sure you do not know?" Van Helsing says, with a wry smile. "I suspect you do. But just in case, I have something for you."

Then, he reaches down and hands me a rectangular object wrapped in newspaper. I don't know what it is. I mean, Van Helsing has never given me anything before. And when I unwrap it there is a framed photo of my dad!

It's the same picture that was on his profile!

"That is your father, Gabriel," Van Helsing says. "I found the remnants of his profile in your sweatshirt. As you can imagine, it was not easy to find the original photograph in my office, but I was determined. It was taken the day we admitted him to the academy. He was young and full of energy, just like you."

"So," I say stunned. "A-Are you saying that gray mist… was him?"

"Yes," Van Helsing says. "Since your father was killed by men and not a vampire, his spirit lives on. It is a miracle he has found you again."

"I… I don't know what to say," I respond, my eyes getting watery.

I look out the window at the blue sky. So, that means my father is still out there, watching over me.

Protecting me.

"I know he is proud of you," Van Helsing says. "And so am I."

"That means a lot," I say, wiping my eyes. "You know, it's funny, but with Count Dracula finally gone I'm not sure what I'm supposed to do next."

"Well," Van Helsing says. "I have been thinking about that very topic. I happen to have an opening on my staff for a Survival Skills professor, and I was thinking there is no one more expert in the subject than you."

"Wait, what?" I say.

"You are still a bit young now," Van Helsing says, "But while you continue your studies here at the academy, I would like to invite you to be a Teaching Assistant to Crawler who will fill the role until you are old enough to assume the position on your own. The students would learn a great deal from you, and I know Professor Hexum would be honored to have you as his eventual successor."

"Seriously?" I say.

"Seriously," Van Helsing says. "Professor Hexum may not have always shown it, but he had great respect for your work ethic, character, and courage."

"Wow," I say. "I-I'm honored. But you really want me to be a teacher here?"

"I could not think of anyone more qualified for the job," Van Helsing says. "Unless, of course, you do not want it."

"No!" I say. "I… I would love to. Thank you."

"You are very welcome," Van Helsing says. "And thank you for everything you have done. The entire world is indebted to you. You have saved us all from a most terrible fate."

"Gee, thanks," I say.

"You are a hero," Van Helsing says. "And though we have purged the world of one crisis, there is still much work to do to convince Naturals that monsters are not a threat and we can all live in peace."

"That's for sure," I say, thinking about monster hunters like Agent M. "And you can count on me."

"I know I can," Van Helsing says. "And I will always be here for you."

And then Van Helsing leans in and hugs me.

At first, I'm so shocked I don't know what to do. I mean, I don't remember any adult ever hugging me before. But then I realize how nice it feels and I lean in, hugging him back tightly.

"I am proud of you," Van Helsing says, finally letting go. "Now we should share the good news of your awakening with the others."

Van Helsing stands up, opens the door, and my friends come storming in. Aura, Rage, and the whole gang circle my bed and I can't stop smiling.

"Take it easy on him," Van Helsing says. "He has been through a lot." Then, he winks and leaves.

"Bram," Aura says, "I'm so happy you're okay."

"Thanks," I say, "you have no idea how happy I am to see you guys."

"You really did it," Rage says, slapping the bed railing. "You defeated Count Dracula. I knew you could do it!"

"Well, that makes one of us," I say. "But really, we all did it, together."

"The best part is that it's over," Aura says, smiling at me. "And you can finally get some peace of mind."

"Are you kidding?" InvisiBill says. "The best part is that we'll never have to take Survival Skills again!"

"For sure!" Hairball says, high-fiving Stanphibian.

I smile and decide to keep my mouth shut.

At least for now.

And as I look at my friends gathered around me, and the picture of my father in my hands, I feel happy knowing that for once in my life, I'm finally home.

YOU CAN MAKE A BIG DIFFERENCE

Calling all monsters! I need your help to get Monster Problems in front of more readers.

Reviews are extremely helpful in getting attention for my books. I wish I had the marketing muscle of the major publishers, but instead, I have something far more valuable, loyal readers, just like you! Your generosity in providing an honest review will help bring this book to the attention of more readers.

So, if you've enjoyed this book, I would be very grateful if you could leave a quick review on the book's Amazon page.

Thanks for your support!

R.L. Ullman

DON'T MISS EPIC ZERO!

Growing up in a superhero family is cool, unless you're powerless…

Gold Medal Winner - Readers' Favorite Book Awards

Don't miss this bestselling series collection with over 2,000 five-star series reviews on Amazon and Goodreads!

Get Epic Zero Books 1-3 today!

ABOUT THE AUTHOR

R.L. Ullman is the bestselling author of the award-winning EPIC ZERO series and the award-winning MONSTER PROBLEMS series. He creates fun, engaging page-turners that captivate the imaginations of kids and adults alike. His original, relatable characters face adventure and adversity that bring out their inner strengths. He's frequently distracted thinking up new stories, and once got lost in his own neighborhood. You can learn more about what R.L. is up to at rlullman.com, and if you see him wandering around your street please point him in the right direction home.

For news, updates, and free stuff, please sign up for the Epic Newsflash at rlullman.com.

***

As always, I would like to thank my Supernatural wife, Lynn, and my freakishly creative kids, Matthew and Olivia, for their undying support.

Made in the USA
Middletown, DE
28 February 2021

34519897R00340